MUSICALIA

Sources of Information in Music

Elliot Zuckerman
Cambridge
October 1970

MUSICALIA

sources of information in music

BY

J. H. DAVIES

Music Librarian, British Broadcasting Corporation

SECOND EDITION
Revised and enlarged

THE QUEEN'S AWARD
TO INDUSTRY 1966

PERGAMON PRESS

OXFORD · LONDON · EDINBURGH · NEW YORK
TORONTO · SYDNEY · PARIS · BRAUNSCHWEIG

Pergamon Press Ltd., Headington Hill Hall, Oxford
4 & 5 Fitzroy Square, London W.1

Pergamon Press (Scotland) Ltd., 2 & 3 Teviot Place, Edinburgh 1

Pergamon Press Inc., Maxwell House, Fairview Park, Elmsford,
New York 10523

Pergamon of Canada Ltd., 207 Queen's Quay West, Toronto 1

Pergamon Press (Aust.) Pty. Ltd., 19a Boundary Street,
Rushcutters Bay, N.S.W. 2011, Australia

Pergamon Press S.A.R.L., 24 rue des Écoles, Paris 5^e

Vieweg & Sohn GmbH, Burgplatz 1, Braunschweig

First edition 1966
Second edition, revised and enlarged 1969
Library of Congress Catalog Card No. 76-77013

Printed in Great Britain by A. Wheaton & Co., Exeter

08 006356 X (flexicover)
08 006357 8 (hard cover)

To my Wife

Contents

Preface

Hang it all! I cannot express it more simply.

RICHARD STRAUSS

THE documentation of music has hitherto been regarded by librarians, research workers and teachers as ill-organized in comparison with that for the literary and technological fields. It does not take long to discover that it exists in great profusion, but also to confirm that it lacks co-ordination. Effort has been mainly of three kinds: by the trained librarian, by the trained musicologist and by the enthusiastic musician or bibliographer (amateur or professional) sometimes working in ignorance of each other. Of these categories, the music librarian and musicologist have scarcely more than a couple of generations of tradition. The professional bibliographer has much more experience to draw upon, but he is likely to be at most an amateur musician, and rarely that. This volume juxtaposes every such kind of effort, since they often form natural complements.

Thus, in this short survey I have attempted to select from and formulate the maze of specialist activity which has gone into the sign-posting of music over the past 100 years or so. When a single hand tackles what should be the work of a group of specialists, it is inevitable that omissions result, and I shall be glad to hear of them. My aim has been not so much to add to the already copious scratchings of the *rats de bibliothèque*, nor try to teach the bibliophile (cruelly and unfairly dubbed "an idiotic class" by Housman) and his counterparts their business, but rather to make it easier for various groups of busy practising musicians and music-lovers to flick the right switches quickly and confidently on a rather elaborate and confusing dashboard.

Exhaustive and exhausting guides abound, but those which courageously attempt selection and grading of repertories, etc., have been given priority where possible, and I have given first place to the ways and means of documenting the music itself—the associated literature of each topic taking a secondary, if important, place.

One distinction I have consistently and deliberately avoided, as far as possible, is that between professional and amateur. In the Latin countries "dilettante" may be almost a dirty word, but "amateur", "Liebhaber" are honourable ones in English-speaking, Teutonic and Scandinavian lands. Moreover, the professional conductor may well be a mere amateur in jazz, the ethno-musicologist an amateur in all other music; in my experience many of the best amateurs are often more knowledgeable than some of their narrowly-specialist professional counterparts.

This book, then, is intended to facilitate the work of all who need systematic help in exploring the musical repertory, whether they be performers, teachers, musicologists approaching new paths, organizers, or librarians bent on providing tools for the job. It is to librarians, primarily, that those who are seriously curious about music must eventually turn, for most research-tools are primarily reference works, frequently expensive, out of print or very hard to come by. And it is librarians in particular who should make every effort to become bibliographically competent to meet the rising need. Musical frontiers are being extended every year, and up-to-date documentation becomes more necessary to plot newer and larger maps.

All essential information for tracing a book or an organization has been given, for the most part, at each mention, to avoid tiresome references back and forwards. The specimen pages have been chosen mainly from works which might normally escape attention or are rare, expensive or out of print.

Preface to the Second Edition

MANY details have been corrected, all discoverable new editions have been included together with much fresh material, mainly covering 1964–8. "The Gramophone Record Collector" in particular has been substantially extended, and "Children's Music and Teaching" has been expanded into a separate Chapter 8.

References to current material occur in my quarterly "Musicalia" articles in the *Library World*, which may be read as a running supplement to the present volume.

Acknowledgements

I AM grateful for much useful help and advice from my willing staff in the B.B.C. Music Library, together with the following: Dr. Gerald Abraham, Hermann Baron, Dr. A. Bentley, Jane Corbett, Charles Cudworth, R. J. C. Davies, Karl Haas, Max Hinrichsen, A. Hyatt King, Mark Lubbock, Alec Robertson, Brian Rust, Dr. Denis Wright and K. A. Wright.

Dr. Vincent Duckles and Dr. B. Trowell have very kindly made extensive suggestions.

CHAPTER 1

The Ordinary Listener

I have a reasonable good eare in musicke:
Let us have the tongs and the bones.

SHAKESPEARE, *A Midsummer Night's Dream*

THERE must be thousands of mere listeners for every performer or specialist. Therefore, he deserves his own chapter, the first, in a book of this kind. Of this great "cloud of witnesses" the majority may well enjoy a lifetime's listening without ever reading a word about music, and some will be actively hostile to the idea. These are unlikely to open this book. The important remainder of lay music-lovers will find a growing need for a few basic books, whether for quick reference, browsing or extended reading.

If cost is of first consideration, the English-speaking layman may wish to begin with paperbacks—with these he may easily fill his first shelf. Whitaker's *Paper-backs in Print* gives the full range of titles in print in the U.K. Penguin Books lead the field with A. Jacobs' *New Dictionary of Music* and with histories such as the *Pelican History of Music* by Robertson and Stevens (in progress), and E. Blom's *Music in England*, supported by special topics such as R. Simpson's *The Symphony*, E. J. Dent's *Opera*, A. Jacobs' *Choral Music*, A. Robertson's *Chamber Music*, G. B. L. Wilson's *Dictionary of Ballet*, G. B. Shaw's *On Music*, and A. Baines' *Musical Instruments through the Ages*. The Oxford University Press follow with Imogen Holst's *ABC of Music*, E. Blom's *Some Great Composers*, D. Cooke's *The Language of Music*, E. J. Dent's *Mozart's Operas* and Emily Anderson's translation of *Mozart's Letters*. Many other publishers have the occasional musical paperback, e.g. Arrow Books with P. Gammond's *Music on Record*, S. Williams' *Come to the Opera* and Beecham's *A Mingled Chime*; Methuen with R. Donington's *The Instruments of Music*; Macmillan with *The Savoy Operas (Words)*; Duckworth with Esther Meynell's *Bach* and W. H. Allen with Hindemith's *A Composer's World*.

Already our mere listener is deeply, albeit economically, involved in the literature of music. Besides the foregoing he could well add what is almost certainly the best single-volume dictionary—E. Blom's *Dictionary of Music* (Dent), which has behind it the mature expertise which later went into the fifth edition of Grove's *Dictionary* (Macmillan), and deals succinctly with many of the marginal aspects of music such as musical settings of literary works. He could usefully add that admirable bedside book, P. A. Scholes' *Oxford Companion to Music* (O.U.P.), self-indexing, well-illustrated and beguilingly arranged to convert an intended one-minute reference to a timeless browse. The ordinary terminology of music is already reasonably covered by the foregoing titles, but there are various dictionaries devoted to terms alone—T. Wotton's *Dictionary of Foreign Musical Terms* (Breitkopf, 1907) is a standard work, but clearly cannot reach those terms which have emerged from electronic music. Good general Italian, German and French–English dictionaries are, of course, an essential ballast for any basic library, but W. J. Smith's *Dictionary of Musical Terms in Four Languages* (Hutchinson, 1961) provides a short cut. It is recent enough to include some electronic terms.*

For younger readers, general approach books like L. Salter's *Going to a Concert* (Phoenix House, 1950) and *Going to the Opera* (Phoenix House, 1955) make pleasant introductions, and sources for further reading are given in Ch. 17. Two very attractive recent works of general musical appreciation are R. Fiske's *Listening to Music*, 2nd edn. (Harrap, 1966), and A. Hopkins' *Music All Around Me* (Frewin, 1967). Opera and operetta plots are covered by Kobbé–Harewood's *Complete Opera Book* (Putnam, 1954), M. Lubbock's *Complete Book of Light Opera* (Putnam, 1962), and the

* A polyglot *Worterbuch* in seven languages is under preparation by the International Association of Music Libraries.

Decca Book of Ballet (Muller, 1958) is the most up-to-date single-volume survey in its field. (See also Ch. 3.)

The listener's pleasure and instruction will be far from complete without a few volumes of the Master Musician's series (Dent). These are under regular revision—examples of thorough recasting being the *Debussy*, *Haydn* and *Schumann* volumes.

"Score reading" is a sorely abused term. Vaughan Williams professed that he never could, but learned the repertory by the Victorian method of piano-duet reading. When the layman talks of score reading he is likely to mean *following* a score without getting too much lost. This emphatically does not imply that the non-performer, or the "one-line" player (to whom the hearing in depth of the printed page may forever remain a mirage) will not benefit considerably from following broadcasts and records with a score. The Penguin scores, and a few others save him from the doubtful pleasures of mentally transposing certain instruments, since they thoughtfully put all such into "concert" pitch (as actually heard but not as written). The general classical repertory is richly covered, from string-trios to symphonies, by the Eulenburg, Kalmus and Lea pocket-scores, while each publisher can add a useful list of study-scores from his own catalogue.

Popular music and jazz may lend itself least of all to support from books. Their literatures are specifically described in Ch. 12. Here, however, the current gramophone catalogues and current reviewing will form ready guides. The record-lending services of public libraries for light music and jazz may not be taken for granted—indeed, many exclude this field as a policy, but there is a small and growing number of authorities which do cover those jazz idioms which have already received respectability as being "seminal".

For any further help over the sources and documentation of music and its literature, the listener, along with his amateur and professional counterparts, had best repair speedily to his music dealer and local library, brandishing the present volume and insisting on action. He should also arm himself with E. T. Bryant's *Music* (Readers' Guides Series, C. Bingly, 1965).

RECENT PAPERBACKS

ABRAHAM, G. *A Hundred Years of Music*, Methuen.
B.B.C. Music Guides (ed. Abraham):
    Bach Cantatas. J. A. WESTRUP.
    Beethoven Piano Sonatas. D. MATTHEWS.
    Haydn String Quartets. R. HUGHES.
    Haydn Symphonies. H. C. R. LANDON.
    Monteverdi Madrigals. D. ARNOLD.
    Mozart Chamber Music. A. H. KING.
    Schubert Piano Sonatas. P. RADCLIFFE.
    Schubert Songs. M. J. E. BROWN.
COPLAND, A. *What to Listen for in Music*, New England Library.
HARMAN, C. *Popular History of Music*, Mayflower.
HOPKINS, A. *Talking About Symphonies*, Pan.
HUGHES, G. *Pan Book of Great Composers*, Pan.
JACOBS and SADIE. *Pan Book of Opera*, Pan.
LAMBERT, C. *Music, Ho!*, Faber.
MYERS, R. H. *Twentieth Century Music*, Calder.
SALZMAN, E. *Twentieth Century Music*, Prentice-Hall.
SEAMAN, J. (ed.). *Great Orchestral Music*, Collier.
SESSIONS, R. *Musical Experience*, Athenaeum.
SHARP, C. *English Folk Songs*, 4th edn, by Karpeles, Heinemann.
STEARNS, M. *The Story of Jazz*, New England Library.
STRAVINSKY and CRAFT. *Conversations*, Penguin.
WESTUP, SIR J. *An Introduction to Music History*, new edn., Hutchinson.

CHAPTER 2

The Orchestral and Band Conductor

*Le Chef d'orchestre, qui a été parfait d'intelligence, de précision
et de verve, mord son mouchoir à belles dents pour contenir son émotion.*

H. BERLIOZ, *Les Soirées de l'orchestre*

THE well-organized conductor, be he virtuoso or tyro, will, in the course of his training and subsequent career, have built his own personal library of well marked scores (if not also of band-parts), and along with it indexes of instrumentations, timings, first performances, sources, etc., supported by a range of publishers' catalogues. The tyro will have done well to read A. Boult's *Handbook on the Technique of Conducting*, 7th edn. (O.U.P.), and H. Scherchen's *Handbook of Conducting* (O.U.P., 1956), for their technical advice, and P. Young's *World Conductors* (Abelard–Schuman, 1965) for its historical and "personality-cult" aspects. But, however rich his library, he will constantly need extra help from reference books. The most generally useful is *The Catalogue of the E. A. Fleisher Library* (Philadelphia, revised 1966, and Suppt. covering 1945–55, 1957) (see Fig. 1), which gives orchestrations, timings and first performances of a vast repertory, and has a section for concerti, classified by solo instrument. The library gives a nation-wide service throughout the U.S., as a complement to commercial services. It controls and even commissions MS. works, most of which are American and form the substance of vol. 2. A forerunner, covering somewhat similar ground, but unrelated to any actual library service

5

is W. Altmann's *Orchester-Literatur Katalog*, 2 vols., (Leuckart, 1926–36) covering publications 1850–1935 and classified into symphonies, suites, overtures, concerti, etc., with timings and orchestrations. This is brought up to 1960 by W. Buschkötter's *Handbuch der musikalischen Konzertliteratur* (Berlin, de Gruyter, 1961) with similar detailed information. The modern repertory (with band-parts on hire from individual publishers) is also collated in certain general trade-catalogues—firstly, for Europe (and Germany in particular), by the *Bonner Katalog* (Musikhandel-Verlagsgesellschaft, 1959–) (see Fig. 2), and secondly, for the U.S., by the ASCAP *Symphonic Catalog* (New York, 1959) (see Fig. 3), and the *Symphonic Music Catalog* (New York, Broadcast Music Inc., 1963). The Kranichsteiner Musikinstitut's (now renamed Internationales Musikinstitut) *Katalog* (Darmstadt, 1966–) gives the holdings of an organization pledged to reflect contemporary trends, and is described in *Fontes artis musicae*, 1958/2 (Bärenreiter). Russian orchestral scores are listed currently in *Musikalnya Literatura*, *Meszhdunarodnya Kniga* and are obtainable direct or through agencies such as Collett's Holdings, Anglo-Russian Music or Musica Rara (London) and Chant du Monde (Paris). Boosey and Anglo-Soviet (London) control and republish certain works, particularly Prokofiev and works commissioned by the Koussevitsky Foundation. For the Communist countries, the Internationale Leihbibliothek (Berlin, D.D.R.) runs a special service (with published catalogues) of MS. works, and thus complements their commercial services.

The chamber orchestra is specially served by Saltonstall & Smith's *Catalogue of Music for Small Orchestra* (Washington, Music Library Association, 1947) which provides, in its system of grouping by instrumentation, a partial answer to recurrent questions such as "what exists for orchestra without trombones, or without trumpets and drums?" A small study by M. Pincherle, *L'Orchestre de chambre* (Larousse, 1948), lists the principal works written since 1880.

Publishers' catalogues, of course, form an essential guide to available material. A comprehensive list of firms, their associates and agencies, forms Appendix IIA. For the classical orchestral repertory, the lists of Breitkopf and Peters (along with the American reprinters

Broude, E. Kalmus, A. Luck, etc.) are still the most generally useful. Antiquarian dealers' catalogues (see Ch. 11), some of which give splendid bibliographical value, are an essential complement, since at any given moment much is out of print. Some countries, where commercial publishing is minimal, form composer's guilds, which help with performing materials, and issue their own catalogues. Donemus (228 Amstel, Amsterdam) is an outstanding example, as witness in its *International Selection of Contemporary Music* (1968). The collecting agencies associated with these organizations are listed in Apepndix IIC. The assumption that such lists are full of dross which no reputable publisher will touch is fortunately not uniformly true. Activities are co-ordinated by the Music Information Centre's group of the International Association of Music Libraries.

AMATEURS

Amateurs need special guidance and carefully graded lists. Publishers' catalogues frequently give help of this kind, featuring special supplements for school ensembles, etc., and reflect the works of many distinguished composers (Hindemith, Marx, Orff, Britten, Vaughan Williams, Crosse, Williamson, Cole, Gardner, etc.) who have written specifically for amateurs. The London firms of Novello and O.U.P. among others, are commissioning series of such works. L. Duck's *The Amateur Orchestra* (Dobson, 1953) is a thoroughly sensible and practical manual with a useful repertory list, and the International Music Council's *Symphonic Music*: 1880–1954 (Peters, 1957) was compiled with particular reference to amateur capability. The most up-to-date repertory is listed in J. Dalby's *School and Amateur Orchestras* (Pergamon, 1966).

TIMINGS

Works by Fleischer and Buschkötter already described include these, but the following devote themselves specifically to the subject. S. Aronowsky's *Performing Times of Orchestral Works* (Benn, 1959) is

based on a wide experience of actual performances, and the compiler
sensibly draws attention to the inevitable variations of perfectly
reputable timings, even by the same conductor. Timings of separate
movements of symphonies, suites, etc., are usefully given and there
are comprehensive lists of publishers and fee-collecting societies. A
much smaller but quite reliable work is W. R. Reddick's *The
Standard Orchestral Repertoire* (New York, Doubleday, 1947).

PREMIÈRES

Most dictionaries and encyclopaedias mention famous first performances whether orchestral, operatic or ballet. This information
appears also in *Fleisher* and in such works as N. Slonimsky's *Music
Since 1900*, 3rd edn. (New York, Coleman–Ross, 1949), M. Séné-
chaud's *Concerts Symphoniques* (Lausanne, Marguerat, 1947), D.
Ewen's *Encyclopaedia of Concert Music* (Owen, 1961) and his *Complete
Book of 20th Century Music* (New York, Prentice-Hall, 1952),
Upton & Borowski's *Standard Concert Guide* (Chicago, McClurg,
1930) and the Victor Books of *Concertos, Symphonies, Overtures*, etc.
(New York, Simon & Schuster). In a special category are the
accounts of famous organizations such as M. B. Foster's *History of the
Philharmonic Society of London: 1813–1912* (Lane, 1912) and its
successor R. Elkin's *Royal Philharmonic . . . 1912–45* (Rider, 1946),
both listing many famous first performances.

BAND-PARTS

Early music often survives in published parts but not in score.
Paradoxically, most modern copyright music may be bought in
study-score form only; the parts must be hired from their publisher.
Fortunately, the core of the (non-copyright) repertory can be bought
(new) from publishers, reprinters and dealers or (second-hand) from
antiquarians. It may also be hired from publishers and from general
commercial hire-libraries such as J. & W. Chester Ltd., Goodwin &
Tabb Ltd., Novello & Co. Ltd., etc., for the U.K., and from the
Fleisher Library (see p. 5) under special limitation, for the U.S.A.

In the U.K., also, the Central Music Library, Westminster, Liverpool and Manchester Public Libraries and some county libraries run loan or subscription services for orchestral and choral materials, while lists of the private holdings of amateur orchestral societies belonging to the National Federation of Music Societies (4 St. James's Square, S.W. 1) are circulated to facilitate inter loan or hire by members.

Conductors such as Boult and Beecham are at opposite poles over the endless question of personal markings, and Inghelbrecht in *The Conductor's World* (P. Neville, 1933) has an amusing chapter on *graffiti*.

CONCERT GUIDES

These and programme notes are discussed in Ch. 17, on the assumption that deputing these chores to someone else will leave the conductor more time with his scores.

HISTORY

The major studies in English are A. Carse's *The Orchestra in the 18th Century* (Heffer–Broude, 1950) and *The Orchestra from Beethoven to Berlioz* (Heffer–Broude, 1950).

ORCHESTRATION

Prototypes are H. Berlioz's *Treatise on Instrumentation*, enlarged and revised by Richard Strauss (Kalmus, 1948) and Rimsky-Korsakov's *Principles of Orchestration*, ed. Steinberg (Kalmus, 1930) together with its *Digest* by Schmid (Boosey, 1950). The standard British works are C. Forsyth's *Orchestration*, 2nd edn. (Macmillan, 1948) and G. Jacob's *Orchestral Technique*, 2nd edn. (O.U.P., 1940), complemented by F. Collinson's *Orchestration for the Theatre* (Lane, 1941). American writers keep abreast of later developments with volumes such as W. Piston's *Orchestration* (Gollancz, 1958) which follows mainly traditional lines, J. Wagner's *Orchestration* (McGraw-Hill, 1959), and H. Mancini's *Sounds and Scores* (Northridge Music

Inc., 1962) which, with examples in print and on disc, exploits the newer symphonic-jazz type of sound. Leibowitz and Maguire's *Thinking for Orchestra* (Schirmer, 1960) sets a wide range of typical problems and provides the solutions made by master composers. Mancini together with R. Garcia's *The Professional Arranger-Composer* (Hackensack, N.J., Wehman Bros.) seem to be the only works dealing with the problems of microphone techniques as applied to music.

EDITING

For a general discussion of musicological aspects see Ch. 9. Meanwhile, salutary reminders of the fallibility of the printed score are N. del Mar's "Confusion and error" (*The Score*, Oct. 1957; Feb. and (July 1958) and C. Sartori's "Mr. Vaughan's Crusades" (*Opera*, April, 1963).

PERIODICALS

Among all the musical journals which deal incidentally with orchestral matters, one in particular devotes itself to them entirely: *Das Orchester* (Mainz, Musikzeitschriften-Verlag), though its emphasis is largely on German domestic affairs.

MILITARY BAND

Band worlds are again quite distinct from the orchestral sphere, even though their protagonists may occasionally nod acquaintance across the stadium platform. The London publisher Boosey & Hawkes holds the key to most of the practical problems, and this firm is officially charged with supplying British and Commonwealth Army bands with the latest versions of national anthems, regimental marches, etc., besides the normal run of military and brass music. The Boosey and the Chappell catalogues accordingly deploy the British repertoire, while E. Berger's *Band Music Guide*, 3rd edn. (Evanston, Ill., The Instrumentalist, 1963) lists current works by title, with indexes of instrumental solos, fanfares, etc., and quotes over 100 publishers, mostly American. It should be made quite clear that the American "band" has its own instrumentation—an amalgam of the British military and brass bands. The most comprehensive historical treatise is that now in preparation by K. Haas: *Three Hundred Years of Military Music* (Hutchinson)—the work of a practical musician and scholar. This will contain sixty-four pages of complete examples from early times to Rossini, and a thirty-four-page bibliography. Further scholarly studies include the rare *Die Militär-musik* of P. Panòff (Berlin, A. Parryhysius, 1938), H. G. Farmer's *Rise and Development of Military Music* (Reeves, 1912) and the articles in *Grove* on "Military band" and in *MGG* under "Janitscharen Musik" and "Militär Musik", rounded off by H. G. Farmer's "Turkish music" article in the *Encyclopedia of Islam*. British surveys include W. Wood's *Romance of Regimental Marches* (Clowes, 1932) and Mackenzie-Rogan's *Fifty Years of Army Music* (Methuen, 1926). A vast documentation by W. C. Tanner (63 Links Side, Enfield, Middx.): *Military Band Encyclopaedia of Bandmasters and Bands in H.M. Army, Royal Marines and R.A.F.*, which is kept up to date with new appointments, etc., remains in typescript. H. W. Schwartz's *Bands of America* (Bailey & Swinfen, 1957) deals with developments from 1860 onwards.

The standard manual for British practice is H. E. Adkin's *Treatise On the Military Band*, rev. edn. (Boosey, 1945), supported, for American practice, by J. F. Wagner's *Band Scoring* (McGraw-Hill, 1960). Each country has its military schools, often with historic archives, that for the U.K. being the Royal Military School of Music (Kneller Hall, Twickenham), whose large working library includes many specially commissioned works, particularly fanfares in MS. The American pioneer of concert band conducting, Edwin Franko Goldman, has his life-work reflected in the following books by his son R. F. Goldman: *The Concert Band* (New York, Rinehart, 1946), and *The Wind Band* (Boston, Allyn & Bacon, 1961).

Pipe, fife and drum music has its own publishers. Fife and drum bands are catered for by Henry Potter Ltd., 36 West St., W.C. 2. Highland bagpipe music is published by Paterson's Publications,

36–40 Wigmore St., W. 1. There is a growing demand, especially in Canada, for combined bagpipe and military band music. Apparently no published arrangements exist as yet, but the Director of Music of the Guards' Depot, Pirbright has some in MS.

BRASS BAND

D. Wright's *Complete Bandmaster* (Pergamon Press, 1963) provides an excellently graded repertory list, not confined to British editions. F. Wright's *Brass Today* (Benson, 1957) is a collection of articles, and the *Bandsman's Everything Within* (Hinrichsen, 1950) is a miscellany, with much biographical detail. The Salvation Army publishes full scores and bandparts of all its specially commissioned works but use is limited to its own bands (Salvationist Publishing Co., Judd St., W.C. 1). An example of an American specialist publisher–dealer's catalogue is *Music for Brass* (King, 7 Canton St., N. Easton, Mass.).

See also Chapter 6.

CHAPTER 3

The Theatre Conductor
and Researcher

(A l'Opéra) on continue à faire un singulier bruit que des gens qui ont payé pour cela appellent de la musique . . . il ne faut pas les croire tout à fait.

C. DEBUSSY, *Monsieur Croche*

THEATRICAL music covers nearly four centuries, and there exists a complex documentation for it. The Society for Theatre Research (1948–, 103 Ralph Court, London W. 2) and its continental counterparts deal only incidentally with music, but must not be overlooked. Other, not primarily musical, reference books include *The Stage Cyclopedia* (1909) with its still useful chronologies and *Who's Who in the Theatre*, 14th edn. (Pitman, 1967). This is almost exclusively British in scope (with some New York data), and lists notable productions and important revivals on the London stage, obituaries, together with a section on centres for theatre research and on public and private collections here and abroad. The *Deutsches Bühnenjahrbuch* (Hamburg, Genossenschaft Deutscher Bühnen-Angehörigen, 1889–) currently performs a similar function for the two Germanies, and includes film, radio and television. Further key works in the theatrical field yielding much incidental musical value are Blanch M. Baker's *Theatre and Allied Arts* (H. W. Wilson, 1952), *The Oxford Companion to the Theatre* (O.U.P., 1951), Kürschner's *Biographisches Theater-Handbuch* (Berlin, De Gruyter, 1956), and the magnificently illustrated *Enciclopedia dello spettacolo* (Rome, 1954–). For general

13

background D. Grout's *A Short History of Opera*, 2nd edn. (Columbia U. Press, 1966), is seminal.

One of the very few works devoted specifically to theatre music is L. Bridgewater's *Music in the Theatre* (Pergamon Press, in preparation), which is at once scholarly and supremely practical in outlook. A smaller, but again completely practical treatise in R. Settle's *Music in the Theatre* (Jenkins, 1957), with its lists of Shakespeare songs and their stage background, and its catalogue of "mood music". Among the few studies in English of the continental scene is H. M. Brown's *Music in the French Secular Theater* (Harvard U.P., 1963).

OPERA

The Music

Opera scores vary considerably in their accessibility. Published full orchestral scores account for only a part of the repertory. Two reliable guides to these are library catalogues (both giving collations): O. Sonneck's *Dramatic Music Catalogue* (Library of Congress, 1908), and the *Katalog der Musikbibliothek Paul Hirsch, Band 2: Opernpartituren* (Berlin, Breslauer, 1930) (see Fig. 4). In both appear many rarities of two kinds: (a) the score which is rare by mere age: early editions of Gluck, Spontini, Donizetti, and (b) those rare because they have never been formally published, but deposited in numbered sets, controlled by their publishers and deposited on restricted contract ("revers") in the opera houses of the world—Verdi, Puccini, Wagner, Richard Strauss, etc. A few full scores have been published in miniature form by Ricordi, etc. The conductor relies on opera-house archives or loan/hire from publishers. The researcher must rely on the same sources or on the very few great libraries lucky enough to have been able to acquire scores. A useful independent source is the Theater Leihbibliothek Emil Richter (Holm-Sappensen, Harburg, Todstedter Weg).

Vocal scores are much easier of access, though a great proportion of them remain obstinately out of print (e.g. Donizetti and early Verdi operas), while others (e.g. the German stage versions by Oscar Hagen of Handel operas) vary radically from original versions, with altered recitatives and even occasional new roles. The B.B.C.'s *Choral and Opera Catalogues*, 2 vols. (1965–), are probably the richest in performing editions, and include many rarities, while a useful basic collection is listed in the (London) Central Music Library's *List of Operas Available* (1955). Some public libraries (e.g. Dagenham, Liverpool, Newcastle-upon-Tyne and Essex County) have published catalogues or hand-lists. The London firm of music publishers and library suppliers, J. B. Cramer & Co. Ltd., quotes over 200 repertory scores in print in their *Basic and Standard Music Library List*, and most antiquarian dealers regularly offer a wide selection. (See Ch. 11.)

Production

A reliable British treatise still apparently remains to be written. Meanwhile M. Graf's *Producing Opera for America*, and Q. Eaton's *Opera Production* (both Univ. of Minnesota Press, 1961) explore the scene in the U.S.A. Eaton's book is particularly valuable for its data about casting, performing rights, availability of materials; it even quotes translations where these have been traced, and has useful appendices for long operas, short operas and some unpublished operas. The Viennese annals are described in W. Beetz' *Das Wiener Opernhaus, 1869–1945* (Panorama, 1949).

Television opera production is, of course, clearing its own special path at such a pace that there is virtually no settled documentation as such. Meanwhile the International Music Centre, Vienna, forms a useful reference point.

LIBRETTI

Early libretto collections of various sizes exist in most of the state and conservatory libraries, one important example being in the Fétis collection at the Brussels Conservatoire. A rare example of a published catalogue is O. Sonneck's *Catalogue of Opera Librettos before 1800*, 2 cols. (Washington, Library of Congress, 1914, reprinted by Johnson, 1968). The recording companies, particularly Decca, have begun to issue original texts with parallel English translations to

complement their albums, though the latter are *not* singing translations. An interesting, if limited, anthology has been gathered
by H. H. Stückenschmidt in his *Spectaculum: Texte moderner Opern*
(Frankfurt, Suhrkamp, 1962), and a useful, apparently unique, list
of extant translations (though inevitably far from complete) is
W. Dace's *Survey of Opera in Modern Translation* (Eastman School
of Music, 1956). The Metropolitan Opera Council, New York,
has recently issued its own compilation of *English Translations of
Foreign Operas* (Central Opera Service Bulletin, November–
December 1966). There seems to be only one manual on the tech-
nicalities of writing—E. Istel's *The Art of Writing Opera Librettos*
(Schirmer, 1922), but both *Grove* and *MGG* have excellent general
articles. Though not primarily operatic, the information being
collected by the Translations Center at Brooklyn College City
University of New York will include some opera material.

Dictionaries, etc.

D. E. Baker's *Biographia dramatica*, 3 vols. (Longman, Hurst, 1812),
though not primarily concerned with opera, covers much theatrical
ground. Examples of works in dictionary form exclusively devoted
to opera are:

> CLÉMENT and LAROUSSE. *Dictionnaire des opéras . . . tous les
> opéras, opéras-comique, opérettes et drames lyriques . . . jusqu'à
> nos jours.* Rev. Pougin (Larousse, 1904).
> H. RIEMANN. *Opern-Handbuch: Opern, Operetten, Ballete,
> Pantomimen . . .* (Leipzig, c. 1892).
> J. TOWERS. *Dictionary-Catalogue of Operas and Operettas* (1910,
> Reprint: DaCapo Press, 1967) (a bare title, composer and
> date list).

Handbooks, Plots

The most comprehensive work in English is Kobbé's *Complete
Opera Book*, revised by the Earl of Harewood (Putnam, 1954): "the

stories of the operas, together with four hundred of the leading airs and motives in musical notation". A feature not systematically attempted in most other similar dictionaries is the casting for major productions in the leading European and American opera houses. The next most comprehensive work is *The Decca Book of Opera* (Laurie, 1956), which gives biographies, critical commentaries by specialists, plots, first performances, librettists and discographies. An American equivalent is D. Ewen's *Encyclopaedia of the Opera* (Wyn, 1955) covering over 100 works.

Directories, Annuals, etc.

The Opera Directory (Calder, 1961) continues where most other opera reference works leave off. International in the fullest sense (using six languages) it classifies organizations, festivals, colleges, conductors, singers, etc., provides a current casting index and a list of operas by contemporary composers. Its counterpart and fore-runner, *Opera Annual* (Calder, 1954–) adds premières, and obituaries. More current data for amateurs is to be found in the *Yearbook* (1965–) of the National Operatic and Dramatic Association. A most valuable reference work for conductors, managers, etc. is G. E. Lessing's *Handbuch des Opernrepertoires* (Boosey & Hawkes, 1952) since it gives copyright details, with full data of provenance of orchestral and vocal material together with full instrumentations of varying versions, plus the required casting, and adds a useful chart classifying the principal roles by type of voice. If it were as strong in the Latin and Anglo–Saxon as in the Teutonic repertoire, it would be even more useful. A list of characters (description, famous exponents, sources) makes *The Handbook of World Opera* by F. L. Moore (Barker, 1961) another welcome tool. The monthly *Opera* (Rolls House Pub. Co.) attempts international coverage, current and future, while *Der Spielplan* (Bärenreiter) details the immense activity of the two Germanies and Austria with some news of current affairs in France and England.

Chronology

Two key works are planned chronologically: A. Loewenberg's *Annals of Opera*, 2nd edn., 2 vols. (Geneva, Societas Bibliographica, 1955), lists over 4000 operas, 1597–1940, with location of performance, length of run, librettists, versions, and (importantly) translations with indexes by composer, title and librettist; W. H. Seltsam's *Metropolitan Opera Annals* (New York, Wilson, 1947) chronicles artists and performances 1883–1947.

Shakespeare Music

The celebrations of 1964 produced at least two valuable works which give special aid to documenting the music. Phyllis Hartnoll's *Shakespeare in Music* (Macmillan, 1964) contains an eighty-page catalogue of works based on the plays and poetry, with a check-list of composers, the joint work of the compilers and the librarian of the Society for Theatre Research. This covers opera (over 180, published and MS.), published incidental music, with some reference to film and radio, and concert works. Dates are given but unfortunately no publishers. A Boustead's *Music to Shakespeare* (O.U.P., 1964) is "a practical catalogue of current incidental music, song settings and other related music", giving publishers but no dates. These may be supported by the resources of the Shakespeare Memorial Library, Birmingham, and the annual volumes of the *Shakespeare Survey* (O.U.P.).

Among the various volumes quoting musical texts are L. C. Elson's *Shakespeare in Music: a collation of chief allusions* (Boston, L. C. Page, 1900), J. H. Long's *Shakespeare's Use of Music* (Gainesville, Univ. of Florida Press, 1963) and E. W. Naylor's *Shakespeare Music* (Curwen, 1912). F. W. Sternfeld's *Music in Shakespearean Tragedy* (Routledge, 1963) gives exhaustive attention to instrumental music and has an index of lyrics.

Much specially arranged music continues to be written for current productions, of course, the archive of the Royal Shakespeare Theatre, Stratford-on-Avon, being especially important. Novello's *Stratford* series reflects the long association of Leslie Bridgewater with this theatre and with many London productions. For those who want some recorded contemporary settings *Music of Shakespeare's Time*, ed. Diana Poulton (EMI records, CLP 1633–4) is recommended.

OPERETTA

Hitherto rather neglected, this field has recently received much systematic documentation and now has reasonably good coverage. M. Lubbock's *Complete Book of Light Opera* (Putnam, 1962) is a worthy counterpart to Kobbé in its scope and wealth of detail, and gives particular attention to the American scene. It covers the Paris, Vienna, Berlin, London and New York repertories, but excludes "opéra comique" and, unfortunately, no publishers are quoted. G. Hughes' *Composers of Operetta* (Macmillan, 1962) is a general survey with an index covering 1824–1960, and is supported by S. Mackinlay's *Origin and Development of Light Opera* (Hutchinson, 1927). S. Czech's *Das Operettenbuch*, 4th edn. (Stuttgart, Muth'sche, 1960) has evolved from a prototype, and still holds the lead for the purely German repertory, including Singspiele, being complemented by the *Operetten-Führer* by Steger & Howe (Hamburg, Fischer Bücherei) and a similarly named volume by A. Würz (Stuttgart, Reclam). Vienna naturally has its own annals, described by F. Hadamowsky and H. Otte in *Die Wiener Operette* (Bellaria, 1947). For France, L. Oster's *Les Opérettes du répertoire courant* (Editions du Conquistador, 1953) usefully supplements the basic Clément and Larousse (see p. 16), while similar small volumes from the same press for opera and ballet round out the repertory. *MGG* has a useful bibliography of the subject under "Operette".

GILBERT AND SULLIVAN

The publishing rights in vocal scores have long been vested in Chappell's, who have recently issued excellent, well-cued and cheap chorus scores. The authentic band-parts remain on hire from D'Oyly Carte, though some amended American versions are on sale. No full scores (except for *Mikado*, Gregg International, 1968), but cued vocal scores are supplied by D'Oyly Carte with the hired parts. The emergence of the music from copyright in 1951 resulted in one major re-working of the tunes: *Pineapple Poll*, a ballet with music based on Sullivan arranged by C. Mackerras, from which a popular concert suite has been published (Chappell).

Two primary centres of information are the D'Oyly Carte Company Ltd. (1 Savoy Hill, W.C. 2) itself, and the Gilbert and Sullivan Society (273 Northfield Av., W. 5). Both maintain libraries, and the latter, which does not confine its activity to the operettas alone, issues a journal. Gilbert and Sullivan bibliography runs to sixty or so major studies, including a concordance: *The Gilbert and Sullivan Operas* by F. J. Halton (New York, Bass Publishers, 1935), and *The Gilbert and Sullivan Dictionary* by G. E. Dunn (Allen & Unwin, 1936). The standard treatise is L. Baily's *The Gilbert and Sullivan Book*, 4th edn. (Cassell, 1956) while more recent major contributions to Savoyard literature are Rollin & Will's *The D'Oyly Carte Company: a record of productions, 1875–1961* (Joseph, 1962) and M. Green's *Treasury of Gilbert and Sullivan* (New York, Simon & Schuster, 1961) which gives complete libretti of the operettas and the words and music of 102 favourite songs.

MUSICAL COMEDY, VARIETY, ETC.

This ground is no less well covered than opera and operetta, though there is no single volume which does what Kobbé and Lubbock respectively do for them. Most musical comedies, whether native or imported from America, are controlled (and, for the most part, published in vocal score and orchestral selection of "hit" tunes) by Chappell of London, whose catalogues are in themselves a history of the musical stage. Two London organizations supplement Chappell's service, particularly for amateurs: Samuel French issues current *Guides to Selecting Plays*, of which *Part 9: musical plays (1962–63)* annotates, with full commercial detail of staging, copyright, costume-hire, etc., about fifty shows released from their West End runs. The National Operatic and Dramatic Association covers primarily the older type of work: *Plays: a guide to the works in the library of NODA* (1929) and *Operas Old and New*, by Page &

Billings (NODA, 1932) are basic but only reflect a limited part of its current service to amateurs, which is described in NODA's *Directory* (1960) and its *List of Operas and Operettas for Schools and Youth Clubs* (1957).

The American scene is even more fully documented. Narrative types of work range from J. W. McSpadden's *Operas and Musical Comedies* (biographies, themes, characters, etc.) (New York, Crowell, 1951) to J. Burton's *Blue Book* series, culminating in *The Blue Book of Tin Pan Alley* (New York, Century House, 1962–) and I. Goldberg's *Tin Pan Alley* (New York, Ungar, 1961) with a supplement *From Sweet and Swing to Rock 'n Roll* by Jablonski. L. A. Paris's *Men and Melodies* (New York, Crowell, 1954) is excellent for background information on Romberg, Kern, Berlin, Gershwin, Cole Porter, Rodgers and Hammerstein, etc. Quick-reference works include Lewine & Simon's *Encyclopaedia of Theatre Music: 4,000 songs from Broadway and Hollywood, 1900–1960* (New York, Random House, 1961), D. Ewen's *American Musical Theatre . . . from 1866 to the Present . . .* (New York, H. Holt, 1958), J. Mattfeld's *Variety Music Cavalcade, 1620–1961*, rev. edn. (New York, Prentice-Hall, 1962) and his *Handbook of American Operatic Premières, 1731–1962* (Detroit Information Service Inc., 1963) which includes much musical comedy. A further attempt to bridge the gap between classical music and jazz is Gammond and Clayton's *Guide to Popular Music* (Phoenix, 1960), in dictionary form, with much biographical data and a good chronological index, 1725–1960.

BALLAD OPERA

Some special problems arise from the nature of this hybrid form which produced some 120 works between John Gay's success of 1728 and 1750. E. D. Gagey deals intensively with this outcrop, listing published and unpublished specimens, and noting sixteen which survived up to 1835 in his *Ballad Opera* (New York, Columbia U.P., 1937). A revival, not limited to, but stimulated by the post-war major recensions of Bliss, Britten and Bukofzer, among others, of the *Beggar's Opera*, is reflected in *John Gay and Ballad Opera*, by

M—B

Handley-Taylor and Granville-Barker (Hinrichsen's 9th Music Book, 1956). Due attention is given here to original airs and their many settings, and to the historical importance of Playfair's and Bax & Austin's resuscitations of *The Beggar's Opera* (1920) and *Polly* (1922) respectively. B. Squire in his introduction to "An index of tunes in the ballad-operas" (*Musical Antiquary*, Oct. 1910, pp. 1–17) shows how incomplete was the background of his 700 popular tunes of the day. Contemporary scores were of these airs alone, with a thorough-bass accompaniment and sketchy indications of string or wind instrumentation. An overture might survive in full score occasionally (Dr. Pepusch's for the *Beggar's Opera*) but very few fully scored, complete ballad operas seem to have survived apart from *Love in a Village* (Royal College of Music), unless one includes Storace's *No Song, No Supper* (Musica Britannica, 16, Stainer & Bell), or the British Museum's MS. band-parts of Shield's *Rosina*. Persistent research, however, is still yielding results as evidenced by R. Fiske's article (*Music and Letters*, April 1961) "A score for *The Duenna*") which traces to Egerton 2493 in the British Museum a manuscript full score by Thomas Linley, Jr. The gaps therein have more recently been traced to the Gresham Library, Guildhall, London. "Favourite airs", with new symphonies and accompaniments as rehashed in Boosey & Co's small series of English Ballad Operas (*Love in a Village, Rosina*, etc.) were virtually the only scores bringing dialogue and music together in performing versions, until a new lease of life was given by the Brecht–Weill *Dreigroschenoper* (Universal, 1928). By the time of the appearance of Weill's *Down in the Valley* (Schirmer, 1948) radio had produced some brilliant examples of the form, and the B.B.C. had added in post-war years, such land marks as *Johnny Miner, The Dark-eyed Sailor, The Ballad of John Axon* and *Blind Raftery*. Dozens of "radio features", closely akin to folk-opera, now remain in MS. in the B.B.C. Music Library. (See also Ch. 13.)

BALLET

"En quel ton jouez-vous, messieurs?" dit *(le danseur) en suspendant son vol. "Il me semble que mon morceau me fatigue plus que de coûtume." "Nous jouons en* mi." *"Je ne m'étonne plus maintenant . . . je ne puis le danser qu'en ré."*

H. BERLIOZ, *Les Grotesques de la musique*

The evidence of the theatre itself that music in ballet is a necessary, expensive and reprehensible nuisance is borne out by ballet literature. R. Fiske's *Ballet Music* (Harrap, 1958) (one of the very few attempts to rescue the subject from the decent obscurity of the pit) emphasized what ballet conductors were already fully aware of, viz. that few full ballet scores have ever been published. *Giselle*, in its various, fully scored forms remains in MS., and the only piano reduction of the original (Meissonnier) has been out of print for generations. Latterly, the position has improved and from firms like Broude, Kalmus, and Musurgia of New York, full scores of *Swan Lake* and *Casse Noisette* are now available, but in 1968 excellently printed full scores such as *Swan Lake* and *Sleeping Beauty* began to appear, separate from the Tchaikowsky collected edition, from Russian State Music. The Tchaikowsky Foundation of New York, fortunately, is both a publishing and research centre, and is steadily making available the key scores and band-parts of the non-copyright repertoire, though not with all the scholarship to be desired. Even now, however, complete orchestrations of Chopin music for *Les Sylphides* have to be hired from their various "publishers" or controllers, while *La Sylphide* (either Loewenskjöld or Schneitzhöffer) is not even commercially hireable at all. Apparently, the only other work devoted to ballet music itself is H. Searle's *Ballet Music: an introduction* (Cassell, 1957), which gives more emphasis than Fiske to modern examples.

Contrast this with the relative surfeit of ballet *literature*, and the point is made that in ballet the stage is all, just as in television the music (even sometimes in opera itself) has to bow to the demands of the picture. C. W. Beaumont's *Complete Book of Ballets* (Putnam, 1937, 3 suppts. to 1955) leads the way, supplemented by Gadan and

Maillard's *Dictionary of Modern Ballet* (Methuen, 1955), the *Victor Book of Ballets and Ballet Music* (Simon & Schuster, 1950), E. B. L. Wilson's *Dictionary of Ballet* (Penguin, 1957), the *Decca Book of Ballet* (Muller, 1958) (which shows a sense of values by beginning with "ballets to specially-composed scores"), and V. Arvey's *Choreographic Music* (New York, Dutton, 1941). The classics are steadily being reprinted by such firms as Gregg International. Apart from numerous "coffee-table" books consisting almost solely of illustrations, special national studies include:

> Denmark: FOG, D. *The Royal Danish Ballet, 1760–1958*, and *Auguste Bournonville* (Copenhagen, Fog, 1961).
>
> England: BRINSON, P. *Ballet in Britain* (O.U.P., 1962).
>
> France: MCGOWAN, M. *L'Art du Ballet de Cour en France, 1581–1643* (Centre National de la Recherche Scientifique, 1963).
>
> > OSTER, L. *Les Ballets du Répertoire Courant* (édns. du Conquistador, 1955).
> >
> > PREMIÈRES, H. *Le Ballet de Cour* (Laurens, 1963).

EARLY DANCE FORMS

These have at least two notable modern chroniclers: Mabel Dolmetsch, with her *Dances of Spain and Italy 1400–1600* and *Dances of England and France, 1450–1600* (both Routledge, 1954), and Melusine Wood, with *Some Historical Dances* and *Advanced Historical Dances* (Imperial Society of Teachers of Dancing, 1952 and 1960).

CHAPTER 4

The Choral Conductor

> *Le programme se compose exclusivement d'un immense oratorio, que le public vient d'entendre par devoir religieux, qu'il écoute avec un silence religieux, que les artistes subissent avec un courage religieux, et qui produit sur tous un ennui froid, noir et pesant comme les murailles d'une église protestante.*
>
> H. Berlioz, *Les Soirées de l'orchestre*

GENERAL BIBLIOGRAPHY

Probably the most comprehensive statement of the vast repertory in both performing and critical editions is the B.B.C.'s *Choral and Opera Catalogue*, 2 vols. (B.B.C., 1967). In addition, most works on choral topics as listed, for example, in R. D. Darrell's *Schirmer's Guide to Books on Music* (New York, Schirmer, 1951) (see Fig. 5), include repertory-lists, some of them doubly valuable for their percipience in grading works by difficulty, such as L. Woodgate's *The Choral Conductor* (Ascherberg, 1949), L. and R. Rhea's *Choral Program Planning* (Southern, 1947) and R. Manning's *From Holst to Britten* (Workers' Music Association, 1949). A work with particular personal association, but containing very valuable chapters on choral technique and training is H. S. and K. Roberton's *Orpheus with his Lute: a Glasgow Orpheus Choir anthology* (Pergamon, 1963). A key-work for the average English choral society is the National Federation of Music Society's *Catalogue of Choral Works . . . Performed . . . 1936–53*, 2nd edn. (4 St. James's Sq., S.W. 1, 1953), with its apparatus of timing, publisher, orchestration. This is supplemented, most practically, by more recent typescript lists of the members' nation-wide holdings of choral stocks. An equivalent U.S. service is given by the Association of American Choruses (Drinker Choral Library, c/o Westminster Choir College, Princeton, N.J.). One of the basic expositions of the enormous German repertory was G. Schünemann's *Führer durch die deutsche Chorliteratur*, 2 vols. (Wölfenbüttel, 1935–6). Then came E. Valentin's *Handbuch der Chormusik*, 2 vols. (Bosse, 1953–8). These are still further extended by the *MGG* articles: "Frauenchor" and "Männerchor". E. Velentin classifies the vast repertory according to sacred and secular, accompanied and *a cappella*, but is heavily Teutonic and does not evaluate. Three American works are of especial value precisely because of their gradings. M. J. Knapp's *Selected List of Music for Men's Voices* (Princeton U.P., 1952), Locke and Fassett's *Selected List of Choruses for Women's Voices*, 3rd edn. (Northampton, Mass., Smith College, 1964) and lastly C. C. Burnsworth's *Choral Music for Women's Voices* (Scarecrow Press, 1968).

G. W. Stubbings' *Dictionary of Church Music* (Epworth Press, 1947) makes a useful approach to terminology, while the B.B.C. Gramophone Library's *Liturgical and other Church Music on Commercial Gramophone Records* (B.B.C., 1960) is an expert survey. For manuscripts and early editions see Ch. 9. Apart from the main repertory published by internationally famous firms, there are many specialist publishers (see Appendix IIA), such as Cary and Faith Press in the U.K., Boehm, Pustet and Schwann in Germany, Desclée and Schola Cantorum for Belgium and France respectively, Van Rossum for Holland, and Carisch in Italy, who collectively put out a vast range of performing editions. The American Institute of Musicology in Rome is responsible for the formidable series *Corpus mensurabilis musicae*, "and associated series", while *Tudor Church Music* (O.U.P., reprinted by Broude, currently under revision by Le Huray and Willcocks) (see Fig. 6), and *Musica Britannica* (Stainer & Bell) stand at the head of numerous British series, the most recent being *Early English Church Music* (Stainer & Bell, 1963–). Historical surveys include W. H. Parry's *Thirteen Centuries of English Church Music*, 2nd edn. (Hinrichsen, 1946) and E. H. Fellowes' *English Cathedral Music from Edward VI to Edward VII* (Methuen, 1941).

D. Stevens' *Tudor Church Music* 2nd edn. (Faber, 1966) is one of the few studies which takes the trouble to list and annotate modern performing editions. The glories of English church music are yet further illustrated in R. Wilkes' *English Cathedrals and Collegiate Churches and Chapels* (Friends of Catholic Music, Faith House, 1968) and in Bower and Wicks, *Repertory of English Cathedral anthems* (Church Music Society–O.U.P., 1965). St. Michael's College, Tenbury, and the Royal School of Church Music (Addington Palace, Croydon) attempt to keep alive the traditions of the medieval song-schools, the latter's *English Church Music* (1963) giving a fair survey of present problems and recent developments. France and Italy have their major scholarly anthologies (with choral music predominating) in H. Expert's *Les Maîtres musiciens de la Renaissance française*, 23 vols. (Leduc, reprinted New York, Broude, 1963); *Monuments de la musique française*, 11 vols. (Salabert–Broude), and L. Torchi's *L'Arte musicale in Italia*, 7 vols. (Ricordi, 1897–1907) respectively, and other nations have their equivalents. These are listed in the *Hirsch Katalog*, Band IV, the *Harvard Dictionary* under "Editions, historical", A. H. Heyer's *Historical Sets* (A.L.A., 1968), and, most recent of all, in L. B. Spiess's *Historical Musicology* (Brooklyn, Institute of Medieval Music, 1963). Research coverage is brought further up to date in K. R. Hartley's *Bibliography of Theses and Dissertations in Sacred Music* (Detroit Information Coordinators, 1966).

PLAINSONG AND PSALMODY

Interpretation (very roughly the choice between free or mensural rhythms) has its own literature, with Alec Robertson's *Interpretation of Plainchant* (O.U.P., 1949) and Dom Gregory Murray's *Gregorian Chant* (Cary, 1963) taking differing views. Meanwhile, the School of Solesmes has in progress a work which reflects the latest researches on the manuscript sources: *Le Graduel Romain* (Abbaye Saint-Pierre de Solesmes, 1957–). The current Roman Catholic service manuals: *Liber brevior* (Gregorian Institute of America, 1954) and *Liber usualis* (Desclée, 1924–) have Gregorian chant notation, and M.

Frost's *Historical Companion to Hymns Ancient and Modern* (Clowes, 1962) has a useful index of plainsong in which all usages are visibly juxtaposed. This volume is intended to supersede W. H. Frere's edition of 1909. The Plainsong and Mediaeval Music Society maintains a useful specialist library (deposited in the University of London library) and keeps certain of its publications in print (Faith Press). The Anglican extension of plainsong is first reflected in Sternhold and Hopkins' *Whole Booke of Psalms Collected into Englysh Metre* (1562 onwards) to be followed in Scotland by *The Forane of Prayers* . . . (1564 onwards.)

HYMNODY

This, in its more generalized sense, is covered for the U.K. by the Hymn Society (c/o The Royal Society of Church Music), and for the U.S. by the Hymn Society of America (475 Riverside Drive, New York 27). The bibliography of hymn-books and their many companion volumes seems not to have been tackled seriously as yet, but a representative listing is given under Hymn Collections in the B.B.C.'s *Choral Catalogue*. The literature of hymnody from Greek to modern times is to be found in the usual music bibliographies and the encyclopaedic articles. J. Julian's *Dictionary of Hymnology*, rev. edn. (Murray, 1915, reprinted New York, Dover, 1957) (presently under revision by the Rev. L. H. Bunn, 125 Monkmoor Rd., Shrewsbury, for the Hymn Society), is a key work, and K. Mummery's trade catalogue *Hymnology, 16th–19th century* (*c*. 1955) remains, in spite of its commercial origin, a useful source of quick reference. Recent trends are described in E. Routley's *Twentieth Century Church Music* (Jenkins, 1964). The Church of England Liturgical Commission more recently called upon the Poet Laureate to put traditional words into modern English. The results appear in *Modern Liturgical Texts* (S.P.C.K., 1968).

CAROLS

The literature stretches from scholarly work treating the carol as a form, e.g. J. Stevens' *Mediaeval Carols* (Musica Britannica, vol. 4,

Stainer & Bell, 1952) and R. L. Greene's *Early English Carols* (O.U.P., 1962), the latter including the later rediscovered examples in the Egerton MS., to the *Oxford Book of Carols* (O.U.P., 1928) and on to extremely popular treatments such as *The Trapp Book of Christmas Songs* (Pantheon, 1950). Further simple expositions with emphasis on the modern carol include E. Duncan's *Story of the Carol* (Scott, 1911) and E. Routley's *The English Carol* (Jenkins, 1958). An extensive list of performing editions appears under "Carols" in the *B.B.C. Choral* and *Song Catalogues* (see Figs. 7 and 11). Two recent attempts to revitalize the repertory by commissioning new arrangements and new settings are *Carols for Choirs* (O.U.P., 1961) and *Sing Nowell* (Novello, 1963) both of which reflect the work of eminent composers like Britten, Fricker, Kodály, Rubbra, etc. Elizabeth Poston's *Penguin Book of Carols* (1965) concentrates on returning to earlier and simpler settings. Scholarly studies include R. L. Greene's *Early English carols* (O.U.P., 1935).

NATIVITY PLAYS, ETC.

Most publishers' catalogues carry sections devoted to Christmas music, including nativity plays. There is a scarcity of editions of authentic medieval music, however, such as the recent versions of N. Greenberg and W. L. Smoldon, *The Play of Daniel* and *The Play of Herod* (O.U.P., 1959 and 1965), I. Gundry's *Medieval Music Dramas* (O.U.P.) and W. L. Smoldon's *Three Medieval Music Dramas of Easter* (O.U.P.). In fact, Greenberg, Gundry, and Smoldon between them are responsible for the most scholarly modern editions. J. Stevens' *Music in Medieval Drama* (Royal Musical Association, Proceedings, 1957–8) surveys this "ghost-subject" expertly.

PROHIBITIONS

The Catholic Church has, intermittently since the Council of Trent, 1545–63, expressed its views on the use of music, usefully summarized in *An Instruction by the Sacred Congregation of Rites on*

Sacred Music and Liturgy (Herder Publications, 33 Queen Square, W.C. 1, 1959), based on the "Motu proprio" of 1903 together with the "Divini cultus" of 1928 and the "Musicae sacrae disciplina" of 1955. This has more than an academic or historic significance today. Certain vocal scores have been edited in accordance with such edicts, e.g. the Novello edition of Schubert's Masses, which quotes the Papal decree of 1894 as authority for amending the composer's setting of the text. In this instance, it results in the Breitkopf editions being the only ones which are musically accurate. This rivalry of liturgical and musical claims is neatly touched upon, with particular reference to Schubert, by A. Robertson in "The Mass in the nineteenth century" (*The Listener*, 19th Dec. 1963). N. Slonimsky's *Music since 1900*, 3rd edn. (New York, Coleman–Ross, 1949) gives the actual text of Pope Pius X's "Motu proprio" on sacred music and adds a "Black list of disapproved music"—declaring as liturgically unfit the sacred works of Cherubini, Haydn, Mozart, Rossini, Schubert and Weber. Breaks with the hieratic view continue, the *Twentieth Century Folk-mass* of G. Beaumont (Paxton, 1957) being merely one of the more spectacular.

SECULAR MUSIC

The major repositories of secular, as of sacred music, are the various critical editions such as the *Denkmäler, Corpus mensurabilis musicae*, etc., series, which are intended as sources for performance rather than performing editions. The amount of hitherto buried treasure here enshrined is virtually endless. Italian madrigals have received their exhaustive study in A. Einstein's *The Italian Madrigal*, 3 vols. (Princeton U.P., 1949) of which the third volume gives the music (unfortunately using obsolete clefs) of ninety-seven complete examples. This is now supplemented by J. Newman's *Index to Capoversi* . . . (Renaissance Society of America, 1967). Its English counterpart is E. H. Fellowes's *English Madrigal School* (Stainer & Bell), now revised by Thurston Dart as *The English Madrigalists*. A reliable single-volume anthology is now available in *The Penguin Book of English Madrigals for four voices* by D. Stevens (Penguin, 1967).

Principal complementary studies as Fellowes's *The English Madrigal Composers*, 2nd edn. (O.U.P., 1948) and J. Kerman's *The Elizabethan Madrigal: a comparative study* (New York, American Musicological Society, 1962). The Madrigal Society deposited its library in the British Museum in 1954 and its catalogue is now published as Part 59 (1955) of the British Museum's *Accessions of Printed Music*. The extensive working library of the now defunct Oriana Society has been deposited in the Central Music Library, Westminster. A bibliographical study covering madrigals, ballets, ayres, canzonets, etc., is E. F. Rimbault's *Bibliotheca madrigaliana* (J. R. Smith, 1847, reprinted by B. Franklin, 1968).

The remainder of the secular repertory is described in the General Bibliography (see pp. 25–27).

THE CHORAL FRINGE

The conductor may find he can divide his choir into a double-choir (for Bach motets, etc.) or into ten parts, for the D. Scarlatti *Stabat mater*, or yet into twenty-four, for Robert Carver's *O Bone Jesu* (Musica Britannica, 15, and Corpus Mensurabilis Musicae, 16), or miraculously into forty "real" parts, for Tallis's *Spem in alium* (O.U.P.). Lists of such works are hard to find, but the B.B.C.'s *Choral Catalogue* deals with them in an appendix. This, also, has a select list of choral works with obbligato instrumental accompaniment (i.e. chamber ensemble) such as Schubert's *Gesang der Geister*, and *Nachtgesang im Walde* or Bruckner's *Abendzauber*, the latter complete with yodeller. Other published lists of this marginal, but occasionally useful, repertory seem not to exist.

CHAPTER 5

The Singer

*Une admirable cantatrice avait inventé une phrase qu'elle
substituait à la phrase originale. Son exemple fut bientôt suivi;
il était trop beau pour ne pas l'être.*

H. BERLIOZ, *Les Grotesques de la musique*

THE singer's shelf is likely to wear a weary look—the albums and
separate song-copies, tattered, torn and patched by singer and
anxious accompanist alike. Ballad, lieder, opera and oratorio volumes
will have been acquired naturally in the course of training. Since the
basic repertory is kept in print as part of publishers' bread-and-butter
there is no particular difficulty of access. The singer, however, is
ʲust as much at the mercy of poor tools in the shape of inept or down-
right bad editions as any other performer, and should always be
fully on guard. He can be reasonably sure that songs of this century
represent their composers' intentions as accurately as the mere
printed page can hope to do, but he must look quizzically at the rest,
using his own judgement if he feels he knows enough, or asking
competent advice.

For the general problem of editing music see Ch. 9. Most of the
aspects there commented upon apply to songs. The trouble is more
likely to concern keyboard accompaniments of eighteenth-century
and earlier songs, though the vocal line itself may also be betrayed by
a complete ignoring of appoggiaturas and various other "gracings".
The intelligent singer is becoming more and more aware of the
exciting possibilities (and the pitfalls) of the all-but-lost art of
embellishment or ornamentation by cadential trill, cadenza, etc.
The problem is not new. P. F. Tosi wrote his *Observations on the*

Florid Song in 1723 (reprints by W. Reeves and by H. Baron), H. Klein his *Bel canto* (O.U.P.) in 1923, and each generation debates the topic anew, e.g. C. Mackerras' "Sense and the appoggiatura" (*Opera*, Oct. 1963). It must suffice here to mention a few examples of attempts to indicate this by scholarly and imaginative editing, while emphasizing that the best of editors must hope to rely in the last resort on the executant's sense of style, supported by technical accomplishment. Elaborate cadenzas, whether genuinely improvised or "written-out" may well only add an unwelcome strain, both for the singer and his audience, by being plastered on to an already elaborate *da capo* aria of Handel or Mozart. Accompaniments may easily betray the singer's stylishness if these are ineptly "strengthened" by anachronistic thickenings and misplaced chromatic harmonies.

Specimen Reliable Editions

Dowland. *English Lute Songs*, ed. Fellowes, rev. Dart (Stainer & Bell)
Haydn. *Arien für Sopran, etc.*, ed. Landon (Haydn Mozart Press)
H. Keller, ed. *Arien und Kanzonetten des 17. und 18. Jahrhunderts* (Bärenreiter)
Mozart. *Konzert-Arien*, ed. L. Lehmann (Peters)
Purcell. *Fifteen Songs and Airs*, ed. G. Cooper (Purcell Society)
E. Reichert. *Lieder und Gesänge* (Oesterreichischer Bundesverlag)
Varied illustrations are given on the discs *The Art of Ornamentation* . . . (Vanguard VSL 11044–5).

FOLK-SONG

Folk-song accompaniments in particular may be breeding grounds of ineptitude. There is force in Constant Lambert's jibe that the only thing to be done with a folk-song is to play or sing it once *forte* and repeat it *piano*. In general, the more elaborate a folk-song accompaniment, the more suspect, but many a singer may be positively helped, if, towards the eighth verse, the accompaniment sounds less primitively than it began. Do Britten's *Folk-song Arrangements: British Isles:*

34 *Musicalia*

France (Boosey & Hawkes), for instance, beguile or irritate by their sophistication? This is a matter of taste, not forgetting that "recitals" of folk-song, already so far from their genuine context of hearth, fairground or village green, are an artificiality in themselves. Sir Arnold Bax's shuddering revolt against all folk-song, however, is unlikely to be shared by most singers, otherwise the searching appeal of one of the most natural manifestations of man's reaction to life would be lost to us. The documentation of folk-music is dealt with separately in Ch. 12.

TECHNIQUE

The young singer does not need to look far for technical advice (in so far as this can be conveyed by the printed word) since many international artists from Lilli Lehmann and Tetrazzini to Plunket Greene and Sir George Henschel have written their books. A more recent statement of singers' problems on the concert platform and the stage, the splendours and miseries of career-building, and the challenge of serial music is G. Baker's *The Commonsense of Singing* Pergamon Press, 1963).

REPERTORY

The "main stream" of international song is readily accessible, as already stated, through the current editions of Peters, Breitkopf, etc. These range from the multi-volume editions of single composers like Brahms, Schubert and Wolf (Peters), to the anthologies gathered by famous singers, such as Elizabeth Schumann's *Album* (Universal) or by mere editors, for varying types of voice, like the *Soprano, Contralto, Tenor* and *Bass Albums* (Boosey & Hawkes) and such period-volumes as *Arie antiche* (Ricordi), *Alte Meister des Bel-canto* (Hinrichsen-Peters), *La Flora* (Hansen–Chester) or the song anthologies now in progress as part of *The Anthology of Music* (Arno–O.U.P.).

Several attempts have been made to list or classify the vast repertory of song, which follow in order of usefulness to the ordinary singer, as distinct from the song-researcher (though they naturally help the latter very considerably): B. Coffin's *The Singer's Repertoire*, 2nd edn., 5 vols. (New York, Scarecrow Press, 1960) (see Fig. 8) which quotes accurate voice-ranges, and deals separately with coloratura, lyric and dramatic soprano songs, mezzo and contralto, lyric and dramatic tenor, concluding with baritone and bass, and a volume (5) of programme notes. S. Kagen's *Music for the Voice* (Indiana U.P., 1969) is a much smaller effort, though as "a descriptive list of concert and teaching material" it has an added interest for its evaluative comments, besides giving *tessiture* and vocal compass. Its four sections are (1) Songs and arias before the nineteenth century; (2) Songs: nineteenth and twentieth centuries; (3) Folk-songs; (4) Operatic excerpts. In the field of Lieder a work which gives unusually full performing details is F. A. Stein's *Verzeichnis deutscher Lieden seit Hayden* (Francke Verlag, 1967). This gives poets, *tessiture*, first lines, etc. M. E. Sears' *Song Index* (New York, 1926–34, reprint Shoe String Press) (see Fig. 9) performs the complementary function of analysing the contents of anthologies (362 collections in all, and 19,000 separate titles). Its thoroughness in quoting authorship of poems and in cross-referencing first lines, translations and variants, has been appreciated by librarians and researchers for a generation. It is a pity that no further supplements ever appeared. In some sense, however, Sears is extended by Helen G. Cushing's *Children's Song Index* (New York), which covers 22,000 songs from 189 collections. A further partial extension to Sears is de Charms' and Breed's *Songs in Collections* (Detroit Information Service, 1966). The New York Public Library's song index can now be partially checked through the reprint of its *Dictionary Catalog* (Hall, 1964–).

BIBLIOGRAPHY

Other important song-indexes exist as part of printed library catalogues. The most recent of these is the British Broadcasting Corporation's series of *Song Catalogues* (B.B.C., 1966), comprising two volumes of composers and two volumes of titles, with appendices for (a) national and folk-songs, by country, and (b) song collections, arranged by country and by topic (drinking songs, negro, Shakespeare, soldier, work songs, etc.). Thirty thousand songs are catalogued, representing one of the world's largest collection of performing editions. A certain amount of analysis of anthologies is attempted. This scope extends to two and occasionally even four solo voices with up to three accompanying instruments; differing versions and translations in variants are brought together under original headings as far as is feasible. Another library catalogue with many song entries, including analytics, is that of the Boston Public Library's *Allen A. Brown Collection*, 4 vols. (1908–16). Early songs are reflected in the British Museum's music catalogues. The *Catalogue of Printed Music, 1487–1800* (1912, and 2nd Suppt. 1940) includes many songs printed in periodicals, while the *Catalogue of Manuscript Music*, 3 vols. (1906–9) contains very extensive "initial-words-and-title" indexes to the main entries for secular and sacred vocal music. Its "names and subjects" index quotes, country by country, the songs associated with the various sovereigns. Another major index to pre-1800 song is included in Edythe N. Backus's *Catalogue of the Huntington Library* (1949). The English periodical *Notes and Queries* extends the performance of such catalogues by locating and annotating under "Songs and ballads", over 2500 songs, often found in collections not indexed elsewhere.

National indexes tend inevitably to limit themselves to particular periods. Day and Murrie's *English Song-books, 1651–1702* (Bibliographical Society, 1940) (see Fig. 10) gives full bibliographical descriptions of 225 items published during Commonwealth, Restoration and Jacobean periods, with composers, authors, first lines, singers, actors, tunes, etc., while the *British Union Catalogue of Early Music*, 2 vols. (Butterworths 1957), also describes and locates copies. A further major contribution (though short) to Jacobean research is P. Warlock's *The English Ayre* (O.U.P., 1926) while F. Zimmermann's *Henry Purcell*, 2 vols. (Macmillan, 1963–7), adds greatly to the scholarly documentation of the period. For America, O. Sonneck's *Bibliography of Early Secular American Music* (i.e. eighteenth century), rev. Upton (Library of Congress, 1945) locates copies of early song-editions. This is now supplemented by R. J. Wolfe's

Secular Music in America, 1801–25, 3 vols. (New York Public Library 1965).

An attempt at international coverage is E. Challier's *Grosser Lieder-Katalog*, 3 vols. (Berlin, Challier, 1885–1914), which lists by title all German and foreign songs published in Germany or Austria, and "alles wissenswerte anderer Länder", whether singly or in anthology form.

THE SUBJECT-APPROACH TO SONGS

Apart from purely lyrical or dramatic songs, many (and they are not necessarily either comic or vulgar) are "about" a specific topic—drink, aeroplanes, transport, ships, etc. The B.B.C. *Song Catalogues* (see Fig. 11) are the fullest guide to such as have appeared in anthology form. Stecheson's *Classified Song Directory* (Hollywood, Music Industry Press, 1961) (see Fig. 12), "Sports and recreations in American popular songs", (*Notes*, July 1949, Sept. 1950, Dec. 1951, and Sept. 1957) and *Aeronautical Music* (Royal Aeronautical Society, 1959) are typical specimens of special aids. The *Notes* series includes an amusing "break-down" of drinking songs (whisky, water, coca-cola, etc.!). The descriptive literature of song topics is thinly and widely spread over the general literature of song, from which B. Coffin's *The Singer's Repertoire*, already quoted, is probably the most helpful for normal concert use.

OBBLIGATI

Obbligato and chamber accompaniments are described in Chamber Music (Ch. 6).

THEMES

For identifying the opening themes of songs by musical notation, transposed to C, Barlow and Morgenstern's *Dictionary of Vocal Themes* (New York, Crown, 1950) is apparently the only general work of its kind. The search may be continued indefinitely in the numerous thematic catalogues devoted to individual composers, such as Köchel–Einstein's *Mozart*, Deutsch's *Schubert* (see Fig. 13), Schmieder's *Bach*, etc. (See Ch. 9).

Finally, the commercial gramophone catalogues (Ch. 14) provide a wealth of miscellaneous information on songs—not least on their relative popularity.

VARIETY AND MUSIC HALL

The Music

A comprehensive statement of popular song albums will be found in Appendix I of the B.B.C.'s *Song Catalogue* (1966). This lists the rich harvest garnered since late Victorian times in the annuals published by Francis, Day & Hunter, and by Feldman, Chappell, Campbell–Connelly, Southern Music and Peter Maurice.

The Literature

The British scene is dealt with in D. C. Calthrop's *Music Hall Nights* (Bodley Head, 1925); C. Pulling's *They Were Singing* (Harrap, 1952) with its indexes of singers, songs and actors; M. W. Disher's *Victorian Song* (Phoenix House, 1955); R. Nettel's *Seven Centuries of Popular song: urban ditties* (Phoenix House, 1956); and Gammond & Clayton's *Guide to Popular Music* (Phoenix House, 1960).

America is equally, if not better covered, by the Mattfeld and Burton works mentioned more fully under Musical Comedy (Ch. 3) and in Hazel Meyer's *The Gold in Tin Pan Alley* (New York, Lippincott, 1958), Lewine & Simons' *Encyclopaedia of Theatre Music: 4,000 songs from Broadway and Hollywood, 1900–60* (New York, Random House, 1961), and J. Fuld's *American Popular Music, 1875–1950* (Philadelphia, Musical Americana, 1955). (See also Chs. 3 and 12.)

THE VOICE IN CHAMBER MUSIC

See p. 51.

SONG TEXTS

Few catalogues and bibliographies go so far as to index by the authors of song texts—poets, librettists, etc., otherwise catalogues would be almost doubled in size. E. Blom's *Everyman's Dictionary*, 2nd edn. (Dent, 1958), and *Grove* give useful lists of well-known settings under poets. The publishers of copyright authors should have details of settings for which permission will (hopefully) have been required. Useful anthologies of texts only are Douliez and Engelhard's *Das Buch der Lieder und Arien* (Munich, Winkler-Verlag, 1956), the *Penguin Book of Lieder* edited and translated by S. S. Prawer (1964) with notes on the poets, and P. L. Miller's *The Ring of Words* (New York, Doubleday, 1963).

CHAPTER 6

The Chamber Musician
and
Instrumental Soloist

The lonely music-maker is indeed a figure of pathos.
AULICH and HEIMERAN, *The Well-tempered String Quartet*

THOSE knowledgeable amateur chamber players Aulich and
Heimeran (however dated their social outlook) have described the
cream of the classical repertory in their whimsical little book *The
Well-tempered String Quartet* (Novello, 1964), and make well-
considered recommendations of string trios, string and piano
quintets, etc., to suit "emergency" and "wind-fall" occasions.
Earlier than this Herter Norton's *String Quartet Playing* (C. Fischer,
1935) and J. Léner's *The Technique of String Quartet Playing* had
become landmarks. One of the latest additions in this particular
field is A. Page's *Playing String Quartets* (Longman, 1964). The
standard reference work, however leisurely and personal in approach,
is still W. W. Cobbett's *Cyclopaedic Survey of Chamber Music*, 3 vols.
(O.U.P., 1963) especially as the third volume makes many cor-
rections to the original of 1929–30, and has full-length evaluative
surveys of European and Russian chamber works since 1929 and of
U.S. and Latin American output over a similar period, with a most
carefully considered bibliography. The latter is particularly useful in
its "Books and articles on individual composers". Other general
surveys include H. Ulrich's *Chamber Music* (Penguin, 1957) and A.

H. King's short study *Chamber Music* (Chanticleer, 1948). E. H. Meyer's *English Chamber Music* (Lawrence & Wishart, 1946) covers the Middle Ages to Purcell only, but is not equalled by any other single study. The musicologist, so far as the fifteenth and sixteenth centuries go, is now superbly catered for by H. M. Brown's *Instrumental Music Printed before 1600: a bibliography* (Harvard U.P., 1966).

BIBLIOGRAPHY

Fortunately, the published repertory (which is vast) is well organized in bibliographies classified by instrumental grouping. Chief among these is the magnificent series of catalogues by W. Altmann: the *Handbuch für Streichquartettspieler*, 4 vols. (Hesse, 1928–31), the *Kleiner Führer durch die Streichquartette* (Deutscher Musikliteratur–Verlag, 1950) and the *Handbücher für Klaviertriospieler . . . für Klavierquartettspieler . . . für Klavierquintettspieler*. The latter three, all published by the Verlag für musikalische Kultur at Wolfenbüttel, 1934–7, have thematic appendices. This immense labour is paralleled by the *Kammermusik-Katalog*, whose sixth edition (Hofmeister, 1945) spans publication from 1841 to 1944, and is supplemented by J. F. Richter's *Kammermusik-Katalog: 1944–58* (Hofmeister, 1960). Both of these adopt the practical plan of dividing the repertory into works with and without piano, and then classifying in descending sizes of combination, e.g. quintets for piano and wind, for piano and wind and strings, wind quintets, mixed wind and string quintets, etc. Composers have been more alive than is popularly supposed to writing "the only other work" which exactly fits, for instance, the combination of the Schubert octet, Beethoven septet, or Brahms horn trio. Catalogues such as Altmann and Richter reveal how many "only other works" have in fact been published.

The foregoing are as exhaustive as Teutonic patience can make them. Anglo-Saxon reticence has produced a work of perhaps greater general value because of its selectiveness: The National Federation's *Catalogue of Chamber Music* (rev. Watson Forbes, 1964) which limits itself to the main stream of the repertory likely to be played in normal concert-giving, but contains some suggestions of works for the average amateur group. A fully graded list, with all its hazards, has tended to defeat compilers. Useful on account of the early music included, though it omits any mention of publishers, is F. A. Stein's *Verzeichnis der Kammermusikwerke von 1650 bis zur Gegenwart* (Bern, Franke Verlag, 1962). The B.B.C.'s *Chamber Music Catalogue* (1965) (see Fig. 14) also includes some MS. works and special transcriptions of early compositions, gives timings as far as possible and is divided into chamber music (decet to trio, indexed on the Altmann–Richter plan), violin and piano, 'cello and piano, and miscellaneous instrumental solos and duos. The British Museum's Music Room maintains on cards (already over 30,000 entries) a broadly classified catalogue of instrumental music (see p. 307 of O. E. Deutsch's *Festschrift* (Bärenreiter, 1963)). More recent (New York, R. M. Bowker, 1965 and Suppt.) is M. K. Farish's *String Music in Print*—an expansion of *Violin Music in Print* (1962). This covers solo and ensemble music for violin, viola, 'cello and bass. Another American work, somewhat wider in scope, is the guide published by the National Music Camp, Interlochen, *A List of Instrumental Ensembles*. The only British subscription-library of chamber music was apparently that maintained by J. & W. Chester Ltd., London, who published a *Handbook and Guide* (1949). This collection has now been bought by Sussex University (1966).

THE KEYBOARD PLAYER

Apart from songs, the keyboard repertory (see also pp. 48–49) is the largest. The terms cembalo, clavecin, harpsichord, Klavier, spinet, virginals, fortepiano, piano, organ, reflect a European growth of seven centuries, and are not easily disentangled. Though Debussy may only be performed on the modern piano, Bach is still played on almost all the above instruments. The majority of the works mentioned below do not attempt to discriminate among these historical and linguistic niceties. E. Closson's *History of the Piano* (Elek, 1947) forms a good introduction to the subject.

PIANO, ETC.

Early keyboard music is published in a variety of editions, good and bad. (See Ch. 9.) Recent reliable examples include those in *Musica Britannica* (Stainer & Bell) and the *Anthology of Music* (O.U.P., in progress), the very earliest examples being epitomized in such works as the *Historical Anthology of Music*, 2 vols. (Harvard, 1947), A. Schering's *Geschichte der Musik in Beispielen* (New York, Broude, 1950) and W. Apel's *Corpus of Early Keyboard Music* (American Institute of Musicology). An historic collection, now an antiquarian rarity, is A. and L. Farrenc's *Le Trésor des pianistes*, 23 vols. (Farrenc, 1861–72).

Analyses

From a long list, the following merit special attention: W. Apel's *Masters of the Keyboard* (Harvard U.P., 1947) and E. Hutcheson's *The Literature of the Piano . . . for Amateur and Student* (Knopf, 1949). A. Cortot's *La Musique française de piano*, 3 vols. (Presses Universitaires de France, 1930–2), of which vol. 1 only is translated (O.U.P., 1932) has few, if any, direct equivalents for other countries.

Repertory, etc.

This is closely graded by difficulty in H. Parent's *Répertoire encyclopédique . . .* , 2 vols. (Hachette, 1907–26).

Concerti

The *Fleisher Catalogue* lists concerti for one to four pianos and orchestra.

Left-hand; Right-hand

P. Scholes' *Oxford Companion*, 9th edn. (O.U.P., 1955) under "Pianoforte, 21" summarizes the repertory, which is certainly not confined to the well-known works by Ravel, Richard Strauss, Britten and Bax. Godowsky pleaded for more cultivation of the left-hand (*Musical Quarterly*, July 1935) and Alkan and York Bowen wrote occasional pieces for the right-hand only. A select bibliography is included in the B.B.C. *Piano and Organ Catalogue* (1965).

ORGAN

Two recent major works form technical and historical surveys: W. L. Sumner's *The Organ*, 3rd edn. (Macdonald & Co., 1962) and Clutton & Niland's *The British Organ* (Batsford, 1963). The latter has a gazetteer of historic organs covering the British Isles. Similar information for other countries has to be sought in numerous special studies, and encyclopaedia articles (e.g. "Orgel" and various place-name entries in *MGG*), or could be had from the various national organists' societies, though Westerby (see below) includes brief notes on internationally famed instruments. More detailed information is now collected (for the first time, apparently, in English) into a single column by D. W. Williams in *The European Organ* (Batsford, 1966).

Analyses

J. Klein's *First Four Centuries of Organ Music* (Associated, 1948) covers from Dunstable to Bach—1370–1749, with elaborate notes on registration and interpretation.

Repertory, etc.

B. Weigl's *Handbuch der Orgelliteratur* (Leuckart, 1931) has immensely detailed lists of all types of music, including works for four hands, with orchestra, with voices, etc., and grades works by difficulty. H. Westerby's *The Complete Organ Recitalist: international repertoire guide* (Musical Opinion, 1933) (see Fig. 15) groups British and American works by type, and foreign works by national schools. M. Hinrichsen's *Organ and Choral Aspects and Prospects*

(Hinrichsen, 1962) forms a useful miscellany of rather fugitive information. The work which brings the repertory most up to date is Reclam's *Orgelführer* by V. Lukas, 2nd edn. (Reclam, 1967).

Concerti

Weigl (above) is supplemented by an exhaustive survey by R. H. Sartorius: *Concertos for Organ and Orchestra* (Evanstown, The Instrumentalist, 1961). The main repertory is given in the *Fleisher Catalogue*, now supplemented by Reclam, above.

WIND MUSIC

The Bible of wind-music is E. Gorgerat's *Encyclopédie . . . pour instruments à vent*, 2nd edn. (Lausanne, Editions Rencontre, 1955), vol. 3 listing the repertory (see Fig. 16). Another of the few extant catalogues devoted to wind is S. M. Helm's *Catalog of Chamber Music for Wind Instruments* (Michigan, National Association of College Wind and Percussion Instrument Instructors, 1952) (see Fig. 17). Useful sectional bibliographies for woodwind occur in the *Woodwind Magazine*, 1948–56 (Box 747, Long Beach Island, N.Y.).

The (British) Wind Music Society's founder, Bryan Fairfax, developed an impressive list of works (including those of symphonic size) which has now been deposited with the Central Music Library, Westminster. It locates sets of certain fugitive pieces and includes a proportion of MS. items. Symptomatic of the growing popularity of the recorder is the appearance of a new British journal devoted to its interests: *Recorder and Music Magazine* (Schott, May, 1963–).

BRASS MUSIC

The British firm of R. Smith (210, Strand, W.C. 2) now specializes on brass band repertory and can be regarded as a point of reference for most queries. *The Brass Quarterly* (Box 111, Durham, New Hampshire) is almost compulsory reading for the expert and specialist, not least for its bibliographies (see pp. 195–6 of vol. 3 of

Cobbett). Publishers and dealers' catalogues yield a rich haul, of course, in new and second-hand materials, especially those of such firms as Musica Rara (London) and the Cambridge Music Shop, whose catalogues of *Brass with Organ* and *Brass with Voices*, etc., are exemplary. See also Chapter 2.

INDIVIDUAL INSTRUMENTS: REPERTOIRE LISTS, ETC.

Accordion

Accordion Times (J. J. Black, Somerset House, Cranleigh, Surrey).

Banjo

SHARPE, A. P. *A Complete Guide to the Banjo Family* (Clifford Essex Music, 1966).

Bass (String)

GRODNER, M. *Comprehensive Catalog* . . . (Bloomington, Indiana Univ., 2nd edn., 1964).

Bassoon

BARTLETT, L. W. *Survey and Check List . . . 18th Century Concertos and Sonatas for Bassoon* (Univ. Microfilms, 1963).

CAMDEN, A. *Bassoon Technique* (O.U.P., 1962). (Repertoire-list by W. Waterhouse.)

KLITZ, B. K. *Solo Sonatas, Trio Sonatas . . . for Bassoon before 1750: musical suppt.* (Univ. Microfilms, 1963).

LANGWILL, L. *The Bassoon and Contrabassoon* (Solo repertoire.) (Benn, 1965).

Bells, Handbells

FLETCHER, H. J. *The First Book of Bells* (E. Ward, 1965).

WATSON, D. *The Handbell Choir* (Gray–Novello, 1959).

Bells, Church

STEPHENS, E. C. *The Sound of Bells* (Record Books, 1964).
WILSON, F. G. *Change Ringing* (Faber, 1965).

Clarinet

FOSTER, L. W. *A Directory of Clarinet Music* (Pittsfield, Mass., A. E. Johnson, 1940).
OPPERMANN, K. *Repertory of the Clarinet* (New York, Ricordi, 1960).
RENDALL, F. G. *The Clarinet* (Williams & Norgate, 1954).
Répertoire . . . des conservatoires: enseignement, morceaux de concours, etc. (Leduc, 1953).
THURSTON, F. *Clarinet Technique*, 2nd edn. (O.U.P., 1964).

Flute and Recorder

ALKER, H. *Blockflöten Bibliographie*, 2 vols. (Wien, Universitäts Bibliothek, 1960–61).
BOUSTED and CHAMBERS. *Essential Repertoire for Flute* (Universal, 1964).
CHAPMAN, F. B. *Flute Technique*, 2nd edn. (O.U.P., 1951).
GIRARD, H. *Histoire et richesses de la flûte* (Librairie Gründ, 1953).
HUNT, E. *The Recorder and its Music* (Jenkins, 1962).
Internationale Flötenliteratur (Hug, 1961) (see Fig. 18).
MILLER, D. E. *. . . Collections Relating to the Flute* (Cleveland, privately printed, 1935).
PRILL, E. *Führer durch den Flötenliteratur*, 2 vols. (Zimmermann, 1913).
QUANTZ, J. *Versuch einer Anweisung die "Flûte traversière" zu spielen, 1752.* (Bärenreiter, 1953).
RIGBY, F. F. *Playing the Recorders* (Faber, 1958).
ROWLAND-JONES, A. *Recorder Technique* (O.U.P., 1959).
VESTER, F. VON. *Flute Repertoire Catalogue* (Musica Rara, 1967).
WINTERFELD and KUNZ. *Handbuch der Blockflötenliteratur* (Bote & Bock, 1959).

Guitar

APIAZU, J. DE. *The Guitar and Guitarists* (Ricordi, 1960).

BONE, P. J. *The Guitar and Mandolin: biographies* . . . (Schott, 1954) (see Fig. 19).

JANHEL, F. *Die Gitarre und ihr Bau* (includes lute, mandolin, etc.) (Frankfurt, Das Musikinstrument, 1963).

PRAT, D. *Diccionario de guitarristas* (Buenos Aires, 1961).

ZUTH, J., *Handbuch der Laute und Gitarre* (Vienna, Goll, 1926–8).

The Altmann and Richter catalogues have a section "Für Gitarre (Laute) und andere Instrumenten".

Harp

ISRAELI MUSIC INSTITUTE. *Contemporary Harp Music* (Universal, 1965).

O'SULLIVAN, D. *Carolan: the life, times and music of an Irish harper* (Routledge, 1958).

ZUNIGEL, H. J. *Verzeichnis der Harfenmuzik* (Hofmeister, 1965).

The Altmann and Richter catalogues have a section "Für Harpe und andere Instrumenten".

Horn

COAR, B. *The French Horn* (De Kalle, Ill., 1950).

GREGORY, R. *The Horn* (Faber, 1961).

SCHULLER, G. *Horn Technique* (O.U.P.).

Keyboard

(a) *Various*

ALKER, H. *Literatur für alte Tasteninstrumente*, 2. Aufl. (Vienna, Geyer, 1967).

(b) *Piano, harpsichord, etc.* (see also p. 43).

BOALCH, D. H. *Makers of the Harpsichord and Clavichord, 1440–1840* (Cardiff, E. Ronald, 1955).

BosQUET, E. *La Musique de clavier* . . . (Brussels, Les Amis de la musique, 1953) (Includes early organ music).

B.B.C. *Piano and Organ Catalogue* (B.B.C., 1965) (see Fig. 20).

FAVRE, G. *La Musique Française de Piano avant 1830* (Didier, 1953).

FRISKIN and FREUNDLICH. *Music for the Piano: concert and teaching material 1580–1962* (New York, Rinehart, 1954) (see Fig. 21).

LOCKWOOD, A. *Notes on the Literature of the Piano* (Michigan U.P., 1940).

PROSNITZ, A. *Handbuch der Klavier-Literatur, 1450–1830*, 2nd edn. (Doblinger, 1908).

RICHTER, J. F. *Kammermusik-Katalog* . . . *1944–58* (piano and organ appendices) (Hofmeister, 1960).

RUSSELL, R. *The Harpsichord and the Clavichord* (Faber, 1959).

RUTHARDT, A. *Wegweiser durch die Klavier-Literatur*, 5th edn. (Hug, 1900).

SÄCHSISCHE LÄNDESBIBLIOTHEK. *Klaviermusik der sozialistischen Länder* (1962).

TEICHMULLER and HERRMANN. *Internationale Moderne Klaviermusik*, 2 vols. (Hug, 1927–34).

WOLTERS, K. *Handbuch der Klavierliteratur zu zwei Händen* (Francke, 1967).

(c) Four hands, etc.

ALTMANN, W. *Verzeichnis von Werken für Klavier* (4, 6 hands, 2 and more pianos) (Leipzig, Hofmeister, 1943) (see Fig. 22).

B.B.C. *Piano and Organ Catalogue* (1965).

GANZER and KUSCHE. *Vierhändig* (Munich, Heimeran, 1954).

MOLDENHAUER, H. *Duo-pianism* (Chicago, Musical College Press, 1950).

ROWLEY, A. *Four Hands—One Piano* (O.U.P., 1940).

Lute (see also *Guitar*)

BosQUET, E. *La Musique de clavier et par extension de luth* (chronological and by country) (Les Amis de la Musique, 1953).

CAMBRIDGE LUTE SERIES (Cambridge, Gamut Publications, 1963–).

Le Luth et sa musique (Paris, Centre de la recherche scientifique, 1958).
THE LUTE SOCIETY (5 Wilton Square, London N. 1).
THE LUTE SOCIETY OF AMERICA (128 Norwood Ave., Upper Montclair, New Jersey 07043).

Mandolin

See *Guitar*.

Oboe

ROTHWELL, E. *Oboe Technique*, 2nd edn. (O.U.P., 1962).

Percussion

BLADES, J. *Orchestral Percussion Technique* (O.U.P., 1961).
MOORE, S. S. *Percussion Playing*, 2nd edn. (Paxton, 1959).

Pipes (Bamboo)

GALLOWAY, M. C. *Making and Playing Bamboo Pipes* (Leicester, Dryad Press, 1958).
Pipers' Guild Handbook (4 Oakway, Rayne's Park, London S.W. 20).

Strings

FARISH, M. K. *String Music in Print* (New York, Bowker, 1965 and Suppt.).
FEINLAND, A. *The Combination of Violin and 'Cello, without Accompaniment* (Paramaribo, J. H. Oliveira, 1944).

(a) Viol family

The Consort: journal of the Dolmetsch Foundation (The Foundation, Haslemere, Surrey).

THE VIOLA DA GAMBA SOCIETY. *Bulletin* (5 Ravenslea Rd., London S.W. 12).

(b) Violin

Altmann series (see p. 41).

BAUDET-MAGET. *Guide du violoniste* (Foetisch, *c.* 1920).

TOTTMANN-ALTMANN, *Führer durch die Violinliteratur* (Schuberth, 1935).

(c) Viola

ALTMANN and BORISOWSKY. *Literaturverzeichnis für Bratsche u. Viola d'amore* (Verlag für musikalische Kultur, Wolfenbüttel, 1937).

MOREY, G. *A List of Selected Works for Viola* (N. Texas State College, 1957).

ZEYRINGER, F. *Literatur für Viola* (Hartberg, Schönwetter, 1963).

(d) Violoncello

KINNEY, G. J. *The Musical Literature for Unaccompanied Violoncello*, 3 vols. (Univ. Microfilms, 1962).

WEIGL, B. *Handbuch der Violoncell-Literatur*, 3rd edn. (Vienna, Universal Edition, 1929) (see Fig. 23).

Zither

BRANDLMEIER, J. *Das Handbuch der Zither*, 2 vols. (Munich, Suddeutscher Verlag, 1963–).

THE VOICE WITH INSTRUMENTAL OBBLIGATI

The best analyses of the unexpectedly large repertory are the Altmann, Richter, and B.B.C. catalogues already quoted, which give the necessary grouping by instrument (voice and one, two, three instruments, with or without piano, etc.). A short list of about thirty such works also appears in the *Chester Chamber Music Library Catalogue*, and B. Coffin's *The Singer's Repertoire*, 2nd edn., 2 vols., (New York, Scarecrow Press, 1960) classifies this repertory by type of voice. Such are the works the singer should consult when companions to favourites like the Brahms songs for voice and viola or Schubert's *Shepherd on the Rock* are needed.

AMATEUR OPPORTUNITY

Amateur players who travel a great deal should be aware of the excellent organization maintained by Miss Helen Rice, 15 West 67th St., New York 23. She issues to members a directory (with self-gradings!) so that amateurs may, whilst on their travels, contact others. Her English counterpart is Mrs. C. Salaman, Flat 2b, 77 Anson Rd., London N. 7, who also maintains a similar directory. The simpler side of amateur repertory is outlined in W. Altmann's *Kleine Führer . . . für Haus und Schule* (Deutscher-Musiklit. Verlag, *c.* 1950).

CHAPTER 7

The Professional and Amateur

It's good to try things you can't do. It helps to keep you humiliated.

AGATHA CHRISTIE, *On Composing*

THE PROFESSIONAL

The *splendeurs et misères* of a musician's training and career have both their age-old and their topical aspects. These are described superficially in a host of "career" volumes, but in sympathetic and realistic detail in R. Elkin's *A Career in Music*, rev. edn. (Novello, 1960), and in R. E. Carter's *Your Future in Music* (Burns & McEachern, 1962). For young people the most thorough-going and down-to-earth guide is L. Salter's *The Musician and his World* (Gollancz, 1963).* British agent sand their managements are listed in Kemp's *Music and Record Industry*, 1966–). Each country has its academies and conservatoires with their appropriate calendars, and published syllabuses. Two special training-schools lying outside the scope of the academies are the London Opera Centre (Commercial Rd., E. 1) and the Central Tutorial School for Young Musicians (Morley College, S.E. 1). The established orchestral player is organized in the U.K. by the Musician's Union (29 Catherine Place, S.W. 1) which issues to its members an annual handbook. The Union also looks after the interests of arrangers and copyists. The professional chorister is represented by Equity (8 Harley St., W. 1) or (for light music) the Songwriter's Guild (32 Shaftesbury Ave., W. 1). The equivalent for the conductor and soloist is the Incor-

* To be supplemented by P. Hindemith's *Elementary Training for Musicians* (Schott, 1949).

porated Society of Musicians (48 Gloucester Place, W. 1) which issues currently a *Handbook and Register*. The British composer may join the Composer's Guild (10 Stratford Place, W. 1) which has begun to publish its catalogue, keeping this current in its journal *Composer*.* Societies abound to further the work of individual composers. They spring frequently from the enthusiasm of one man for one composer, are sometimes shortlived, but have occasionally borne substantial fruit in publications (e.g. the Berlioz, Bruckner and Mahler societies) or in recordings (the Hugo Wolf Society). An international list appears in *M.G.S.* under "Gesellschaften und Vereinen", and a British list called One Man Shows by R. L. E. Foreman (*Library Association Record*, February 1967) gives details of current societies for the following: Bantok, Bax, Beecham, Berlioz, Delius, Elgar, Glazunov, Ireland, Merrick, Poulenc, Scott, Johann and Richard Strauss, Sullivan, Verdi, Wagner and Warlock.

The Arts Council (4 St. James's Square, S.W. 1) co-operates with these bodies in the uneasy task, now shared by local authorities, of granting subsidies and assigning guarantees. The British Council (65 Davies St., W. 1) has music officers to promote the interest of British music abroad and to act as host to visiting musicians. All these activities are summarized in *Who's Who in Music*, 5th edn. (London, Burke's Peerage, 1969) (see Fig. 24). The professional musicologist's training is described in Ch. 9. Music critics may belong to the Critics' Circle—their names and the papers they represent are listed in *World's Press News* (9 Old Bailey, E.C. 4). Incidentally, the more valuable of their pronouncements have been gathered together by N. Demuth in *An Anthology of Music Criticism* (Eyre & Spottiswoode, 1947), by M. Graf in *Two Hundred Years of Music Criticism* (Norton, 1946) and also in E. Hanslick's reprinted *Music Criticisms, 1846–99* (Penguin, 1963). Spanning both professional, student and amateur organizations is the UNESCO-sponsored International Music Council, Paris, which has its own journal, *The World of Music* (1957–) to describe its efforts at stimulating international co-operation.

* British agents and managements are listed in Kemp's *Music and Record Industry* (1966–).

THE AMATEUR

Amateur activity varies greatly from country to country, but is nowhere more vital to national life than in the U.K. The Music Teachers' Association (106 Gloucester Place, W. 1) reaches a fair proportion of the thousands of British teachers, most of whose pupils are amateurs. Current topics are aired in *The Music Teacher* (Evans Bros., Montague House, Russell Square, W.C. 1). The Associated Board of the Royal Schools of Music (15 Bedford Square, W.C. 1) co-ordinates examinations in the U.K., Dominion and Commonwealth Countries, and publishes *The Piano Teachers' Yearbook* together with a vast range of its own standard and current editions. The journal of the Schools Music Association (*Music*, 1966–) now fills a distinct gap with a regular feature "Where to hear your exam. music", while the National Federation of Music Societies (29 Exhibition Rd., S.W. 7) forms a rallying point, with its conferences, *Bulletin*, and its *Graded List of Orchestral Music for School and Amateur Orchestras* (1961) for the corporate music-making of hundreds of amateur bodies, and assists them by maintaining location-lists of orchestral and vocal materials available for interchange. The Standing Conference for Amateur Music (26 Bedford Square, W.C. 1) makes an annual recommendation of suitable music. Much pioneer work has been done for the more remote areas by the Rural Music Schools Association (Little Benslow Hills, Hitchin, Herts.) which has its own journal, *Making Music* (1946–). Alongside these there is the musical side of adult education in Britain, which is summarized in *Who's Who in Music* by a chapter, "Music in Adult Education", describing the functions of the University Extra-mural departments, the Workers' Educational Association and the local authorities. A glance at the prospectuses of the fifty or sixty authorities in the greater London area offering evening-institute courses, for example, shows a phenomenal range of orchestral and choral groups, listening groups, appreciation classes, etc. Music-teaching in schools is outlined in Ch. 8.

The British (amateur) musical festival may well be almost unique. Much of the enthusiastic work of the foregoing societies is channelled into these annual gatherings, which are co-ordinated by the British

Federation of Music Festivals (106 Gloucester Place, W. 1), whose *Yearbook* gives details of amateur competitive events. A further list appears in *Who's Who in Music*.

SUMMER SCHOOLS, ETC.

No happier grounds exist for the pollination of professional skill and amateur talent than the many holiday courses, some of quite long-standing. These vary from the gargantuan Interlochen Music Camp in the U.S.A. to the more intimate gatherings at places such as Canford and Downe House, or those run by bodies like the Workers' Music Association where amateurs and students join for orchestral, choral and chamber rehearsal under professional conductors. Among the more sophisticated is the Dartington Summer Music School, directed for many years by William Glock, which celebrated its twenty-first birthday in 1968, and attracts galaxies of international talent to perform and expound, and includes masterclasses and some chamber-music making. In contrast is the even more venerable Music Camp, which held its 73rd and 74th meetings in 1968, with membership by invitation from its founder Dr. Bernard Robinson. This is unique in completely avoiding a didactic element and remaining purely a rehearsal ground for the cream of amateur and some professional talent. The standard is such that virtually no holds are barred in choice of repertory. It stands as yet another example of dedicated enthusiasm working entirely without official aid.

CHAPTER 8

The Music Educator

THERE is much music written especially with children in mind or particularly to appeal to children, but there is a dearth of music genuinely written for playing by (particularly) small children. In piano music as in children's opera, once the "lollipops" such as Bartók's *For Children*, and some of the *Mikrokosmos* (Boosey & Hawkes) are tackled there is a severe drop in quality and apparently little real effort to write interesting music for small hands and young minds. Lengnick for piano music, and Novello and O.U.P. for opera, are rather more aware of this than most British publishers.

Ensemble music fares better, since quite recently composers like Britten, Vaughan Williams, Maxwell Davies, Kodály, Orff and Marx have approached the problem imaginatively, and given a salutary lead. Current output is advertised, of course, in the educational sections of publishers' catalogues, and reviewed in journals such as *The Music Teacher*.

Musical opportunity in schools is described by the Colston Research Society in its symposium *Music in Education* (Butterworth, 1964) and in the *Handbook for Music Teachers*, 2nd edn. (Novello, 1968), edited by B. Rainbow in conjunction with the University of London Institute of Education. Rainbow is particularly useful as a classified and graded repertory-list of music (songs grouped by age and type of school, orchestral music, instrumental ensemble music, percussion, recorder). Its 2nd edn. has added chapters on comprehensive and public schools, on music in the school assembly and the primary schools, brass bands, the guitar in education, music for stage productions, etc. Both of these surveys recognize, perhaps inadequately, the immense influence wielded by the B.B.C.'s broadcasts (radio and television) and reflected in many attractive handbooks (B.B.C. Publications, 35 Marylebone High St., W. 1). Two Pergamon volumes form valuable additions to the foregoing: J. Dalby's *School and amateur orchestras* (1966) and H. Wiseman's *The Singing Class* (1966). A further centre of lively activity is The University of Reading where Dr. A. Bentley holds international seminars on experimental research. The University Library has, in this connection, compiled a 37-page reading list of books and periodicals in which, among many national contributions, work sponsored by the International Society for Music Education commands special attention. The Society's conference reports go back to 1953, and current data appears in its journal *International Music Educator* (Schott). Yet other journals interested in this rapidly developing field are *Journal of Research in Music Education* (1953–), *Living Music*, *Making Music* (1946–) and the Schools Music Association's *Music* (1966–).

The British impetus of Burt, Wing and Mainwaring earlier in the century is thus flowering widely. In Reading and London, and in Novello's *Music Education Research Papers* (1966–) are to be seen some of its most recent and substantial fruits.

The examination machinery for the theoretical side of children's musical education in the U.K. is shared between the Associated Board and the various universities, and there is no lack of "coaching" literature (regularly reviewed in *The Music Teacher*). There seems to be only one work, so far, specifically devoted to the G.C.E.: Corbett and Yelverton's *Music for G.C.E. "O" Level* (Barrie & Rockliff, 2nd edn., 1967). The American scene in "music education" is vigorously reflected in a wide variety of official bodies, journals and monographs, exemplified by the Music Teachers' National Association, the Music Educators' National Conference, etc., though these are not, of course, confined to actual school-teaching.

For lists of children's books on music the reader should consult Rainbow, (see p. 57), together with the School Library Association's *Primary School Library Books* (1961) and the music section of their *Guide to Book Lists and Bibliographies* (1961). J. B. Cramer of London have compiled their own list. *The British Catalogue of Music* has regular entries under "Children", and an extensive older list appears in Schirmer's *Guide*. Songs are very exhaustively indexed by Helen G. Cushing in her *Children's Song Index* (New York, H. W. Wilson, 1936) which analyses 189 anthologies. Annual surveys of various classes of children's music now appear in *Notes*.

Films and film-strips for children are summarized in Rainbow. The fullest information can be had from The Educational Foundation for Visual Aids, 33 Queen Anne St., London W. 1.

CHAPTER 9

The Musicologist

*Spontini s'écria: "C'est indigne! affreux! Mais on me corrigera
donc aussi, moi, quand je serai mort? . ." Ce à quoi je répondis
tristement: "Hélas! cher maître, vous avez bien corrigé Gluck!"*

H. BERLIOZ, *A travers chants*

"[THE musicologist] is there primarily to get things right" said
Professor Westrup in his paper "Practical musicology" to the
Cambridge congress of the International Association of Music
Libraries (*Music Libraries and Instruments*, Hinrichsen, 1961). His
short survey both showed the need and provided the justification for
a science which has only in the last generation gained more than a
foot-hold. *Grove* ignored the topic until the fifth edition. *Die Musik
in Geschichte und Gegenwart* (Bärenreiter) has a lengthy article and
bibliography under "Musikwissenschaft". J. La Rue's article
"Musical exploration" (*Library Trends*, vol. 8, no. 4, University of
Illinois, 1960) describes the present-day challenge to librarians, and
an evaluation of basic text-materials is attempted by V. Duckles'
article "The teaching of music bibliography" (*Notes*, vol. 20, no. 1,
Music Library Association). K. E. Mixter's *General Bibliography for
Musical Research* (Detroit Information Service, 1962) is a broadly
based approach, leading to single-volume surveys such as G.
Haydon's *Introduction to Musicology* (University of N. Carolina,
1959) and J. Chailley's *Précis de musicologie* (Presses Universitaires de
France, 1958), for non-specialists and L. B. Spiess' *Historical
Musicology* (Brooklyn, Institute of Mediaeval Music, 1963), for
students. The latest survey balancing American and Western development is *Musicology* by Harrison, Hood & Palisca (Prentice-Hall,

1964). This is now supplemented by Columbia University's *Current Musicology* (1965–).

The trained musicologists' Bible is G. Adler's *Handbuch der Musikgeschichte*, 2 vols., 2nd edn. (Berlin, Keller, 1930, reprint announced by Schneider, Tutzing) while E. Bücken's *Handbuch der Musikwissenschaft*, 13 vols., (Musurgia, 1949) is a splendidly illustrated general history, with volumes devoted to instruments and "Aufführungspraxis". Certain other works on early music stand out as landmarks in the post-war extension of musical horizons, notably G. Reese's *Music in the Middle Ages* (Dent, 1941) and *Music in the Renaissance* (Dent, 1954), together with M. Bukofzer's *Music in the Baroque Era* (Dent, 1948) and *Studies in Medieval and Renaissance Music* (Dent, 1951). The seminal *New Oxford History of Music* (O.U.P., 1957–) (see Fig. 25) is only now beginning to get into its stride (5 vols., to 1968), but its companion, *The History of Music in Sound*, 10 vols., (O.U.P., 1953–9) and the accompanying HMV records are complete. An American counterpart, *The Norton History of Music*, (Norton, 1949–) has progressed more quickly (5 vols. out of 7 by 1963), but is not on such an elaborate scale. From a vast literature devoted to interpretation, R. Donington's *The Interpretation of Early Music* (2nd edn., Faber, 1965) is the most recent major treatise, highly practical (in the direct Dolmetsch tradition), not least as concerns the use of instruments. In his series *Style and Interpretation* (O.U.P., in progress), Howard Ferguson is one of the latest to expound and attempt to reflect accurately in performing editions the intentions of early keyboard composers.

SOURCE-MATERIALS

A recent bibliographical starting-point is Duckles' *Music Reference and Research Materials* (New York, Free Press of Glencoe/London, Collier–Macmillan, 1967), which has 1150 fully annotated bibliographical entries. Following this is Rita Benton's prototype for R.I.S.M.'s eventual world dictionary of contributing libraries: *Directory of Music Research Libraries*, Part 1: *Canada and U.S.* (University of Iowa, 1967). A useful German forerunner was Kahl and Luther's *Repertorium der Musikwissenschaft: Musikschrifttum*,

Denkmäler und Gesamtausgaben in Auswahl: 1800–1950 (Bärenreiter, 1953). L. B. Spiess (p. 60) also covers some of the same ground and includes an up-to-date list of "modern editions of theoretical sources". A volume particularly directed to American college students is Ruth Watanabe's *An Introduction to Musical Research* (Prentice-Hall, 1967). Works which give the contents of historical editions are W. Apel's *Harvard Dictionary of Music* (Harvard U.P., 1944), A. H. Heyer's *Historical Sets . . .* (American Library Association, 1957), and the *Katalog der Musikbibliothek Paul Hirsch*, Band 4 (O.U.P., 1947), the two latter indexing such sets analytically by composer. A project is now gathering momentum, under the auspices of the International Music Libraries Association and the International Musicological Society, which will eventually provide a completely new basis for both manuscript and printed sources, replacing R. Eitner's *Quellen-Lexikon*, 10 vols. (Reprint, Graz, Akademische Drucks und Verlagsanstalt, 1960) (see Fig. 26) and its supplements, by the work of national research teams. This is the *Répertoire international des sources musicales* (Bärenreiter/Henle) (see Fig. 27), planned in two main series (composer and subject, totalling up to twenty volumes) and described in detail in a series of communiqués issued by Bärenreiter.

The reprinting programmes of the publishers responsible for the great nineteenth century *Gesamtausgaben* are now getting fully under way. Breitkopf, Broude, Ewards and (for revised collected editions of the masters, Bärenreiter) lead the field here. In addition, the extensive *Denkmäler* series are now again available (mainly Breitkopf), while a newcomer in this field, Gregg International Publishers, has made a start with Vittoria (8 vols.) and Handel-Chrysander (complete in 97 vols., 1966). The last is particularly welcome in view of the inevitably slow progress of Bärenreiter's *Hallische Handelausgabe*.

Microfilm archives of musicological sources are steadily growing, one of the prototypes being the Deutsches Musikgeschichtliches Archiv (Kassel), described in *Fontes artis musicae*, 1954/2. Two of many specialist projects concern liturgical archives: the St. Louis, Missouri, University's Vatican Films in the Pius XII Memorial

Library (see *Notes*, June 1957) and the Monastic Manuscript Microfilm Library in St. John's University, Collegeville, Minnesota (see *Notes*, Sept. 1958). Another is the Isham Memorial Library at Harvard. The Hoboken Photogrammarchiv in the Vienna National Library was described in the *Journal of Renaissance and Baroque Music*, vol. 1 (1946).

EARLY PRINTED MUSIC

Bibliographies of early music and of early music in modern editions are listed by Duckles, while the scores themselves are listed in the British Museum's annual *Accessions Lists* (fairly comprehensively) and *Fontes artis musicae* (selectively). An exposition of United Kingdom printed holdings is provided by the *British Union Catalogue of Early Music (before 1801)*, 2 vols. (Butterworth, 1957) (see Fig. 28), of which an annotated master-copy is maintained in the British Museum's Music Room.

MANUSCRIPTS

British manuscripts are described in a number of library catalogues such as those of the British Museum, Bodleian and Christ Church, Oxford, but a nation-wide inventory awaits the completion of work by a British team for the *Répertoire international des sources musicales*. For the U.S., O. E. Albrecht's *Census of Autograph Music Manuscripts of European Composers in American Libraries* (Univ. of Pennsylvania, 1953) is unique in its scope, and already under major revision. Some modern private collectors have published catalogues which include many manuscripts, e.g. *Manuskripte . . . von Scarlatti bis Stravinsky: Musikautographen–Sammlung Louis Koch* (Stuttgart, F. Krais, 1953), and A. Meyer, *Collection musicale* (Abbeville, F. Paillart, 1961).

FACSIMILES, ETC.

Many masterworks have been published in replica, wholly or in part, particularly since the collotype process made this so splendidly possible. A few specimens follow—their use is primarily, of course, to save the trouble and expense of seeing the originals (though the latter may naturally yield secrets which the best replica misses), but they have their marginal uses for reproduction in concert-brochures, television programmes, etc.:

> Drei Masken Verlag, Munich (Mozart, Schubert, Wagner, Weber, etc.).
> HANDEL, G. F. *Messiah* (London, 1868; Hamburg, 1892).
> The Harrow replicas: Purcell, Handel, etc. (Heffer).
> Bärenreiter (Bach).
> SIMPSON, C. *The Division Viol* (Curwen).
> ÖSTERREICHISCHE BIBLIOTHEK, *Katalog des Archivs für Photogramme Musikalischer Handschriften* (Öst, Bib., 1967).
> VERDI, G. *Falstaff*, *Requiem* (Ricordi).
> WINTERNITZ, E. *Musical Autographs from Monteverdi to Hindemith*, 2 vols. (Princeton U.P., 1955).

The International Association of Music Libraries' *Documenta musicologica* is a series of annotated facsimiles of major treatises such as those by Quantz, Walther, Praetorius. The first is devoted to German works of which seventeen had been published by 1962. Two recent anthologies drawn from these and more modern sources are W. O. Strunk's *Source-readings in Music History* (Norton, 1950) and P. Nettl's *Book of Musical Documents* (New York, Philosophical Library, 1948), while the works which annotate and "place" the landmarks are J. E. Matthew's *The Literature of Music* (Stock, 1896) (see Fig. 29) and G. Reese's *Fourscore Classics of Music Literature* (New York, Bobbs–Merrill, 1957). The latter confines itself to works not available in English, and quotes early and modern editions. Biographical source material relating to individual composers has its own growing literature, exemplified by the work of David and Mendel for Bach (Norton, 1945), Deutsch for Schubert (Dent, 1946) and Mozart (Bärenreiter, 1961) and by Arnold and Fortune for Monteverdi (Faber, 1968). Firms such as Gregg International Publishers, Fritz A. M. Knuf (Nieuwe Spiegelstraat, 70, Amsterdam) and more recently, the Robert Owen Lehman Foundation of Washington (London, Quaritch) specialize on reprints of major treatises or outstanding scores. The full extent of this field is nowhere more clearly laid out than in the Library of Congress *Catalogue of Early Books on Music* (before 1800), whose two volumes cover acquisitions to 1942, and include for good measure a "list of books on music in Chinese and Japanese". In this latter connection, Spiess (see p. 60) contains sections on Chinese, Japanese and Slav musicological terms. From September 1966 *Notes* has carried a semi-annual feature on "Reprints and forthcoming reprints". Sources and collected editions are listed in Blum's *Music Serials in Microfilm and Reprint Editions* (*Notes*, June 1968).

EDITING

No single topic has more bitterly divided the practical musician from the pedantic editor, but slowly the validity of the conclusions of those musicologists who are also practical musicians (as, ideally, they should all be) is gaining ground. The matter is emphatically not confined to early music or the classics. The "process of corruption" lurks in nineteenth century as in Renaissance and Baroque scores: Bach, Handel, Haydn, Bruckner, Puccini and Verdi are all battlegrounds.

Early Music and Classics

W. Emery's *Editions and Musicians* (Novello, 1957) is "a survey of the duties of practical musicians and editors towards the classics", and deals cavalierly, even cynically, with past standards, questioning the validity of so-called "Urtexte", and Collected Editions which have passed as sacrosanct for 100 years. More calligraphically technical is its companion *Editing Early Music* (Novello, 1963)— "notes on the preparation of printers' copy", issued by Emery, Dart & Morris on behalf of Stainer & Bell, Novello and O.U.P. The topic was still more closely argued by D. Stevens at the New York congress of the International Musicological Society, recorded in the

Report (Bärenreiter, 1961–62), and more recently extended by
Dadelsohn's *Richtlinien* (Bärenreiter, 1967). After these, the crucial
question "what is a good edition?" may best be answered prag-
matically by directing the reader to some good and bad examples—
such a list is given in T. Dart's *The Interpretation of Music* (Hutchinson, 1967). J. Tobin's *Handel at Work* (Cassell, 1964) provides one
modern example of applied research, in this case devoted to *Messiah*.
Additionally, the student will find some general problems of music
editing aired absorbingly in A. Tyson's *The Authentic Editions of
Beethoven* (Faber, 1963).

Modern Music

Problems of the composer's written or printed intentions should
not be so taxing as in earlier music. Wagner set a standard of meticulousness, which composers like Richard Strauss and Elgar have
emulated, yet Bruckner, for instance, has been constantly at the
mercy of "friend" and editor alike for 80 years or so, as H. Redlich
describes in Chapter VII of his *Bruckner and Mahler* (Dent, 1955) and
R. Simpson in *Bruckner and the Symphony* (B.B.C., 1963). N. Del
Mar's "Confusion and error" (*The Score*, Oct. 1957, Feb. and
July 1958) shows again the corruptions still extant in many accepted
scores of the normal concert repertory, while C. Sartori's *Mr.
Vaughan's Crusade* (Opera, April 1963) sums up a protracted dispute,
almost an Italian *cause célèbre*, over accuracy in Puccini and Verdi
scores, and shows a salutory sense of perspective.

THEMATIC CATALOGUES

The Music Library Association's *Check List of Thematic Catalogues*
(New York Public Library, 1954), together with B. S. Brook's
Supplement (Queen's College, New York, 1966), give the key to an
unexpectedly wide range of music, and this is brought more up to
date by L. B. Spiess (see p. 60). The classical repertory is covered by
numerous separate catalogues, of which the *Breitkopf Thematic
Catalogue, 1762–87* (reprint, Broude, 1967, followed in 1962 by
Köchel–Einstein's *Chronologisch-thematisches Verzeichnis sämtliche*

Tonwerke W. A. Mozarts (Ann Arbor, Edwards, 1947 (Fig. 30), and Wiesbaden, Breitkopf, 1964 (Fig. 31)) are the prototypes. Schmieder's *Bach-Werke-Verzeichnis* (Leipzig, Breitkopf, 1958– (Fig. 32)), Kinsky and Halm's *Beethoven*, and O. E. Deutsch's *Schubert* are outstanding modern examples. These are complemented by Barlow and Morgenstern's *Dictionary of Musical Themes*, and *Dictionary of Vocal Themes* (Benn, 1949 and 1956 respectively). Difficulties begin when departing from the "main stream". Boccherini and Vivaldi are cases in point. Boccherini, Clementi and Vivaldi were, until recently, cases in point, though these particular gaps have now been filled by de Rothschild, Tyson and Pincherle respectively. Where even more fugitive works, especially *anonyma* are concerned, musicologists are at a loss for lack of *incipits*. The scope here is endless, and many catalogues do in fact exist, mostly in musicologists' card-indexes, and unlikely to see publication. One attempt to make such findings accessible is that described by J. La Rue (*Fontes artis musicae*, 1960–2), covering 18th-century chamber music and concertos. Inquiries to New York University (New York, 3) will be followed up. The computer is being pressed into service in other ways than for thematic identifications, and the present state of development is described by A. T. Hickman in *Electronic Apparatus for Music Research* (Novello, 1968). The Computer Museum Network in New York directed by Everett Helm is a recent sign of growing activity. A still more recent effort to aid identification in a specific field is Duckles and Elmer's *Thematic Catalogue of a Manuscript Collection of Eighteenth Century Italian Instrumental Music . . .* (Univ. of California Press, 1963). Yet another is the thematic index of over 1200 works which forms vol. 2 of B. S. Brook's *La Symphonie française dans la seconde moitié du XVIII*, 3 vols. (Université de Paris, 1962), distributed by H. Baron, London. Current developments in the thematic field will be found spread over the musicological periodicals in general and in *Fontes* in particular, important recent contributions being N. Bridgman's "Nouvelle visite aux incipits musicaux" (*Acta musicologica*, 23, 11–IV, 1961) and Lansky and Suppan's *Der neue Melodien-Katalog des deutschen Volksliedarchivs* (*Fontes*, 1963/1–2).

DISSERTATIONS AND THESES

Those which achieve normal publication present no particular search-problems. The (typescript) majority, however, remain on deposit in various university faculties and libraries, though partially available through such agencies as University Microfilms. Chapter 8, Bibliographies of Dissertations, of K. Mixter's *General Bibliography*, referred to earlier, covers the ground internationally for the general indexes, which, of course, include musicological items. Examples of bibliographies limited to music theses are Helen Hewitt's *Doctoral Dissertations in Musicology*, 3rd edn. (American Musicological Society, 1961), and R. Schaal's *Verzeichnis deutschsprachiger musikwissenschaftlicher Dissertationen, 1860–1960* (Bärenreiter, 1963). These are supplemented by the lists in *Musical Quarterly* and by *Current Musicology*'s "Dissertations from abroad" (1965–). America also has K. R. Hartley's *Bibliography of Theses and Dissertations in Sacred Music* (Information Coordinators, 1966). For the rest, the various national musicological societies (see *Organizations*) form the best approach, though German dissertations are listed independently in the *Deutsches Jahrbuch für Musikwissenschaft* (Peters–Hinrichsen); and England now has P. Doe's *Register of Theses on Music* (Royal Musical Association Research Chronicle no. 3, 1966) covering the past 25 years, with a classified index.

FESTSCHRIFTEN

These useful volumes of collected essays in honour of one individual contain a world of specialist information. The Festschriften themselves are listed in Spiess (see p. 60) and E. C. Krohn's "Musical Festschriften and related publications" (*Notes*, 2nd series, vol. 21, nos. 1–2) describes the present state of research into their scope and contents. H. F. Williams published an *Index of Medieval Studies in Festschriften* (Univ. of California Press, 1951). Later documentation includes Karl and Luther's *Repertorium der Musikwissenschaft* (Bärenreiter, 1958), J. B. Coover's provisional list of 1958, and W. Gerboth's index in the Reese Festschrift, *Aspects of Medieval and*

Renaissance Music (O.U.P., 1967). The latter gives 1,500 titles and a subject index.

TRANSLATIONS

The joint enterprise of the International Association of Music Libraries and the American Musicological Society is responsible for a new Translations Centre for musicological studies and documents. Its scope is described in *Current Musicology*, no. 6 (1965).

SPURIOSA

The discovery of doubtful, spurious or misattributed compositions is part of the very lifeblood, if not the livelihood, of the musicologist. The "Beethoven" funeral march regularly played and so-called in military ceremony, but more probably by J. H. Walch; and the "Jena" symphony by J. F. Witt; the "Mozart" *Wiegenlied* by B. Flies; the tenuous connection of J. Haydn with the *St. Antoni chorale*—these are a few of the better-known cases. The two most accessible treatments of such matters in general are in the *Oxford Companion* (Mis-attributed Compositions) and in *Notes*, vol. 12, nos. 1 and 4 (Ye Olde Spuriosity Shoppe, or, Put it in the Anhang, by C. L. Cudworth). Cudworth's articles, dated as they are, nevertheless show very clearly the dangerous shoals which remain to be navigated as a result of the foibles or mischiefs of composers, publishers, editors and musicologists themselves. Wherever the ground has not been conveniently covered by an Einstein, a Deutsch, a Schmieder, etc., or by the above surveys, there is still no substitute for painstaking individual research. (See also Ch. 17, Curiosa.)

ETHNOMUSICOLOGY

This is one of the newer branches of research. It already has its own growing bibliography, e.g. B. Nettl's *Reference Materials in Ethnomusicology* (Detroit, Information Coordinators, 1967) the separate section of the bibliography to the "Musikwissenschaft" article in

Die Musik in Geschichte und Gegenwart, and the *Bibliography of Asiatic Musics* which appeared serially in *Notes*, 1947–51. These are now supplemented by L. J. P. Gaskin's *Select Bibliography of Music in Africa* (International African Institute, 1965) and Gillis and Merriam's *Ethnomusicology and Folk-music: an international bibliography of dissertations and theses* (Wesleyan University, 1966). Leading periodicals include: *Ethnomusicology* (The Hague, 1959–) and *Journal of the Society of Ethnomusicology* (Wesleyan University 1947–). The preponderance of American effort can further be judged from the projects regularly described in *Current Musicology* (Columbia University, 1965–). The principal treatise is J. Kunst's *Ethnomusicology*, 3rd edn. (The Hague, Nijhoff, 1959) (see Fig. 33) which also has a very extensive bibliography. Two organizations have existed for some time: the Los Angeles Institute of Ethnomusicology described by its Director, Mantle Hood, in the Prentice-Hall volume already quoted, and (as a section of the Sorbonne) the Institut de Musicologie under Alain Daniélou. The latter has recently assumed charge of the Berlin Institute for Comparative Music Studies, with the aim of avoiding any undue independence on racial theory. Over vast areas covered by these institutions and their journals, the music remains mostly unwritten, but is becoming more readily accessible through recordings such as UNESCO's *Musical Anthology of the Orient*, and the Library of Congress *Archive of Folk-song*. Research in the Orient itself has mostly centred around the Society for Research in Asiatic Music under Prof. Hisao Tanabe for the past 30 years, while America has its own focal point in the American Ethnomusicological Society.

The evolution of instruments also engages the attention of such bodies as the Galpin Society (*Journal*, 1948–) while folk-song and dance likewise has its own international and national organization (Ch. 12). The first two volumes of Besseler and Schneider's *Musikgeschichte in Bildern* (Leipzig, Deutscher Verlag, 1964–) and W. Bachmann's *Die Anfänge des Streichinstrumentenspiels* (Breitkopf, 1964) also provide first-class surveys. Current activity can further be followed in *The World of Music* (International Music Council). See also p. 123.

ORGANIZATIONS

The International Musicological Society co-ordinates national activities and reflects these in *Acta musicologica* (1928–) and its triennial conference proceedings (Bärenreiter). National bodies include:

Belgium	Société belge de Musicologie. (Publications, 1947–.)
France	Société de Musique d'Autrefois. (Revue de Musicologie, 1917–.)
	Société Française de Musicologie. (Annales Musicologiques, 1963–.)
Germany	Gesellschaft für Musikforschung. (Die Musikforschung, 1948–.)
Holland	Vereeniging vor Nederlandsche Musikgeschiedenis. (Bouwsteenen, 1869–.)
Italy	La Società Italiana de Musicologia. (La Rassegna musicale, 1928–.) (Rivista musicale italiana, 1894–.)
Japan	Japanese Musicological Society. Tokyo University of Arts. (1952–.)
Spain	Instituto Español de Musicologia. (Anuario musical, 1946–.)
Sweden	Svenska Samfundet för Musikforskning. (Svensk tidskrift . . . 1919–.)
U.K.	(Royal) Musical Association. (Proceedings, 1874–; Index v. 1–90).
U.S.A.	American Musicological Society. (Journal, 1948–.)
U.S.S.R.	Soyuz Sovetskikh Kompozitorov. (Sovetskaia musyka, 1933–.)

TRAINING

Conservatoires, colleges and academies still concentrate on instrumental training and general musicianship, but some now include courses in the history of music, Extended musicological studies leading to a degree are mostly left, in the English-speaking world at least, to the universities.

CHAPTER 10

The Music Librarian

I love vast libraries; yet there is a doubt
If one be better with them or without.

J. G. SAXE, *The Library*

THE paths of the layman, the professional and amateur musician, and the musicologist having been eased in the foregoing chapters as regards sources, what remains for the music librarian—or rather the general librarian, since the majority of smaller libraries will rarely have a trained music librarian on their staff? (Of the 600 or so municipal and county library systems in Great Britain, probably not more than one-tenth have an assistant who can give his entire time to music service, even after the encouraging post-war development of gramophone record departments, and most other countries are far less well served.) Most of the reference works already discussed will be found only in libraries, and of these only the large, well-established and interested library is likely to possess the expensive and out-of-print items.

The music librarian might well become first acquainted with the basic terms of his job from C. Hopkinson's "The fundamentals of music bibliography" (*Fontes*, 1955/2) and from A. Van Hoboken's "Probleme der musikbibliographischen Terminologie" (*Fontes*, 1958/1), and then proceed to read one of the sanest short expositions (unaccountably overlooked in recent bibliographies): E. A. Savage's "One way to form a music library" in his *Special Librarianship in General Libraries* (Grafton, 1939).

Statements of problems, scope and opportunities have appeared in *Fontes* 1959/2 (A. H. King's "The music librarian and his tasks") and in *Library Trends*, vol. 8, no. 4, where Duckles, La Rue and others cover the technical, administrative and bibliographic areas in a challenging manner. Current developments are summarized by The Library Association's *Five Years' Work* series, and by J. H. Davies in *Progress in library science*, 1965, ed. R. L. Collison (Butterworths, 1965). The latter contributes quarterly notes on current developments ("Musicalia") to *The Library World* (W. H. Smith & Son).

BIBLIOGRAPHY

About 100 key references are quoted and their relevance discussed by the present writer in his music chapter of the symposium *Special Materials in the Library* (L. A., 1963). Other basic lists (annotated) are given in C. M. Winchell's *Guide to Reference Books*, 7th edn. (American Library Association, 1951 and Suppts.) and A. J. Walford's *Guide to Reference material* (L.A., 1955 and Suppt., 1963), but by far the most comprehensive and up-to-date statement is V. Duckles' *Music Reference and Research Materials* (New York, Free Press of Glencoe/London, Collier–Macmillan, 1964) which consolidates and supersedes three other similar surveys. The best brief general expositions are E. C. Krohn's "Bibliography of music" (*Musical Quarterly*, vol. 5, 1919) and A. H. King's "Recent work in music bibliography" (*The Library*, 4th series, vol. 26, 1945), followed by J. B. Coover's "The current status of music bibliography" (*Notes*, vol. 13, no. 4, 1956). The most recent years are also covered to some extent by L. B. Spiess in the bibliographical section of his *Historical Musicology* (Brooklyn, Institute of Medieval Music, 1963). K. E. Mixter's *General Bibliography for Music Research* (Detroit Information Service 1962) makes a good background to these studies.

For many librarians, particularly in municipal and county libraries, the primary tools are McColvin and Reeves' *Music Libraries* (Grafton, 2 vols., 1937–8; 2nd edn., much enlarged by J. Dove, Deutsch, 1964) together with E. T. Bryant's *Music Librarianship* (J. Clarke, 1959) (see Fig. 34) which latter it deliberately complements, and B. Redfern's *Organising Music in Libraries*

(C. Bingley, 1966). The gramophone librarian has Ch. 5 of Bryant together with the International Association of Music Libraries (U.K. Branch) *Handbook of Gramophone Record Libraries*, ed. H. Currall, 2nd edn. (Crosby, Lockwood, 1969). (See also Ch. 15.)

PUBLISHED CATALOGUES

Many major catalogues date from the early part of this century, and some are becoming available again in reprint. The article "Musikbibliotheken" in *MGG* quotes catalogue details and Duckles (2nd edn.) provides a clearer list, alphabetically by town in the section "Catalogs of Music Libraries and Collections" (nos. 817–1138).

DICTIONARIES AND ENCYCLOPAEDIAS

The basic works in English such as *Grove* (Macmillan) and *Oscar Thompson* (Dent) are adequately annotated in the bibliographies already quoted, and have been mentioned *seriatim*. The completion of F. Blume's *Die Musik in Geschichte und Gegenwart* (Bärenreiter, 1949–68) (see Fig. 35) is too important not to be emphasized separately. Its editor described the achievement and the supplement which is planned to wind up the whole set in *Notes*, Dec. 1967. On at least two counts, this work is far ahead of other encyclopaedic works: the profuseness of its illustrations and the thoroughness of its bibliographical apparatus. Still essential for detailed coverage is F. J. Fetis' *Biographie universelle des musiciens*, 2nd edn., 1873–80 (reprinted Brussels, Culture et Civilisation, 1963). More recent, though smaller projects, need mention, viz. Riemann's *Musiklexikon*, 12th edn., 3 vols. (Schott, 1959–68), *Larousse de la musique*, 2 vols. (Larousse, 1957) and, latest of all, the *Enciclopedia della musica*, 4 vols. (Ricordi, 1963–4). Some works usefully concentrate on biographical data, among which a special place must be given to Baker's *Biographical Dictionary of Musicians*, 5th edn. (Schirmer, 1958), reprinted (1966) with a substantial supplement by Slonimsky. For today's composers there is S. Bull's *Index to Biographies of Contemporary Composers* (Scarecrow Press, 1964).

The full extent of such works is surprisingly large. R. Schaal lists over 200 "Lexika", 1473–1949 in *Das Jahrbuch der Musikwelt* (Bayreuth, J. Steeger, 1949), but the most thorough study is J. B. Coover's *Bibliography of Music Dictionaries* (Denver, Bibliographical Center, 1952) which quotes 811 items and has a useful Topical Index. Over thirty dictionaries, for instance, are given as devoted to instruments and their makers.

SOURCE-MATERIALS

See Ch. 9.

MODERN EDITIONS

The traditional guide (and still useful, in spite of its age) remains F. Pazdirek's *Universal-Handbuch der Musikliteratur*, 10 vols. (Vienna, [1904–1910?]) (reprinted, Knuf) (see Fig. 36). As a checklist of about half a million items in print at that time it covers ground which has never similarly been attempted on a world basis. When the full range of the British Broadcasting Corporation's catalogues (songs, choral and chamber music, 1965–) is available, a great gap in knowledge of the provenance of performing editions (both of Pazdirek's era and since, including much antiquariana) will have been filled. Current national bibliographies are fully described by K. E. Mixter (see p. 73). It must suffice here to emphasize the supra-national nature of three of them: *The British Catalogue of Music* (British National Bibliography, 1957–), (see Fig. 37), the U.S. *Catalog of Copyright Entries Pt. 5a: Published Music* (Library of Congress, 1947–) (see Fig. 38), and The Library of Congress's *Music and Phonorecords* (1953–). The first and second have a large coverage outside their own countries by reason of copyright deposit, direct or through agencies, while the third lists works represented by Congress printed cards, and, therefore, knows no boundaries. The remainder are almost exclusively national affairs, though the famous prototype, A. Hofmeister's *Handbuch der Musikliteratur* (1844–) (see Fig. 39), claimed (at least originally) to cover "Deutschland und die angrenzenden Ländern" for published music, books and periodicals.

The best *select* lists of the repertory, including its literature are in the new McColvin & Reeves and in Bryant. The "Listes selectives internationales" which appear regularly at the end of issues of *Fontes artis musicae* (see Fig. 40) and the British Museum's annual accessions lists form excellent current check-lists of scores, while *Notes* gives possibly the fullest available international coverage to current musical literature, and rather less to current scores. The average public library is better served by J. B. Cramer's *Basic and Standard Music Library Lists*, their current *Library Bulletins*, and by similar services offered by Hainauer of London and other music dealers (see Ch. 11).

MUSIC LITERATURE

Current international output of the literature of music (including periodicals) is covered by the *Bibliographie des Musikschrifttums* (Hofmeister/Novello, 1936–) begun by Taut and continued by Schmieder. The serious time-lag (up to 6 years or more) must be filled by national bibliographies and by reviews. The advent, however, of R.I.L.M. *Abstracts of Musical Literature* (American Musicological Society, 1967–) will change the face of current documentation, and music now begins to enjoy the kind of abstracting service which the sciences and some of the humanities enjoy.

A short but lively exposition of British and American literature, mainly in current editions, is E. T. Bryant's *Music* in the Readers' Guide Series (Bingley, 1965), and *Modern Music and Musicians: 1900 to the present day*, 2nd edn. (Library Association, 1968).

CLASSIFICATION AND CATALOGUING

A librarian may at any time inherit a badly organized collection or be called upon to start a new one. For classification he should master relevant chapters of McColvin and of Bryant, and study closely the facet classification (1960) developed by Coates for the *British Catalogue of Music* together with the simpler scheme of Schmieder (see above). The Universal Decimal Classification has a new English edition in preparation by the British Standards Institution, and the Library of Congress revised its Class M, Music and Books on Music, in its 2nd edn. of 1963. A further attempt has been made by I. Pethes in his *Flexible Classification for Music and the Literature of Music* (Budapest Centre of Library Science, 1967). A revealing comparison by the compiler of the Hirsch catalogues is Kathi Meyer-Baer's "Classifications in American music libraries" (Hirsch, Dewey, Congress) in *Music Review*, Feb. 1951.

For cataloguing, the same works should be carefully studied, followed by the specialist *Code International de Catalogage* . . . (International Association of Music Libraries, Peters–Hinrichsen, 1957–) which will have covered, when complete, the finest points of the craft (including treatment of manuscripts and recordings) in a series of graded manuals. The best examples of each kind of catalogue should be considered in detail, and the differences of approach noted between the bibliographically meticulous British Museum, Hirsch, Huntingdon, etc., catalogues and the practical handlists such as those of the B.B.C. and the Liverpool, Dagenham, Ealing and Newcastle Public Libraries. The cataloguing of musical manuscripts has been sorely neglected, perhaps owing to a failure of experts to agree. Vol. 4 of the *Code International de Catalogage* will be devoted to manuscripts. Apart from this one of the very few published statements is W. Altmann's *Die Katalogisierung musikalischen Handschriften* (Kongress der deutschen Musikgeschicht, Bericht, Leipzig, 1926).

Subject-headings, whether for full dictionary-cataloguing (a declining art) or for subject indexing of classified catalogues, need the most careful study. The Library of Congress *Music Subject Headings* (1952) and the New York Public Library *Music Subject Headings* (Boston, G. K. Hall, 1959) deserve comparison with those devised for other classification schemes.

PROFESSIONAL ORGANIZATION

The International Association of Music Libraries (Secretariat, Ständeplatz 16, Kassel) has made itself during its first dozen years a rallying-point for professional matters. It has working commissions covering research, public libraries, radio, records, cataloguing etc., whose specialist activities are regularly reported in *Fontes artis musicae* (Bärenreiter, 1954–); its national branches (of which the U.K. and American are the largest) span the world. IAML acts as a link not only between the various types of music librarian, but with musicological organizations, one of its principal activities being to organize, jointly with the International Musicological Society, the *Répertoire international des sources musicales* (Bärenreiter–Henle, 1960–) (see Ch. 9). Its published conference proceedings form major statements of current policy and activity (Brussels, 1955: The Hague, Nijhoff, 1958; Cambridge, 1959: *Music Libraries and Instruments*, Hinrichsen, 1960; Stockholm, 1962: *Fontes*, 1964; Dijon, 1965: *Fontes*, 1965; and New York 1968: *Fontes*, 1969) and the U.K. branch has recently launched its own journal *Brio* (1964–) as a mirror for, *inter alia*, British policy and practice.

Training for music librarianship is slowly developing under the auspices of examining bodies such as the Library Association, the American Library Association, the State library administration in France and under the Radio-Diffusion-Télévision Française in association with the national branches of the International Association of Music Libraries. A thorough knowledge of the sources and methods of approach described in the present volume will go a fair way towards equipping librarians to meet future demands. The latter will certainly intensify with the growth of musicological and practical training now in evidence. The present writer has reviewed the needs for training in *Brio*, Spring 1965, supplementing the principles outlined (but so imperfectly realized as yet) by Susanne Clercz-Lejeune in *Le Bibliothécaire Musicale, International Congress of Libraries . . . Brussels*, vol. 3 (Nijhoff, 1958) and IAML's training symposium, Stockholm 1962 (*Fontes artis musicae*, 1964).

Current Musicology (Columbia University, 1965–) shows a development of teaching music bibliography in American universities which is not so far paralleled elsewhere.

CHAPTER 11

The Collector and Dealer

THE private collector of music and its literature has little to guide him except his own taste and personal experience. J. E. Matthew's *The Literature of Music* (Stock, 1896), based on a lifetime's collecting, and C. B. Oldman's *Collecting Musical First Editions* (Constable, 1938) together with the chapter "Private Music Collecting" in McColvin & Reeves' *Music Libraries*, vol. 2 (Grafton, 1938 and Deutsch, 1964) were rather solitary contributions until A. Rosenthal dealt with historical aspects in "The Music Antiquarian" (*Fontes artis musicae*, 1958/2), and H. Baron followed this with *The Music Antiquarian of Today* (*Brio*, no. 2, 1964). To these may be added G. Thibault's "Les Collections privés . . ." (*Fontes artis musicae*, 1959/2) and A. H. King's *Some British Collectors of Music, c.1600–1960* (C.U.P., 1963). The same author's *English Pictorial Musical Title-pages, 1820–85* (Bibliographical Society, 1950) short as it is, reflects a revival of an earlier fashion in collecting, as does his *Sheet Music Covers Yesterday and Today* (Graphis Annual, 1953–4).* The standard works in this field are J. Grand-Carteret's *Les Titres illustrés . . .* (Turin, Bocca, 1904) and Zur Westen's *Musiktitel aus vier Jahrhunderten* (Leipzig, Röder, *c.*1910), both superbly illustrated. A more recent review of a related field is Beck and Roth's *Music in Print* (New York Public Library, 1965).

The constant migration of collections of all kinds continues to fascinate and frustrate the specialist, to tease the dealer and to astound the layman. Current discoveries, not all so promptly revealed as that of the present state of the Cummings music in the

* A later survey is G. S. Fraenkel's *Decorative Music title-page* (Dover/Constable, 1968).

Nanki Music Library (*Musical Times*, Oct. 1963), continue to render out of date some of the information even in comparatively recent articles such as O. E. Deutsch's "Collections, private" in *Grove* V. The recent wanderings of the Cobbett chamber music collection serve to underline this point. Dispersal, theft, to say nothing of the ravages of war, make this an area where precise and up-to-date documentation is extremely hazardous.

Some very rich private collections still remain intact, however. The Koch (autographs) and Meyer collections are among the very few of which published catalogues can currently be bought, though the former is already partly dispersed either privately or at auction, particularly the Beethoven section. The great Paul Hirsch collection (now in the British Museum) has its four-volume catalogue, now out of print, and there has never been a published catalogue of the famous Hoboken collection. Only the first volume of the catalogue of the Cortot collection was published: *Bibliothèque Alfred Cortot, Première partie . . .* (Société Internationale de Musicologie, 1936) and the whole collection is now in various private and institutional hands. One of the largest collections to be sold in modern times was that of Werner Wolffheim, whose sale-catalogue still appears from time to time in antiquarian catalogues (*Versteigerung der Musikbibliothek . . .* 2 vols., Breslauer & Liepmannssohn, 1928). The long list of Sotheby catalogues includes some famous music-sales, and again the catalogues may occasionally be bought from dealers, e.g. Cummings, 1917; Earl of Aylesford, 1918; Christie-Miller, 1919; Willmott, 1935; Arkwright, 1939; A. F. Hill, 1947 and Baron Landau, 1949. These, especially if they carry prices, form part of the collector's or dealer's apparatus. He may, in any case, confirm prices from the auctioneer, or from such series as *Book Auction Records* for the U.K. and the *Jahrbuch der Auktionspreise* (Hamburg, Hauswedell) for Germany, Austria, Switzerland and the Netherlands.

Antiquarian music-dealers' current catalogues are regularly summarized in *Notes* (Washington, Music Library Association), and both Oldman and Rosenthal (see p. 79) draw attention to their extreme value, in bibliographical detail, to the collector. There are probably not more than 100 established firms in the world, of which about a dozen are British—and these are listed in *Who's Who in Music*, 5th edn. (Burke's Peerage, 1969).

The literature of the book trade includes music antiquarians, of course, particularly the *International Directory of Antiquarian Booksellers* (International League of Antiquarian Booksellers) and the series published by the Sheppard Press: *A Dictionary of Dealers in Second-hand and Antiquarian Books: the British Isles; S. America; Canada and U.S.A. etc.* "Permanent wants-lists" do not seem to be divulged as they are for books in the foregoing series, though the *Clique* (170 Finchley Rd., N.W. 3) is a potential British vehicle for these, and the *Bookman* similarly serves the U.S.A. Many U.S. libraries issue their own (often very formidable) "wants-lists" to dealers, etc.

For a tentative list of private collections now in British public institutions see Appendix I.

The current "sheet music" retail trade, in general, is in a parlous state, and if music publishers encourage direct dealing with institutional and private customers, the music shops have only themselves to blame. Central London has suffered from the absorption of such general agents as Augener into publishing consortiums working from the provinces. The West End in particular has been steadily eroded of music-sellers (other than antiquarian), and the retirement of the Galliard complex to the country has put still greater pressure on firms such as J. B. Cramer and the London Music Shop, the latter specializing with particular usefulness on educational music. Probably the most complete account in tabloid form of the organization of antiquarian and modern music-dealing is the "Musikverlag und Musikalienhandel" article in Band 9 of *Die Musik in Geschichte und Gegenwart* (Bärenreiter). For the U.K. a current buyer's guide is *The Music Trade Directory* (Tofts & Woolf, 1968/9–). For further notes on commercial publishing see Ch. 16 and for a list of publishers and agencies see Appendix IIA.

CHAPTER 12

The Folk Singer and Jazzman

You should make a point of trying every experience once, excepting incest and folk-dancing.

ANON (*from* ARNOLD BAX, *Farewell my Youth*)

To index a folk-song is only a little less impossible than to index a cluster of daisies.

M. DEAN-SMITH, *Index of English Songs*

THE scholarly pursuit of music in its racial aspects is dealt with under Ethnomusicology in Ch. 9, where attention is drawn to the extensive bibliography prepared by Jaap Kunst. The research worker has various national organizations (and their journals) to turn to, such as the English Folk Song and Dance Society (2 Regent's Park Rd., N.W. 1) with its *Folk Directory: folk service yearbook* (Cecil Sharp House, 1965–), and their co-ordinating body, the International Folk Music Council (35 Princess Court, Queensway, W. 2) which has published a useful guide *The Collection of Folk-music* (1958) and the Library of Congress "Archive of folk-song" (described in *Library Journal*, vol. 88, no. 18, Oct. 1963). UNESCO has also given a lead with *Archives of Recorded Music* (1949–) divided into western, oriental, ethnic and folk-music, its *World Collection of Recorded Folk-music* (1952–), and its *International Directory of Folk-music Record Archives* (Recorded Sound, 10/11, 1963). This chapter is intended to help with the more normal requirements of the singer and folk-dancer.

The problem of what is genuine folk-music, as distinct from the composed or arranged music which often passes for it, is best approached *ad hoc* by research into each folk-tune in question.

Rescue of fast-disappearing tunes began in the late nineteenth century by collectors whose published work is reflected in the list below. These researchers were probably too late to catch some tunes, and a little too early, at first, for full use of recording techniques. Today, a modicum can be traced in the gramophone catalogues by title or exponent and from *The International Catalogue of Recorded Folk-music* (O.U.P., 1954) (see Fig. 41), while radio organizations mostly have their own very considerable archives on disc or tape. The latter, however, are not usually accessible to the public. An example is the B.B.C.'s *Folk and National Music Recordings* (1958–). The rapidly consolidating national sound-archives are also, of course, natural sources for much material not otherwise accessible. One very specialized example is the Frank C. Brown *Collection of North Carolina Folk-lore*, 7 vols. (Duke University Press, 1952–). Another is the *Deutsches Volksliedarchiv* in Freiburg im Breisgau. The handling of over 200,000 songs recorded in the field, in addition to the enormous published archive, together with the notation-classification is described by Lansky and Suppan in "Der neue Melodien Katalog des deutschen Volksarchivs" (*Fontes artis musicae*, 1963/1–2).

Among the companies which have specialized on the urban and industrial songs which are ousting the old kind are Topic Records (27 Nassington Rd., N.W. 3), Waverley Records (23 Earl Grey St., Edinburgh 3), Folkways (121 West 47th St., New York 36) and Elektra Records (189 West 10th St., New York 14).

NATIONAL AND FOLK SONGS

Besides the popular community-song anthologies, a fairly wide range of international and national song books is always in print. Some typical examples among many are:

International

Botsford Collection of Folk-songs (Original and English text), 3 vols. (Schirmer–Chappell).

BROWN and MOFFATT. *Characteristic Songs and Dances of All Nations* (English), (Bayley & Ferguson).

E. LUND. *Book of Folk-songs* (Original and English text), 2 vols. O.U.P.).

Great Britain

BOULTON and SOMERVELL. *Our National Songs*, 4 vols. (Cramer).

BROADWOOD and FULLER-MAITLAND. *English County Songs* (Cramer).

HATTON and FARING. *Songs of England*, 3 vols. (Boosey & Hawkes).

D. MACMAHON. *New National and Folk-song Book*, 2 vols. (Nelson).

SEEGER and McCOLL. *The Singing Island* (Mills Music).

SEEGER and McCOLL. *Songs for the Sixties* (Workers' Music Association).

SHARP and WILLIAMS. *Folk-songs* (various), (Novello).

WILLIAMS and LLOYD. *English Folk-songs* (Penguin).

Ireland

COLUM, P. *A Treasury of Irish Folklore*, 2nd edn. (Crown).

HATTON and MOLLOY. *Songs of Ireland* (Boosey & Hawkes).

H. HUGHES. *Irish Country Songs*, 4 vols. (Boosey & Hawkes).

O'KEEFE, D. *First Book of Irish Ballads* (Mercier Press).

PETRIE, G. *The Petrie Collection of the Ancient Music of Ireland* (Gregg International).

Scotland

KENNEDY-FRASER. *Songs of the Hebrides*, 3 vols. (Boosey & Hawkes).

McLEOD and BOULTON. *Songs of the North*, 3 vols. (Cramer).

Wales

A. MOFFATT. *The Minstrelsy of Wales* (English text) (Augener).

B. RICHARDS. *Songs of Wales* (Welsh and English text) (Boosey & Hawkes).

America

B. IVES. *Albums*, 2 vols. (Leeds Music).
A. LOMAX, *Penguin Book of American Folk-songs* (Penguin).
C. SANDBURG. *American Songbag* (Harcourt, Brace).
I. SILBER. *Songs of the Civil War* (Columbia Univ. Press).
I. SILBER. *Songs of the Old West* (Columbia Univ. Press).
   See also the journal *Sing Out* (N.Y., 1950–).

Australia

B. IVES. *Folio of Australian Songs* (Southern Music).

Canada

FOWKE and JOHNSTON. *Folk-songs of Canada* (Waterloo Music Co., Ontario).
FOWKE and JOHNSTON. *Folk-songs of Quebec* (Waterloo Music Co., Ontario).

France

B. BRITTEN. *Folk-song Arrangements* (French and English text) (Boosey & Hawkes).
J. TIERSOT. *Chants de la vieille France* (Heugel).

Germany

L. ANDERSEN. *Deutsche Heimat* (Schott).
M. FRIEDLAENDER. *100 Deutsche Volkslieder* (Peters–Hinrichsen).

Greece

BOURGAULT-DUCOUDRAY. *Mélodies Populaires de Grèce* (Lemoine).
PYM, HILARY. *The Songs of Greece (poems only)* (*Sunday Times*).
SPATHY. *Chansons Populaires Grècques* (Sénart).

M—D

Hungary

B. Bartók. *Magyar nepdal*, 4 vols. (Universal).
Z. Kodály. *Hungarian Folk Music*, Bks. I–XI (Universal).
F. Korbay. *Hungarian Melodies*, 3 vols. (Schott).

Italy

F. Burkhard. *Bella Italia* (Italian and German), (Universal).
A. Parisotti. *Arie antiche*, 3 vols. (Ricordi).

Poland

A. Harasowski. *Golden Book of Polish Songs* (Polish State).

Spain and Latin America

F. J. Obradors. *Canciones clasicás espanolas*, 2 vols. (Unión Musical Espanola).
Sandoval. *Favourite Latin American Songs* (Schirmer).
(Peer International–Southern Music specialize on arrangements of Latin American music. The most recent survey of the literature of the area is G. Chase's *Guide to the Music of Latin America*, 2nd edn. (Pan American Union–Library of Congress, 1962).)

Sweden

G. Hagg. *Songs of Sweden* (Schirmer).
J. Sahlgren. *Svenska Folkvisor*.

Negro Spirituals

H. T. Burleigh. *Plantation Melodies Old and New* (Schirmer).
H. A. Chambers. *Treasury of Negro Spirituals* (Blandford Press).
R. N. Dett. *Religious Folk-songs of the Negro* (Hampton Inst., Virginia, 1927).

Sea Shanties

J. C. COLCORD. *Songs of American Sailormen* (Putnam).
R. R. TERRY. *Shanty Books*, 2 vols. (Curwen).

The above all have keyboard accompaniment at most. For orchestral accompaniments, two useful collections are *Tunes and Toasts for All Times* (Boosey, 1948) which covers the U.K., U.S.A., Canada, Ireland, etc., and includes music for parades and fanfares, and *Mammoth Orchestra Collection of Songs of the World* (C. Fischer). Basic international lists of recordings (available in the Schwann catalogue) appeared in the *Library Journal*, vol. 88, no. 9, May 1963.

Apart from these mixed products of research and commercial arrangement, there remains a large section of anthologies more clearly collected at first-hand. Most are out of print. Some typical examples are S. Baring-Gould's *Songs of the West*, rev. edn. (Methuen, 1905), Bartók & Kodály's *Magyar nepzene tara*, 4 vols. (Kiado Academy of Budapest), Idelsohn's *Thesaurus of Oriental Hebrew Melodies*, 10 vols. (Harz, 1925) and Weckerlin's *Echos du temps passé*, 3 vols. (Durand). They are listed fairly exhaustively in an appendix to the B.B.C.'s *Song Catalogues*. For English folk-song, the work of Margaret Dean-Smith deserves special mention. Her *Index of English Songs* (English Folk Dance and Song Society, 1951) covering those contributed to the Society's journals, 1899–1950, and based on E. A. White's index, shows the enormous degree of variation in title, first lines, and tunes (e.g. *The Bitter Withy* has at least six alternative titles, nine first lines, and over twenty melody-variants). Her groupings of carols, shanties, game-songs, street-cries, wassail songs, etc., are particularly useful as carrying the *cachet* of authenticity derived from the Society's collectors. Her *Guide to English Folk-song Collections, 1822–1952* (Univ. of Liverpool Press, 1954) (see Fig. 42) first annotates in great detail a chronological list of collections and then indexes their contexts, thus forming a direct complement to the data on original versions given in her *Index*. The most famous anthology of traditional English music is Chappell's *Popular Music of the Olden Time*, harmonized by Macfarren, 2 vols. (Cramer, Beale &

Chappell, 1858–9). This, with its liberal descriptive matter, suffered much abbreviation in Wooldridge's edition of 1893, and it is unfortunate that the current reprint (New York, J. Brussel, 1961) is of the latter recension, though it makes some amends by including F. Kidson's *Traditional Tunes* (1891) as an appendix. Twice as many tunes and wider background notes are now gathered in C. N. Simpson's *The British Broadside and its Music* (Rutgers Univ., 1966). For ballad texts, the Child MS. collection at Harvard forms a primary source, now added to by the Cecil Sharp MSS. and later field-work. Published in parts as *English and Scottish Popular Ballads*, 5 vols. in 10 (1898) and in a single volume edited by Sargent and Kittredge (1904), the important allocation of tunes, based upon the above sources, is now in progress as B. H. Bronson's *Traditional Tunes of the Child Ballads* (Princeton U.P., 4 vols. to 1966), supplemented by H. H. Flanders' *Ancient Ballads traditionally sung in New England* (O.U.P./Univ. of Pennsylvania, 1962–) also based on Child. Some splendid recreative talent has been poured into the B.B.C.'s "radio-ballad" programme, produced by C. Parker and incorporating folk-song settings arranged by Peggy Seeger and Ewan McColl.

FOLK-DANCE

As a comprehensive guide *An Index to Folk-dances and Singing Games* (Chicago, American Library Association, 1936) appears to be unique. Some anthologies double their value by giving as clear guidance as possible to the dance movements, e.g. M. Dolmetsch's *Dances of England and France from 1400 to 1600 with their Music and Authentic Manner of Performance* (Routledge, 1949) which reconstructs from contemporary treatises the basse-danse, branle, pavan, galliard, coranto, etc. A primary English source is J. Playford's *English Dancing Master, 1651* (Facsimile, Schott, 1959). The English Folk Song and Dance Society publishes two popular manuals: D. Kennedy's *Country Dancing for Elementary Schools*, and *Community Dance Manuals*, the latter for adults. Ram Gopal's *Indian Dancing* (Phoenix, 1951) is a similarly authoritative statement of the origins, movements and gestures of the four schools. A. S. Barnes & Co.

(101 Fifth Avenue, New York 3) is a specialist publisher with a comprehensive list both of international folk dances (*The Folk-dance Library*, 5 vols.) and old-time and square-dances, listed in Schirmer's *Guide*.

JEWISH MUSIC

Eric Mandell, in *A Collector's Random Notes on the Bibliography of Jewish Music* (Fontes, 1963/1–2) rightly quotes A. Sendrey's *Bibliography of Jewish Music* (Columbia U.P., 1951) as being the key work, so that NIS has come to mean "not in Sendrey". This work covers both the music and its literature and includes extensive sections of "music having Jewish character or based upon Jewish thematic material" and of recordings. C. Vinaver's *Anthology of Jewish Music* (Marks, 1955–) and A. W. Binder's *Pioneer Songs of Palestine* (Marks, 1942) provide different approaches. For organizations, Sendrey quotes the relevant ones, to which can now be added the Central Music Library in Tel Aviv, the Haifa Music Library and the Jewish National and University Library in Jerusalem. The Mayerowitsch collection in the Jews' College (11 Montagu Place, W. 1) is devoted to synagogue music, and in this particular field the *Out of Print Classics Series of Synagogue Music*, 25 vols. (New York, Sacred Music, 1953–4) is important. The Mandell collection was described to the American Conference of Cantors in 1961, and a further American collection is that of Jacob Michael at 120 Wall St., New York.

GYPSY MUSIC

In A. Szöllösy's *Bartók Béla Válogatott zenei vrásai* (Budapest 1948) Bartók's article "Gypsy music? Hungarian music?" tends to discredit Liszt's theories (*The Gypsy in Music* (Reeves, 1930)) on the influence of the "Hungarian gypsy music" which mostly passes for genuine. The "gypsy" index-heading in J. Kunst's *Ethnomusicology* refers to a dozen or so serious studies. L. A. Smith's *Through Romany Songland* (Slott, 1889) describes and quotes apparently authentic tunes, while K. Bendl's *Gypsy Songs*, 2 vols. (Novello) adds formal keyboard accompaniments to the type of tune easily found also in anthologies of Rumanian and Hungarian songs.

NATIONAL ANTHEMS

Some useful special studies have been made, and these are listed in the bibliographies attached to Wakeling and de Fraine's "National anthems" (*Music Review*, vol. 3, nos. 3 and 4, 1942) and P. Nettl's *National Anthems* (2nd edn., New York, F. Ungar Publishing Co., 1967). The former, short as it is, gives the essential details of historical provenance and the sources. The latter is an extended survey. Both quote only melody-lines. Harmonizations in piano score are given in *Die National-hymnen der Erde* (Munich, Max Heuber, 1958) and Shaw and Coleman's *National Anthems of the World*, 2nd edn. (Blandford Press, 1963) (see Fig. 43). Both give original texts (though not of all 158 verses of the Greek anthem), with short historical notes. The latter is more complete, more up to date (Algeria, Bahrein and Qatar are included) and gives copyright data, but the former adds dates of achieving independence and national celebration days. Orchestrations of these anthems were published by Boosey as *National Anthems of All Nations* (1910) and by Breitkopf as *Hymnen der Völker* (1936). Revisions and new anthems have been scored as they arise by Boosey & Hawkes, who are charged by the Army Council with keeping military bands up to date. Many orchestral settings, as distinct from military band, remain in MS., which complicates the life of the impresario responsible for orchestral salutes to visiting dignitaries from the many new independencies.

The British anthem has its own complicated history, told first by R. Clark, *An Account of the National Anthem* (1822) and rounded off by P. Scholes in *God Save the Queen* (O.U.P., 1954). Its settings vary from Arne's (B.M. Add. MS. 29,466), (apparently the first recorded performance, 1745, of what Scholes regards as the world's first national anthem) to those of Costa, Elgar, Bartók, Wood, etc., exhaustively listed by Scholes. Since then Britten has scored a new version (MS. Boosey & Hawkes) and Raymond Leppard has prepared a wind arrangement from the earliest known version of the melody *c.* 1740 (Cambridge, Gamut Publications, 1962).

JAZZ

Recorded performances of jazz are, naturally enough, mainly American, though in recent years Europe, and especially Great Britain, has overhauled the U.S.A. in actual issues of the discs. For the documentation of jazz the emphasis has likewise shifted to Europe.

BIBLIOGRAPHY OF JAZZ

The first major attempt was apparently A. P. Merriam's *Bibliography of jazz* (American Folklore Society, 1954). No single comprehensive study seems to have been attempted since.

JAZZ ENCYCLOPAEDIAS

The two principal ones are L. Feather's *Encyclopaedia of jazz* (Barker, 1961) and its smaller counterpart: *Dictionary of jazz* by Panassié and Gautier (Cassell, 1956). These, in turn, are supplemented by the *Encyclopaedia Yearbook of jazz* (Barker, 1967), the *New Yearbook of jazz* (Barker, 1959) and *Encyclopaedia of jazz in the sixties* (Horizon, 1966).

GENERAL STUDIES ON JAZZ

The most recent general survey is C. Fox's *Jazz in perspective* (B.B.C., 1969) which carries a bibliography and discography, authoritatively annotated by one of the foremost of British jazz journalists and broadcasters. F. Newton's *The Jazz scene* (MacGibbon and Kee, 1959; Penguin, 1961) describes the economic background as well as studying the musicians. The relation of jazz to other kinds of American music is brilliantly analysed by W. Mellers in *Music in a new found land* (Barrie & Rockliffe, 1964), while Shapiro and Hentoff tell the story of jazz in the words of the musicians themselves in *Hear me talkin' to ya* (Davies, 1955; Penguin, 1962). G. Schuller provides "the best musicological study so far" (Fox) in *Early jazz* (O.U.P., 1968) which takes the story to 1931 and is to be followed by a further volume. In *Jazz* (Cassell, 1960) the editors Hentoff and McCarthy present new historical perspectives by twelve foremost critics and scholars.

Afro-American music in general is covered by H. Courlander in *Negro folk music, U.S.A.* (Columbia University Press, 1963).

JAZZ DISCOGRAPHIES, etc.

Cherington and Knight's *Jazz catalogue: a complete discography*, with a bibliography by C. A. Johnson (Jazz Journal, 1965) was a pioneer effort, now being surpassed by the project, still incomplete after eight volumes, launched by J. G. Jepsen (Knudsen, 1963–) in extension of McCarthy and Carey's *Jazz directory* (Delphic Press/Cassell, 1950).

A further general discography is B. Rust's *Jazz records: 1897–1942*, 2nd edn. (N.Y., Arlington House, 1969) covering the 'pre-Jepsen' years.

Blues
Dixon and Godrich. *Blues and gospel records* (Storyville, 1969).
Leadbitter, M. *Blues records, 1943–66* (Hanover Books, 1968).
Oliver, P. *Blues fell this morning* (Cassell, 1959).
Rust, B. *Negro, blues and Gospel records* (Rust, 1965).

The discography section of Fox (above), usefully divided into: "Beginnings, New Orleans, Chicago and Kansas City, New York, Swing, Beboppers and revivalists, Modern jazz, An International music" is particularly useful and up-to-date in extending the above lists.

INDIVIDUAL JAZZ MUSICIANS
Cassell's *King of jazz* series, 12 volumes, 1959–63.
Macmillan's *Jazz masters* series, 1965– *in progress*.
Green, B. *The Reluctant art* (MacGibbon & Kee, 1962).
Lomax, A. *Mister Jelly Roll* (Cassell, 1962).
Smith, W. *Music on my mind* (MacGibbon & Kee, 1965).
Spellmann, A. B. *Four lives in the bebop business* (*Coleman, McLean, Nichols, Taylor*) (MacGibbon & Kee, 1967).

JAZZ PERIODICALS

The principal American journals are *Downbeat* and *Music, U.S.A.* while Britain has *Jazz Journal*, *Jazz Monthly*, and *Storyville*. Canada has *Coda*, reflecting the interest newly centred in Toronto.

JAZZ RESEARCH

The New Orleans Jazz Museum under its curator Clay Weston is an obvious reference point, as can be judged from its journal *The Second Line* (1950–). Other, rather larger, centres of research are Tulane University and the Institute of Jazz Studies at Rutgers, Newark, which is based on the collections of Marshall W. Stearns.

JAZZ TECHNIQUES

The actual techniques of jazz as distinct from its highly personal historical background, have developed a sturdy literature over the past 10 years. Here the names Dankworth, Mancini, Mehegan, Paparelli and Russo stand out with such works as J. Mehegan's *Jazz Improvisation*, 4 vols. (Guptill, 1959–65), and F. Paparelli's *Eight to the Bar* (Leeds Music, 1941), and *Four to the Bar* (Music Corporation of America, 1967) in particularly heavy demand.

CHAPTER 13

The Broadcaster

You little box, held to me when escaping
So that your valves should not break,
Carried from house to ship from ship to train,
So that my enemies might go on talking to me
Near my bed, to my pain
The last thing at night, the first thing in the morning,
Promise me not to go silent all of a sudden.

BERTHOLD BRECHT

Music has always been the backbone of radio, and everything points to its remaining so. After 20 years, television's presentation of music is still vigorously experimental, the picture itself remaining a more or less dominant factor.

For 40 years the B.B.C. and other major radio organizations have risen to the immense challenge offered by the opportunity (with the means) to promote music of all kinds on an unparalleled scale, so that, for instance, the B.B.C.'s annual 2000 hours of serious music transmission has long ceased to be a miracle and become an accepted part of life. Radio effort has resulted in such an unprecedented patronage of music (by repertory-playing, commissions of new music, creation of its own symphony, etc., orchestras, under-writing of other orchestras, and by generally providing an un-rivalled shop-window for composers, living or dead, and artists) that the level of public appreciation and awareness is now on an almost unrecognizably higher level than formerly, and is continually rising. The world's largest libraries of music for performance are now those developed by these radio organizations (the B.B.C.

employs, for instance, about 100 full-time staff, with many part-time arrangers, copyists, etc.) and these libraries contain, besides the most liberal representation of the various repertories, a wealth of unpublished works in MS.—special commissions of original music, special versions and editions of existing works, etc. The European Broadcasting Union is setting-up a "radio-publishing house" based on the Nederlands Radio-Unie, Hilversum, and an orchestral materials interloan bureau (Radiodiffusion-Télévision Belge, Brussels).

It is logical, in these circumstances, to regard radio libraries (whether of music, commercial recordings or recorded programmes) as primary sources of information in the relevant documentary fields. In fact, they are the *only* reliable sources for detailed data on much of their own output, but their general documentation serves to answer many general practical and musicological queries. The Radio Commission of the International Association of Music Libraries has published (for members) a *Catalogue of Rare Orchestral Materials*, edited by F. Lindberg (1959) and a much expanded edition is in preparation. A number of such libraries issue catalogues in book form for domestic consumption (France, Sweden, Holland, Canada, Australia, New Zealand, Switzerland, etc.), but the B.B.C.'s published series (1965–), mentioned serially throughout this book, breaks fresh ground and forms a major contribution to music bibliography.

The literature of music-in-radio grows steadily. *British Broadcasting: a bibliography* (B.B.C., 1958–60) includes works by Gielgud, McNeice and Sieveking which treat music incidentally, but probably the first separate attempt at a bibliography was W. Rubsamen's "Bibliography of books and articles on music in film and radio" (*Hinrichsen's Yearbook*, vol. 6, 1949–50) and the most recent is that attached to the article "Rundfunk und Fernsehen" in *Die Musik in Geschichte und Gegenwart* (Bärenreiter, 1963). The latter article gives an international list of commissioned operas, radio and television, including the winners of the Italia Prize 1948–62 and the Salzburg Television opera prizes. G. Chase's *Music in Broadcasting* (McGraw-Hill, 1946) is a general treatise which touches on marginal topics such as arranging, continuity, performing rights, musicology and television problems. Two general books on radio art have substantial chapters dealing with music. F. Felton's *The Radio Play* (Sylvan Press, 1949) discusses its differences from theatre music and, in support of certain theses, discusses the suitability of such incidental music as that for *Hassan*, *Peer Gynt*, *The Bluebird*, *L'Arlésienne*, etc., while D. McWhinnie's *The Art of Radio* (Faber, 1959) discusses the music written for such landmarks of B.B.C. radio-drama and feature as *The Dark Tower*, *The Rescue*, *The Odyssey*, and includes radiophonic effects music. This latter topic was specially treated in the issues of *Gravesanerblätter* (Ars Viva/Schott), which reflected the technical experiments carried out by Hermann Scherchen and his engineers. Since then most radios have formed their own experimental "radiophonic workshops". A. Hopkins' article "Incidental music on the wireless" (*B.B.C. Quarterly*, vol. 19, no. 2, 1954) quotes forty composers commissioned during a period of 3 years. This, added to other radios' contributions, plainly signifies a vast area of expertise in this marginal use of music.

Current B.B.C. television opera (besides being surveyed retrospectively in the annual *B.B.C. Handbook*) is reviewed, of course, in the normal music press and especially in *Opera*. German output is surveyed in the *Deutsches Bühnen-Jahrbuch*, and *Der Spielplan* attempts international current and prospective coverage. The International Music Centre (Lothringerstrasse, 18, Vienna) was founded in 1957 as a co-ordinating point for radio and television opera, ballet, etc., and arranges conferences to compare output and stimulate aesthetic and technical ideas. *Films for Music Education and Opera Films: an international select catalogue* (International Music Centre/UNESCO/H.M.S.O., 1962) is its first publication.

CHAPTER 14

The Gramophone Record Collector

> *When lovely woman stoops to folly and*
> *Paces about her room again, alone,*
> *She smooths her hair with automatic hand,*
> *And puts a record on the gramophone.*

T. S. ELIOT, *A Theatre Sermon*

FOR the mass of the general musical public, gramophone records are probably more important than concert-going or even than broadcasting. The serious gramophile's opportunities are very substantial; as a private collector he has a range limited almost solely by his purse, with plenty of finding-lists and critical guides to help him. The basic encyclopaedic work for "78" and the initial output of "33" records is likely to remain Clough and Cuming's *World's Encyclopaedia of Recorded Music* and its three supplements (Sidgwick & Jackson, 1952–57) (see Fig. 44), on account of its detailed accuracy. This claims to be virtually a full list of "all acoustically and electrically recorded music of serious interest" from 1925 to 1955. Its American counterpart is the *Guide to Long-playing Records*, 3 vols. (Knopf, 1955), which carries evaluative and comparative notes. Supplementary to both is the *Stereo Record Guide* (Longplaying Record Library, 1960–) again with critical notes. Since the latter seems to be an established serial publication it may rank as the primary critical guide, though *The Record Guide* (Collins, 1955), a revised edition overhauling the previous volumes of 1951–3, has not been surpassed

Musicalia

in its standards of criticism. A similar and more up-to-date guide, apparently to be systematically revised, is Gammond and James' *Music on Record*, 4 vols. (Hutchinson, 1962–4). Other annotated guides include E. Greenfield's *Guide to the Bargain Classics* (Longplaying Record Library, 1965) and his *Penguin Guide* (1966). Specialist works include the Vienna Akademie der Wissenschaften Phonogrammarchivs-*Kommissions Katalog der Tonbandaufnahmen* (1964) and T. Bescovy-Chambers'. *The Archives of Sound* (Oakwood Press, 1966) which concentrates on his tone recordings, including those of many composers themselves. A non-critical list which grows in importance as a finding-tool as the series grows is the Library of Congress *Catalog: music and phonorecords* (1954–), which cumulates the entries served by their printed catalogue-cards. Another excellent guide is the E.M.G. *Monthly Letter*, whose findings are sifted and cumulated in successive editions of *The Art of Record Buying* (E.M.G., 13 editions to 1968). E. T. Bryant's *Collecting Gramophone Records* (Focal Press, 1962) makes a good approach for the tyro, with a later complement in I. March's *Running a Record Library* (Longplaying Record Library, 1965).

COMMERCIAL CATALOGUES

Decca, E.M.I., Philips, Pye, and Deutsche Grammophon form the principal British Groups and all issue elaborate catalogues. The U.S. output is cumulated by the *Schwann Catalogue*, while Europe had *Disques* (France), until its demise, and there remain *Diapason* (France), *Langspielplatte* (Germany) and *Santandrea* (Italy) to represent the current scene. Great Britain maintains an unsurpassed range which includes *The Classical Record Catalogue and Recommended Recordings*, *Stereo Record List* and the *Popular Record Catalogue*. Apart from these there are over 1700 foreign and domestic catalogues covering the past, according to the B.B.C. Gramophone Librarian's "Record lists and information sources" (*Gramophone Record Libraries*, ed. Currall, Crosby Lockwood, 2nd edn., 1969). The *Billboard Music-record Directory* (New York, Billboard) lists these by country along with much other information on promotion and distribution.

REVIEWING

P. W. Plumb ("The Record review" in Currall) annotates the British output, and briefly lists the American. A regular feature of the periodical *Notes* (Washington, Music Library Association) is Myers' "Record ratings" (1948–), which has been cumulated up to 1955 (New York, Crown Publications, 1956). A vast number of journals review records regularly but none more authoritatively and in detail than *The Gramophone*.

COLLECTING

The British collector of antiquariana is well served by Collectors' Corner (62 New Oxford St., W. 1), the International Record Collector's Agency (20 Newport Court, W.C. 2) Record Specialities (14 Dukes Rd., W.C. 1) and their progenitor The Gramophone Exchange (80 Wardour St., W. 1). During its run (1942–57) the U.S. journal *The Record Changer* was the best forum for the exchange of American jazz recordings, and a typical American equivalent of the London Gramophone Exchange in the general field of deleted recordings is The Record Hunter Shop (507 Fifth Avenue, New York 17). Discurio (9 Shepherd St., W. 1) concentrates on tracing and supplying the fugitive disc which is currently in print, while the serious jazz collector has, for example, Dobell's Record Shop (77 Charing Cross Rd., W.C. 2).

MOOD MUSIC

Most of the established commercial catalogues feature this to some extent. Boosey & Hawkes and Chappell in addition issue catalogues of such music, contractually limited to use in radio, television and in licensed halls. Such services are now extended by a growing number of firms, such as Impress, de Wolfe, Bosworth, Paxton, Harmonic, Conray, Southern and Emba, but these are principally limited to use on radio, television and film sound tracks. To these may now be added Weinberger, Syncro Fox, Keith Prowse, Ember and Transworld.

SUBJECT DISCOGRAPHIES

A typical example, among many, is J. Coover and R. Colvig's *Medieval and Renaissance Music on Long-playing Records* (Detroit Information Service, Inc., 1964). Smaller studies are likely to appear alongside the traditional bibliographical apparatus of any relevant monographs, but they are a regular feature of such journals as the *Record Review, Record Collector, Recorded Sound, American Record Guide, Jazz Monthly*, etc. They may also intermittently be met in *Records and Recording, High Fidelity* and *Audio Record Review*. R.I.L.M.'s *Abstracts of Musical Literature* (International Musicological Society, 1967–) is including discographies in its new service.

UNESCO's *Archives de la musique enregistrée*, planned as a monumental series, began in 1949. The scope of this topic increases apace, as is shown by the extent of the individual performer-discographies (over 200) listed by Brunn and Gray in their *Bibliography of Discographies* (Recorded Sound, 7, 1962). This worthy effort is reduced in value by apparently ignoring the vast mass of discographies which appear, as hinted above, as part of literary monographs. Moreover, there is at least one series of extended monographs solely devoted to special discographies, viz. J. B. Lippincott's *Keystone Books in Music*, of which the following have so far appeared:

J. Briggs. *The Collector's Tchaikowsky and the Five* (1959).
C. G. Burke. *The Collector's Haydn* (1959).
A. Cohn. *The Collector's 20th-century Music in the Western Hemisphere* (1961).
H. C. Schonberg. *The Collector's Chopin and Schumann* (1959).

HISTORIC RECORDINGS

With singers absorbing the main interest, and the other artists, orchestras, etc., taking a more modest place, the various special sections of the commercial catalogues give details of currently available works. Some useful general cumulations are: *Voices of the Past* (Oakwood Press, 1956–), R. Bauer's *New Catalogue of Historical*

Records, 1898–1909 (Sidgwick & Jackson, 1947) and *Edison Aubert Cylinder Records* (S. H. Carter, 7 Abbott's Close, Worthing, 1963). For biographical detail of the great singers of the past Kutsch and Riemens' *Unvergängliche Stimmen* (Bern, Francke Verlag, 1962) (see Fig. 45) is probably the most complete, though weakened by serious inaccuracies. Further sources are Celletti's *I Grandi Voci* (Rome, Istituto per la Collaborazione Culturale) and the British Institute of Recorded Sound.

INTERNATIONAL ARCHIVES

The great corpus of non-commercially recorded sound is in the hands of the various national "phonotèques" now co-ordinated by the Fédération Internationale des Phonotèques (Brussels, Phonotèque Nationale), whose provenance and constitution is given in *Fontes*, 1963/1–2. For the U.S., the Library of Congress assumes this function, while for the U.K. the British Institute of Recorded Sound (38 Russell Sq., W.C. 1) is the responsible body. Both aspects are described by P. Saul in "Museums of sound" and the "British Institute of Recorded Sound" (Currall, see p. 98). A short survey by P. Miller discusses both historic records, and the contribution recording has made to early music: "Musicology and the phonograph" (International Musicological Society, *8th Congress Report* (Bärenreiter, 1961)).

The Library of Congress recently secured another valuable archive in the Secrist collection, while the New York Public Library's Rodgers and Hammerstein Foundation steadily develops its Record Archive. The Association for Recorded Sound Collections has made a start with its *Preliminary Directory of Sound Record Collections in the U.S. and Canada* (1967).

HI-FI

After about 15 years of vigorous development the hi-fi world has become quite elaborately exotic. Amateur interest is intense. In a primarily technical area the musical element remains strong enough to avoid being swamped, and presumably will always provide the major impetus to recording. In addition to the journals already mentioned, the British *Hi-Fi News* and the American *High Fidelity* may be singled out as of interest to professional and layman alike. The amateur is further catered for by such journals as *The Tape Recorder* (Link House) and *The Tape Recording Magazine* (Print and Press Services). A British Amateur tape-recording contest is held annually and this contributes to an international contest. The results are listed in *Sound Archives* issued to members by the Federation of British Tape-Recordists and Clubs.

POPULAR MUSIC

Non-commercial attempts to anthologize the contents of the old and new specialized catalogues, include B. Rust's *London Musical Shows on Records, 1894–1954* (British Institute of Recorded Sound) and his *Top-tunes of 1912–58* (B.B.C., internal).

This carried a Supplement, 1959–62, but has since been incorporated into *The Melody Maker*, which has now launched into a *Yearbook* (Longacre Press). Useful reference works not primarily concerned with discs include J. Fuld's *Book of World Famous Music* (Crown, 1966), J. H. Chapman's *Index to* [American] *Top-Line Tunes* (Bruce Humphries, 1962); The [British] Songwriters' Guild's *Sixty years of British Hits, 1917–66* and *Standard British Popular Songs and Melodies, 1907–66* (Mayfield, 1968); and N. Shapiro's *Popular Music: an annotated index* (Adrian Press, 1964–5). See also Chapter 11.

COPYRIGHT

The legal aspect of the use of records is summarized in *Who's Who in Music*, 5th edn. (Burke's Peerage, 1969) which quotes the Mechanical Copyright Protection Society Ltd. (310 Streatham Rd., S.W. 16) as dealing with royalties on sales and on broadcast recordings, and Phonographic Performance Ltd. (62 Oxford St., W. 1) as dealing with rights of makers regarding public performance. These matters are dealt with by individual firms in the U.S., and controlled internationally by BIEM, 28 rue Ballu, Paris 8. Fuld (above) combines some useful marginal historical comments on copyright arising out of his bibliographical researches.

CHAPTER 15

Periodicals, Yearbooks, etc.

A CERTAIN proportion of periodical literature is of lasting importance, particularly as a reflection of topical matters. Schumann, Berlioz, Prunières, Fox Strangways, H. F. Chorley, Philip Heseltine, Ernest Newman, Richard Capell and Eric Blom are but a few distinguished musical journalists, and their traditions are far from dead.

BIBLIOGRAPHY

The most recent statement is in the *MGG* article "Zeitschriften", which renders the "Periodical" article in *Grove* V sadly out of date. The latter quotes W. Freystatter's *Die musikalischen Zeitschriften*, covering 1722 to 1844 (1844, reprinted Knuf, Amsterdam, 1963) as being still the only book of its kind. This must be supplemented by later specialist studies such as J. B. Coover's "Bibliography of East European music periodicals" (*Fontes artis musicae*, 1956/2, 1957/2, 1958/1–2, 1959/1, 1960/1–2, 1962/1–2, and indexed in 1963/1–2), and F. Blum's "East German music journals: a checklist" (*Notes*, June 1962). To this can now be added E. Rohles' *Die deutschsprachigen Musikperiodika, 1945–57* (Bosse, 1961), and I. Fellinger's *Verzeichnis der Musikzeitschriften des Neunzehntenjahrhunderts* (Bosse, 1968).

Basic lists are also found in the *Harvard Dictionary* and in *MGG*, while current lists are found in *Willing's Press Guide*, annually, for the U.K., and, for the world, in Ulrich's *Periodicals Directory* (R. R. Bowker). Current indexing is done in the *Music Index* (Detroit Information Survey, 1949–) which continues to increase its coverage, and, over a smaller, more academic area, by Tauts' and later

Schmieder's *Bibliographie des Musikschrifttums* (Hofmeister, 1936–). A new British project, intended to improve on existing indexing now appears serially, compiled by C. Wallbaum, in the journal, *Brio*, (1964–) of the U.K. Branch of the International Association of Music Libraries. Several journals not analysed by the *Music Index*, *Schmieder* or the *British Humanities Index*, are included. Musical articles appearing in non-musical journals are only partially covered by general indexes. Two studies supplement these: the British Museum's *Handlist of Music published in Some British and Foreign Periodicals between 1787 and 1848* (1962), and *Articles Concerning Music in Non-musical Journals, 1949–64* by S. Thiemann (Current Musicology, Columbia U.P., 1955–66).

Many early sets of musicological journals, including defunct series, are now extremely rare and expensive antiquarian items. Firms such as Swets and Zeitlinger (471 Kaisergracht, Amsterdam) make a speciality of attempting to complete gaps for libraries. Musurgia of New York offers a microfilm service for any or all sections of such runs as the *Allgemeine Musikalische Zeitung* (reprint, Fritz A. M. Knuf, Nieuwe Spiegelstr. 70, Amsterdam C) and *Neue Zeitschrift für Musik*. Sets or excerpts may also be had from Schnase Facsimile Reprints, 120 Brown Road, Scarsdale, New York. E. C. Krohn's *History of Music* (Washington Univ., 1952) indexes many historic periodicals among the thirty-nine musicological works annotated.

Locations for over 100 U.S. libraries can be found in O. W. Strunk's *State and Resources of Musicology . . .* (Michigan U.P., 1942) supplemented by A. H. Heyer's *Check-list of Publications* (Michigan U.P., 1944).

A breakthrough for musicologists and librarians alike has been achieved by B. S. Brook, responsible for the launching of R.I.L.M. *Abstracts of Musical Literature* (International Musicological Society, 1967–). With the help of national co-ordinators a systematic attempt is being made to provide précis of a very wide range of music articles in periodicals, and eventually of musical books.

There are over 150 established journals extensively surveyed by Ruth Watanabe in her *Introduction to Music Research* (Prentice-Hall,

1967). The principal serious ones in English are *Music and Letters* (1920–), with a cumulative index for 1920–59 (O.U.P.), *Music Review* (1940–), *Musical Quarterly* (1915–) with cumulative indexes 1915–62 (New York, Goodkind Press, 1960) and the *Musical Times* (1844–). Cumulative indexes to musicological journals are quoted in L. B. Spiess's *Historical Musicology* (New York, Inst. of Mediaeval Music, 1963).

The question of locating sets of these journals is partially solved for the U.K. by the *British Union Catalogue of Periodicals*, 4 vols. and suppt. (Butterworths, 1955–62) and for the greater London area by the *London Union List of Periodicals*, 2nd edn. (Library Association, 1958) now under revision. Both these sources will eventually give place to the *Index to the Holdings of Music Periodicals in the Libraries of the British Isles*, by Garratt and Sheard, now in preparation for the U.K. Branch of the International Association of Music Libraries. For America and Canada, the primary location-list is the *Union List of Serials*, 2nd edn. (New York, H. W. Wilson, 1943–).

Specialist interest is frequently self-evident (*Accordion News*, *Brass Quarterly*, *Piano-maker*, *Strad*, etc.). This is not always so obvious; e.g. that *Caecilia* is devoted to Catholic church music, or that *Melos*, *Tempo*, *Die Reihe* and the *Score* (1949–61) are primarily concerned with contemporary works. Such details are usefully given by Ulrich (see p. 103).

For the music-lover anxious to obtain a general impression of the journalist's contribution to the British musical scene, the most useful periodicals are probably the *Musical Times*, *Music and Musicians*, *The Gramophone*, *Records and Recording* and *Opera*. Subscription and delivery details are given in W. Dawson and Sons' *Guide to the Press of the World* (10 Macklin St., W.C. 2). Yet further interests are catered for by *Music Industry* (Tofts & Woolf, 1964–), "a monthly trade magazine for everything musical".

Over the centuries much music has appeared (often for the first, occasionally the only time) in periodicals. The *Musical Times* and *La Revue musicale* are but two of the modern periodicals to carry musical supplements. For the research-worker on earlier music, the British Museum's *Handlist of Music Published in some British and Foreign*

Periodicals . . . 1787–1848 . . . (1963) needs special note, as a complement to the *Catalogue of Printed Music (1487–1800)* (British Museum,
1912).

YEARBOOKS, ETC.

Such musical yearbooks and almanacs as there are tend to be
limited to special topics. One useful general example which did not
achieve annuity despite its title was *Das Jahrbuch der Musikwelt*
(Bayreuth, J. Steeger, 1949), which attempted academic and professional coverage; much of the information, if not the detail of
personnel, is still relevant. *Who's Who in Music*, 4th edn. (Burke's
Peerage, 1962) is useful for its miscellaneous information about
British musical organizations as well as for its potted biographies.
Hinrichsen's *Music Yearbooks* (1944–), attempted encyclopaedic
stature, became irregular after the first six volumes, and are now
devoted to special topics. The directories quoted earlier list such
works fairly completely, but for details of series such as the Bach,
Chopin, Handel, Haydn, Mozart, R. Strauss, Verdi and Wagner
Yearbooks the researcher must consult the composer-bibliographies,
and the *Repertorium der Musikwissenshaft*, or, more recently, L. B.
Spiess (see p. 60), and Duckles' *Music Reference and Research Materials*
(see p. 73).

CHAPTER 16

Printing, Publishing
and Copying

FROM the earliest efforts of Petrucci in Venice, John Rastell in London, Attaingnant in Paris, to the application of lithography by Senefelder and to the modern photo-engraving and lithographic processes and their "near-print" successors, is a story well documented in encyclopaedias. The technical detail of printing, water marks, publishing, etc., might well be absorbed as a discipline valid for much musicological research (see Ch. 9).

HISTORICAL AND BIBLIOGRAPHICAL

Duckles' *Music Reference and Research Materials* quotes sixty-two works on the history of music printing, and many more come to light in the best bibliography of the subject: A. Davidsson's *Die Literatur zur Geschichte des Notendruckes* (Musikbibliographische Beiträge, Uppsala, 1954). The outlines of development can readily be gained from *Scholes*, *Grove* and the *Harvard Dictionary* under "Engraving", "Printing", "Publishing", and in *MGG* under "Musikverlag–Musikalienhandel and "Notendruck". Both articles are by R. Schaal and the former carries a comprehensive international list of firms, with dates.

Historical and technical treatises on special aspects abound. A major pioneer effort for Great Britain was F. Kidson's *British Music Publishers, Printers and Engravers . . . to George IV* (1900, reprinted, New York, Bloom, 1967), but this is largely superseded by Humphries and Smith's *Music Publishing in the British Isles . . . to the Middle of the Nineteenth Century* (Cassell, 1954) (see Fig. 46), which includes music-sellers. R. Steele's *Earliest English Music Printing to the close of the Sixteenth Century* (Bibliographical Society, 1903) and W. C. Smith's *Bibliography of the Musical Works Published by J. Walsh* (2 vols., Bibl. Soc., 1948–68) are further examples of special studies of English practice, and a recent monograph by Kathi Meyer-Baer: *Liturgical Musical incunabula* (Bibliographical Society, 1962) provides a good specimen of international studies. Nineteenth-century England is reflected in Novello's *Short History of Cheap Music* (1887) and France has C. Hopkinson's *Dictionary of Parisian Music Publishers, 1700–1950* (the author, 1954) with the more limited, but intensive study by C. Johannsen: *French Music Publishers' Catalogues of the Second Half of the Eighteenth Century*, 2 vols. (Stockholm, Royal Swedish Academy of Music, 1955), the second volume being devoted to facsimiles. Italy has C. Sartori's *Dizionario Degli Editori Musicali Italiani* (Florence, Olschki, 1958) (see Fig. 47) and other more limited studies by the same compiler. American publishing-history is covered by a number of special studies listed under "American Music", "Sheet Music" etc., in Schirmer's *Guide*, pre-eminent among which are Sonneck and Upton's *Bibliography of Early Secular American Music* (Library of Congress, 1945) and Dichter and Shapiro's *Early American Sheet Music* (Bowker, 1941) which includes a directory of publishers, with lists of lithographers and artists before 1870. The Central European area is dealt with by A. Weinmann (below). Probably the only attempt in English to tackle Russian publishing history is C. Hopkinson's *Notes on Russian Music Publishers* (the author, 1959).

The dating of music by publishers' plate-numbers and paper-makers' watermarks begins to achieve some degree of accuracy, but its limitations need always to be kept in view. Most national libraries have developed their own apparatus for such work. The best general list in published form is O. E. Deutsch's *Musikverlagsnummern*, 2nd edn. (Merseburger, 1961) which covers forty firms, 1710–1900, and this is supported by special studies like A. Weinmann's series, commencing with *Vollstandiges Verlagsverzeichnis Artaria* (Vienna,

Krenn, 1952) continuing with studies on Huberty, Toricella, Kozeluch, etc. (listed by Duckles) and supplemented by R. H. Hill's *Plate-numbers of C. F. Peters' Predecessors* (American Musicological Society, 1938) and Neighbour and Tyson's *English music publishers' plate numbers* (Faber, 1965). E. Heawood's *Watermarks* (Hilversum, Paper Publications Society, 1950) is important though it has no specific reference to music manuscripts as such, and J. La Rue's "Water-marks and musicology" (*Acta Musicologica*, vol. 23) begins to outline a largely unmapped area. C. B. Oldman's "Watermark dates in English paper" (*The Library*, 4th series, vol. 25, nos. 1–2, 1944) draws attention to the dangers of relying on watermarks alone to determine dates of publication. Somewhat unexpectedly, there are useful hints on this topic in J. Fuld's *The Book of World Famous Music* (Crown, 1966). A. H. Shorter's *Paper Mills and Paper-makers in England, 1495–1800* (Paper Society, 1957) will stand as a permanent work of reference.

Exhibition catalogues form some of the most useful reminders of landmarks in music printing. Examples are the *Guide to the Exhibition in the King's Library Illustrating the History of Music Printing and Bookbinding* (British Museum, 1939), *The Printed Note: 500 years of music printing and engraving* (Toledo Museum of Art, 1957), and (shortest, cheapest and most recent) A. H. King's *Four Hundred Years of Music Printing* (British Museum, 1964), with a useful select bibliography.

MODERN

Economic trends naturally affect publishing. In the U.K. at least, sale of sheet-music, whether popular balladry or church anthem, is but a pale shadow of its Victorian self. The *British Catalogue of Music* and the *U.S. Catalog of Copyright Entries*, however, show thousands of new titles annually. Normal printing, mostly litho, continues, but is being invaded by near-print processes (see p. 111: "Photo-copying") of many kinds. The classics are constantly being reprinted by Breitkopf, Peters, Bärenreiter, Broude, Gregg, E. Kalmus, etc., or re-edited and published *ad hoc*. Generally speaking, modern orchestral material (i.e. band-parts) may only be hired from the publisher, who prints and sells a study score (see also Ch. 2). Each country has its own organization (listed in Appendix IIB) and these are co-ordinated by the International Publishers' Association. Smaller countries (e.g. Scandinavian) lacking a native publishing industry, form composers' societies to exploit their composers' works. A prototype of these is Donemus (51 Jacob Obrechtstraat, Amsterdam), which issues catalogues of photocopies and discs of contemporary Dutch works. This activity has latterly been co-ordinated by the Music Information Centres Commission of the International Association of Music Libraries (Canadian Music Centre, 33 Edward St., Toronto 7, Ontario). A further source of information in this marginal field of not-formally-published music is the group of national collecting-societies (see Appendix IIC) such as ASCAP for the U.S. and the Performing Right Society for the U.K. There are, however, few equivalents of the ASCAP *Symphonic Catalogue* (1959).

"Who published what?" "Is there a national agent?" and "Is the music still in print?" are constant problems. In this highly individualistic sphere take-over bids, mergers, transfers of copyright, stocks and agencies present a fluid situation. Provincial music-dealers often rely on collecting-agencies such as Blackwell of Oxford and the London Music Shop, W.C. 2. Public libraries rely additionally upon Paxton (30 Old Compton St., W. 1) and J. B. Cramer (99 St. Martin's Lane, W.C. 2), who have amassed a vast slip-index of music in and out of print. Out-of-print stocks, especially of more popular music of bygone years may sometimes be traced to the shelves of Francis Music Supplies, 12 Gerard St., W.C. 1.

Leipzig has lost its pride of place as a world centre for music publishing and engraving, and its stocks (still considerable in spite of bombing and looting) have to be tapped via official western agencies in Bonn, Kassel or Wiesbaden or by private enterprise such as Musica Rara (2 Gt. Marlborough St., W. 1). Appendix IIA gives a comprehensive list of established publishers and agencies but does not include, in detail, the world of Tin Pan Alley.

MANUSCRIPT COPYING

There are several short treatises helpful to the would-be copyist, of which the most useful are A. Jacob's *Music Handwriting*, 2nd edn. (O.U.P., 1947) and H. Chambers' *Musical Manuscript* (Curwen, 1951) each giving practical advice on materials, writing, notation, lay-out of orchestral and vocal scores and parts. A. Donato's *Preparing Musical Manuscript* (Prentice-Hall, 1963) does the same but adds chapters on reproduction and binding and on (American) copyright.

PHOTO-COPYING

Publisher and private individual alike are increasingly turning to a multiplicity of devices for avoiding the high costs of engraving and printing. These "near-print" systems range from studio-photographic processes of the traditional "photostat" type, to dye and heat processes, microfilming, microcards, etc. Recent landmarks in this rapidly expanding field are touched upon in successive issues of *Five Years' Work in Librarianship* (Library Association). The most recent comprehensive treatise is apparently W. R. Hawken's Copying methods manual (A.L.A., 1966). Microfilming techniques are common to all literary, technical and musical fields alike. Single specimen prints can be produced by every photo-copier on the market. For the reproduction of bulk materials for orchestras and choirs, however, a large proportion of machines are unsuited because they are limited to single-sided printing of little more than foolscap size. Xerox, Verifax, Thermofax and such processes have these limitations. This leaves the Azoflex type of machine as the most practical for band-parts, etc., since it will print a double-sided double-spread with ease. There are two organizations specifically charged with fostering technical development and co-ordination: for the U.S., the Council on Library Resources, Inc., and for the U.K., the Council for Microphotography and Document Reproduction, which issues a *Directory of British Photo-reproduction Services*.

MUSIC TYPEWRITERS

Three machines have been publicly offered. The Pavey Musigraph is under production by the Imperial Typewriter Co. Ltd. of Leicester, and its inventor Lily Pavey (29 Laing House, Combergrove, S.E. 5) is still improving it. The American "Musikwriter" (City Reproduction Centre, 4 Denmark St., W.C. 1 for the U.K.) is slowly gaining some ground, particularly for making master-sheets of short vocal and piano items. The extremes of flexibility commanded by good hand-copying, however, seem likely to elude their capabilities.

COPYRIGHT

Control of what is reproduced is as essential in the documentary as in the recording field. Very broadly, the commonsense view of the situation as distinct from the legal view, is that no harm ensues from the "fair-copying" for private use of single copies of short specimens and excerpts. Indeed this can no more be prevented than the private tape-recording of broadcasts and commercial discs. The trouble begins with republishing or resale of copied music. This is definitely illicit and actionable where copyright music is concerned. For the U.K., guidance can be had from the *Copyright Act* (HMSO, 1956), the Board of Trade's *Copyright (libraries) Regulations* (HMSO, 1957) and the Royal Society's *Fair Copying Declaration*, 3rd edn. (1957). There is an easily assimilable statement, including recent decisions, in *Who's Who in Music* (Burke's Peerage, 1969). The most recent British study of the protection of intellectual property with special reference to music is D. Thomas's *Copyright and the Creative Artist* (Institute of Economic Affairs, 1967).

For other countries the copyright position is similar only if they subscribe to the Bern Convention. A notable abstainer is the U.S.S.R. which results in lack of protection of Russian scores unless these are simultaneously published elsewhere. Boosey & Hawkes of London, Chant du Monde of Paris and Leeds Music of New York, for instance, claim control over certain contemporary Russian works under these conditions.

Two international studies demand attention. The first (almost alone as a review of historic procedures), is H. Pohlmann's *Die Frühgeschichte des musikalischen Urheberrechts, c. 1400–1800* (Kassel, Bärenreiter, 1962), while the other (modern and practical, but already out of date for the U.K. at least) is S. Rothenberg's *Copyright and Public Performance of Music* (The Hague, Nijhoff, 1954).

CHAPTER 17

Miscellany

NEW MUSIC

Le droit de jouer en fa *dans une symphonie en* re.

H. BERLIOZ, *Grotesques de la musique*

I have nothing to say—I am saying it.

JOHN CAGE

THIS brief note must be confined almost exclusively to the post-Schoenberg period, though the seeds of the "new" harmony were sown in H. Schenker's *Harmonielehre* of 1906 (English trans. Chicago U.P., 1954)—a work interpreted by F. Salzer in *Structural Hearing*, 2 vols. (Dover, 1962). Such seeds are watered by E. Krenek's *Studies in Counterpoint* (Schirmer, 1940), together with P. Hindemith's slightly more traditionally rooted *Craft of Musical Composition*, 4th edn., 2 vols. (Associated Music Publishers, 1941–2), and A. Honegger's *I am a Composer* (Faber, 1966). L. Spinner's *Short Introduction to the Technique of Twelve-tone Composition* (Boosey, 1960), J. Rufer's *Composition with Twelve Notes . . .* (Barrie & Rockliff 1954) and H. Searle's *Twentieth Century Counterpoint* (Williams & Norgate, 1954) are all for the musician with a keen enough ear to separate sense from nonsense and the logical from the ludicrous, while H. Hartog's *European Music in the Twentieth Century* (Routledge, 1957) and D. Mitchell's *The Language of Modern Music* (Faber, 2nd edn. 1966) are not so fiercely technical. Two further introductions attempting to satisfy the bewildered layman are P. Yates' *Twentieth Century Music* (Allen & Unwin, 1968) and

F. Routh's *Contemporary Music: an Introduction* (English Universities Press, 1968). The range of this literature is usefully summarized in *Modern Music and Musicians: readers' guide* (Library Association, 1961). The "concrete" idiom is expounded with reference to its principal precursors, Varèse, Cage and Messiaen, by P. Schaeffer, extensively in *Traité des Objets Musicaux* (Éditions du Seuil) and more briefly, for university students, in *La Musique Concrète* (Presses Universitaires Françaises). The literature of electronic music begins to grow, M. Wilkinson's *An Introduction to Electronic Music* (Barrie & Rockliff, 1961) being among the first general surveys, and the subject is included in Ann P. Basart's *Serial Music* (Univ. of California Press, 1961), probably the first bibliographical study of its kind. Most radios now have their own "radiophonic workshops", but, apart from H. Scherchen's *Gravesanerblätter* (Ars Viva/Schott, 1955–62), their findings, by their very nature, tend to elude publication. This renders the more valuable the first journal specifically devoted to electronic topics, *The Electronic Music Review* (New York Electronic Music Center, 1967–), nos. 2–3 (April–July 1967) carried an "International electronic music catalog" compiled by H. Davies for the Independent Electronic Music Center at Trumansburg, New York.

It is fair to say that some current experimental music of the Stockhausen, Boulez, Nono type would be virtually still-born if it were not heavily underwritten, or actually commissioned by the European radios, who pour their expensive rehearsal time very liberally into it. As it is, only a few specimen study-scores reach publication, and these mostly by Schott, Universal Edition and Faber Music.

The present extent of development is described by Hugh Davies in "A discography of electronic music and musique concrète" (*Recorded Sound*, vol. 14, April 1964 and April–July 1966), which covers scores, books and tapes. Over 200 composers have composed over 1000 works using tape as a medium, during the past 15 years, and over fifty companies have issued discs. This growth is even more recently reflected in the 1500 items described in L. M. Cross's *Bibliography of Electronic Music* (Univ. of Toronto, 1967).

Topical comment, of course, comes in periodical literature, the most recent of all being the Fromm Music Foundation's *Perspectives of New Music* (Princeton U.P./O.U.P., 1963–). In addition to established journals such as the *Journal of Music Theory*, *Melos*, *Die Reihe* and *Tempo* (see Ch. 15), *le dernier cri* can also be seen discussed in such papers as the *Darmstädter Beiträge* (Mainz), being the year book (Band V, 1962) of the Darmstadt Summer courses, *Nutida Musik* (Stockholm), the journal of Sveriges Radio, *La Revue musicale de la Suisse Romande* (Lausanne), the *Schweizerische Musikzeitung* (Zurich), the *Boletino Latinamericano de Musica* (Washington), and the Handbook of Latin-American Studies (Univ. of Florida Press, 1936).

Some documentary landmarks of this period which might otherwise be hard to trace are usefully given in N. Slonimsky's *Music Since 1900*, 3rd edn. (Coleman–Ross, 1949), in a section "Letters and Documents". This gives the full text of such pronouncements as Schoenberg's letter on the origin of the twelve-tone method, and the Soviet musical policy resolution of 1948, Zhdanov's speech, statements by Shostakovich, Khachaturian, etc., which have so influenced the recent course of Russian music.

Each country has its organizations for the promotion of contemporary music, those for the U.K. being primarily the B.B.C., together with the 20-year old Society for the Promotion of New Music (4 St. James's Square, S.W. 1) and the New Opera Company (c/o Sadler's Wells Theatre). These are complemented by the International Society for Contemporary Music (K. A. Hartmann, Wilelmstr. 23, Munich 3) which has held its gatherings since 1923.

CONCERT PROMOTION

Perhaps not unnaturally, the mysteries of promotion lie outside the range of normal documentation. There seems to be no reference book with genuinely international coverage. The nearest is Musical America's *Annual Booking Edition*, which has a measure of European data. Kemp's *Music and Record Industry* (1966–) covers the British field.

PROGRAMME NOTES AND ANALYSES

Useful background is given in *Grove* V under "Programme notes" and in P. A. Scholes' *Oxford Companion* under "Annotated programmes", which quotes Arne, 1768, as the earliest example. The classic examples of modern times are, of course, D. Tovey's *Essays in Musical Analysis*, 6 vols. (O.U.P., 1935) (see Fig. 48), supplemented by Rosa Newmarch's *Concert-goers' Library of Descriptive Notes*, 6 vols. (O.U.P., 1928–48). One of the few works which attempts anaylsis of music of the past 20 years is G. von Westerman's *Concert guide* (Thames & Hudson, 1963).

Extended concert-guides and specialized analytical volumes have been mentioned *seriatim*. Prototypes of this form of literature include F. Niecks' *Programme Music* (Novello, 1906), Sir G. Grove's *Beethoven and his Nine Symphonies* (Novello, 1896), and E. Evans' *Analytical Account of the Entire Works of Johannes Brahms*, 2 vols. (Reeves, 1912). The gramophone sleeve-note and analytical brochure form further useful sources of information, and the Deutsche Grammophon Archiv series is especially commendable for the meticulousness with which MS. and printed sources are quoted.

NICKNAMES

Everyone can identify the *Moonlight Sonata* but few know its other nickname—the *Laube Sonata*. There are a couple of comprehensive lists of such names: F. P. Berkowitz's *Popular Titles and Subtitles of Musical Compositions* (New York, Scarecrow, 1962) and P. Mies' *Volkstümliche Namen musikalischer Werke* (Bonn, Musikhandel, 1960). P. A. Scholes' *Oxford Companion*, under "Nicknamed compositions", gives a short, well-annotated list and describes the origin of the (mostly unauthorized) attributions.

CURIOSA

The oddities of music have frequently acquired their status or flavour through age, for a normality of one age often becomes an oddity in the eyes of a succeeding era. Many curiosities are incidentally revealed in surveys such as P. A. Scholes' *The Mirror of Music, 1844–1944* (Novello and O.U.P., 1947) merely in the course of tracing British musical life as reflected in *The Musical Times* magazine. The same may be said for almost any backward glance at music, if not, indeed at certain present manifestations.

A few books have emphasized or especially gathered together the "curiosa" of music. L. C. Elson's *Curiosities of Music* (Boston, O. Ditson, 1880) is one such, though dealing only with ancient works. N. Slonimsky's *Lexicon of Musical Invective* (New York, Coleman, 1953) and his *A Thing or Two about Music* (New York, Crown, 1949) are further examples, the latter being a gallimaufry of limericks, paradoxes, anecdotes, etc. The French contribution to this off-beat sector is exemplified by J. B. Weckerlin's *Musiciana* (Garnier, 1877), which includes "extraits d'ouvrages rares ou bizarres", and, of course, by almost any page of Berlioz (*Les Soirées de l'orchestre*; *A travers chants*; *Les Grotesques de la musique*). The *Soirées* have recently appeared in a new translation by C. R. Fortescue (Penguin, 1963).

The German contribution is a bibliography which reveals some intriguing headings such as: Böses, Hässliches, Negatives, Teufliches, Unheimliches; Humor, Ironie, Komik, Parodie, among much serious reference to aesthetic, medicinal and psychopathic, etc., aspects. This is Zu Mecklenburg's *Bibliographie einiger Grenzgebiete der Musikwissenschaft* (Baden-Baden, Heitz, 1962). It lists and classifies 3500 items drawn from a wide range of literature as garnered in the *Jahrbuch der Musikbibliothek Peters*, etc. Hermann Baron, the London antiquarian, has a substantial catalogue of curiosities in preparation. (See also Ch. 9 (Spuriosa).)

LETTERS

The Gesellschaft der Freunde des Int. Musiker-Brief-Archivs, Berlin was founded as an intended world-centre for research. Its director, Müller von Asow, had plans for a Gesamtkatalog der Musiker-Briefe, and, before his death, had completed German editions of the letters of Bach, Gluck, Haydn, Mozart, Monteverdi, etc. Musicians' letters have, of course, been collected, translated and published regularly for many years, major recent examples being Meyerbeer's *Briefe und Aufzeichnungen* (De Gruyter, 1960–), and *Mozart-Briefe und Aufzeichnungen* (Bärenreiter/Novello, 1963–). Some outstanding recent specimens of English translations are those by Emily Anderson and C. B. Oldman: *Mozart and his Family*, 2nd edn. by King & Carolan (Macmillan, 1966); *Beethoven*, 3 vols. (Macmillan, 1961), by Emily Anderson; O. E. Deutsch's *Schubert* (Dent, 1946) and H. C. R. Landon's *Haydn* (Barrie & Rockliffe, 1959).

There are several anthologies, among them Norman and Shrifte's *Letters of Composers, 1603–1945* (Knopf, 1946), M. Pincherle's *Musiciens peints par eux-mêmes* (Cornau, 1939), and J. Tiersot's *Lettres de musiciens écrites en français*, 2 vols. (Bocca, 1924–36). Dealers and auctioneers such as Stargardt of Marburg and Christie and Sotheby of London regularly issue catalogues, often lavishly illustrated, of autograph letters, etc.

PICTURES

The collector, the musicologist and ethnomusicologist, the marginally interested musician, the television producer—all may need help or information from musical pictures. The standard work for many years was G. Kinsky's *History of Music in Pictures*, new edn. (Dent, 1937) but this will gradually give place to Besseler and Schneider's *Musikgeschichte in Bildern* (Deutscher Verlag für Musik, 1964–) whose four volumes are planned to cover ancient, medieval and modern times. A recent one-volume survey has appeared with alternative French, English and German texts: F. Lesure's *Music in Art and Society* (Pennsylvania University Press, 1968). Further important studies include M. Pincherle's *An Illustrated History of Music* (Macmillan–Reynal, 1960) and Collaer and Vander Linden's *Historical Atlas of Music* (Harrap, 1968). Portraits are specifically covered by G. McCory's *Portraits of the World's best known Musicians* (Presser, 1946) together with the A.L.A. *Portrait Index* (Library of Congress, 1906) and the exhaustive *Allgemeiner*

Bildniskataloge, 19 vols., (Leipzig, Hiersemann, 1930–38) which includes composers, etc. Under the editorship of H. C. Wolff an imaginative plan for the iconography of opera has been started. Details appear in *Fontes*, 1968/1. Iconography also features as a heading in R.I.L.M., 1968–.

Die Musik in Geschichte und Gegenwart (Bärenreiter, 1949–) is probably the best illustrated full-scale encyclopaedia, and P. A. Scholes' *Oxford Companion* is well served for its size. Many dealers' catalogues carry sections devoted to musical prints, especially portraits. Intending reproducers of these prints should take care to check copyright aspects.

The following is a short selection from the very considerable range of published composer-iconographies, chosen mainly for their current availability:

> *J. S. Bach* by W. Neumann (Verlag der Nation, 1957).
> *Beethoven* by R. Bory (Atlantis, 1960).
> *Bruckner* by W. Abendroth (Munich, Kindler Verlag, 1958).
> *Chopin* by A. Boucourechliev (Thames & Hudson, 1963).
> *Chopin* by K. Kobylanska (Cracow, Polish Music Publishing House, 1955).
> *Dvořák* by A. Hořejš (Artia, 1955).
> *Handel* by Rackwitz and Steffens (Leipzig).
> *Liszt* by Weilguny and Handrick (Weimer, Volksverlag, 1958).
> *Mozart* by O. E. Deutsch (Bärenreiter, 1961).
> *Mozart* by R. Bory (Geneva, Editions contemporaines, 1948).
> *Verdi* by C. Gatti (Milan, Garzanti, 1941).
> *Wagner* by R. Bory (Geneva, Editions A. Jullien, 1938).

MUSICAL NOVELS

Novels in English with music (mainly about a real or imaginary composer) as a principal theme now run to over 100. Apparently no full-scale study of this aspect of fiction has yet been made, but the novels themselves are traceable through the standard Baker and Packman *Guide to the Best Fiction* (Routledge, 1932) supplemented by

Colton and Glencross's *Cumulated Fiction Index, 1945–60* (Association of Assistant Librarians, 1960) under Musicians and Singers. It would seem one cannot be both. Further sources are *The Readers' Guide to Prose Fiction* (Appleton–Century, 1940) and the *Fiction Catalogues* (1941–) issued by H. W. Wilson. The latter attempt some degree of classification—Harpists, Singers, etc.

ANNIVERSARIES: CHRONOLOGIES

Many organizers, from the important impresario to the secretary of a local gramophone society, find the need for precise chronological data about musicians, performances, etc. Grove's *Dictionary*, 5th edn. (Macmillan) gives, in an easily overlooked Appendix I (vol. 9 and supplementary volume) a Chronology of Composers and Contemporaneous Artists, 1400–1955, where names are repeated every 10 years from the age of 20 throughout their lives. Many works of the "annals" type, quoted *seriatim* throughout this book, cover similar ground, often in great detail. J. Detheridge's *Chronology of Musical Composers*, 2 vols. (Birmingham, Detheridge, 1936) complements Grove by beginning at the year 820. N. Slonimsky's *Music since 1900*, 3rd edn. (Coleman-Ross, 1949) and La Revue Musicale's *La Musique 1900–1950: tableau chronologique des principales oeuvres . . .* (R. Masse, 1952) are examples covering the past generation. Various calendars (e.g. Peters edn.) and diaries (*Musician's Diary*) also give much curious and often very fugitive information in this form.

FESTIVALS

British festivals were mentioned in Ch. 7. The fullest description of international festivals is in D. G. Stoll's *Music Festivals of the World* (Pergamon, 1963). Travel agencies and their federations supply current details.

FILM MUSIC

The music itself lies in the archives of the various film studios and is more than usually subject to the hazards of dispersal and destruction. Only a tiny proportion achieves publication in anything like original form. Some survives in successful concert arrangements, and these are listed currently in the *British Catalogue of Music* (British National Bibliography, 1957–). The commercial gramophone catalogues list recorded versions.

The use of film in teaching is reflected in the International Music Centre, Vienna's selective catalogue: *Films for Music in Education and Opera Films* (UNESCO/HMSO, 1962), supplemented by K. A. Wright's "Available Films on Music" in *Music*, Spring, 1968.

For the U.K. the British Film Institute (81 Dean St., W. 1) runs a general information service, and the Sound Film Music Bureau Ltd. (380 Streatham High St., S.W. 16) deals with the use of copyright music in films.

A modest but useful little guide is F. Rawlings' *How to Choose Music for Amateur Films*, 2nd edn. (Focal Press, 1961), which covers not only general background music but national and international mood-music (see also Ch. 14, p. 99), music for special occasions, sound-effects, recording companies and their distributors, and copyright restrictions.

Most writing on the cinema, including such classic pronouncements as those of Eisenstein and Pudovkin, have something, however brief, to say about the use of music. Probably the earliest general survey was K. London's *Film Music* (Faber, 1936), just late enough to reflect on the demise of the silent film. Since then, there have been a few contributions including G. Cockshott's *Incidental Music in the Sound Film* (Dobson, 1947), H. Colpi's *Défense et illustration de la musique dans le film* (Lyons, Serdoc, 1963) and M. Arnold's *Film Music* (Recorded Sound, no. 18), but they rarely include any useful documentation. For this, one must rely on J. Huntley's *Film Music* (Skelton Robinson, 1947) with its biographical index, sections on B.B.C. film music, and recordings of British film music, Huntley and Manvell's *Technique of Film Music* (Focal Press, 1957) which has a good bibliography and list of film-music recordings, G. D. McDonald's "Songs of the silent film: 1905–27" (*Notes*, Sept. 1957) and on C. McCarty's *Film Composers in America: a checklist of their work* (Glendale, Calif., Valentine, 1953). Film music criticism is largely ignored, the only systematic but short-lived attempt being H. Keller's in *Music and Letters*. Probably the only separate bibliography is Nelson and Rubsamen's "Books and articles on music in film and radio" (*Hinrichsen's Musical Yearbook*, vol. 6, 1951). Regular surveys began to appear in *Notes* from 1966.

INSTRUMENTS

Both *Grove* V and *Die Musik in Geschichte und Gegenwart* carry good general articles, the former adding a useful index of illustrations; each gives international lists of public collections (*Grove* adding important private ones for the U.K.) but *MGG* quotes published catalogues. The full extent of the literature of instruments is given in the bibliographies to the above articles, and of that to J. Kunst's *Ethnomusicology* (see Ch. 9). Classics in English include R. Donington's *The Instruments of Music* (Methuen, 1949), F. W. Galpin's *Textbook of European Musical Instruments* (Dutton, 1937), K. Geiringer's *Musical Instruments* (Allen & Unwin, 1945) and C. Sachs' *The History of Musical Instruments* (Norton, 1940). To these must be added A. C. Baines' *Woodwind Instruments*, 3rd edn. (Faber, 1967), E. Winternitz's *Musical Instruments of the Western World* (McGraw-Hill, 1967) and the Galpin Society's successful general survey *Musical Instruments through the Ages* (Penguin, 1961). As a recent example of a reliable catalogue of an historic collection the Horniman Museum's *Descriptive Catalogue* (1958) of the Carse collection is recommended. An obvious reference point of specialist knowledge is the Comité International des Musées de Collections d'Instruments (CIMCIM). This body has now published provisional recommendations for *Preservation and Restoration of Musical Instruments* (Evelyn, Adams & Mackay, 1967).

Each class of instrument has its documentary literature, such as R. Vannes' *Dictionnaire Universel des Luthiers*, 2 vols. (Brussels, Les

Amis de la musique, 1951–56) and L. G. Langwill's *An Index of Musical Wind Instrument Makers*, 2nd edn. (Edinburgh, the author, 1962), supplemented by monographs of the kind Bate, Rendall and Gregory have produced for oboe, clarinet and horn, and Herzog for piano manufacturers' numbers.

Current research is reflected in specialist journals such as that of the Galpin Society, 7 Pickwick Rd., London, S.E. 21, the Stradivarius Association, 1170 Aubonne, Switzerland, or the *Woodwind Journal*, now superseded by the *Woodwind World* (Gerstner Publications, Bedford Hills, New York).

Systematic classification has become one of the ethnomusicologists' main tasks. Various systems have been evolved by specialists such as Hornbostel and Schaeffner (details in Kunst) but the simple statement in P. A. Scholes' *Companion to Music*, for the average reader, or, for librarians, the appropriate schedules of the various general classification schemes are recommended.

Instrumentation is dealt with in Ch. 2, and experiments in the electronic field in *New Music* (see pp. 114–16).

Patent specification for instruments are easily accessible by consulting the "music" volumes at the Patent Office Library, which covers U.K. and U.S. output.

Germany appears to retain its traditional lead in instrument-making, and the periodical *Das Instrument* (Frankfurt, 1, Kluberstrasse, 9) reflects topical affairs in this field.

PITCH

Articles such as those in *Grove*, *MGG* and *The Oxford Companion*, survey the two aspects of this subject which have immediate practical applications for musicians and writers on music, viz. standardization and notation.

In spite of international agreements in 1939 and 1953 on a standard of A=440, it is still possible for a Czech orchestra to find its pitch sufficiently at variance, for instance, with a British piano to cause embarrassment. The latest survey gives the clue to this situation, and quotes a table of variations in measurements of standard tuning-frequency effected in various countries over the past three centuries. This is C. Van Loo's "On the standardization of musical pitch" (*European Broadcasting Union Review*, Dec. 1962) which pleads for retaining A=440 but points out that this still has no legal enforcement.

A similar degree of variety also applies to pitch notation, and no one system is generally accepted. *The Oxford Companion* quotes the variants and comments on their relative worth.

MUSIC IN HOSPITALS

A group of doctors at Michigan University . . . recommend Handel for weak hearts, Mozart for rheumatism, Schubert . . . for sleeplessness.

Woodwind Magazine, Oct. 1953.

A detailed description of the work and resources of the Council for Music in Hospitals (East Dean, N. Eastbourne, Sussex) is given in *Who's Who in Music*, 5th edn. (Burke's Peerage, 1969). The associated problem of teaching music to handicapped children is dealt with in a separate chapter of B. Rainbow's *Handbook*, vol. 1 (see p. 57). In the U.S., the American National Association for Music Therapy has consolidated its work since 1950, and has published annually its findings as *Music Therapy* (1951–). An English expert is Juliette Alvin whose *Music for the Handicapped Child* (O.U.P., 1965) and *Music Therapy* (Baker, 1966) are pioneering works. The (British) Society for Music Therapy and Remedial Music and the Rudolf Steiner Association are further bodies covering these interests. The Schools Music Association's *Report on Music in Special Schools* is also important.

THE BLIND

To see a blind chorister among his or her fellows, happily singing from a Braille chorus part is a sobering, yet cheering, sight. The existence of complete choirs of blind singers such as the Pro Cantu of

London is even more heartening. The fact is that a library of over 40,000 items, not limited to classics, has been transcribed into Braille. The responsible agencies are, for the U.K., the National Library for the Blind (35 Gt. Smith St., S.W. 1) and the Royal National Institute for the Blind (224 Gt. Portland St., W. 1) and, for the U.S., the Division for the Blind of the Library of Congress working through distributing libraries in the various states. No complete and up-to-date published catalogue exists of what is available, but, if enough time is allowed, almost any simple score can be transcribed.

MECHANICAL INSTRUMENTS

Old mechanical musical instruments have themselves been the subject of wide research since the turn of the century, and the revival of interest in the music written for them has led to many and varied arrangements and transcriptions, particularly of flute-clock pieces. *Grove* refers to a small handful of articles on individual instruments, while *MGG* (Mechanische Musikinstrumente) provides a thorough-going general introduction, with a bibliography of over fifty items published since 1909. Albert Protz has written a major treatise—*Mechanische Musikinstrumente* (Cassel, 1943) and this is now extended by E. Simon's *Mechanische Musikinstrumente früherer Zeiten und ihre Musik* (Wiesbaden, Breitkopf, 1960). A standard work in English is J. E. T. Clark's *Musical Boxes*, 3rd edn. (Allen & Unwin, 1961).

The British Piano Museum, Brentford, Middlesex reflects the lifelong enthusiasm of F. W. Holland, its founder-curator, and concentrates on collection and restoration of automatic, reproducing pianos and organs. These play the music exactly as recorded by the great recording artists early in this century.

APPENDIX I

Principal Music Collections, formerly in Private Hands, and now to be found in Institutions and Libraries of Great Britain

The function of this list is merely to locate certain collections. These may only partly be represented, particularly where they were acquired piece-meal at auction, etc. For further details about their scope, history, migrations, dispersal, etc., see A. H. King's *Some British Collectors of Music, c. 1600–1960* (C.U.P., 1963). Besides listing sales and sale-catalogues *c.* 1711 onwards of both named and un-named collectors, this work also lists alphabetically "Collectors whose music has been conserved intact, in whole or part" and "Collectors whose music was dispersed". *Grove* V's article "Libraries and collections" arranges some of the same information by place and library, but only the most outstanding collectors can be traced in this and similar encyclopaedias under their own names.

ALDRICH, HENRY. Oxford, Christ Church.

ALLAN, ERSKINE. Cambridge, Union Society.

ALLEN, SIR HUGH. Oxford University, Faculty of Music.

ARNOLD, F. T. (17th–18th cent. chamber music). Cambridge University.

AYLESFORD, EARL OF (Handel). Manchester Public Library.

AYLWARD, THEODORE (English sacred music and organ music). Cardiff Public Library.

BALFOUR, A. J., FIRST EARL. Edinburgh, National Library of Scotland.

BARRY, C. A. Royal Academy of Music.

BAX, ARNOLD. British Museum; Chappell & Co. Ltd.

BENSON, L. Royal College of Music.

BLOM, ERIC. Central Music Library.

BLUNT, JANET (folk material). English Folk Dance and Song Society.

BONAVIA, F. British Broadcasting Corporation.

BOUGHTON, RUTLAND (autograph MSS.). British Museum.

BOULT, SIR ADRIAN (orchestral parts). British Broadcasting Corporation. (Orchestral scores). Royal College of Music.

BOURNE, T. W. (Handel and contemporaries). Oxford, Bodleian.

BRIAN, HAVERGAL. B.B.C.; British Museum (autographs).

BRIDGE, SIR FREDERICK. Trinity College of Music.

BROADWOOD, LUCY (folk-song MSS.). English Folk Dance and Song Society.

BUTTERWORTH, GEORGE S. K. (folk-song MSS.). English Folk Dance and Song Society.

CAMM, JOHN B. M. (orchestral scores, etc.). Bournemouth, Public Library.

CARL ROSA (opera materials). Liverpool Public Library; Royal College of Music.

CHAPEL ROYAL (MSS.). British Museum.

CHAPPELL, WILLIAM (folk-song MSS.). English Folk Dance and Song Society.

CHARLOTTE, QUEEN, Wife of George III. British Museum.

CHELLE, W. (MS. treatises). Lambeth Palace.

CHESTER CHAMBER/MUSIC LIBRARY. Sussex University.

CHRISTIE-MOÓR, MRS. WINIFRED (Edwin Evans and Gerald Cooper collections). Central Music Library.

CHURCH HOUSE, Westminster (Julian and Mann collections). British Museum.

COLLES, H. C. C. Addington, Royal School of Church Music; Cambridge, King's College.

CONCENTORES SOCIETY. Guildhall Library.

CONCERTS OF ANCIENT MUSIC. Royal College of Music.

COOPER, GERALD M. Cambridge, Fitzwilliam Museum, Pendlebury Library. Central Music Library.

COSIN, JOHN, DR. (17th cent. church music). Cambridge, Peterhouse College.

CROSS, PERCY ("Siddell" orchestral library, Manchester). British Broadcasting Corporation.

CROTCH, W. (MS. scores, sketchbooks, etc.). Norwich, City Library.

DANNREUTHER, EDWARD. Royal College of Music.

DENT, EDWARD.
   (Opera scores, letters, and MSS. of own compositions). Cambridge, King's College. Sadler's Wells Theatre.
   (Transcripts). Cambridge, Pendlebury.

DRAGONETTI, D. (operas). British Museum.

DRYSDALE, LEARMONT (own compositions). Glasgow University.

EINSTEIN, A. (Smith College archive of Italian madrigals and instrumental music: film). British Broadcasting Corporation.

ELLA, JOHN. Royal College of Music.

ELVEY, SIR GEORGE. London University.

ENGLISH BACH SOCIETY. Royal Academy of Music.

ENGLISH FOLK DANCE AND SONG SOCIETY (MSS.). Clare College, Cambridge.

EUING, W. (MSS., early printed music, etc.). Glasgow University.

EVANS, EDWIN. Central Music Library.

FARMER, H. G. (Scottish and Oriental music). Glasgow University.

FITZWILLIAM, RICHARD, 7th Viscount (Handel autographs, etc.). Cambridge, Fitzwilliam Museum.

FLOWER, SIR NEWMAN (Handel MSS.). Manchester Public Library.

FOLK SONG SOCIETY. English Folk Dance and Song Society.

FORREST, WILLIAM (Tudor masses). Oxford, Bodleian.

FOX STRANGWAYS, A. H. British Broadcasting Corporation.

FROST, MAURICE (church music: part collection). Addington, Royal School of Church Music.

FULLER-MAITLAND, J. A. (English church music MSS.). Liverpool, Public Library.

GARDINER, G. B. (folk-music). Glasgow, Mitchell Library. English Folk Dance and Song Society.

GARDINER, H. BALFOUR (folk-song MSS.). English Folk Dance and Song Society.

GATTY, R. A. (folk-songs). English Folk Dance and Song Society.

GEORGE III, IV. British Museum.

GILCHRIST, ANNE G. (folk material). English Folk Dance and Song Society.

GLEN, J. (Scottish music). Edinburgh, National Library of Scotland.

GOETZ, ANGELINA (full scores). Royal Academy of Music.

GOODSON, R. (early English and foreign music). Oxford, Christ Church.

GORDON, J. B. (vocal scores). Sadler's Wells Theatre.

GOSTLING, W. (17th cent. choirbooks). York Minster.

GRAINGER, PERCY (folk-song MSS.). English Folk Dance and Song Society.

GRANVILLE, BERNARD (Handel MSS.). British Museum.

GRESHAM COLLECTION. Guildhall Library.

GRIFFIN, R. Cambridge, Fitzwilliam Museum.

GURNEY, IVOR (MSS.). Gloucester Public Library.

HADOW, SIR HENRY. Oxford University, Faculty of Music.

HALLIWELL, W. Wigan, Public Library.

HALLIWELL-PHILLIPS, J. O. (songs). Manchester, Chetham's Library.

HAMMOND, H. E. D. (folk-songs). English Folk Dance and Song Society.

HAMOND, T. Oxford, Bodleian.

HANDEL OPERA SOCIETY (performing materials). Novello & Co.

HARTY, SIR HAMILTON. Belfast, Queen's University.

HARVARD, LAWRENCE. Cambridge, King's College.

HAWKINS, SIR JOHN (treatises, part-books, MSS.). British Museum.

HEATHER (HEYTHER), WILLIAM (Tudor masses). Oxford, Bodleian.

HERON-ALLEN, EDWARD (books on the violin). Royal College of Music.

HESS, DAME MYRA. Central Music Library, Westminster.

HILL, A. F. (selected early editions). British Museum.

HIRSCH, PAUL. British Museum.

HOOK, JAMES (autograph MSS. and printed music). Cambridge University.

HOPKINSON, CECIL (Berlioz). Edinburgh, National Library of Scotland.

INGLIS, A. W. Edinburgh, National Library of Scotland.

JASPER, JOLY. Dublin, National Library of Ireland.

JENNENS, CHARLES (Handel MSS., via Aylesford collection). British Museum.

JULIAN, J. (hymnology, ex-Church House, Westminster). British Museum.

KALISCH, A. (vocal scores). Royal Academy of Music.

KEMBLE, FANNY (17th cent. keyboard and vocal music). Hereford Cathedral.

KENNEDY, PETER (folk-song recordings). English Folk Dance and Song Society.

KENNEDY-FRASER, MARJORIE (Gaelic song). Edinburgh University.

KIDSON, FRANK. Glasgow, Mitchell Library. Leeds, Public Library.

KIMPTON, G. (orchestral music). Royal Academy of Music.

KING'S MUSIC LIBRARY (now Royal Music Library). British Museum.

KURTZ, A. G. (autograph letters of musicians). British Museum.

LAMBERT, CONSTANT (orchestral music). British Broadcasting Corporation.

LANDAU, BARON HORACE DE (selected MSS. and early editions). British Museum.

LEATHER, MRS. E. M. (folk-songs). English Folk Dance and Song Society.

LEIGH OF STONELEIGH (17th and 18th cent. printed music). Oxford, Oriel College.

LENNARD, H. B. (Handel MSS.). Cambridge, Fitzwilliam Museum.

LITTLETON, A. H. (early music and treatises). London University.

LOMAX, ALAN (folk-song recordings). English Folk Dance and Song Society.

MACKWORTH, SIR HENRY (Bonner Morgan collection). Cardiff, Public Library.

MADRIGAL SOCIETY. British Museum.

MANN, A. H. Cambridge, King's College.

(East Anglian music). Cambridge University. Norwich City Library.

MARR, R. A. (18th cent. music). Edinburgh, Public Library.

MARSHALL, JULIAN (Handel scores and libretti). Edinburgh, National Library of Scotland.

MAYEROWITSCH, H. (Jewish liturgical music). Jews' College.

MEE, J. H. Oxford University, Faculty of Music.

MEYERSTEIN, E. H. W. (autographs: part of collection). British Museum.

MOODY, F. and MANNERS, C. (opera scores and parts). Glasgow, Mitchell Library.

MORGAN, BONNER (17th and 18th cent. music). Cardiff, Public Library.

NEWMAN, ELDRIDGE (orchestral music). British Broadcasting Corporation.

NEWMARCH, ROSA (vocal scores). Sadler's Wells Theatre.

NICHOLSON, SIR SYDNEY. Addington, Royal School of Church Music.

NIECKS, FRIEDRICH. Edinburgh, Reid Music Library.

NOVELLO AND CO. (vocal scores). Sadler's Wells Theatre.

OAKELEY, H. S. Edinburgh, Reid Music Library.

OLDMAN, C. B. British Museum.

ORD, BORIS. Cambridge, Pendelbury and Rowe.

ORIANA MADRIGAL SOCIETY. Central Music Library, Westminster.

OUSELEY, SIR FREDERICK (MSS. and printed books). Tenbury, St. Michael's College.

PARKER, REV. JOHN (MS. Continental madrigals). British Museum.

PARRY, SIR CHARLES H. H. (autographs and printed music). Royal College of Music.

PENDLEBURY, RICHARD. Cambridge University, Faculty of Music.

PEPYS, SAMUEL (early vocal music). Cambridge, Magdalene College.

PERABO, E. (MSS.). British Museum.

PHILIDOR, ANDRÉ (MSS. to end of 17th cent.). Tenbury, St. Michael's College.

PITT, PERCY (orchestral music). British Broadcasting Corporation.

PLAINSONG AND MEDIAEVAL MUSIC SOCIETY. London University.

PRENDERGAST, H. (church music). Royal Academy of Music.

PROUT, EBENEZER. Dublin, Trinity College.

REID, JOHN. Edinburgh, Reid Music Library.

RIESS, FERDINAND. Royal Academy of Music.

RONALD, SIR LANDON (orchestral music). British Broadcasting Corporation.

ROWE, L. T. Cambridge, King's College.

ROYAL MUSIC LIBRARY (formerly King's music library). British Museum.

ROYAL PHILHARMONIC SOCIETY

    (MSS.). British Msueum.

    (Printed scores and parts). Royal Academy of Music.

RUGGLES-BRISE, LADY DOROTHEA L. Edinburgh, National Library of Scotland. Perth, Public Library.

SACRED HARMONIC SOCIETY (printed music and MSS.). Royal College of Music.

SARGENT, SIR M. (orchestral music, etc.). Royal College of Music.

SCHOLES, PERCY. National Library of Canada; Central Music Library, Westminster.

SCOTT, CHARLES KENNEDY (Oriana Madrigal Society). Central Music Library, Westminster.

SCOTT, MARION M. Cambridge University.

SHARP, CECIL (folk-song material). British Museum. English Folk Dance and Song Society. Cambridge, Clare College.

SIDDELL, F. W. (orchestral hire library). British Broadcasting Corporation.

SLOANE, SIR HANS (MSS.). British Museum.

SMITH, J. C. (Handel transcripts). British Museum. Cambridge, Fitzwilliam Museum.

STANFORD, SIR CHARLES (autographs). Royal College of Music.

STATIONERS' HALL. Oxford University, Bodleian.

STEVENS, R. J. S. (MSS. printed editions). Cambridge, Fitzwilliam Museum. Glasgow University. Royal Academy of Music.

STILLIE, Y. L. Glasgow University.

TAPHOUSE, T. W. (portion of library). Leeds, Public Library.

TAYLOR, W. L. (psalm books). Aberdeen University.

TERRY, C. S. (Bach collection, ex-R.C.M.). Oxford University, Faculty of Music.

THOMAS, A. GORING. Royal College of Music.

TOULOUSE-PHILIDOR (*see* Philidor).

TOVEY, SIR DONALD. Edinburgh, Reid Music Library.

TREFUSIS, LADY MARY (hymnals and psalters). Addington, Royal School of Church Music.

TURNBULL, R. Glasgow, Mitchell Library.

U.S. EMBASSY (scores and records). University of London.

VICTORIA, QUEEN. British Museum.

WALEY, S. W. Royal College of Music.

WALKER, ERNEST. Oxford University, Faculty of Music.

WATSON, HENRY. Manchester, Public Library.

WEISS, PROF. P. (Beethoven relics). Edinburgh, Reid Music Library.

WESTMORLAND, 11th EARL OF. Royal Academy of Music.

WHITE, REV. E. H. (folk-song index). English Folk Dance and Song Society.

WIGHT, REV. OSBORNE (16th and 17th cent. MS. and printed music). Oxford, Bodleian.

WIGHTON, A. J. (Scottish music). Dundee, Free Library.

WILLIAMS, R. VAUGHAN
  (Folk-song MSS.). English Folk Dance and Song Society.
  (Autograph MSS.). British Museum.

WINDSOR, J. M. Royal College of Music.

WOOD, SIR HENRY J. (orchestral music). Royal Academy of Music.

ZAVERTAL, V. H. (Mozart relics, etc.). Glasgow University.

APPENDIX IIA

Music Publishers and Agents

THE following is a list of the principal established music-publishers and their
U.K. and U.S. agents. An exhaustive international list covering all music
publishers, particularly in the popular music field would be impracticable,
especially on account of their often ephemeral nature. For a more complete
statement on the latter, reference can be made to the annual *Billboard Music-
record Directory* (N.Y. Billboard) or to the national publishers' organizations, e.g. The Music Publishers' Association (73 Mortimer St., W. 1) and
The Music Publishers' Association of the U.S. (609, 5th Avenue, Fourth
Floor, N.Y. 17). (See Appendix IIB.) International lists are also given in the
B.B.C.'s Music Catalogues and in *MGG* (Band 5, 1956).

Publisher and Address	*Agents in U.K. and/or U.S.A.*
AFAS MUSIK VERLAG (HANS DUNNEBEIL)	
See Bote & Bock	
AFFILIATED MUSIC PUBLISHERS, LTD.	
138/140 Charing Cross Rd., W.C. 2	
AHN & SIMROCK	
Meinekestr. 10, Berlin 15, Germany	
Schützenhofstr. 4, Wiesbaden, Germany	
ALKOR EDITION	
See Bärenreiter	
ALSBACH, G. & CO.	Hinrichsen (Purchase) *U.K.*
Raamsgracht 10, Amsterdam, Holland	Novello (Hire) *U.K.*
	Peters *U.S.A.*
AMERICAN INSTITUTE OF MUSICOLOGY	Hinrichsen *U.K.*
P.O. Box 12233, Dallas 25, Texas, U.S.A.	
AMICI DELLA MUSICA DA CAMERA, GLI	Hinrichsen *U.K.*
Via Bocca di Leone 25, Rome, Italy	
AMPHION ÉDITIONS MUSICALES	United Mus. Publishers *U.K.*
5 Rue Jean-Ferrandi, Paris 6, France	Elgan-Vogel *U.S.A.*
AM-RUS EDITION	
See Leeds Music Ltd.	

Publisher and Address	*Agents in U.K. and/or U.S.A.*
ANDRAUD, ALBERT J.	Southern *U.S.A.*
2871 Erie Av., Cincinnati 8, Ohio, U.S.A.	
ANDRÉ, JOHANN	
Frankfurterstr. 28, Offenbach am Main, Germany	
ANGLO-FRENCH MUSIC PUBLISHERS	
See Oxford University Press	
ANGLO-SOVIET MUSIC PRESS (LONDON) LTD.	
295 Regent Street, London, W. 1	
ARNOLD, EDWARD (PUBLISHERS) LTD.	
See Novello	
ARROW MUSIC PRESS	Boosey & Hawkes *U.S.A.*
250 W. 57th St., New York 19, N.Y., U.S.A.	
ARS VIVA	Associated Mus. Publishers
See Schott	*U.S.A.*
ARTIA VE SMEČKÁCH 30, PRAHA	Boosey & Hawkes; Kalmus A. (orchestral) *U.K.*
ASCHERBERG, HOPWOOD & CREW, LTD.	Big 3 *U.S.A.*
16 Mortimer St., London, W. 1	
ASHDOWN EDWIN, LTD.	
19 Hanover Sq., London, W. 1	
ASSOCIATED BOARD OF THE ROYAL SCHOOLS OF MUSIC	Mills *U.S.A.*
14 Bedford Sq., London, W.C. 1	
ASSOCIATED MUSIC PUBLISHERS INC.	Schott *U.K.*
1 W. 47th St., New York 36, N.Y., U.S.A.	
AUGENER LTD.	Galaxy *U.S.A.*
See Galliard	
BANK, ANNIE, EDITIONS	Chester *U.K.*
Anna Vondelstr, Amsterdam, Holland	
BÄRENREITER	
Heinrich Schütz Allee 29–37, Kassel-Wilhelmshöhe, Germany	
P.O. Box 115, New York 34, N.Y., U.S.A.	
32 Gt. Titchfield St., London, W. 1	
BARON, N., CO.	
Box 149, Oyster Bay N.Y., U.S.A.	
BAYLEY & FERGUSON LTD.	
54 Queen St., Glasgow C. 1, Scotland	
16, Mortimer St., London, W. 1.	

Publisher and Address	*Agents in U.K. and/or U.S.A.*

BELAIEFF, ÉDITIONS
  10 Sq. Desnouettes, Paris 15, France
  Kronprinzenstr. 26, Bonn, Germany
	Boosey & Hawkes *U.K. and*
	U.S.A.

BELWIN INC. Rockville Centre, L.I., U.S.A.	Bosworth *U.K.*

BENJAMIN, ANTON J. LTD.
  239/241 Shaftesbury Av., London, W.C. 2
  Werderstrasse, 44, Hamburg 13, Germany
	Associated Mus. Publishers
	U.S.A.

BERLIN, IRVING, LTD.
  14 St. George St., London, W. 1
  1650 Broadway, New York 19, N.Y.,
  U.S.A.	

BESSEL, W. & CO. LTD.
  c/o B. Bessel, 22 Farley Court,
  Melbury Rd., London W. 4.
  78 Rue de Monceau, Paris 8, France
	Boosey & Hawkes *U.K.*
	Ricordi *U.S.A.*

BIG 3 MUSIC CORP.
  1540 Broadway, New York 36, N.Y.,
  U.S.A.	

BIRCHARD, C. C. *See* Summy-Birchard	

BIRNBACH, RICHARD
  Dürerstr. 28a, Berlin–Lichterfelde–West,
  Germany	

BLACK, A. AND C. *See* Ascherberg, Hopwood & Crew	
BÖHM, ANTON UND SOHN Ludwigstr. 3, Augsburg D, Germany	Hinrichsen *U.K.*
BOILEAU, CASA EDITORIAL DE MUSICA Provenza 285–287, Barcelona, Spain	
BOMART MUSIC PUBLICATIONS INC. Hillsdale, New York, U.S.A.	
BONGIOVANNI, FRANCESCO Via Rizzoli 28e, Bologna, Italy	Hinrichsen *U.K.*

BOOSEY & HAWKES LTD.
  295 Regent St., London, W. 1
  4 Rue Drouot, Paris, France
  Kronprinzenstr. 26, Bonn, Germany
  30 W. 57th St., New York 19, N.Y.,
  U.S.A.	

BORNEMANN, ÉDITIONS 15 Rue de Tournon, Paris 6, France	United Mus. Publishers *U.K.* Gray *U.S.A.*

Publisher and Address	*Agents in U.K. and/or U.S.A.*
BOSTON MUSIC COMPANY 116 Boylston St., Boston, Mass. 16, U.S.A.	Chappell *U.K.*
BOSWORTH & CO. LTD. 14–18 Heddon St., London, W. 1 Hohestr. 133, Köln, Germany	Belwin *U.S.A.*
BOTE, E. and G. & BOCK, A. G. Hardenbergstr. 9a, Berlin– Charlottenburg, Germany	Schott *U.K.* Associated Mus. Publishers *U.S.A.*
BRANDUS & CIE *See* Joubert	United Mus. Publishers *U.K.*
BREITKOPF & HÄRTEL Burgstr. 6, Wiesbaden, Germany	British & Continental *U.K.* Associated Mus. Publishers *U.S.A.*
BRITISH & CONTINENTAL MUSIC AGENCIES, LTD. 64 Dean St., London, W. 1	
BROADCAST MUSIC INC. 589, 5th Av., New York 17, N.Y., U.S.A.	
BROCKHAUS, MAX Mühlestr. 14, Lörrach, Baden, Germany	Novello (Orchestral only) *U.K.*
BROEKMANS & VAN POPPEL Van Baerlstr. 92, Amsterdam, Holland	Hinrichsen *U.K.* Peters *U.S.A.*
BROUDE BROS. 56, W. 45th St., New York 36, N.Y., U.S.A.	Schott *U.K.*
BRUCKNERVERLAG *See* Bärenreiter	
CAMPBELL, CONNELLY & CO. LTD. 10 Denmark St., London, W.C. 2 565, 5th Av., New York 19, N.Y., U.S.A.	
CARISCH, S.P.A. Via General Fara N. 39, Milan, Italy	Hinrichsen (Purchase) *U.K.* Chester (Hire) *U.K.* Mills *U.S.A.* Boosey & Hawkes *U.S.A.*
CARY, L. J. & CO., LTD. 16 Mortimer St., London, W. 1	
CASA EDITORIAL DE MUSICA BOILEAU *See* Boileau	
CAVENDISH MUSIC CO. LTD. 295 Regent St., London, W. 1	Boosey & Hawkes *U.S.A.*

Publisher and Address	*Agents in U.K. and/or U.S.A.*
CEBEDEM FOUNDATION 3 Rue Du Commerce, Bruxelles, Belgium	Lengnick *U.K.*
CHANT DU MONDE, ÉDITIONS LE 32 Rue Beaujon, Paris 8, France	United Mus. Publishers *U.K.* Leeds *U.S.A.*
CHAPPELL & CO. LTD. 50 New Bond St., London, W. 1 86 Bd. Haussmann, Paris, France 609, 5th Av. New York 17, N.Y., U.S.A. Schwanthalerstr. 51, München, Germany	
CHESTER, J. & W. LTD. Eagle Court, London, E.C. 1	G. Schirmer (Rental) *U.S.A.*
CHOUDENS, ÉDITIONS PARIS 138 Rue Jean Mermoz, Paris 8, France	United Mus. Publishers *U.K.* Peters *U.S.A.*
CHURCH, JOHN, CO. Bryn Mawr, Pennsylvania, U.S.A.	Kalmus *U.K.* Presser *U.S.A.*
CINEPHONIC MUSIC CO. LTD. 10 Denmark St., London, W.C. 2	
CLOWES, WILLIAM & SONS, LTD. Little New St., London, E.C. 4	
CONCORDIA PUBLISHING HOUSE 3558 South Jefferson Av., Saint Louis 18, Missouri, U.S.A.	
COSTALLAT, ÉDITIONS 60 Rue De La Chaussée D'Antin, Paris 9, France	United Mus. Publishers *U.K.* Baron (Orchestral) *U.S.A.*
CRAMER, J. B. & CO. LTD. 99 St. Martin's Lane, London, W.C. 2	
CRANZ, ALBERT 22 Rue D'Assault, Bruxelles, Belgium	Weinberger (Theatrical Material) *U.K.* Southern *U.S.A.*
CRANZ (AUG.) G.M.B.H. Elise-Kirchner-Str. 15, Wiesbaden- Biebrich, Germany	c/o United Mus. Publishers *U.K.*
CURCI, EDIZIONI, S.R.L. 4 Galleria Del Corso, Milan, Italy	Big 3 *U.S.A.*
CURWEN, J. & SONS LTD. 29 Maiden Lane, London, W.C. 2	G. Schirmer *U.S.A.*
CZECH STATE MUSIC *See* Artia	
DANIA, EDITION Kronprinsessegade 26, Copenhagen, Denmark	Chester *U.K.* Peters *U.S.A.*

138   *Appendix IIA*

Publisher and Address	*Agents in U.K. and/or U.S.A.*
DAREWSKI, HERMAN, MUSIC PUBLISHING CO.	
64 Dean St., London, W. 1	
DASH, IRWIN, MUSIC CO. LTD.	
10 Denmark St., London, W.C. 2	
DE RING	
17 Laurierstraat, Antwerp, Belgium	
DE SANTIS	Hinrichsen *U.K.*
Via Cassia 13, Rome, Italy	
DELRIEU & CIE	Galliard *U.K.*
41 Avenue De La Victoire, Nice, France	
DESCLÉE & CIE	Chester *U.K.*
13 Rue Barthélémy Frison, Tournai, Belgium	
DESSAIN, H.	United Mus. Publishers *U.K.*
Bleekstraat 9, Mechelen, Belgium	
DEUTSCHER VERLAG FÜR MUSIK	British & Continental *U.K.*
Karlstr. 10, Leipzig C.1, Germany	
DISNEY, WALT, MUSIC CO. LTD.	
52 Maddox St., London, W. 1	
2400 W. Alameda Av., Burbank, California, U.S.A.	
DITSON, OLIVER	Kalmus *U.K.*
Bryn Mawr, Pennsylvania, U.S.A.	Presser *U.S.A.*
DIX LTD.	
16 Soho Sq., London, W. 1	
Trade: 64 Dean St., London, W. 1	
DOBLINGER, MUSIKVERLAG	Kalmus *U.K.*
Dorotheergasse 10, Wien 1, Austria	Associated Mus. Publishers *U.S.A.*
DONEMUIS-FOUNDATION	Lengnick *U.K.*
Jacob Obrechtstr. 51, Amsterdam, Holland	Peters *U.S.A.*
DURAND & CIE	United Mus. Publishers *U.K.*
4 Place De La Madelaine, Paris, 8, France	Elkan–Vogel *U.S.A.*
ELKAN–VOGEL CO. INC.	United Mus. Publishers *U.K.*
1712–1716 Sansom St., Philadelphia 3, Pennsylvania, U.S.A.	
ELKIN & CO. LTD.	Galaxy *U.S.A.*
Borough Green, Sevenoaks, Kent	
ENGSTRØM & SØDRING MUSIKFORLAG	Hinrichsen *U.K.*
Palaisgade 6, Copenhagen K, Denmark	Peters *U.S.A.*

Publisher and Address	*Agents in U.K. and/or U.S.A.*
ENOCH & CIE 27 Boulevard Des Italiens, Paris 2, France	United Mus. Publishers *U.K.* Associated Mus. Publishers *U.S.A.*
ENOCH & SONS 19 Hanover Sq., London, W. 1	Boosey & Hawkes *U.S.A.*
ESCHIG, MAX 48 Rue De Rome, Paris 8, France	Schott *U.K.* Associated Mus. Publishers *U.S.A.*
EULENBURG, EDITION, G.M.B.H. Flössergasse 8, Zürich, Switzerland	Eulenburg *U.K.* Peters *U.S.A.*
EULENBURG, EDITION, INC. 373 Park Av. Sth., New York 16, N.Y., U.S.A.	Eulenburg *U.K.*
EULENBURG, ERNST, LTD. Cobbs Wood Estate, Brunswick Rd., Ashford, Kent	Peters *U.S.A.*
FABER MUSIC, LTD. 24 Russell Square, London, W.C. 1	G. Schirmer *U.S.A.*
FAITH PRESS, LTD. 7 Tufton St., London, S.W. 1	
FAZERIN MUUSIIKKIKAUPPA OY Aleksanterinkatu 11, Helsinki, Finland	Hinrichsen *U.K.*
FEIST, LEO INC. 799, 7th Av., New York 19, N.Y., U.S.A.	Big 3 *U.S.A.*
FELDMAN, B. & CO. LTD. 64 Dean St., London, W. 1	
FISCHER, CARL, INC. 62 Cooper Sq., New York 3, N.Y., U.S.A.	Hinrichsen *U.K.* (except Webern: Boosey)
FISCHER, J. & BRO. Harristown Rd., Glen Rock, New Jersey, U.S.A.	
FOETISCH FRERES 5–7 Rue Caroline, Lausanne, Switzerland	Chester *U.K.*
FORBERG, ROBERT Sedanstr. 18, Bad Godesberg, Germany	Hinrichsen *U.K.* Peters *U.S.A.*
FORLIVESI, A. CASA MUSICALE Via Rome 4, Firenze, Italy	Hinrichsen *U.K.* Ricordi *U.S.A.*
FORSYTH BROS. LTD. 190 Gray's Inn Rd., London, W.C. 1	
FOX, SAM, MUSIC PUBLISHING CO. 1841 Broadway, New York 23, N.Y., U.S.A.	Prowse *U.K.*

Publisher and Address	*Agents in U.K. and/or U.S.A.*
FRANCIS, DAY & HUNTER, LTD.	Big 3 *U.S.A.*
138 Charing Cross Rd., London, W.C. 2	
FREEMAN, E. H. LTD.	
95a St. George's Rd., Brighton, Sussex, England	
FRENCH, SAMUEL, LTD.	
26 Southampton St., London, W.C. 2	
FÜRSTNER, LTD.	Boosey & Hawkes *U.K.*
Flat 6, 40 Hyde Park Gate, London, S.W.	
GALAXY MUSIC CORP.	
2121 Broadway, New York 23, N.Y., U.S.A.	
GALLIARD, LTD.	
Queen Anne's Rd., Southtown, Great Yarmouth, Norfolk	
GAUDET, E., ÉDITIONS	Ricordi *U.S.A.*
4 Boulevard Bonne-Nouvelle, Paris 10, France	
GAY, NOEL, MUSIC CO. LTD.	
24 Denmark St., London, W.C. 2	
GEHRMANS, CARL, MUSIKFORLAG	Boosey & Hawkes (Orchestral only) *U.K.*
Vasagatan 46, Stockholm 1, Sweden	Boosey & Hawkes *U.S.A.*
	Elkan-Vogel *U.S.A.*
	Southern *U.S.A.* (Orchestral)
GLOCKEN VERLAG, LTD.	
33 Crawford St., London, W. 1	
Theobaldgasse 16, Wien 6, Austria	
GOODWIN & TABB, LTD.	Mills *U.S.A.*
36 Dean St., London, W. 1	Peters *U.S.A.*
GRAHL, H. L.	Hinrichsen *U.K.*
Günthersburger Allee 46, Frankfurt am Main, Germany	Peters *U.S.A.*
GRAY, H. W. CO. INC.	Novello *U.K.*
159 E. 48th St., New York 17, N.Y., U.S.A.	
GREGG INTERNATIONAL PUBLISHERS LTD.	
1 Westmead, Farnborough, Hants.	
GRUS, L. & CIE	
65 bis, Rue de Miromesnil, Paris 8, France	

Publisher and Address	*Agents in U.K. and/or U.S.A.*
GUTHEIL, A. G.M.B.H. 22 Rue d'Anjou, Paris 8, France Dessauerstr. 17, Berlin S.W. 11, Germany	Boosey & Hawkes *U.K. and U.S.A.*
GWYNN PUBLISHING CO. Llangollen, North Wales	
HAINAUER, JULIUS, LTD. 29 Cranbourne Gdns., London, N.W. 11	
HAMELLE, J. 22 Bd. Malesherbes, Paris 8, France	United Mus. Publishers *U.K.* Elkan-Vogel *U.S.A.*
HANSEN'S, WILHELM, MUSIKFORLAG Gethersgade 9, Copenhagen, Denmark	Chester *U.K.* G. Schirmer *U.S.A.*
HARGAIL MUSIC PRESS 157 W. 57th St., New York 19, N.Y., U.S.A.	
HARMS INC. 488 Madison Av., New York 22, N.Y., U.S.A.	Chappell *U.K.* Mus. Pub. Holding Corp. *U.S.A.*
HARMS, T. B. & CO. 1270, 6th Av., New York 20, N.Y., U.S.A.	Chappell *U.K. and U.S.A.*
HARRIS, FREDERICK, MUSIC CO. LTD. 14 Berners St., London, W. 1	
HASLINGER, CARL Tuchlauben 11, Wien 1, Austria	
HAWKES & SONS LTD. *See* Boosey & Hawkes	
HAYDN INSTITUT Karlsplatz 6, Wien 1, Austria	Kalmus *U.K.*
HAYDN-MOZART PRESSE Karlsplatz 6, Wien 1, Austria	Kalmus *U.K.* Associated Mus. Publishers *U.S.A.*
HEINRICHSHOFEN'S VERLAG Bremenstr. 52–58, Wilhemshaven, Germany	Hinrichsen *U.K.* Peters *U.S.A.*
HENLE, G., VERLAG Schöngauerstr. 24, München 55, Germany	Novello *U.K.* C. Fischer *U.S.A.*
HENN, ÉDITIONS 8 Rue de Hesse, Geneva, Switzerland	
HEUGEL & CIE (AU MÈNÈSTREL) 2 bis, Rue Vivienne, Paris 2, France	United Mus. Publishers *U.K.* Presser *U.S.A.*
HEUWEKEMEIJER, A. J. Bredeweg 21, Amsterdam-O, Holland	

142 *Appendix IIA*

Publisher and Address	*Agents in U.K. and/or U.S.A.*
HINNENTHAL, J. P. Königsbrügg 22, Bielefeld, Germany	Musica Rara *U.K.*
HINRICHSEN EDITION LTD. 10–12 Baches St., London, N. 1	Peters *U.S.A.*
HOFMEISTER, FRIEDRICH Eppsteinerstr. 43, Frankfurt am Main, Germany	Novello *U.K.*
HUDEBNI MATICE *See* Artia	
HUG & CO. Limmatquai 26–28, Zurich, Switzerland	Hinrichsen *U.K.* Peters *U.S.A.*
HUGHES & SON (PUBLISHERS) LTD. 29 Rivulet Rd., Wrexham, Denbighshire, N. Wales	
HUNGARIAN STATE MUSIC P.O.B. 149, Budapest 62, Hungary	Boosey & Hawkes *U.K.*
INTERNATIONAL MUSIC CO. 509, 5th Av., New York 17, N.Y., U.S.A.	
INTERNATIONAL MUSIC CO. LTD. 16, Mortimer St., London, W. 1	
INTERNATIONALE MUSIKLEIHBIBLIOTHEK, Brunnenstr. 188/190, Berlin, N. 54, Germany	
ISRAEL MUSIC INSTITUTE P.O. Box 6011, Tel-Aviv	Kalmus *U.K.*
ISRAELI MUSIC PUBLICATIONS P.O. Box 6011, Tel-Aviv, Israel	Chester *U.K.* Leeds *U.S.A.*
JOBERT, JEAN, ÉDITIONS 44 Rue Du Colisée, Paris 8, France	United Mus. Publishers *U.K.* Elkan-Vogel *U.S.A.*
JOUBERT & CIE 25 Rue D'Hauteville, Paris 10, France	United Mus. Publishers *U.K.*
JUNGNICKEL, ROSS 165 E. 35th St., New York	
JUNNE, OTTO Nerotal 16, Wiesbaden, Germany	
JÜRGENSON, P. *See* Russian State	
KAHNT, C. F. An Der Hofstatt 8, Lindau Bodensee, Germany	Novello *U.K.* Associated Mus. Publishers *U.S.A.*
KALLMEYER, GEORG, VERLAG *See* Möseler Verlag	

Publisher and Address	*Agents in U.K. and/or U.S.A.*

KALMUS, ALFRED A. LTD.
  2/3 Fareham St., London, W. 1
KALMUS, EDWIN F.   Kalmus, A. *U.K.*
  1345 New York Av., Huntington
  Station, Long Island, N.Y., U.S.A.
KEITH PROWSE
  See Prowse
KERR, JAMES S.
  79 Berkeley St., Glasgow C.3, Scotland
KING, ROBERT, MUSIC CO.
  7 Canton St., Nth. Easton, Mass,
  U.S.A.
KISTNER FR. & SIEGEL C. F., & CO.   Novello and Hinrichsen *U.K.*
  Luisenstr. 8, Lippstadt, Germany   Concordia (Organum series)
                                                  U.S.A.
KNEUSSLIN VERLAG   Musica Rara *U.K.*
  Amselstr. 43, Basel, Switzerland   Peters *U.S.A.*
KRENN, LUDWIG   Bosworth *U.K.*
  Reindorfgasse 42, Wien 15, Austria
KULTURA   Boosey & Hawkes *U.K. and*
  P.O.B. 149, Budapest 62, Hungary   *U.S.A.*
LAFLEUR & SON   Boosey & Hawkes *U.S.A.*
  See Boosey and Hawkes
LARWAY, J. H.
  19 Hanover Sq., London, W. 1
LAUDY & CO.
  See Bosworth
LAWSON–GOULD, MUSIC PUBLISHERS INC.   Curwen *U.K.*
  609 Fifth Avenue, New York 17
  N.Y., U.S.A.
LEDUC, ALPHONSE, & CIE   United Mus. Publishers *U.K.*
  175 Rue St. Honoré, Paris 1, France   Elkna-Vogel *U.S.A.*
LEEDS MUSIC CORPORATION   Leeds Music Ltd. *U.K.*
  322 W. 48th St., New York 36, N.Y.,
  U.S.A.
LEEDS MUSIC LTD.
  25 Denmark St., London, W.C. 2
LEMOINE, HENRI, & CIE   United Mus. Publishers *U.K.*
  17 Rue Pigalle, Paris 9, France   Elkan-Vogel *U.S.A.*
LENGNICK, ALFRED, & CO. LTD.   Mills *U.S.A.*
  Purley Oak Studios,
  421a Brighton Rd., S. Croydon, Surrey

Publisher and Address	*Agents in U.K. and/or U.S.A.*
LEONARD, GOULD & BOLTTLER *See* Cramer	
LEUCKART, F. E. C.	Novello *U.K.*
Prinzenstr. 7, München 19, Germany	Associated Mus. Publishers *U.S.A.*
LIBER-SOUTHERN, LTD.	Southern *U.S.A.*
8 Denmark St., London, W.C. 2	
LIENAU, ROBERT	Hinrichsen *U.K.* (except
Lankwitzerstr. 9, Berlin–Lichterfelde–	Sibelius, O.U.P.)
Ost., Germany	Peters *U.S.A.*
LITOLFF, HENRY, VERLAG	Hinrichsen *U.K.*
Forsthausstr. 101, Frankfurt am Main,	Peters *U.S.A.*
Germany	
LUNDQUISTS, ABRAHAM, MUSIKFÖRLAG	
Drottninggatan 26, Stockholm, Sweden	
LYCHE, HARALD, & CO.	Hinrichsen *U.K.*
Drammen, Norway	Peters *U.S.A.*
LYREBIRD PRESS	
See Oiseau–Lyre, Éditions De L'	
McGINNIS & MARX	Hinrichsen *U.K.*
408, 2nd Av., New York 10, N.Y., U.S.A.	Peters *U.S.A.*
MARGUERITAT, ÉDITIONS	
7 Cour Des Petites Ecuries, Paris 10, France	
MARKS, EDWARD B. MUSIC CORPORATION	Boosey & Hawkes
136 W. 52nd St., New York 19, N.Y., U.S.A.	
MAURICE, PETER, MUSIC CO. LTD.	
21 Denmark St., London, W.C. 2	
MERCURY MUSIC CORPORATION	Schott *U.K.*
47 W. 63rd St., New York 23, N.Y., U.S.A.	Presser *U.S.A.*
MERSEBURGER VERLAG	Hinrichsen *U.K.*
Alemannenstr. 20, Berlin–Nikolassee,	Peters *U.S.A.*
Germany	
METROPOLIS, S.P.R.L.	Hinrichsen *U.K.*
Avenue de France 24, Antwerp, Belgium	
METZLER & CO. LTD. *See* Cramer	
MILLS MUSIC, LTD.	
20 Denmark St., London, W.C. 2	
1619 Broadway, New York 19, N.Y., U.S.A.	

Publisher and Address	*Agents in U.K. and/or U.S.A.*
MODERN, EDITION	
Walhallastr. 7, München 19, Germany	
MOECK, HERMANN, VERLAG	Schott *U.K.*
Hannoverschestr. 43a, Celle, Germany	
MORRIS, EDWIN, & CO. LTD.	
52 Maddox St., London, W. 1	
35 W. 51st St., New York 19, N.Y., U.S.A.	
MÖSELER VERLAG	Novello *U.K.*
Gr. Zimmerhof 20, Wolfenbüttel, W. Germany	Presto *U.S.A.*
MOWBRAY, A. R. & CO. LTD.	
28 Margaret St., London, W. 1	
MURDOCH & CO.	Chappell *U.S.A.*
See Chappell	
MUSIC PRESS	Presser *U.S.A.*
See Mercury Music Corporation	
MUSIC PUBLISHERS HOLDING CORP.	
619 W. 54th St., New York 19, N.Y., U.S.A.	
MUSICA RARA	Presser *U.S.A.*
2 Gt. Marlborough St., London, W. 1	
MUSICALES TRANSATLANTIQUES, ÉDITIONS	United Mus. Publishers *U.K.*
14 Avenue Hoche, Paris 8, France	Presser *U.S.A.*
MUSICUS, ÉDITION	
333, W. 52nd St., New York 19, N.Y., U.S.A.	
MUSIKWISSENSCHAFTLICHER VERLAG	
See Hinrichsen	
NAGELS VERLAG	Associated Mus. Publishers *U.S.A.*
See Bärenreiter	
NOËL, PIERRE	United Mus. Publishers *U.K.*
24 Bd. Poissonnière, Paris 9, France	
NORDISKA MUSIKFÖRLAGET	Chester *U.K.*
Pipersgatan 29, Stockholm 0, Sweden	Novello (Orchestral) *U.K.*
NORSK MUSIKFORLAG	Chester *U.K.*
Karl Johansgt. 39, Oslo, Norway	Novello (Orchestral) *U.K.*
NOVELLO & CO. LTD.	Gray *U.S.A.*
Borough Green, Sevenoaks, Kent	
OERTEL, L.	
Kärntner Platz 2, Hannover–Waldhausen, Germany	

Publisher and Address	*Agents in U.K. and/or U.S.A.*
OISEAU-LYRE, ÉDITIONS DE L' Les Remparts, Monaco	United Mus. Publishers *U.K.*
OLSCHKI, LEO S. Via Delle Caldaie 14, Firenze, Italy	Hinrichsen, *U.K.*
OXFORD UNIVERSITY PRESS 44 Conduit St., London, W. 1 417, 5th Av., New York 16, N.Y., U.S.A.	
PARAGON MUSIC PUBLISHERS 57, 3rd Av., New York 3, N.Y., U.S.A.	Hinrichsen *U.K.*
PATERSON'S PUBLICATIONS LTD. 36–40 Wigmore St., London, W. 1	C. Fischer *U.S.A.*
PAXTON, W. & CO. LTD. 36–38 Dean St., London, W. 1	
PEER INTERNATIONAL 1619 Broadway, New York 19, N.Y., U.S.A.	Southern *U.K. and U.S.A.*
PEER MUSIKVERLAG G.M.B.H. Klärchenstr. 11, Hamburg 39, Germany	Liber-Southern *U.K.* Southern *U.S.A.*
PETERS, C. F. Forsthausstr. 101, Frankfurt am Main, Germany	Hinrichsen *U.K.* Peters *U.S.A.*
PETERS, C. F. CORPORATION 373 Park Av. Sth., New York 16, N.Y. U.S.A.	Hinrichsen *U.K.*
PETERS EDITION 10–12 Baches St., London, N. 1	Peters *U.S.A.*
PIGOTT & CO. LTD. 112 Grafton St., Dublin	Mills *U.S.A.*
POLSKIE WYDAWNICTWO MUZYCZNE Warszawa, Foksal 18, Poland	Kalmus *U.K.*
PRESSER, THEODORE, CO. Bryn Mawr, Pennsylvania, U.S.A.	Kalmus *U.K.*
PRESTO MUSIC SERVICE Box 10704, Tampa, Florida, U.S.A.	
PRO MUSICA VERLAG Leipzig, Germany	
PROWSE, KEITH, MUSIC PUBLISHING CO. LTD. 21 Denmark St., London, W.C. 2 *Trade:* 46 Gerrard St., London, W. 1	Fox *U.S.A.*
PUSTET, FRIEDRICH Gutenburgstr. 8, Regensburg, Germany	Hinrichsen *U.K.*

Publisher and Address	*Agents in U.K. and/or U.S.A.*
RAHTER, D.	Associated Mus. Publishers
See Benjamin	*U.S.A.*
REID BROS. LTD.	
See Ascherberg, Hopwood & Crew	
RICORDI, G. & CO. LTD.	Ricordi *U.S.A.*
The Bury, Church St., Chesham, Bucks.	
3 Rue Requepine, Paris 8, France	Ricordi *U.S.A.*
Via Berchet 2, Milan, Italy	Ricordi *U.S.A.*
16 W. 61st St., New York 23, N.Y., U.S.A.	
RIES & ERLER MUSIKVERLAG	Hinrichsen *U.K.*
Charlottenbrunnerstr. 42, Berlin-	Peters *U.S.A.*
Grünewald, Germany	
ROBBINS MUSIC CORP. LTD.	Big 3 *U.S.A.*
23 Denmark St., London, W.C. 2	
1540 Broadway, New York 36, N.Y., U.S.A.	
ROGERS, WINTHROP	
295 Regent St., London, W. 1	
ROUART, LEROLLE & CIE	
29 Rue D'Astorg, Paris 8, France	
ROZSAVÖLGYI	
See Kultura	
R.S.M.V.	
See Russian State Publication Co.	
RUSSE DE MUSIQUE, ÉDITION	Boosey & Hawkes *U.K. and*
22 Rue D'Anjou, Paris, France	*U.S.A.*
RUSSIAN STATE PUBLICATION CO. (MUSIC)	Leeds *U.S.A.*
Moscow 200, U.S.S.R.	
SALABERT, FRANCIS, ÉDITIONS	
22 Rue Chauchat, Paris 9, France	
SCHAUER, RICHARD	
239/241 Shaftesbury Av., London, W.C. 2	
SCHIRMER, E. C., MUSIC CO.	
600 Washington St., Boston 11, Mass. U.S.A.	
SCHIRMER, G. INC.	Chappell *U.K.*
609, 5th Av., New York 17, N.Y., U.S.A.	
SCHLESINGERSCHE MUSIKHANDLUNG	
See Lienau	

Publisher and Address	*Agents in U.K. and/or U.S.A.*
SCHMIDT, C. F.	Hinrichsen *U.K.*
Cäcilienstr. 62, Heilbronn, Germany	
SCHOLA CANTORUM, ÉDITIONS	United Mus. Publishers *U.K.*
76 bis, Rue Des Saints-Pères, Paris 7, France	Elkan–Vogel *U.S.A.*
SCHOTT & CO. LTD.	
48 Gt. Marlborough St., London, W. 1	Associated Mus. Publishers *U.S.A.*
30 Rue St. Jean, Bruxelles, Belgium	Peters *U.S.A.*
Weihergarten 5, Mainz, Germany	Associated Mus. Publishers *U.S.A.*
SCHULTHEISS, C. L., MUSIKVERLAG	Hinrichsen *U.K.*
Denzenbergstr 35, 74 Tübingen, Germany	
SCHWANN, L., MUSIKVERLAG	Hinrichsen *U.K.*
Charlottenstr. 80–86, Düsseldorf, Germany	
SÉNART, MAURICE, ÉDITIONS	United Mus. Publishers *U.K.*
See Salabert	Ricordi *U.S.A.*
SIKORSKI, HANS, VERLAG	Prowse *U.K.*
Johnsallee 23, Hamburg 13, Germany	
SIMROCK, N.	Associated Mus. Publishers *U.S.A.*
239/241 Shaftesbury Av., London, W.C. 2. *See also* LENGNICK	
Dorotheenstr. 176, Hamburg 39, Germany	
SIRIUS VERLAG	Hinrichsen *U.K.*
Wiclefstr. 67, Berlin N.W. 21, Germany	
SKANDINAVISK MUSIKFORLAG	Chester *U.K.*
Borgergade 2, Copenhagen, Denmark	
SONZOGNO, CASA MUSICALE	Ascherberg *U.K.*
Via Bigli 11, Milan, Italy	Associated Mus. Publishers *U.S.A.*
SOUTHERN MUSIC PUBLISHING CO. LTD.	
8 Denmark St., London, W.C. 2	
1619 Broadway, New York 19, N.Y., U.S.A.	
STAINER & BELL, LTD.	Galaxy *U.S.A.*
Lesbourne Road, Reigate, Surrey	
STEINGRÄBER VERLAG	Bosworth *U.K.*
Auf der Reiswiese 9, Offenbach am Main, Germany	

Publisher and Address	*Agents in U.K. and/or U.S.A.*

STERLING MUSIC PUBLISHING CO. LTD.
  50 New Bond St., London, W. 1
SUECIA, EDITION
  See Gehrmans Musikforlag
SUMMY–BIRCHARD PUBLISHING CO.   A. Kalmus *U.K.*
  1834 Ridge Av., Evanston, Illinois, U.S.A.
TISCHER & JAGENBERG
  Prinzenweg 3, Starnberg, Germany
TRANSATLANTIQUES, ÉDITIONS   United Mus. Publishers *U.K.*
  14 Av. Hoche, Paris 8, France   Presser *U.S.A.*
UGRINO VERLAG   Hinrichsen *U.K.*
  Elbchausee 499a, Hamburg–Blankensee,
  Germany
UNIÓN MUSICAL ESPAÑOLA S.A.   United Mus. Publishers *U.K.*
  Carrera de San Jeronimo, 26 Y Arenal   Associated Mus. Publishers
  18, Madrid, Spain   *U.S.A.*
UNITED MUSIC PUBLISHERS LTD.
  1 Montague St., London, W.C. 1
UNIVERSAL EDITION A.G.   Kalmus *U.K.*
  Karlsplatz 6, Wien, Austria   Associated Mus. Publishers
                                         U.S.A.

UNIVERSAL EDITION (LONDON) LTD.
  2/3 Fareham St., London, W. 1
URBÁNEK, FR. A.
  See Artia
VAN ROSSUM, J. R.   Hinrichsen *U.K.*
  Minnebroederstr. 1–3, Utrecht K,   World Library *U.S.A.*
  Holland
VICTORIA MUSIC PUBLISHING CO. LTD.
  52 Maddox St., London, W. 1
  1650 Broadway, New York 19, N.Y.,
  U.S.A.
VIEWEG VERLAG   Musica Rara *U.K.*
  Ringstr. 47a, Berlin–Lichterfelde-   Peters *U.S.A.*
  West, Germany
VIKING MUSIKFORLAG
  Norrebrogade 34, Copenhagen N.,
  Denmark
WALSH, HOLMES & CO. LTD.
  See Galliard
WEEKES, A. & CO. LTD.
  See Galliard

Publisher and Address	*Agents in U.K. and/or U.S.A.*
WEINBERGER, JOSEF, LTD.	
Steinweg 7, Frankfurt am Main, Germany	
33 Crawford St., London, W. 1	
Mahlerstr. 11, Wien 1, Austria	
WEINTRAUB MUSIC CO.	
240 W. 55th St., New York 19, N.Y., U.S.A.	
WILLIAMS, JOSEPH, LTD.	Mills *U.S.A.*
See Galliard	
WILLIAMSON MUSIC, INC.	Chappell *U.S.A.*
1270, 6th Av., New York 20, N.Y., U.S.A.	
14 St. George St., London, W. 1	
WITMARK, M. & SONS	Mus. Pub. Holding Corp.
488 Madison Av., New York 22, N.Y., U.S.A.	*U.S.A.*
WOOD, BRADBURY LTD.	
52 Maddox St., London, W. 1	
WORKERS' MUSIC ASSOCIATION	
136a Westbourne Terrace, London, W. 2	
WORLD LIBRARY OF SACRED MUSIC	
1846 Westwood Av., Cincinnati 14, Ohio, U.S.A.	
WRIGHT, LAWRENCE, MUSIC CO. LTD.	
19 Denmark St., London, W.C. 2	
YEAR BOOK PRESS	
See Ascherberg, Hopwood & Crew	
ZANIBON, G. C.	Hinrichsen *U.K.*
Piazza Dei Signori, Padova, Italy	Peters *U.S.A.*
ZERBONI, SUVINI, EDIZIONI	Hinrichsen *U.K.*
Galleria Del Corso 4, Milan, Italy	Associated Mus. Publishers *U.S.A.*
ZIMMERMANN, WILHELM, MUSIKVERLAG	Novello *U.K.*
Kronbergerstr. 30, Frankfurt am Main, Germany	Peters *U.S.A.*

APPENDIX IIB

Music Publishers' Organizations

INTERNATIONAL	Union Internationale des Éditeurs, Section des Éditeurs de Musique, 1 rue de Courcelles, Paris 8.
AUSTRIA	Verband der Bühnenverleger Österreichs, Kiningergasse 6, Wien 12.
BELGIUM	Chambre Syndicale des Éditeurs de Musique de Belgique, 13 rue de la Madeleine, Brussels.
DENMARK	Dansk Musik Forlaeggerforening, Borgargade 2, Copenhagen.
FINLAND	A. B. Fazers Musikhandel, Alexandersg. 11, Helsinki.
FRANCE	Chambre Syndicale des Éditeurs de Musique, 44 rue du Colisée, Paris 8.
GERMANY	Deutscher Musikverleger Verband, Vivatgasse 2, Bonn.
HOLLAND	Vereeniging van Muziekhandelaaren en Uitgevers in Nederland, Leidsegracht 11, Amsterdam.
ITALY	Unione Nazionale degli Editori di Musica (U.N.E.M.), via F. Sforza 1, Milan.
NORWAY	Norsk Musikkforleggerforening, Musik Huset A.S., Karl Johansgate 45, Oslo.
SWEDEN	Svenska Musikförläggare Föreningen, Postbox 16358, Stockholm.
SWITZERLAND	Association des Marchands et Editeurs de Musique en Suisse, 39 Avenue des Collèges, Pully-Lausanne.
UNITED KINGDOM	The Music Publishers' Association Ltd., 73 Mortimer Street, London W. 1.
U.S.A.	Music Publishers' Association of the U.S., 2 East 71st Street, New York 21.

APPENDIX IIC

Performing Rights and Collecting Societies

GENERALLY speaking, performing rights for all music (except large-scale choral works and musico-dramatic works) are vested in the national "performing right" society. Long choral works and stage works generally, including ballet, are controlled (during their term of copyright), both as to performing right and orchestral hire, directly by their publishers, or in the case of unpublished works by their individual copyright-owners. Concert-promoters are, therefore, advised to work through these agencies and the associated bodies, such as the Mechanical Copyright Protection Society Ltd., and Phonographic Performance Ltd., which handle recording rights. Revised lists, giving changes of address and much other non-musical information, appear from time to time in the journal *Interauteurs* (Paris, Confédération Internationale des Sociétés d'Auteurs et Compositeurs).

PERFORMING RIGHTS AND COLLECTING SOCIETIES

ARGENTINA	SADAIC	Sociedad Argentina de Autores y Compositores de Música, Lavalle 1547, Buenos Aires.
AUSTRALASIA	APRA	Australasian Performing Right Association Ltd., Box 4007, VV., G.P.O., Sydney, N.S.W.
AUSTRIA	AKM	Staatlich Genehmigte Gesellschaft der Autoren, Komponisten und Musik-verlage, Baumannstrasse 8, Vienna 3.
BELGIUM	SABAM	Société Belge des Auteurs, Compositeurs et Editeurs, 61 rue de la Loi, Brussels.
BRAZIL	UBC	Uniao Brasileiria de Compositores, 134, Rua Visconde de Inhauma, Rio de Janeiro.

154 *Appendix IIC*

CANADA	CAPAC	Composers, Authors and Publishers Association of Canada Ltd., 1263 Bay Street, Toronto 5, Ontario.
CHILE	UDC	Director del Departamento del Derecho de Autor de la Universidad de Chile, San Antonio No. 427, 2° piso, Santiago.
COLOMBIA	SAYCCO	Sociedad de Autores y Compositores de Colombia, 22–40 Avenida Caracas, Bogotá.
CZECHOSLOVAKIA	OSA	Ochranny Svaz Autorsky, Narodini Trida Cs. armady 20, Praha-Bubenec, Prague.
DENMARK	KODA	Internationalt Forbund til Beskyttelse af Komponistrettigheder i Danmark, 26 Kronprinsessegade, Copenhagen.
FINLAND	TEOSTO	Saveltajain Tekijanoikeustoimisto, Teosto p.y., Hietaniemenkatu 2, Helsinki.
FRANCE	SACEM	Société des Auteurs, Compositeurs et Éditeurs de Musique, 10 rue Chaptal, Paris 9.
GERMANY–EAST	AWA	Anstalt zur Wahrung der Aufführungsrechte auf dem Gebiete der Musik, Marx-Engels Platz 7, Berlin 12.
GERMANY–WEST	GEMA	Gesellschaft für Musikalische Aufführungs- und Mechanische Vervielfältigungsrechte, 37/38 Bayreuther Str., Berlin, W. 30.
GREECE	ESSE	Société Héllenique des Compositeurs, Auteurs et Éditeurs, 7 rue Botassi, Athens.
HOLLAND	BUMA	Het Bureau voor Muziek-Auteursrecht, Herengracht 458, Amsterdam-C.
HUNGARY	ARTISJUS	Le Bureau Hongrois pour la Protection des Droits d'Auteur, Naya u. 6, Budapest VII.
ICELAND	STEF	Sambond Tonskalda og Eigenda Flutningsrettar, Freyjugata 3, Reykjavik.
ISRAEL	ACUM	Acum, P.O.B. 11201, Tel-Aviv.
ITALY	SIAE	Società Italiana degli Autori ed Editori, Via Gianturco, 2, Rome.

JAPAN	JASRAC	Japanese Society of Rights of Authors and Composers, Tameike Meisan Building, 30 Akasaka Tameikecho, Minato-Ku, Tokyo.
MEXICO	SACM	Sociedad de Autores y Compositores de Mexico, S.C., Ponciano Arriaga No. 17, Mexico I, D.F.
NORWAY	TONO	Norsk Komponistforenings Internasjonale Musikkbyra, Klingenberg Gt. 5, Oslo 9.
POLAND	ZAIKS	Stowarzyszenie Autorów, 2 rue Hipoteczna, Warsaw 84.
PORTUGAL	SACTP	Sociedade de Escritores e Compositores Teatrais Portuguêses, Avenida Duque de Loulé No. III–IO, Lisbon.
SPAIN	SGAE	Sociedad General de Autores de España, Apartado 484, Calle Fernando VI, 4, Madrid.
SWEDEN	STIM	Föreningen Svenska Tonsättararna Internationella Musikbyra, Tegnerlunden 3, Stockholm.
SWITZERLAND	SUISA	Société Suisse des Auteurs et Éditeurs, Général–Guisan Strasse, 38, Zürich 2.
U.K.	PRS	Performing Right Society Ltd., Copyright House, 29 Berners Street, London, W. 1.
URUGUAY	AGADU	Asociación General de Autores del Uruguay, Calle Canelones No. 1130, Montevideo.
U.S.A.	ASCAP	The American Society of Composers, Authors and Publishers, 575 Madison Avenue, New York 22, N.Y. Broadcast Music Inc., 589 Fifth Avenue, New York 17, N.Y. SESAC Inc. The Coliseum Tower, 10 Columbia Circle, New York 19, N.Y.
YUGOSLAVIA	ZAMP	Zavodza Zaštitu Autorskih Malih Prava, Misarska 12–14, Belgrade.

Index

HOPKINSON, C. (*cont.*)
  Parisian music publishers 108
  Russian music publishers 108
HOŘEJŠ, A.: *Dvořák* 120
Horn 48
HORNBOSTEL, E. M. VON, instrument
  classification 124
HORNIMAN MUSEUM 156
Hospitals, music in 125
HUBERTY 108
HUGHES, G.: *Composers of operetta* 19
HUGHES, H.: *Irish country songs* 84
HUMPHRIES & SMITH: *Music publish-
  ing* 107, fig. 46
Hungarian folk-song 126
HUNT, E.: *The recorder* 47
HUNTINGTON LIBRARY 36
HUNTLEY, J.: *Film music* 122
HUNTLEY & MANVELL: *Technique of
  film music* 122
HUTCHESON, E.: *The literature of the
  piano* 43
HYMN SOCIETY 28
Hymnody 28
Hymns ancient and modern 28

Iconography 119–20
IDELSOHN, A. Z.: *Thesaurus of
  oriental Hebrew melodies* 87
Incidental music
  drama 13
  radio 95–6
Incipits 66–7
INCORPORATED SOCIETY OF MUSICI-
  ANS: *Handbook and register* 53
Incunables 63, 107–8
INDEPENDENT ELECTRONIC MUSIC
  CENTER 115
Indian dancing 88
INGHELBRECHT, D. E.: *The conductor's
  world* 9
INSEL VERLAG 80
INSTITUTE OF JAZZ STUDIES 93

Instrument, Das 124
Instrumentation 9
Instruments
  repertory 40 ff
  research 70, 123–4
Interlochen 42, 56
INTERNATIONAL ASSOCIATION OF
  MUSIC LIBRARIES 2, passim
*International catalogue of recorded folk-
  music* 82
International co-operation 54
*International directory of antiquarian
  booksellers* 80
INTERNATIONAL FOLK MUSIC
  COUNCIL 82, fig. 41
INTERNATIONALE LEIHBIBLIOTHEK 6
INTERNATIONAL MUSIC CENTRE,
  VIENNA 15
INTERNATIONAL MUSIC COUNCIL 54
International music educator 58
INTERNATIONAL MUSICOLOGICAL
  SOCIETY 62, 71
INTERNATIONAL PUBLISHERS' ASSOCI-
  ATION 110
INTERNATIONAL RECORD COLLECTORS'
  AGENCY 99
*International selection of contemporary
  music* (Donemus) 7
INTERNATIONAL SOCIETY FOR CON-
  TEMPORARY MUSIC 116
INTERNATIONAL SOCIETY FOR MUSIC
  EDUCATION 58
INTERNATIONALES MUSIKINSTITUT 6
INTERNATIONALES MUSIKER-BRIEF-
  ARCHIVS 118
Interpretation 27, 32–3, 61, 81
Invective 118
IRELAND, JOHN, SOCIETY 54
Irish folk-song 84
Irish harp 48
ISHAM MEMORIAL LIBRARY 63
ISRAELI MUSIC INSTITUTE: *Contem-
  porary harp music* 48

BARTÓK, Béla—Cont'd

620p **Concerto**..*U. E.*
    Solo—2 (2nd alt. Picc.), 2 (2nd alt. Engl. H.) 2, 2—4, 2, 3—Tymp.,
    Perc. (3 or 4 players)—Str.: 10, 10, 6, 6, 6   **23**
    comp. 1926; 1st perf. Frankfurt-on-Main, July 1, 1927, Furtwängler conducting, the composer at the Piano

BEETHOVEN, Ludwig van   Bonn-on-Rhine 1770—1827 Vienna

366p **op. 15, Concerto I, C major** ....*B. & H.*
    Cadenza to 1st movement by Julius Röntgen (*Alsbach*)
    Solo—1, 2, 2, 2—2, 2—Tymp.—Str.   **37**
    comp. about 1798; 1st perf. Prague 1798, Beethoven at the Piano

377p **op. 19, Concerto II, B♭ major.** ....*B. & H.*
    Cadenza to 1st movement by Julius Röntgen (*Alsbach*)
    Solo—1, 2, 0, 2—2 Horns—Str.   **28**
    comp. 1794/95; 1st perf. at the Vienna Burgtheater, March 29, 1795, Salieri conducting, Beethoven at the Piano; rev. 1798, and 1st perf. in rev. version. Prague, same year, Beethoven at the Piano

368p **op. 37, Concerto III, C minor**...*B. & H.*
    Cadenzas to 1st movement by Julius Röntgen (*Alsbach*) and Gabriel Fauré
    (*Magasin Musical Pierre Schneider*)
    Solo—2, 2, 2, 2—2, 2—Tymp.—Str.   **39**
    comp. 1800; 1st perf. at the Theater on der Wien, Vienna, April 5, 1803, Ignaz von Seyfried conducting, Beethoven at the Piano

369p **op. 58, Concerto IV, G major**..*B. & H.*
    Cadenzas to 1st and last (Rondo) movement by Julius Röntgen (*Alsbach*),
    to Rondo also by Wilhelm Backhaus (*Heinrichshofen*)
    Solo—1, 2, 2, 2—2, 2—Tymp.—Str.   **30**
    comp. 1805, compl. 1806; 1st perf. privately March 1807; in public Vienna, Dec. 22, 1808, Ignaz von Seyfried conducting, Beethoven at the Piano

363p **op. 73, Concerto V, E♭ major (called the "Emperor" Concerto)**...*B. & H.*
    Solo—2, 2, 2, 2—2, 2—Tymp.—Str.   **35**
    comp. 1809; 1st perf. Leipzig, Nov. 28, 1811, J. Ph. Ch. Schulz conducting, Friedrich Schneider at the Piano

*590p **op. 80, Phantasie for Piano, chorus and orchestra, C minor**.......*B. & H.*
    Solo—2, 2, 2, 2—2, 2—Tymp.—Str.—Vocal chorus quartet   **19**
    comp. summer 1808; 1st perf. at the Theater an der Wien, Vienna, Dec. 22, 1808, Ignaz von Seyfried conducting, Beethoven at the Piano

452p **Concerto, D major (1st movement), posthumous work with**
    cadenza by Josef Labor....................................*B. & H.*
    Solo—1, 2, 0; 2—2, 2—Tymp.—Str.   **12**
    comp. between 1788 and 1793

591p **Rondo, B♭ major (posthumous work)**...........................*B. & H.*
    Solo—1, 2, 0, 2—2 Horns—Str.   **10**
    comp. in Vienna about 1795

BENEDICT, Jules (Sir Julius)   Stuttgart (Germany) 1804—1885 London

689p **op. 18, Concertino, A flat major**............................*Hofmeister*
    Solo—2, 2, 2, 2,—2, 2—Tymp.—Str.   Score in MS

BENNETT (Sir) William Sterndale   Sheffield 1816—1875 London

669p **op. 19, Concerto IV, F minor**............................*Kistner & S.*
    Solo—2, 2, 2, 2—2, 2—Tymp.—Str.   Score in MS   **22**
    1st perf. at the Leipzig Gewandhaus, Jan. 17, 1838, the composer at the Piano

668p **op. 22, Capriccio, E major**...............................*Kistner & S.*
    Solo—2, 2, 2, 2—2, 2—Tymp.—Str.   Score in MS   **8**
    comp. at Leipzig 1840/41

FIG. 1. The Edwin A. Fleisher Music Collection. Philadelphia, 1966.

Komponist / Werk	Gattung	Spieldauer	Verlag
A little Symphony	O	20	OUP
Symphonie für Streicher	StO	23	Nov
2. Symphonie C-dur	O	32	JW
Variationen über ein Originalthema	O	23	JW
William Byrd Suite	O	13	Bo & Ha
Jacobi, Frederick			
Indianische Tänze	O	16'30	UE
Konzert für Violoncello u. Orch.	Vc/O	18	UE
Jacobi, Wolfgang			
Capriccio für Klav. u. Orch.	K/O	14'20	Mod
Musik für Streichorch. (Preludio, Elegia, Scherzo, Notturno)	KO	14	Gg
Jacobson, Maurice			
David Ballett, Suite	O	33	Cu
Symphonic Suite	StO	23	Cu
Jahnen, Gerd			
Galante Story! Mod. Impression	O	ca. 5	Ama
Souvenier de France, mod. Impression	O	ca. 5	Ama
Tausend kleine Dinge, mod. Skizze	O	ca. 3	Ama
Janáček, Leos			
Die Abenteuer des Herrn Broucek, Oper in 2 Teilen, Dichtung von V. Dyk u. Fr. Prochazka	Oper	abdf	UE
Adagio für Orch.	O	6	AE
Amarus, Kantate	SiGCh/O	30	AP
Tagebuch eines Verschollenen	Ges/O	38	AP
Aus einem Totenhaus, Oper in 3 Akten (4 Bildern) n. d. Roman von Dostojewsky			
„Memoiren aus einem Totenhaus", deutsch von Max Brod	Oper	abdf	UE
Dostojewsky-Ouvertüre	O	6	UE
Suite a. d. Oper „Aus einem Totenhaus"	O	22	UE
Die Ballade vom Berge Blanik	O	8	AP
Eifersucht	O	6	AE
Das ewige Evangelium	SiGCh/O	21	AP
Festliche Messe für Soloquartett, gem. Chor u. Orch.	SiGCh/O	48	UE
Idylle, Suite für Streichorch.	StO	21	AP
Jenufa, Oper a. d. mährischen Bauernleben in 3 Akten von Gabriele Preissora, deutsch			
von Max Brod	Oper	abdf	UE
Jenufa Rhapsodie, bearb. von Max Schönherr	O	25	UE
Katja Kabanova, Oper in 3 Akten nach Ostrowskijs „Gewitter", deutsch von Max Brod	Oper	abdf	UE
Das Kind des Musikanten	O	12	AP
Kinderreime für Kammerchor u. 10 Instrum.	KaCh/KlO	15	UE
Kozacek	O	4	AE
6 lachische Tänze	O	18'30	UE
6 mährische Tänze	O	25	AE
Die Sache Makropulos, Oper in 3 Akten nach dem Drama von Karl Capek.			
Für die deutsche Bühne übersetzt u. bearb. von Max Brod	Oper	abdf	UE
Sarka, Oper in 3 Akten, Text von Jul. Zeyer	Oper	abdf	UE
Serbischer Kolo	O	3	AE
Sinfonietta	O	25	UE
Suite, op. 3 (aus dem Nachlaß)	O	16	UE
Suite, op. 3 in 4 Sätzen	O	14	AP
Suite für Streichorch.	StO	18	UE
Die Schenke in den Bergen	SMCh/O	8	AP
Schicksal, Oper in Vorspiel, 2 Akten u. Nachspiel	Oper	abdf	AE
Das schlaue Füchslein, Oper in 3 Akten n. Tesnohlideks Novelle, deutsch von Max Brod	Oper	abdf	UE
2 sinfonische Fragmente aus „Das schlaue Füchslein", einger. v. Manfred Willfort	O	ca. 20	UE
Taras Bulba, Rhapsodie für Orch.	O	ca. 25	UE

FIG. 2. *Bonner Katalog*. Bonn, Musikhandel–Verlagsgesellschaft, 1959.

COMPOSER & WORKS	INSTRUMENTATION	DURATION	MATERIAL FROM
COPLAND, Aaron (Continued)			
STATEMENTS (IN 6 MOVTS.)	*3,*3,*3,*3 - 4,3,3,1 - timp.,perc. (4) - str.	18½'	Bo.Hawkes
"STOMP YOUR FOOT" FROM THE OPERA "THE TENDER LAND" (FOR MIXED CHORUS & ORCH.)	2,2,2,2 - 2,2,2,0 - perc. - pf. - str.		Bo.Hawkes
SYMPHONY NO. 1	3,3,3, alto sax.,3 - 8,5,3,1 - timp.,perc., cel. - 2 hp. - pf. - str.	25'	Bo.Hawkes
SHORT SYMPHONY (SYMPHONY NO. 2) 1. Allegro; 2. Lento; 3. Allegro	*3,*3,*3,*3 - 4,2,0,0 - pf. - str.	15'	Bo.Hawkes
SYMPHONY NO. 3 1. Molto moderato; 2. Allegro molto; 3. Andantino quasi allegretto; 4. Molto deliberato (fanfare) - allegro risoluto	3(2 alt. with picc.),*3, E^b cl., *3,*3 - 4,4,3,1 - timp.,perc. (5), cel., glock., xyl. - 2 hp. - pf. - str.	40'	Bo.Hawkes
SYMPHONY FOR ORGAN & ORCH.	3,3,3, alto sax. (ad lib.),3 - 4,3,3,1 - timp., perc., cel. - 2 hp. - org. - str.	25'	Bo.Hawkes
SYMPHONIC ODE (REVISED 1955)	2 picc.,2,*4,1 E^b cl.,*3,*4 - 8,4,3,1 - timp., perc. (4), bells, cel., glock., xyl. - 2 hp. - pf. - str.	21'	Bo.Hawkes
"THE TENDER LAND" (SUITE FROM THE OPERA)	3,2,2,2 - 4,3,3,1 - timp.,perc. - hp. - pf. - str.	18½'	Bo.Hawkes
TWO PIECES FOR STRING ORCHESTRA	str.	11'	Bo.Hawkes
COPLAND, Aaron - FINE, Irving			
OLD AMERICAN SONGS: SET NO. 1 (FOR SOLI, CHORUS & ORCH.)	1,2,1,1 - 1,1,1,0 - hp. - str.	13'	Bo.Hawkes
COPLAND, Aaron - GREEN, Johnny			
FANTASIA MEXICANA (BASED ON "EL SALON MEXICO")	1,1,2,2 - 2,2,3,0 - timp.,perc. (2) - str.		Bo.Hawkes
COPPOLA, Piero			
INTERLUDE DRAMATIQUE	3,3,3,4 - 4,3,3,1 - timp.,perc. - 2 hp. - str.	10'	Ricordi
SYMPHONY IN A MINOR	3,3,3,4 - 4,3,3,1 - timp.,perc., cel. - 2 hp. - str.	30'	Ricordi
CORELLI, A. - BARBIROLLI, John			
CONCERTO FOR OBOE & STRINGS	ob. - str.	10'	Bo.Hawkes
CONCERTO GROSSO (FROM VIOLIN SONATAS OF ARCANGELO CORELLI) (IN 4 MOVTS.)	str..		Oxford
CORELLI, A. - BAZELAIRE			
ADAGIO FOR CELLO & STRING ORCH.	str.	4½'	Baron
CORELLI, A. - BROWN			
SONATA DA CAMERA NO. 7	pf. - str.		Galaxy
SONATA DA CAMERA NO. 8	pf. - str.		Galaxy
SONATA DA CAMERA NO. 9	pf. - str.		Galaxy
SONATA DA CAMERA NO. 10	pf. - str.		Galaxy
CORELLI, A. - BRUNI, M.			
SONATA DA CHIESA, OP. 3, NO. 12 (FOR STRINGS)	str.		Henmar
CORELLI, A. - DORATI, Antal			
CONCERTO GROSSO NO. 1 IN D MAJOR			A.P.R.A
CORELLI, A. - DUBENSKY, A.			
CONCERTO GROSSO IN D MINOR (FOR STRINGS)	str.		Ricordi

FIG. 3. *ASCAP Symphonic Catalog.* New York, 1959.

Majestät dem Könige Friedrich Wilhelm IV. von Preußen in tiefster Ehrfurcht zugeeignet von den Verlegern.

Wien: Artaria & Comp. 178 S. VN: 3163.

Erste vollständige Ausgabe der Partitur nach dem Original-Manuskripte.

43 BEETHOVEN, LUDWIG VAN

Die Ruinen von Athen. Fest- und Nachspiel von August von Kotzebue. Op. 113.
Leipzig: Breitkopf & Härtel.
(Werke. Kritische Gesamtausgabe. Serie 20. Nr. 207ª.)
Riemann 489, Sonneck 13.

44 BEETHOVEN, LUDWIG VAN

König Stephan. Vorspiel von August von Kotzebue. Op. 117.
Leipzig: Breitkopf & Härtel.
(Werke. Kritische Gesamtausgabe. Serie 20. Nr. 207ᵇ.)
Sonneck 13.

45 BELLINI, VINCENZO

Norma. Tragedia lirica in due atti di Felice Romani. Musica di Vincenzo Bellini. Prima rappresentazione: Milano teatro alla Scala 26 dicembre 1831.

Milano: Ricordi. (1915). 4 Bl. 429 S. VN: 115 216. 8⁰.

Clément 786, Riemann 368, Towers 458.

46 BELLINI, VINCENZO

La Sonnambula. Del sige. mro. Bellini. Atto 1. 2. [Text von Felice Romani.]

2 Bde. 290 Bl. [Hs.] qu. 4⁰.

Clément 1040, Riemann 529, Towers 596.

47 BENDA, GEORG

Ariadne auf Naxos. Ein Duodrama von Georg Benda. Vollständige und verbesserte Partitur. Ariane à Naxos. Duodrame par George Benda.

18

FIG. 4. *Katalog der Musikbibliothek Paul Hirsch, Band 2: Opernpartituren.* Berlin, Breslauer, 1930.

Based on Upton's "The Standard Operas" (1885), rev & enl by Borowski 1933.

WILLIAMS, STEPHEN
Come to the opera! Forew Sir Thomas Beecham. 302 p, mus ex. Beechhurst 1948.   3.00

Some 57 operas with an index of characters.

OPERA (4. Metropolitan Opera Company & House)

See also:

America (music in)	Lehmann
I. Cook	Opera-1 (esp Marek)
Galli-Curci	Opera-3 (esp Cross,
Gatti-Casazza	Milligan, Peltz)
History	App IIb (Dike)

Standard works apparently O/P include those by Knight, Peltz, Sanborn, etc.

KOLODIN, IRVING
The Metropolitan opera, 1883–1939. Intro W. J. Henderson. xxi, 646 p, illus. Oxford (1936) 2nd rev enl ed 1940; Knopf new ed 1951, in prep.   △
A detailed record including much original research, with repertory table, record of casts of premières, noted débuts, etc.

PELTZ, MARY ELLIS
Behind the gold curtain: the story of the Metropolitan Opera, 1883–1950. Forew Mrs August Belmont. 96 p, illus. Farrar Straus 1950.   2.50
A history of the Met. illustrated with some 100 photographs.

Metropolitan opera milestones. Forew Mrs August Belmont. v, 74 p, illus, bibl, bds. Metropolitan Opera Guild Inc., N. Y., 1944.   1.00
A brief summary of the Met's history.

PELTZ, MARY ELLIS & LAWRENCE, ROBERT
The Metropolitan opera guide: the standard repertory of the Metropolitan Opera Association, Inc. as selected by Edward Johnson, general manager. Forew Mrs August Belmont. 497 p, illus (Alexandre Serebriakoff), mus ex, 6–p bibl. Modern Library 1939 (7th pr 1947).   2.45
Includes synopses of the plots.

SELTSAM, WILLIAM H. *(compiler)*
Metropolitan opera annals: a chronicle of artists & performances. Intro Edward Johnson. xvi, 751 p, 127 photos. Wilson 1947, 2nd cor pr 1949.   7.00
Published in association with the Metropolitan Opera Guild. Tabulated data, season by season, 1883–1947, of personnel, programs, casts, etc., with excerpts from press reviews.

(Same), Index to composers; lists of errata. 6 p, paper. Wilson 1949.   △
Supplementary material to "Metropolitan opera annals"; bound in the 2nd printing, supplied gratis by the publishers (on application) to purchasers of the 1st edition.

OPERETTA/OPÉRA-COMIQUE

See also:

Amateur Music	History
(Korn)	Opera-1
America (music in)	Opera-3
Appreciation	(esp McSpadden)
California (Gagey)	Poetry (ed Boas)
Community Music	Popular Music
Composers (& under	Program Music
names of individuals)	Rodgers & Hart
Gershwin	School Music
Gilbert & Sullivan	Theater
Hammerstein	

Standard works apparently O/P include those by Beach, Mackinlay, McSpadden (but see Opera-3), etc.

BEACH, FRANK A.
Preparation and presentation of the operetta. Forew Wm. Allen White. 204 p, illus, 2–p bibl. Ditson 1930.   2.00
Practical manual, primarily for school use.

COOPER, MARTIN
Opéra comique. 72 p, 4 col pl, 30 b&ws, mus ex. Chanticleer 1949.   2.50
"World of Music" series No 7. A survey-history, stressing the "golden age" of opéra-comique in France in the 18th century.

GENEST, EMILE. See App Ia.

HADAMOWSKY, FRANZ & OTTE, HEINZ. See App Ib.

JONES, CHARLES T. H. & WILSON, DON
Musico-dramatic producing: a manual for the stage & musical director. 140 p, photos, drwgs (Clark Fiers & Karl Bradley, facs, mus ex, paper. Gamble (1930), 2nd rev enl ed 1939.   1.50
Practical advice, especially for producing school & amateur operettas.

SMITH, CECIL
Musical comedy in America. x, 374 p + 64 pl (pors, facs, etc). Theatre Arts 1950.   5.00
An informal historical survey of the popular musical stage on Broadway from "The Black Crook" to "South Pacific."

UMFLEET, KENNETH R.
School operettas and their production. 128 p, illus, 2–p bibl. Birchard 1929.   2.00
Practical manual, including classified lists of recommended operettas.

FIG. 5. *Schirmer's Guide to Books on Music,* by R. D. Darrell. G. Schirmer, New York, 1951.

MASS

Sine Nomine

GLORIA

MSS. authority see p. lii.   (1) b: om. Pet. 35.   (2) C: Tenb. 357.   (3) b: om. Pet. 35.   (4) F: Pet. 32.   (5) add. ♯: Tenb. 358.   (6) b: om. Pet 27, 32.

FIG. 6. *Tudor Church Music*. O.U.P., 1923.

CARMEN, Johannes (14th. - 15th. cent.)
COMPOSITIONS, 3.
1. Venite adoremus dominum; Salve sancta eterna trinitas.)   ed.Reaney
2. Salve pater, creator omnium; Felix et beata   )   Mus.Ref.Lib.
3. Pontifici decori speculi   )   Copp.Mens.Mus./11.1.
1 only: 2-part, bssn. cont.   ed.Reaney   Lat.   Photo[Corp.Mens.Mus]   3931
2 only: SSTT, & insts.   trans.Reaney, ed.D.Stevens.   Fr.Lat.   MS[Bib.Paris]   6050

CARNAZZI
MASS à 3 concertanti, & cont.   ed.Commer   Lat.Ger.   (in vol.)   Bote & Bock

CARNE, Gerald
The BALLAD OF JOSING FJORD: TTBB, acc.   arr.Woodgate   2'50"   A. H. & C. (1940)   965

CAROLS
These will be most conveniently traced through the Title Index, but below is given
a selection of the bestknown anthologies held in the Library:-

Cambridge Carol Book	ed.Wood & Woodward	Mowbray
Carols, 58 traditional; 1st. & 2nd. Bks.	ed. & arr. Dunstan	Reid
Carols, twice 33.	arr. G.Shaw	Boosey & Hks.
The Carol Descant Book	arr. Chambers	Novello 10622-24
Christmas Carols, 10: SSA	arr. Cope	Boosey & Hks.
Christmas Carols, 12: SATB	arr. Terry	Curwen
Christmas Carols, 24: male voices	arr. Stainer & Bramley	Novello
Chrsitmas Carols, 101	"Star" edition	Paxton (1931)
Christmas Carols	arr. Walford Davies	Novello (4667
Christmas Carols, New & Old	ed. Stainer & Bramley	Novello
Christmas-tide Carols; 1st. & 2nd. series	arr. Martin	Novello
Cowley Carol Book	ed.Wood & Woodward	Mowbray
Czech Folk-carols, 24: unis. & SATB	arr. Grimes	Freeman
English Carol Book	ed. M.Shaw	Mowbray
English Traditional Carols	arr. Vaughan Williams & Shaw	O.U.P.
Flemish & other Christmas Carols	arr. D.S.Smith	S. & Bell (1938)
Folk Carols, 200	ed. Terry	Burns Oates

      English Traditional Carols   French Traditional Carols
      Besancon Noëls   Bearnaise and Burgundian Noëls
      Provençal Carols   Basque Carols
      Dutch and Flemish Carols   Italian Carols
      German, Alsatian & Polish Carols   European Medieval Carols
      English Medieval Carols

Folk-song Carols	arr. Sharp	Novello
An Italian Carol Book	ed. Wood & Woodward	Faith Press 10051
Mediaeval Carols; (Musica Britannica, Vol/4)	ed. J.Stevens	S. & Bell 9948-9956
A Medieval Carol Book	ed.Terry Lat.Eng.	Curwen 10070
Old Christmas Carols	arr. D.Smith	S. & Bell 10056
Old English Carols, 4: soli, & SATB	arr. G.Holst	Bayley & Ferg. 874
Old French & Czechoslovakian Carols	arr. Donovan	S. & Bell 10058
Old French & Franconian Carols	arr. Smith	S. & Bell 10054
Old French & German Carols	arr. Smith	S. & Bell 10055
Old French & Polish Carols	arr. Smith	S. & Bell 10057
Oxford Book of Carols	ed. Dearmer, Williams & Shaw	O.U.P.
Provençal & Russian Carols	arr. Smith	S. & Bell 10060
Traditional Basque & Flemish Carols	arr. Smith	S. & Bell 10059
Traditional Christmas Carols, 8.	arr. Smith	S. & Bell 10053
Traditional French Noëls, 8.	arr. Smith	S. & Bell 10052

CARON, Philippe (15th. cent.)
MASS; L'Homme armé
†   Agnus Dei: SCTB   ed.Smijers   Lat.   (in vol.)   Alsbach

CARPENTER, John Alden (1876 - 1951)
SONG OF FAITH: mixed chorus, acc. orch.   11'45"   G.Schirmer (orch.MS.   8332

CARPENTRAS   see:- GENET, Elzéar

CARON, Philippe
MASS : L'homme armé   SATB   ed.L.Feininger   Mus.Ref.Lib.   Mon.Poly.Lit.I/1-3.(1948)

FIG. 7. *B.B.C. Choral and Opera Catalogue.* B.B.C., 1967.

American Songs Employing Agility

Coloratura Soprano

Beach	Fairy lullaby			ASC
Buzzi-Peccia	Under the greenwood tree	LMH	EF-A	DIT
Charles	Let my song fill your heart	LH	EF-AF	GSC
Clough- Leighter	My lover he comes on on the skee·	HM	D-F	BOS
Crist	O come hither	HM	B-GS	CFI
Curran	Ho! Mr. Piper	LH	D-G	GSC
Gaynor	Pierrot	H	E-B	BOS
La Forge	Come unto these yellow sands	H	FS-B	GSC
Lubin	The piper	H	C-A	GSC
Manning	Shoes	M	EF-F	GSC
Menotti	Lucy's arietta (The Telephone)			GSC
Nordoff	There shall be more joy	M	CS-FS	AMP
Parker	The lark now leaves her watery nest	LH	D-BF	JCH
Treharne	A widow bird sat mourning	H	FS-AF	BOS

British Songs and Arias
Employing Agility

Coloratura Soprano

Arne, M.	The lass with the delicate air	MH	D-G	†
Arne, T.	Where the bee sucks	HM		†
Bainton	The nightingale near the house			CUR
Bax	Shieling song	H	CS-A	CHE
Benedict	The carnival of Venice	H	D-EF	GSC
-----	The gypsy and the bird Flute	H	D-E	GSC
-----	The wren Flute	H	F-C	PRE
Besley	Listening	H	E-AF	CUR
Bishop	Echo song Flute	H	D-C	GSC
-----	Lo! here the gentle lark Flute	H		†
-----	Love has eyes	M		†

43

FIG. 8. *The Singer's Repertoire*, 2nd edn., by B. Coffin. New York,
Scarecrow Press, 1960.

Owre the water to Charlie. See "Come boat me o'er, come row me o'er"

Oxenford, Edward
Funiculi, funicula (Denza)

Oxenford, John .
Around me, blessed image, ever soar (Irish air)
The bell ringer (Wallace)
"Like the lark" (Abt)
Smile, my Kathleen, pray (Irish air)
"'Tis no time to take a wife" (Irish air)

Oxford cries. See "Chairs to mend, old chairs to mend" (Hayes)

The Oxford tragedy. See The miller's apprentice

"Oy, yiboneh yiboneh yiboneh yiboneh hamikdosh." See May the temple be rebuilt

Oysters and wine at 2 A.M. Old song. SW

P

P. T. Barnum's show. Air: Menagerie. SRW

"Pa bryd y deui eto" ("When will you come, my sweeting") Old Welsh song. Modern words by W. Ifan. e.w. WO

"Pa, this same day." C. Lecocq. (Tr of Père adoré, c'est Girofié) e. WLO

Pacini, Giovanni
Ah! con lui mi fu rapita (from Saffo)

Pacius, Friedrich
"Our land." See Vårt land, vårt fosterland
Vårt land, vårt fosterland

A pack of cards. Old song. SW

Paddy Doyle ("To my way-a-y-ay ah") Short drag chantey. WSE
For variants see following songs of similar title

Paddy Doyle's boots ("To my way-ay-ay-ah") Bunt chantey. TSB 1

Paddy Doyle's boots ("To my way-ay-ay-yah") Bunt chantey. SBS

Paddy Duffy's cart. D. Braham. Words by E. Harrigan. SRW

Paddy works on the railway. Capstan chantey. TSB 2
Variant of: Poor Paddy works on the railway

Padilla, José
"Little Princess." See Princesita
Princesita

Page, E. V.
Lardy dah

Page, Edgar
Beulah land (Sweney) Authorship uncertain

"Pai, pai, paitaressu." See Lullaby (Merikanto)

The pain of love. See Heimlicher liebe pein (Weber)

Paine, Robert Treat
Adams and liberty (Smith?)

Paine, T.
The old cabin home

¡Páisdín fionn! An páistín fionn (Blonde Paistín) Irish folk song. g.ir. ML 1

Paisley, William M.
Razorback rootin' song

An páistín fionn. See Páisdín fionn

Un pajarito (A fickle maiden) Mexican folk song. e.s. HE

Paladilhe, Émile
The mandolin song. See Mandolinata
Mandolinata (with words "O I'm a happy creature")

Palestrina, Giovanni Pierluigi da
"Gloria Patri"
"Glory to God." See "Gloria Patri"
The strife is o'er; the battle done (Tr of Finita jam sunt praelia)

"Pali synephias' oyrhanos." See Waisenkind

The Palisades. New York university alma mater. D. M. Genns (music and words) AIS—KU—KV
The grim grey Palisades. AI
"O grim, grey Palisades." LAS

Palm branches ("Sur nos chemins") See Les rameaux (Faure)

Palmer, John F.
The band played on (Ward)

Palmer, John Williamson
Stonewall Jackson's way (Composer unknown) Authorship uncertain

Palmer, Ray
"My faith looks up to Thee" (Mason)

Palmgren, Selim
Autumn. See Höst
"The golden day is dying" Höst
I vassen
In the willows. See I vassen
Liljekonvalje
Lily of the valley. See Liljekonvalje

The palms. See Les rameaux (Faure)

Die palmweide (Raita) Finnish folk song. fi.g. ML 3

La paloma azul (The blue dove) Mexican folk song. e.s. VS

Palomero, M. E.
Princesita (Padilla)

"Pan ddelo'r haf a'i flodau fyrdd." See Blodau'r cwm

"Pan oeddwn ar frig noswaith." See Y gwŷdd

"Pan oeddwn i'n fugail yn hafod y rhyd." See Bugail yr hafod

Pancakes ("Mother off to the market goes") Russian folk song. e. MFF

Pancakes! pancakes! joy and good luck to all at home. See La chanson des beignets

Panchenko, S. W.
Ah, if mother Volga
"Oh, if mother Volga." See Ah, if mother Volga

Pah's holiday. F. Bridge. Words by J. Shirley. CSB 4

Pansies. W. R. Cox. Words by J. W. Riley. BST

FIG. 9. *Song Index*, ed. M. E. Sears. New York, H. W. Wilson, 1926.

the PILGRIM, *being the last* | *Writeings of* M: Dryden. *1700.* |
[triple rule] | *London* | [triple rule] | *Sould by I : Walſh Muſicall
Inſtrument maker in Ordinary* | *to his Majesty, at the Golden Harpe
and Hoboy in Cathe⸗* | *⸗rine Street, near Summerset House in the
Strand* | [fig. 40]

2°. No signatures. 5 leaves, unpaged. f. [1] title-page; f. [1]ᵛ blank. Engraved
throughout, on one side of paper only.

4 songs, by D. Purcell.

S. R.: no entry. T. C.: no entry. Advertised in *The Post Boy* (no. 806) on 8 June
1700.

Copy: HD.

185 [within a double rule] AN | INTRODUCTION | TO THE |
𝕾kill of 𝕸uſick: | In THREE BOOKS: | [rule] | By *JOHN
PLAYFORD.* | [rule] | CONTAINING | I. The *Grounds* and
Principles of MUSICK, | according to the *Gamut*: In the moſt
Ea- | ſie Method, for Young Practitioners. | II. Inſtructions and
Leſſons for the *Treble,* | *Tenor* and *Baſs-Viols*; and alſo for the |
Treble-Violin. | III. The Art of *Deſcant,* or Compoſing *Muſick* |
in Parts: Made very Plain and Eaſie by the | late Mr. HENRY
PURCELL. | [rule] | 𝕿he 𝕱ourteenth 𝕰dition. | Corrected and En-
larged. | [rule] | *LONDON:* printed by *William Pearſon,* at the
Hare and | *Feathers* in *Alderſgate-ſtreet,* for *Henry Playford,* at his |
Shop in the *Temple-Change, Fleet-ſtreet.* 1700.

Title-page of Book II on sig. E7:

AN | INTRODUCTION | To the Playing on the | *Baſs, Tenor,*
and *Treble-Viols;* | And alſo on the | 𝕿reble-𝖁iolin, | [rule] |
BOOK II. | [rule | group of type-ornaments | double rule] |
Printed in the Year M DCC.

Title-page of Book III on sig. H3:

AN | INTRODUCTION | TO THE | 𝕬rt of 𝕯eſcant : |
Or, Compoſing | MUSICK | In *PARTS.* | [rule] | BOOK III. |
[rule] *With the* Additions *of the Late* | *Mr.* HENRY PURCELL. |
[rule] | Printed in the Year M DCC.

8°. π¹ A⁸ χ¹ B–L⁸ M⁴ N² (D4, H3 unsigned). 96 leaves, paged irregularly from B1
to N1ᵛ (180) omitting 81–90. π1 blank; π1ᵛ frontispiece; A1 title-page; A1ᵛ blank;
A2–A2ᵛ preface; A3–A7 introduction; A7ᵛ–A8ᵛ verses; χ1–χ1ᵛ contents; N2–N2ᵛ

FIG. 10. *English Song-books, 1651–1702* by Day and Murrie.
Bibliographical Society, 1940.

REN'S SONGS   see: NURSERY RHYMES

NITY SONGS

ALLAN'S COMMUNITY SONGS		M.Allan	18839
COMMUNITY BOOK OF IRISH SONGS		F.D.& H.	10946
COMMUNITY SING-SONG BOOK 2 vols.	ed.Newton	K.Prowse	R 394-5
COMMUNITY SONG ALBUMS		F.D.& H.	
No. 1			27125
No. 2			27126
No. 3			27128
No. 4			27130
No. 5			27131
No. 6			27133
No. 7			27134
No. 8			27615
No. 9			27616
COMMUNITY SONG BOOK	ed.Sydney Baynes	Boosey	R 591
DAILY EXPRESS COMMUNITY SONG BOOK 2 vols.	ed.Goss	Daily Express	R 346-7
POCKET SING-SONG BOOK		Novello	R 283
POPULAR AND COMMUNITY SONG BOOK No. 1		F.D.& H.	R 316
STAR COMMUNITY SONG BOOK 2 vols.		Paxton	R 12-13

Y SONGS

COWBOY SONGS	Wilf Carter	Thomson	18138
COWBOY SONGS	ed.Lomax	Macmillan	R 7
COWBOY SONGS AND MOUNTAIN BALLADS	G.Autry arr.Manoloff	Cole	13407
COWBOY SONGS FROM THE WESTERN PLAINS, 3	arr.Welbeck	F.Harris	12656-8
RANCH, RANGE AND HOME SONGS	ed.W.Livernash	Stasny-Lang	13507

SONGS

Le BAL CUBERT (Old French dances)	R.Blanchard	Paris	R 679
CANCIONERO POPULAR VASCO (Basque) Vols.4 & 5	ed.D.R.M.de Azkue	Boileau & Bernasconi	R 492-3
CHARACTERISTIC SONGS AND DANCES OF ALL NATIONS	arr.Moffat	Bayley & Ferguson	R 33
CHODSKE (Czech songs and dances)	arr.J.Jindřich	Hudební Matice	19440
CORPUS DI MUSICHE POPOLARI SICILIANE	A.Favara	Accademia di Scienze Lettere	
Vols. 1 & 2		e Arti di Palermo	R 718
CSÁRDÁS, 50	arr.Farkas	Hungarian State	18572
CYPRUS SONGS AND DANCES	C.Apostolides	Apostolides	R 257
DANCING SONGS OF THE WORLD	ed.Duncan	Bayley & Ferguson	R 652
The ENGLISH DANCING MASTER	ed.Playford	Playford	R 576
KRÁLOVNIČKY (Czech folk dances)	arr.Janaček	Czech State	16135
NORWAY MUSIC ALBUM	ed.Forestier & Anderson	Ditson	R 163
O'NEILL'S MUSIC OF IRELAND	ed.O'Neill	Lyon & Healy	R 529
POPULAR MUSIC OF THE OLDEN TIME 2 vols.	arr.Macfarren	Chappell	R 526-7
RONDES AVEC JEUX ET AIR À DANSER	arr.C.Lebouc	Lerolle	9637
SWORD DANCES OF NORTHERN ENGLAND 3 vols.	ed.C.Sharp	Novello	5068-70
ZAHRAJTE MI DO KOLA (Czech folk dances)	arr.Seidel & Spičák	Czech State	21112

(see also NURSERY RHYMES AND CHILDREN'S SONGS)

POPULAR FRENCH SONGS AND MUSICAL GAMES (Fr.& Eng)arr.Helen Taylor		Enoch	R 648
RONDES AVEC JEUX ET DE PETITES CHANSONS	arr.Lebouc	Lerolle	9637
SONG TIME	ed.Dearmer & Shaw	Curwen	R 246

BILLY SONGS AND MOUNTAIN BALLADS (see also Section 1: U.S.A. for songs from the Appalachian Mountains)

BEECH MOUNTAIN FOLK SONGS AND BALLADS	ed.Matteson	G.Schirmer	R 25
COWBOY SONGS AND MOUNTAIN BALLADS	arr.G.Autry & Manoloff	Cole	13407
HILL-BILLY CAMP FIRE SONGS	arr.Pat Pattison	Southern	16650
KENTUCKY MOUNTAIN SONGS, 7	arr.J.J.Niles	G.Schirmer	21249
LONESOME TUNES	arr.Brockman & Wyman	H.W.Gray	25200
MORE SONGS OF THE HILL FOLK	arr.J.J.Niles	G.Schirmer	8646
MOUNTAIN SONGS OF NORTH CAROLINA	arr.Bartholomew	G.Schirmer	317
SONGS FROM THE HILLS OF VERMONT	arr.Hughes	G.Schirmer	18511

FIG. 11. *B.B.C. Song Catalogue.* B.B.C., 1966.

TUNE FOR TEX - Taylor - Hansen

TUNE TOWN SHUFFLE - Basie-Ebbins-Winston - B V C

T U R Q U O I S E - Garner - Goldsen Inc

TUXEDO JUNCTION - Feyne-Hawkins-Johnson-Dash - Lewis

T W I L I G H T - Garner - Goldsen Inc

UNISON RIFF - Rugolo - Leslie

UPTOWN JAZZ - B V C

VOLCANO - Basie - B V C

WALKIN' BASS - Mancini - Northridge

WALKIN' LINE - Brubeck - S P

WALKIN' SHOES - Mulligan Skyview

THE WALTZ - Brubeck - S P

WEEP NO MORE - Brubeck - S P

WHEN I WAS YOUNG Brubeck - S P

WHITE JAZZ - Gifford - A A M

YARDBIRD SUITE - Parker - Criterion

YASHITAKI MIKIMOTO Parker - Colin

YOUNG LOVE - Garner - Goldsen Inc

J E A L O U S

HEY JEALOUS LOVER - Barton

I GET SO JEALOUS - M P H

I'M JEALOUS - Remick

I'M NOT JEALOUS BUT I DON'T LIKE IT - Stasny

I STILL GET JEALOUS - Morris

I WISH YOU WERE JEALOUS OF ME - Lincoln

J A L O U S I E - Harms

JEALOUS - Malie-Little-Finch Mills

JEALOUS BOY FRIEND - Wit

JEALOUS HEART - A R

JEALOUS HEARTED ME - Peer

JEALOUS LADY - Milene Ascap

JEALOUS LOVER - Williams-Wright - Mills

JEALOUS MAN BLUES - Peer

JEALOUS LOVER - Davis - Peer

JEAOLOUS MOON - Kerr-Zamecnik - Fox

JEALOUS OF YOU - Marks

JEALOUS SWEETHEARTS - Peer

JEALOUS WIFE - Ascap

JEALOUSY - Dick-Bishop - Jones Ascap

JEALOUSY - Gordon-Revel - Crawford

J E A L O U S Y - G S

JEALOUSY - Trinkaus - Wit

THERE'S DANGER IN JEALOUSY - Witmark

J E W E L R Y

ACRES OF DIAMONDS - Leeds

BAND OF GOLD - Mills

BAUBLES BANGLES AND BEADS - Frank

BELLS IN HER EARRINGS Simon

BLACK DIAMOND - Hometown Ascap ?

BLACK DIAMOND - Conrad B M I

BLACK PEARL OF TAHITI Robbins

BLOWING THE FAMILY JEWELS AWAY - Robert Ascap

BLUE DIAMONDS - Vogel

C A M E O - Burns - Charling

C A M E O - Montrose - Pell Mell Ascap

CROCE DI ORO - S B

DIAMOND DUST - Robbins

DIAMOND EARRINGS - Robb

DIAMOND HEELS - Mitchell Ascap

DIAMONDS AND PEARLS Lode B M I

DIAMONDS AND RUBIES Juke Box Alley Ascap

DIAMONDS ARE A GIRL'S BEST FRIEND - Consolidated

DIAMONDS IN THE DIRT Feist

DIAMONDS IN THE STAR-LIGHT - Feist

EMERALD EYES - Robbins

EMERALD SONG - Cons

FOURTEEN CARAT FOOL Fanfare Ascap

FRIENDSHIP RING - R J

GOLDEN EARRINGS - Par

GOLDEN LOCKET - Veronique Ascap

HEART AND A RING - Cornell Ascap

HEAVENLY JEWELS - C F

HE WEARS A PAIR OF SILVER WINGS - Harms

I'VE GOT RINGS ON MY FINGERS - Harms

JEWEL SONG - Faust-Gounod Trad

JEWELS FROM CARTIER - Robb

JEWELS OF PANDORA - Feist

JUST A LITTLE GOLD WATCH AND CHAIN - Cole

LITTLE FRATERNITY PIN - W M

LITTLE GOLD CROSS - Carlton Ascap

LITTLE GOLD LOCKET - Mills

LITTLE GOLD RING - Robert Ascap

LITTLE RING - Planetary

MY LITTLE GOLDEN HORSE-SHOE - Alamo

MY MOTHER'S PEARLS - Miller

MY RING OF GOLD - Dubonnet Ascap

OLD FASHIONED LOCKET Plymouth

ONE DIAMOND RING - Chap

PEARL OF THE ORIENT - Robb

P E A R L S - Chappell

PEARLS ON VELVET - Robbins

PERFECT JEWELS - G S

PLAIN GOLD RING - H R

PUT THAT RING ON MY FINGER - A B C

RESTRINGING THE PEARLS Albert Ascap

RING THAT I GAVE TO YOU Champagne Ascap

RINGS ON HER FINGERS W M

R U B Y - Miller

RUBY AND THE PEARL - Famous

RUBY AND THE ROSE - Robb

SAPPHIRE - Mark V11 Ascap

SILVER BELLS - Paramount

SKY FULL OF DIAMONDS Roncom

STAR SAPPHIRE - Robbins

STRING OF PEARLS - Mutual

THE STRING OF PEARLS - Chap

TAKE BACK THE ENGAGE-MENT RING - Cole

TAKE THIS RING - Harms

T O P A Z - Northern

TOPAZ TANGO - Robbins

TURQUOISE - Mark V11 Ascap

TWO LITTLE RUBY RINGS Harms

WEAR YOUR RING AROUND MY NECK - Gladys

WEDDING RING OF GOLD Southern

WHEN YOUR OLD WEDDING RING WAS NEW - Mills

WITH THIS RING - B V C

YELLOW BAND OF 14 CARAT GOLD - H R

JEWISH - HEBREW - ISRAEL

A CHULEM - 1953 - Kammen

ADARIM DODI NATAN - 1942 Zaira - Marks

A D I R H U - Trad

A D M O S S A I - Kammen

A D O N O L A M - Trad

A HEIM A HEIM - 1921 - Meyerowitz - Kammen

AHEIM AHEIM BRIEDERLACH AHEIM - Kammen

ALEI GIVAH - 1942 - Nardi Marks

AM YISRAEL CHAI - Mills

AND THE ANGELS SING B V C

AN OREM YESOIMELE - 1922 Kammen

ANU BANU ARTSA - Mills

ARTSA ALINU - Mills

AVIGAYIL - 1952 - Avigal-Nardi - Marks

A V R E M E L E - Kammen

FIG. 12. *Classified Song Directory* by A. and A. Stecheson.
Hollywood, Music Industry Press, 1961.

MS. Sketch, dated 1st May 1816 (together with 419 and 442)—
Dr. Alwin Cranz, Vienna; final version—lost.

1ST PF. (?) 4th May 1927, Musikvereinssaal, Vienna.

1ST ED. 1892, Gesamtausgabe.

358. ' Die Nacht ' (Uz), Song (XX 235). 1816.

MS. Fragment only (together with 363)—Otto Taussig, Malmö.

1ST ED. *c.* 1848, A. Diabelli & Co., Vienna (no. 8821), as no. 2
of *Nachlass*, book 44.

The first five bars of the voice part and the right-hand part of the acc.
are missing in the MS.; the first chord, however, of the pf. introduction
is genuine.

359. ' Lied der Mignon ' (' Nur wer die Sehnsucht kennt,' from
Goethe's ' Wilhelm Meister '), Song (XX 260). 1816.

MS. Lost (Witteczek's copy).

1ST ED. 1872, J. P. Gotthard, Vienna (no. 337), as no. 13 of
forty songs, this song dedicated by the publisher to Fräulein
Helene Magnus.

For other settings of this poem, see the note to 481.

360. ' Lied eines Schiffers an die Dioskuren ' (Mayrhofer), Song
(Op. 65, no. 1; XX 268). 1816.

MS. Lost.

1ST ED. 24th November 1826, Cappi & Czerny, Vienna (no. 221)
as no. 1 of Op. 65.

Mayrhofer called this poem ' Schiffers Nachtlied.'

FIG. 13. *Schubert Thematic Catalogue* by O. E. Deutsch. Dent, 1951.

BLOCH, Ernest   Continued

String QUARTET No.1 in B min. (1916)	Score only			50'00"	54'30"	G.Schirmer (1929)	CM 296
String QUARTET No.2			31'30"	36'20"	37'10"	Boosey & Hks.(1947)	50909
String QUARTET No.3						G.Schirmer (1953)	52080
Piano QUINTET			33'10"	35'00"	36'00"	" (1923)	50361
Piano QUINTET No.2 (1957)						Broude (1962)	53517
String QUARTET No.4	Not in BBC Library				31'50"	Broude	
String QUARTET No.5 (1956)						Broude (1962)	53519

BLOMDAHL, Karl-Birger (1916 -)

String QUARTET No.2 (1948)		Svenska Tonsättare	51959
TRIO Cl. Cello & Piano		Schott (1956)	52872

BLOW, Dr. John (1649 - 1708)

CO. PERJUR'D MAN 2 Voices, 2 Vlns. & Continue		Photo & MS.	Songs 7071
	ed. & arr. H.Watkins Shaw	[Amphion Anglicus]	
2 SONATAS Vln. Cello & Piano		Oiseau Lyre	50004
1. in A 6'20" 2. in G			

BLUMENFELD, Felix (1863 - 1931)

SARABANDE in G min. from 'Les Vendredis'	String quartet		Belaieff	50111
String QUARTET op.26 in F	Score only		"	CM 425

BLUMER, Theodor (1882 -)

TANZ-SUITE op.53 Fl. Ob. Cl. Hn. Bsn.	Score only	13'30"	Simrock (1925)	CM 37

BOCCHERINI, Luigi (1743 - 1805)

QUARTETS (String quartets)

op.1/1.in C min. (1761)	No score	ed. Upmeyer	IN VOL.	Bärenreiter(1952)	52013
	Score only	ed. Polo	"	Ricordi (1928)	CM 720
op.6/1 in D	Score only	"	"	" "	CM 722
op.6/2 in C min.)					
op.6/3 in Eb)					
op.6/4 in G min.)	"	"	"	" "	CM 723
op.6/5 in F)					
op.6/6 in A)					
op.6/6 in A)	No score	ed. Hofmann	" 9'45"	Peters	50181
op.8/5 in D)					
op.10/1 in C min.	Score only	ed. Polo	"	Ricordi (1928)	CM 721
op.10/2 in D min.	No score	ed. Hofmann	"	Peters	50181
op.10/4 in Eb	Score only	ed. Polo	"	Ricordi (1928)	CM 720
op.10/6 in E	No score	ed. Hofmann	"	Peters	50181
op.11 (6 Quartets)[Divertimenti]	No score			Venier [c.1780]	51122
No.1. in D No.2. in F No.3. in E					
4. in F 5. in Eb 6. in C					
op.25/1 in C)	No scores			de la Chevardiere	52459
op.26/2 in D)				[c.1775]	
op.26/3 in Eb)					
op.26/4 in Bb)					
op.26/5 in A min.)					
op.26/6 in C)					
op.27/2 in G min.	No score	ed. Hofmann	"	Peters	50181
op.27/2 in G min. (Bocch.s Cat. op.24/2)	ed. Sadie			MS.[Sieber 1777]	52800
op.27/3 in C	Score only	ed. Polo	"	Ricordi (1928)	CM 721
op.27/4 in A	"	"	"	" "	CM 720
op.27/5 in D (1778)	No score	ed. Upmeyer	"	Bärenreiter	52013
(Entitled op.24/5 in this edition)					
op.32/1 in Bb)	No score		"	Schmitt [c.1780]	52'60
op.32/2 in G min.)					
op.32/3 in Eb)					
op.32/4 in A)			14'20"		
op.32/4 in A)	"	ed. Hofmann	"	Peters	50181
op.32/5 in F)	"		"	Schmitt [c.1780]	52'60
op.32/6 in F min.)					
op.33 piccola Nos. 1 - 6 (Quartettini)(1781)	Mus.Ref.Lib.			Classici Italiani della Mus.vol.1.	
op.33/3 (Artaria); op.39/3 (Pleyel) in D	ed. S.J.Sadie			MS.[Pleyel]	52803
(Boccherini's cat. op.32/3)					
op.33/4 in C	No score		IN VOL.	Pleyel [c.1795]	50221
op.33/5 in G min.	"		"	"	"
	"	ed.Hoffmann	"	Peters	50181
op.33/6 in A	"	"	"	"	"
"	Score only	ed. Polo	"	Pleyel [c.1795]	50221
"	"	ed. S.J.Sadie	"	Ricordi (1928)	CM 721
(Boccherini's cat. op.32/6)				MS.[Pleyel]	52820

FIG. 14. *B.B.C. Chamber Music Catalogue*. B.B.C., 1965.

Speth (*fl.* 1675). Organist, Cath., Augsburg. Catholic organist. "Ars Magna," 1693. 5 vols. (Leuckart). (1873.)

Pachelbel (1653-1706). South German organist, born in Nuremberg. Works. Univ. Ed. and B.V. Ed. "Chaconne" (Bohm), Pr. and F., and "Chaconne" ("Alte Meister"—Peters, No. 21). Toccata, No. 45, and 39 Nos. in "Orgel Barock" (B. and B.).

Böhm (1661-1773). 4 vols., B. and H. Organist at Hamburg and Lüneberg.

Bruhns (1665-1697). "Alte Meister" (Peters). Organist, Copenhagen. Pupil of Buxtehude.

Walther (1684-1750). Works. B. and H. and B. V. Eds.

In Gray's Historical Series are the following:

Frohberger, Fantasia; *J. H. Bach* (1615-92), Ch. Prelude; *J. M. Bach* (1648-98), Ch. Prelude; *W. F. Bach* (1710-84), Ch. Prelude; *C. P. E. Bach* (1714-88), Fant. and Fugue; *J. B. Bach* (1676-1749), Variations; *J. C. Bach* (1642-1703), Pr. and F. in E flat—all members of the Bach family; also *Marpurg* (1718-95), Prel. and Capriccio; *C. F. C. Fasch*, Fugue in F.

GENERAL COLLECTIONS.

Alte Meister. Ed. 1929. Dr. Straube. 2 vols. (Peters). For Recital see Nos. 2, 3, 6, 12, 15, 16, 27, 29.

Meister des Orgelbarock (Bote and Bock). Recital Nos. 17, 21, 45, 50, 56, 58, 64, 66, 74.

Ecole Classique (Schott). Sweelinck, Murschauser, etc.

Organum Series (Kist), 18 bks. (Böhm to Krieger). 15-16 Cent.

Alte Meister (B. and H., 1913). 17-18 Cent. "German Masters" (Peters).

"Early German" Organ Works, B. and H., 1930.

BACH.

Bach (1685-1750). Various Editions. *Peters* (original), Vol. II appears in a new phrased Edition, with Dr. Straube's notes in English, 1914. Vol. IX, new Edition (Seiffert), 1904. *Augener's* (Dr. Hull), phrased edition; *Novello; B. and H.* (Gesammt Ausgabe); *Schirmer* (Schweitzer); *Durand's* cheap "Ed. Classique—Faure-Bonnet."

Preparatory Selections: Dr. Horner (Williams); and De Lange's Ed. (Peters); Henderson (B. and F.). *Sonatas:* No. 3 in D (Adagio); No. 5 in C (Finale); separate De Lange Edition (Peters). *Concertos:* (Peters), Vol. VIII, first movements of Nos. 1, 2 and 4—interesting as transcriptions of Vivaldi's violin works; also Pastorale, third movement (Gray).

POETRY OF BACH RECITAL.

(1). *The Sands of Time.* Prelude in B minor. (5). Aug Ed. Vol. 2. No. 16.

Typifies the Pilgrimage of Life. This work progresses gradually to a majestic close.

FIG. 15. *The Complete Organ Recitalist* by H. Westerby. Musical Opinion, 1933.

MALIGE, Fred. Quartette pour 4 cors en fa *(Breitkopf)*.
MOULAERT, R. Andante pour 4 cors *(manuscrit auteur)*.
PERILHOU, Albert. Chasse pour 4 cors *(Hengel)*.

TROIS CORS ET TROMBONE

VILLA-LOBOS, H. Chôros N° 4 pour 3 cors et trombone *(Eschig)*.

QUATUOR DE SAXOPHONES

ABSIL, J. Quatuor pour saxophones *(Lemoine)*.
ALBENIZ. 3 pièces pour quatuor de saxophones *(Leduc)*.
BOZZA. Andante et Scherzo pour quatuor de saxophones *(Leduc)*.
CLÉRISSE. Caravane, pour quatuor de saxophones.
    Chanson du rouet, pour quatuor de saxophones.
    Sérénade mélancolique, pour quatuor de saxophones *(Leduc)*.
FRANÇAIX, Jean. Quatuor pour saxophones *(Eschig, Schott)*.
GLAZOUNOV, Alexandre. Quartette pour saxophones *(Boosey)*.
MEULEMANS, Arthur. Pièce pour 4 saxophones *(Gervan, Bruxelles)*.
MOULAERT, Raymond. Andante, fugue et final pour 4 saxophones (sopr., alt., tén., bar.) *(manuscrit de l'auteur)*.
PIERNÉ, G. Chanson d'autrefois — Introduction et variations — Marche des petits soldats de plomb — La Veillée de l'Ange Gardien, pour quatuor de saxophones *(Leduc)*.
SCHMITT, Fl. Quatuor, op. 102, pour 4 saxophones *(Durand)*.

SAXO ALTO, HARPE, CELESTA ET BATTERIE

VELLONES, P. Rhapsodie (op. 92) pour saxo alto, harpe, celesta et batterie *(Lemoine)*.

Cinquième partie

PIÈCES POUR CINQ INSTRUMENTS

CINQ INSTRUMENTS À VENT

BAEYENS, August. Quintette pour flûte, hautbois, clarinette, cor, basson *(manuscrit de l'auteur)*.
BALAY. La Vallée silencieuse, rêverie pour hautbois, clarinette, basson, cor et flûte principale *(Leduc)*.
BALAY. L'Aurore sur la forêt pour flûte, hautbois, clarinette, basson et cor principal. Petite suite miniature dans le style du XVIII° siècle *(Leduc)*.

269

FIG. 16. *Encyclopédie de la Musique pour Instruments à Vent*, vol. 3 by E. Gorgerat. Lausanne, Editions Rencontre, 1955.

Winds: 6 Winds, 1 Perc

ANSSEN   Obsequies of a Saxophone. 6Winds, SnareDr. . . . .
MARCELLI   Music Box. Picc, 2Fl, Ob, 2Cl, Bells. . . . . **Mills**
MOZART   Divertimento #5, 6--C, C; K 187, 188 (1773).
                    Arr: 2Cl, 3Tt, Tb, Tymp by Kahn. . . . . **Marks**
SCHAIKOWSKY   Capriccio Italien, Op 45 (1880).
                    Arr: 2Tt, Hn, Bar, Tb, Tuba, Marimba by Talmadge. . . Belwin
            Intro. & Finale from Swan Lake, Op 20 (1876).
                    Arr: 2Tt, Hn, Bar, Tb, Tuba, Marimba by Talmadge. . . Belwin
VERDI   Triumphal March from Aida (1871).
                    Arr: 2Tt, 2Hn, Tb(Bar), Tuba, Tymp by Gordon. . . Witmark; MPHC

---

7 INSTS. : 7 Winds

WQuar, 3 additional Woodwinds

OLZONI   Minuetto. Plus Cl, AltCl, BsCl. Arr: Conn. . . . . . CFisch
USCH   Ozark Reverie. Plus Cl, 2Hn. . . . . Fitzsimmons
ALLEY   Serenade. Plus Fl, Cl, Bn. . . . . Witmark; MPHC
LAMENT   Fantasia con fugua, Op 28. Plus EH, 2Hn. . . . . . . Andraud
ABERT   Scherzo, Op 107. Plus Bn, 2Hn. . . . . B&H; AMP
INDY   Chanson et Danses--Bb, Op 50 (1898). Plus Cl, Hn, Bn. . . Durand(1899); E-V
KOUQUET   Adagio, Aubade, Scherzo. Plus Cl, Bn, Hn. . . . . . Lemoine(1910); Andraud
IERNE, GABR.   Preludio & Fughetta--c mi, Op 40. Plus Fl, Bn, Hn. Hamelle(1906); Andraud
HENE-BATON   Aubade, Op 53. Plus Cl, Bn, Hn. . . . . Durand; E-V
ÖNTGEN   Serenade--A, Op 14. Plus Bn, 2Hn. . . . . B&H(1878)
CHUMANN   Knight Rupert, from Album for Young for Pf, Op 68#12.
                  Arr: plus Cl, AltCl, BsCl by Cheyette-Roberts . CFisch
OJA   Serenata. Plus Cl, 2Hn. . . . . Ricordi
IND   Serenade Amusante, Op 1339. Plus Cl, 2Hn. . . . . . . Andraud

isc: 7 Woodwinds

ACH, K. P. E.   6 Sonatas--G, F, A, D, Eb, C. 2Fl, 2Cl, Bn, 2Hn.Ed: Leupold . . Litolff(1935-37)
AMEAU   Musette en Rondeau. Arr: 3Cl, 2Bn, 2Hn. . . . . Andraud
         Tambourin. Arr: 3Cl, 2Bn, 2Hn. . . . . Andraud
OSETTI   Parthia--D. 2Ob, 2Cl, Bn, 2Hn. Ed: Kaul, in D. T. B. XXXIII. . . B&H

isc: 7 Brass

EREZOWSKY   Suite, Op 24 (1938). 2Tt, 2Hn, 2Tb, Tuba. . . . . Mills
RABEC   Bläsermusiken. 2Tt, 3Hn, 2Tb. . . . . Ullman(1940)
JONAMENTE   Sonata. Arr: 2Ct, 2Hn, Tb, Bar, Tuba by King. . . . Mus f Brass
OHN   Music for Brass Insts. 3Tt, Tt(Hn), 2Tb, BsTb. . . . . . . SMPC
OMMA   Musik. For 7 Brasses. . . . . Ullmann(1940)
ECAIL   Septet for Brass. Tts, Tbs. . . . . Evette & Schaeffer(1921)
OCKE   Music for King Chas. II. Arr: 3Ct, Hn(Tb), Tb, Bar, Tuba. . Mus f Brass
BORNE, WILLS.   Prelude. 2Ct, Ct(Hn), Tb(Hn), Tb, Bar, Tuba . . Mus f Brass
             2 Ricercari. 2Ct, 2Hn, Tb, Bar, Tuba. . . . . Mus f Brass
UGGLES   Angels, from "Men and Angels." 4 muted Tt, 3 muted Tb. . . . . . NME
HEIN   Gagliarda. Brass Septet[?]. Ed: ? . . . . McG & M
EBOTH   Suite. 4Tt, 3Tb. . . . . Heinrichshofen(1940)
MON   Brass Septet. See Brass Quint, Op 26.

Fig. 17. *Catalog of Chamber Music for Wind Instruments* by S. M. Helm.
Michigan, National Association of College Wind and Percussion Instrument
Instructors, 1952.

Kammermusikwerke für Flöte mit andern Instrumenten
(mit Klavier)

a) Trios

Addison, J., Trio, Fl., Oboe u. Klavier   10.80

Arnold, J., Everybody's favorite easy
flute solos or duets, Serie Nr. 102
2 Flöten und Klavier   8.85

Bach, C. Ph. E., 12 kleine Stücke
(Walther), Flöte, Violine und Klavier   3.90
— Trio Nr. 1 in D-dur
Flöte, Viola und Klavier   10.15
— Trio Nr. 2 in a-moll
Flöte, Viola und Klavier   10.15
— Trio Nr. 3 in G-dur
Flöte, Viola und Klavier   10.15
— Trio in B-dur (Landshoff)
Flöte, Violine und Basso Continuo   9.90
— Trio E-dur (Walther)
2 Flöten und Klavier   3.90
— Trio h-moll (Ermeler), Flöte, Violine,
Klavier mit Cello   3.90
— Trio-Sonate in G-dur (Brüggen)
Flöte, Violine und Klavier   7.50

Bach, J. Chr. Fr., Divertissement
(Moyse), 2 Flöten und Klavier   13.—
— Sonate in A-dur (Frotscher)
Flöte, Violine und Continuo   7.—
— Sonate D-dur (Ruf), konzertierendes
Cembalo, Flöte und Cello   8.20

Bach, J. S., Sonata in G-dur (Geehl)
2 Flöten und Klavier   10.25
— Sonata G-dur (Hermann)
Flöte, Violine und Klavier   7.60
— Triosonate aus dem „Musikalischen
Opfer", c-moll (Hermann), Flöte,
Violine und Klavier (Cello)   4.95
— 3 Trio-Sonaten in C-dur, G-dur
e-moll (Hermann), Klavier, Violine
und Flöte   8.50
— 4 Trio-Sonaten, Bd. 1 und 2
(Landshoff), 2 Flöten (Flöte, Violine),
Cello und Cembalo   à 9.90
— Trio-Sonate Nr. 2 in e-moll (Frotscher)
Flöte, Violine II u. Cembalo (Cello)   4.20
— Trio-Sonate Nr. 5 in G (Frotscher)
Flöte, Violine und Klavier (Cello)   4.20

Bach, W. F., Sonate in D (Leeuwen)
2 Flöten und Klavier   4.90
— Sonate F-dur (Brandts)
Flöte, Violine und Klavier   7.90
— Trio Nr. 1 und 2 in D (Seiffert)
2 Flöten und Basso cont.   à 7.—
— Trio Nr. 3 und 4 in B-dur und
a-moll (Seiffert)
2 Flöten und Cembalo   à 7.—

Beethoven, L. van, Trio in G-dur
(Lyman), Flöte (Violine), Fagott
(Cello) und Klavier   19.—

Beyer, J. S., Partita in C-dur (Gronefeld)
Flöte, Violine u. Cembalo (Cello)   7.65

Bloch, E., Concertino
Flöte, Viola und Klavier   10.40

Boismortier, B. de, 5 Gentillesse
„La Plainville" (Walter), Flöte
Violine u. Klavier (Cello ad. lib.)   5.20
— op. 37, Nr. 2, Sonate e-moll (Ruf)
Flöte, Viola da Gamba und Klavier   6.10

Bononcini, G. B., Trio-Sonaten Nr. 1—4
(Giesbert), 2 Fl. u. Klavier   à 3.90

Burkhard, W., op. 76 a, Canzona
2 Flöten und Klavier   5.90

Califano, A., Sonata a tre (Brinckmann)
2 Flöten und Cembalo   9.75

Cimarosa, D., Konzert (Wollheim)
2 Flöten und Klavier   9.60

Corrette, M., Noel Allemand (Guy)
Flöte, Violine und Klavier (Cello
und 3. Violine ad. lib.)   6.25
— Sonate Nr. 5 in G (Petit)
Flöte, Violine und Basso cont.   16.10

Damase, J.-M., Sonate en concert
Flöte, Klavier u. Cello ad. lib.   8.75

Daube J. F., Trio in d-moll (Neemann)
Laute, Flöte und Klavier   7.—

Drießler, J., op. 34, Nr. 2, Sonata a tre
Flöte, Gambe und Cembalo   12.—

Duruflé, M., op. 3, Prélude,
Récitatif and Variations
Flöte, Viola und Klavier   9.25

Erbse, H., op. 13, 12 Aphorismen
Flöte, Violine und Klavier   8.50

Fesch, W. de, op. 12, Nr. 1—3,
12 Sonaten (Noske)
2 Flöten und Cembalo (Cello)   8.70

Françaix, J., Musique de cour
Flöte, Violine und Klavier   10.25
Orchestermaterial leihweise

Fux, J., Nürnberger Partita
(Hoffmann), Flöte, Oboe und
Cembalo (Cello)
Partitur (Klavierstimme)   3.90
Stimmen   à —.80

Gagnebin, H., Trio in D-dur
Flöte, Violine und Klavier   11.95

Galuppi, B., Triosonate G-dur (Ruf)
Flöte, Oboe und Basso cont.   6.85

FIG. 18. *Internationale Flötenliteratur.* Hug & Co., 1961.

the nineteenth century in Vienna. The A.M.Z. during the years 1828-30 frequently records his concert performances and guitar compositions. He is described on his publications as Member of the Royal Chapel and Professor of the Guitar. He was the author of a *Theoretical and Practical Guitar School*, Op. 1, issued by Artaria, Vienna ; Op. 14, *Bravour Sonata in D*, for guitar and piano, Wienberger, Vienna ; Op. 15, *Caprices for guitar solo ;* Op. 19 and 21 for *Guitar with string quartet ;* Op. 30, *Variations Concertantes, for guitar with orchestra.* A new and revised edition of Seegner's guitar studies has been published by Schott, London.

Segovia, Andres, contemporary, born February 28, 1890, at Linares, Jaen, Spain. His parents removed to Granada when he was a child and shortly after he was placed with an uncle and aunt. His first interest in music was with the piano, violin and 'cello but with indifferent results and it was not until attracted to the guitar that his genius became manifest. With savings from his pocket-money he purchased a guitar from the maker Benito Ferrer, and because his family accused him of wasting his time and money on this instrument he considered it wise to practise secretly. Associating with Flamenco players he consequently adopted their style of playing, and later, after hearing the music of Arcas, Sor, and Tarrega decided to adopt their style so was obliged to re-learn. Many years after, he wrote : " As I had to fight the opposition of my family there was no question of a teacher, a school, or any other of the usual methods of instruction." With no encouragement from his family, or any external stimulus whatever, it was solely the love of the guitar that induced him to rent a small room where he lived alone and diligently studied and practised. His first concert was in Granada in 1909 and he extended his sphere with recitals in the Salle Erard, Paris, where his triumphant successes brought him in friendly acquaintance with many famed musicians, several of whom, amazed and surprised at his virtuosity, dedicated compositions to him. From France he travelled to Russia where in Moscow Conservatoire of Music, on March 2, 1926 his recital elicited high praise from the music press. In 1927 his recitals were acclaimed in bold headlines : " Segovia's fastidious artistry," his " Bewitching guitar," and " Amazing virtuosity." Reporting his London concerts the press said : " Praise is superfluous, his is, in its way, one of the most astonishing displays of musical and technical mastery at the present time. Despite the fact that he had learned of the death of his thirteen year old son, only a few hours before, Segovia insisted on giving his recital—the boy had been electrocuted when crossing an acqueduct near Geneva." For periods Segovia has been a professor of the guitar in Geneva Conservatoire of Music. In 1929 he was receiving applaudits in Japan and the same year flew with Manuel Ponce to the Latin American republics where Ponce conducted his orchestral works, one of which, *Concerto of the South,* a *Concerto for Guitar with full orchestra,* dedicated to Segovia, was given its first performance at Montevideo. This Concerto was

FIG. 19. *The Guitar and Mandolin* by P. J. Bone. Schott, 1954.

BRAHMS, Johannes (cont.)

GAVOTTE in A (Gluck) arr. for the piano	3'00"-3'15"		
	ed.Thümer	Augener	898
	ed. (& simplified) by Geehl	Ashdown	1554
		Breitkopf	2411
	ed.Warner	Bosworth	4184
		Breitkopf	11850
		Hinrichsen (1952)	11701

GIGUES, 2 (1855)
    No.1 in A min.)
    No.2 in B min.)   ed.Herrmann   Breitkopf   11850

HUNGARIAN DANCES (1852-69) (orig. for piano duet)

1.	in G min.	12.	in D min.
2.	in D min.	13.	in D
3.	in F	14.	in D min.
4.	in F-sh.min.(orig. F min.)	15.	in Bb
5.	in F-sh.min.	16.	in F min.
6.	in Db	17.	in F-sh.min.
7.	in F (orig. in A)	18.	in D
8.	in A min.	19.	in B min.
9.	in E min.	20.	in E min.
10.	in E	21.	in E min.
11.	in D min.		

(Nos.5 & 6 were originally composed by Kéler, Béla-)
(M.L.A. 'Notes', Sept.1955)

(original ed.) Bks.1 & 2 (1872) arr.Brahms   Bks.3 & 4 (1881) arr.Kirchner

			Simrock	6654
Book 1	Nos.1-5		Simrock	7003
Book 2	" 6-10		Simrock	11882
Book 3	" 11-16		Simrock	11883
Book 4	" 17-21		Lengnick	4775
Complete:	Nos.1-21		Peters	3251
	Nos.1-21	arr.Singer	Henle (1953)	11881
	Nos.1-10	ed.Georgii	Breitkopf	11850
	"		Reid	615
	"		Paxton	6562
	Nos.1-4	arr.Krenkel		

Easy arrangements:-
    Book 4   Nos.17-21   arr.Keller   Simrock (1881)   11884
    No.7 in A   K.Prowse (1929)   5025

IMPROMPTU op.90/2 by Schubert, arranged as a study for the left hand   Breitkopf   11850
                      (doubtful authenticity)

INTERMEZZI, 3 op.117 (1892)
    1. in Eb (Schlummerlied) 'Schlaf sanft mein Kind'   3'30"-4'45"
    2. in Bb min.   4'00"-4'35"
    3. in C-sh.min.   4'35"-5'35"

Complete sets:	(original edition)	Simrock (1892)	12147
	ed.Sauer	Peters	129
	ed.Mayer-Mahr	Lengnick (1925)	3522
	ed.Mann	Augener (1928)	4024
	ed.Sauer	Peters	6047
	ed.Mann	Augener (1928)	7200
	ed.Georgii	Henle (1952)	11851
Separate copies: No.1	(original edition)	Simrock (1892)	9946
	ed.Samuel	Paterson	510
	ed.Mann	Augener (1928)	9940
	ed.Mayer-Mahr	Schott (1925)	6104
	ed.Warner	Bosworth	4184
No.2	(original edition)	Simrock (1892)	9947
	ed.Warner	Bosworth	4184
No.3	(original edition)	Simrock (1892)	9948

For other INTERMEZZI see the following works:-
        BALLADEN op.10/3
        KLAVIERSTÜCKE op.76/3,4,6,7
        FANTASIEN op.116/2,4,5,6
        KLAVIERSTÜCKE op.118/1,2,4,6
        KLAVIERSTÜCKE op.119/1,2,3

For INTERMEZZO in Bb min. (Rückblick) see SONATA in F min. op.5

INTERMEZZI, 3 op.117 complete set   Novello   5750

FIG. 20. *B.B.C. Piano and Organ Catalogue*. B.B.C., 1965.

The Twentieth Century 196

sisting of a left-hand melodic line accompanied by "twittering" figures in the right—all lying easily.
(Augener)

Sonata

A long, very serious work in three movements, in uncompromising dissonant idiom, showing imagination and deep feeling. It presents formidable technical and interpretative problems.
(Augener)

BENJAMIN BRITTEN (1913-) Great Britain

Holiday Diary (1934)

Suite for piano

Early Morning Bathe

Vivacious, fast 6/8, triplet sixteenth-note figuration. Requires some stamina.

Sailing

Swaying melody, sonorous accompaniment. Animated, agitato middle section.

Fun-Fair

Very brilliant rondo, requiring bravura, command of chords and octaves, sharp rhythmic accentuation.

Night

Tranquil finale, melody in the midst of widely separated intervallic sonorities.
(Boosey & Hawkes)

ROBERT CASADESUS (1899-) France

Twenty-four Preludes

In four books. Essays in a variety of genres: melodic, energetic, brusque, flowing, dans le goût espagnol, atmospheric, tender, intimate, marcia funèbre, dans le style ancien (with musette), Bourrée, etc. A useful collection worth exploring for concertizing or teaching. Oriented toward Ravel (to whom they are dedicated).
(Eschig)

Eight Etudes

Accent on facility. Fairly difficult pieces exploring the following pianistic problems: thirds, octaves, resonance, fourths and fifths, two against three, left hand, chords, lightness of touch.
(Schirmer)

Toccata (1950)

Lengthy essay in double notes and octaves. Requires virtuosity, endurance, precision and power.
(Durand, through Elkan-Vogel)

ALFREDO CASELLA (1883-1947) Italy

The changing character of Casella's piano style gives evidence of a restless, agitated mind constantly exploring new avenues of expression. Both the whimsical character of his shorter pieces and the broad, expansive qualities of his more extended works display a wide variety of musical and

FIG. 21. *Music for the Piano* by Friskin and Freundlich. New York, Rinehart, 1954.

II. FÜR KLAVIER 4HÄNDIG UND ANDERE INSTRUMENTE

NB. ohne nähere Bezeichnung stets mit Violine und Violoncell

A Originalwerke

Berens, Hermann : op. 23 Gesell-schafts-Quartett Nr 1. 1852 Cranz
— op. 48 dgl. Nr 2 (D). 1856 »
— op. 72 dgl. Nr 3 (a). 1863 »
— op. 80 dgl. Nr 4 (f). 1869 »
Fétis, François Joseph : Sextuor (Es) m. StrQuart. P. u. St. 1864 Schott
Godefroid, J. M. : op. 6 Adagio. 1865 Roothaan, Amsterdam
Huber, Hans : op. 54 Walzer. 1882 Rieter-B
Hummel, Ferd. : op. 37 Serenade : Im Frühling (4 Sätze ; D). 1884 Kistner

— op. 39 Lenzreigen. 6 Stücke. 1886 Kistner
Hummel, Joh. Nep. : op. 99 Nocturno (f) m. 2 Hörn. NA. 1860 Peters
Jadassohn, Salomon : op. 100 Sextett (G) m. StrQuart. 1888 Kistner & S
Krug, Arnold : op. 20 Fahrende Musi-kanten. Walzer. 1880 Rob. Forberg
Manns, Ferd. : op. 36 Sonate (C) m. V. od. Vc. od. beiden Instrum. 1883 Rühle
Mohr, Herm. : op. 47 Rondo mignon. 1890 Heinrichshofen

II. B 1 a Sinfonische Werke bearbeitet für Klavier 4händig, Violine und Violoncell

Beethoven, Ludwig van : Nr 1 ; op. 21 (C). 1862 (Karl Burchard) ; VA. 1896 B & H
— Nr 2 ; op. 36 (D). Dgl.
— Nr 3 Eroica ; op. 55 (Es). 1866 ; VA. 1896 (Karl Burchard) B & H
— Nr 4 (B) ; op. 60. 1867 ; VA. 1897 (Karl Burchard) B & H
— Nr 5 (c) ; op. 67. 1867 ; VA. 1897 (Karl Burchard) B & H
— Nr 6 pastorale ; op. 68. (F) 1868 ; VA 1897 (Karl Burchard) B & H
— Nr 7 ; op. 92 (A). 1869 (Karl Burchard) B & H
— Nr 8 ; op. 93 (F). 1870 (Karl Bur-chard) B & H
— Nr 9 ; op. 125 (d). 1879 (Karl Bur-chard) B & H
Brahms, Joh. : Nr 1 ; op. 68 (c) 1878 (Friedr. Hermann) Simrock
— Nr 2 ; op. 73 (D). Dgl.
— op. 80 Akademische Fest-Ouv. 1899 (Friedr. Hermann) Simrock
— op. 81 Tragische Ouv. Dgl.
— Nr 3 ; op. 90 (F). Dgl.
— Nr 4 ; op. 98 (e). 1897 (Stefan Wahl) Simrock
Händel, Georg Friedrich : Wasser- und Feuermusik. Concerto grosso Nr 25 u.

26. 1870 (Friedr. Aug. Kummer : op. 49 Nr 34) Joh. Oertel
Haydn, Josef : 12 Sinf. (Karl Bur-chard). Nr 1 (G mit dem Pauken-schlag). Nr 94 1865 ; 2 (G) Nr 88 1865 ; 3. (Es) Nr 99 1868 ; 4 (G ; Ox-ford) Nr 92 1874 ; 5 (B ; La reine) Nr 85 1872 ; 6 (G ; Militär-Sinf.) Nr 100 1873 ; 7 (B) Nr 102 1874 ; 8 (D) Nr 104 1878 ; 9 (D) Nr 98 1879 ; 10 (c) Nr 95 1880 ; 11 (D) Nr 86 1883 ; 12 (d) Nr 96 1885 Heinrichshofen
— 4 Sinf. 1872/3 (Karl Burchard) Nr 1 (D) Nr 93 ; 2. (C) Nr 97 ; 3 (Es) Nr 103 ; 4. (D) Nr 101 Hofmeister
Mendelssohn-Bartholdy, Felix : Nr 1 ; op. 11 (c). 1888 (Friedr. Hermann) B & H
— Nr 2 ; op. 52 (B) aus der Kantate Lobgesang. Dgl.
— Nr 3 ; op. 56 (a ; schottische). 1875 (F. Hermann) B & H ; 1878 (J. N. Rauch) Litolff
— Nr 4 ; op. 90 (A ; italienische). 1877 (Karl Burchard) B & H
— Nr 5 ; op. 107 (D ; Reformations-Sinf.). 1877 (Friedr. Hermann) B & H
Mozart, W. A. : 12 Sinf. 1863/71 (Karl Burchard) Hofmeister

FIG. 22. *Verzeichnis von Werken für Klavier, 4 und 6 Händig . . .* by W. Altmann. Leipzig, F. Hofmeister, 1943.

MENDELSSOHN, ARN., op. 70 Sonate in fis. M. 3.—. Lpz., Peters. 1917. —ms—s.

Dieser Sonate kann höchstens instruktiver Wert zugesprochen werden, denn ihre musikalischen Qualitäten weisen sie bei aller Anständigkeit der Themengebung und technischen Mache um mindestens 50 Jahre zurück. Es wäre hoch an der Zeit, daß solche Komponisten wie Mendelssohn und Genossen endlich zu Bewußtsein kommen, daß seit dem Tode Schumanns die Musik hinsichtlich ihrer Thematik, ihrer harmonischen und technischen Ausgestaltung denn doch wesentlich andere Ausdrucksformen angenommen hat als jene, die sie in etlichen Varianten noch immer wieder dem Publikum vorzusetzen wagen.

MENDELSSOHN-BARTHOLDY, F., op. 45 u. 58 Zwei Sonaten in B u. D, op. 17 Variations concertantes in D u. op. 109 Lied ohne Worte in D (D. Popper) M. 2.50. Wien, U. E. 1902. — Dgl. (Fr. Grützmacher) M. 2.50. Lpz., Peters. 1878. — Dgl. (L. Grützmacher) M. 3.—. Braunschweig, Litolff. 1870. — Dgl. M. 3.—. Lpz., Breitkopf. 1878. — Dgl. ohne op. 109 (R. Hausmann) M. 3.—. Lpz., Steingräber. 1903. — Dgl. op. 45 u. 58 (C. Liégeois) fr. 12.—. Paris, Lemoine. 1920. — Dgl. einzeln: op. 45 (K. Schröder) M. 1.—, op. 58 (K. Schröder) M. 1.—. Lpz., Schuberth u. Co. — Dgl. op. 45 u. 58 (W. Speidel u. B. Cossmann) je M. 2.—. Bremen, Schweers u. Haake. 1878. —ms—s.

Heutzutage, da die Begeisterung für die Werke von Mendelssohn (1809—1847) einer ruhigeren, durch eine vergleichende Kritik gedämpfteren Anerkennung gewichen ist, ließe sich, wenn es der Raum gestatten würde, neben dem „Für" auch vieles „Wider" bei einer Betrachtung dieser Cellosonaten sagen. Leider muß hier bloß der zusammenfassende Hinweis genügen, daß diese beiden Schöpfungen, trotzdem sie zu den mehr äußerlich, d. h. durch ihre Liebenswürdigkeit und Melodienreichtum und weniger durch die Tiefe und Vornehmheit ihres Inhaltes wirkenden zu zählen sind, sich nichtsdestoweniger einer außerordentlichen Beliebtheit erfreuen, da sie, für das Soloinstrument günstig gesetzt, sich leicht bewältigen lassen und mehr Effekt machen, als es im ersten Augenblick den Anschein hat.

MENDELSSOHN, L., op. 213 Schülerkonzert in D. M. 2.50. Lpz., Junne. —1—ms.

Ein gutes Schulstück, das, dankbar und dabei nicht schwer, besonders bei Schülerproduktionen mit Erfolg gespielt werden kann.

* **MIGOT, G.,** Dialogue en 4 parties. Fr. 16.—. Paris, Senart. 1922.

MJASKOWSKI, N., op. 12 Sonate in D. M. 6.50. Wien, U. E. i. Ausg. d. russ. Staatsvlg., Moskau. 1913. —s.

Eine 1911 entstandene, ganz tonale Schöpfung Mjaskowskis (geb. 1880), der in derselben viele harmonische Berührungspunkte mit Glazunow zeigt.

MOCSONYI, A. v., op. 9 Sonate in G (dzt. vergriffen). Wien, U. E. 1882. —ms—s.

* **MONNIKENDAM, M.,** Sonate. Paris, Senart. 1926.

MOÓR, E., op. 22 Sonate in c. M. 6.—. Wien, Gutmann. 1891. —s.
— op. 55 Sonate Nr. 2 in g. M. 7.50. Lpz., Kistner u. Siegel. 1906. —ms.

Kein moderner, aber kraftvoller Gestalter seiner nicht unwirksamen thematischen Einfälle.

*—op. 76 Sonate in a. Schw. fr. 7.—. Paris, Mathot. 1909.
*—op. 117 Suite in C. Ebenda. 1911.

MOUQUET, J., op. 24 Sonate. Fr. 15.—. Paris, Lemoine. 1907. —ms.
Ein ernstes Werk, das gute Musik, aber wenig Empfindung und Temperament enthält.

FIG. 23. *Handbuch der Violoncell-Literatur* by B. Weigl. Vienna, Universal Edition, 1929.

Cornwall; Henry G. Mills, County Hall, Truro.

Cumberland; Sec.

Derbyshire; Sec.: A. L. Westcombe, 43 Kedlestone Rd., Derby.

Devon; Miss D. H. Senior, A.R.C.M., County Education Office, Larkbeare, Topsham Rd., Exeter; Sec.: W. E. Philip, Esq., M.A., Chief Education Officer, County Education Office, Larkbeare, Topsham Rd., Exeter.

Dorsetshire; Miss Joan Brocklebank, Sutton Waldron, Blandford.

Durham.

East Lothian; Sec: Leslie J. Carnegie, B.L., County Buildings, Haddington.

Ely, Isle of; Sec.: M. G. Martindale, M.A.; 7 Hills Road, Cambridge.

Essex; Sec: W. J. Spurrell, 54 New St., Chelmsford.

Fife C.C. Education Committee; Mr. D. L. Merchant, B.Mus., Education Offices, Wemyssfield, Kirkcaldy, Fife

Gloucestershire; Mr. R. W. Clifford, F.T.C.L., G.T.C.L., Gloucestershire Community Council, Community House, College Green, Gloucester; Sec: Mr. R. J. Tilstone, Gloucestershire Community Council, Community House, College Green, Gloucester.

Hampshire & Isle of Wight; J. D. Lovelock, The Castle, Winchester; Sec: D. Cecil Williams, 92 Upper Shaftesbury Avenue, Southampton.

Herefordshire; Chn: Major F. J. Bullen, O.B.E., Mus.B. (Cantab.), F.R.C.O., Wennetune, Almeley, Hereford; Sec: Lt.-Col. C. W. Dann, M.C., E.D., Community House, 7 St. Owen St., Hereford

Hertfordshire; E. Bimrose, Highbury House, Highbury Rd., Hitchin; Sec.: Miss Deidre Ive, Highbury House, Highbury Rd., Hitchin.

Huntingdonshire; Mrs. Ethel M. Charles, White Willows, Hartford Rd., Huntingdon; Sec: Capt. F. H. L. Lewin, Shepherd's Hall, Godmanchester.

Inverness-shire; J. A. Mallinson, 63 Kingsmills Rd., Inverness; Sec: Miss Jean Sim, 5 Drummond St., Inverness.

Kent; Adviser: Mervyn Bruxner, Springfield, Maidstone; Sec: The County Music Adviser.

Lancashire; O. H. Edwards, D.Mus., H. Horrocks, B.Mus., Education Dept., County Hall, Preston.

Leicestershire.

Lindsey (Lincs.); L. N. C. Barnaby, M.A.(Oxon.), County Offices, Lincoln; Sec.: F. J. Birkbeck, M.A., County Offices, Lincoln; Organiser: L. N. C. Barnaby, M.A.

Middlesex.

Midlothian; Robert R. Stobie, M.A., Mus.B.; Sec: Miss Jane G. White, M.A., 85 New Hunterfield, Gorebridge.

Norfolk; Sidney Twemlow, County Education Office, Stracey Rd., Norwich; Sec: F. Lincoln Ralphs, M.Sc., Ph.D., LL.B., County Education Office, Stracey Rd., Norwich.

Northamptonshire; Adviser: Stanley Thorne, F.R.C.O., Craigleith Park View, Moulton, Northampton.

Northumberland; Dr. J. A. G. Mantz, 17 Ellison Place, Newcastle-upon-Tyne 1; Sec.: Alec Trotter, C.A.M.D.I.N., 17 Ellison Place, Newcastle-upon-Tyne 1.

Nottinghamshire; M. L. Nutley, County Hall, Trent Bridge, Nottingham; Sec: A. Roberts, Rural Community Council, 11 Park Row, Nottingham.

Orkney; J. Mitchell Bawden, L.R.A.M., Education Offices, Kirkwall; T: 614; Sec.: Alex Doloughan, M.A., Education Office, Kirkwall.

Oxfordshire; Miss C. Pilkington, 20 Beaumont St., Oxford; Sec: Miss H. C. Deneke.

Rutland; Sec: Miss Ferguson, 24 High St., Oakham.

Shropshire; Miss K. Schroeder; Sec.: J. Barham Johnson, M.A., Mus.Bac., M.R.S.T., Broomberry, Port Hill Drive, Shrewsbury.

Somerset; Geoffrey R. Self, St. Margarets, Hamilton Rd., Taunton; Sec: F. A. Goodliffe, St. Margarets, Hamilton Rd., Taunton.

Staffordshire; now disbanded.

Stirling, County of; Geo. C. McVicar, Dip.Mus.Ed., R.S.A.M., 22 Queen Street, Stirling; Sec.: John O'Brien, M.A., 38 Meeks Road, Falkirk.

Suffolk, East; Chn: Lady Cranbrook; Sec.: B. J. Reid, County Hall, Ipswich

Surrey; Norman Askew, A.R.A.M., L.R.A.M., A.R.C.M., F.R.C.O., Morningside, Wych Hill Lane, Woking; Sec: A. B. Leach, B.A., Education Dept., County Hall, Kingston-upon-Thames.

Sussex; Sec: Major G. H. Powell-Edwards, Old Bank House, Lewes.

Warwickshire; now disbanded.

Westmorland; Sec.: Miss E. Gilson, Sand Aire House, Kendal.

Wiltshire; Corporate County Music Adviser; Wiltshire Rural Music School (Miss Jean Horsfall, Director), 42 Wingfield Rd., Trowbridge; Sec: G. J. Oakshott, 24 Wingfield Rd., Trowbridge.

Worcestershire; Arthur William Benoy, County Education Offices, Castle St., Worcester.

Yorkshire; Sec: H. S. E. Sneison, 9 Minster Yard, York.

MUSIC ADVISERS AND ORGANISERS

PARTICULARS ARE SET OUT IN THE FOLLOWING ORDER

Authority; Name of Officer; Address; Official Title.

City of Aberdeen; John B. Dalby, B.Mus., F.R.C.O. Chm.), The Music Centre, St. Paul St., Aberdeen; Organiser of Music.

County Borough of Barnsley Education Committee; David John Green, Town Hall, Barnsley; Music Adviser.

Barrow-in-Furness County Borough; G. Uren, B.A., John Whinnerah Institute, Barrow-in-Furness, Lancs.; Teacher Adviser for Music.

Birmingham Education Committee; Dr. Desmond MacMahon, O.B.E., 59 Carless Avenue, Harborne, Birmingham, 17; Music Adviser.

Bradford: Dr. Charles Hooper, M.A., D.Mus., 7 Greencliffe Av., Baildon, Shipley, Yorks.; Master of the Lay Clerks & Choristers, Bradford Cathedral.

Bristol; A. Vaughan Davies, Education Office, College Green, Bristol; Music Adviser & Inspector of Schools.

Buckinghamshire; Kenneth Collingham, L.R.A.M., A.R.C.M. & Barbara Hales, G.R.S.M., Education Dept., County Offices, Aylesbury; Music Advisers.

Burton-upon-Trent; Miss Barbara Brown, L.R.A.M., 2 Main St., Stapenhill, Burton-upon-Trent, Staffs.; Music Organiser.

Cambridgeshire; G. D. Edwards, M.A., Shire Hall, Cambridge; (Home): The Malting House, Newnham Rd.; County Music Adviser: L. D. Stewart.

Carmarthenshire; Elfed Morgan, Education Offices, County Hall, Carmarthen; County Music Organiser.

Cheshire Education Committee; F. W. Mason, B.A., L.R.A.M., Cheshire County Training College, Alsager, Stoke-on-Trent; Senior Lecturer in Music.

Denbighshire; Megan Williams Parry, c/o Education Offices, Ruthin; County Music Organiser.

County Borough of Doncaster; B. William Appleby, M.B.E., M.A., (Private) 53 Thorne Rd., Doncaster; (Official) Education Offices, Whitaker St., Doncaster; Schools Music Organiser.

Durham County Council; L. T. Whaley, 2 Linden Grove, Leadgate, Consett; J. W. R. Taylor, Killowen Towers, Etherley Lane, Bishop Auckland; County Music Organisers.

Edinburgh; John B. R. Whitfield, 3 Bright's Crescent, Edinburgh, 9; Supervisor of Music.

Essex; Frank Burkill & Eric Stapleton, County Education Offices, Chelmsford; Music Advisers.

Gateshead Education Committee; Henry A. Tye, L.T.C.L., Education Office, Prince Consort Rd. S., Gateshead, 8; Music Organiser.

Glasgow; J. Gilmour Barr, 129 Bath St., Glasgow, C.2; Superintendent of Music.

Gloucestershire Education Committee & Gloucestershire Community Council; R. W. Clifford, Community House, College Green, Gloucester; County Music Adviser.

City of Gloucester; Harold Briggs, Education Office, 1 Brunswick Square, Gloucester; City Music Organiser.

Herefordshire County Council; R. Henley James, B.A., B.Mus., L.R.A.M., L.T.C.L., Education Dept., County Offices, Bath St., Hereford; County Music Organiser.

Hertfordshire; E. Bimrose, Highbury House, Highbury Rd., Hitchin, Herts; County Music Organiser.

Huntingdonshire; Eric Rosebury, B.A., B.Mus., Education Offices, Gazeley House, Huntingdon; County Music Organiser.

City of Leicester; Henry G. B. Saunders, F.R.C.O., Education Offices, Newarke St., Leicester; Inspector of Secondary Schools & Adviser in Music.

Lindsey (Lincs.); L. N. C. Barnaby, M.A., Lindsey County Offices, Education Dept., Newland, Lincoln; Music Organiser.

Kent Education Committee; Mr. Mervyn Bruxner, Springfield, Maidstone; County Music Adviser.

FIG. 24. *Who's Who in Music*, 4th edn. London, Burke's Peerage, 1962. (Now superseded by 5th edn., 1969.)

Ex. 212

Evidence of the remarkable accuracy of the oral tradition in Chinese opera is provided by the nearly complete agreement between the *kuencheu* recording in Hornbostel's record-series *Musik des Orients*, and the printed edition of 1792.[1] The intervals agree almost entirely, but there are slight rhythmic deviations—a crotchet in the edition of 1792 may become a dotted crotchet in the recorded version.

FOLK-SONG

The scientific study of Chinese folk-music has scarcely begun, for though many collections are now being made, no collector, so far as is known, has as yet made recordings in the field; all depend on the ear. From personal observations made during a brief stay in central China it seems probable that traces of other and older types of scalar structure survive in the folk-music. This is suggested by street-cries collected in Syhchuan and Gueyjou Provinces. The enharmonic tetrachord (a fourth built up from a major third and a minor second) of the Japanese modes *hirazyoosi*, *kumoizyoosi*, and *iwatozyoosi* (p. 145) is rare in classical Chinese music and *jingshih*; it occurs, however, in the following street-cry:

Ex. 213

Again, chains of thirds, so striking a feature of Western, African,

---

[1] Wang Kwang-chi, 'Über die chinesische klassische Oper 1530–1860', *Orient et Occident, Bibliothèque Sino-Internationale* (Geneva, 1934).

FIG. 25. *New Oxford History of Music*, vol. 1. O.U.P., 1957.

Ave regina 8 voc. und Dne. Deus salutio 4 voc. im Autogr. Ms. 19083, 1—3, P. Hofb. Wien. Ebendort ein Memento Dne. David per voce sola c. org. im Autogr. Ens aeternum (Walte Gott gnädig) 4 voc. c. orch. — O Jesu te invocamus (Allmächtiger, ebenso, 2 Hymnen). P. Lips., Br. & H. je 11 S. [B. B. B. Wagener. Musikfr. Wien die 2. Hymne. B. Lpz. Amst. Lpz. Thomas.

O fons pietatis, pour Basso solo et choeur, c. org. ou orch. Paris, Canaux. 11 S. P. [B. Wagener.

Tantum ergo f. Sopr. u. A. Stb. [Musikfr. Wien.

Gott ist mein Lied; zum Erntefest. P. Ms. 380b. [B. B.

Gott im Winter, in Stb. [Stadtb. Augsbg. Der Versöhnungstod, Cantate. P. im Stich. [Berl. Singakad. Musikfr. Wien (besteht aus 6 Adagios, die J. A. Schulze f. Chor u. Orch. bearb. hat).

3 Gesänge von Gellert f. 4 Stim. mit Clavierbegltg. Offenb., André. P. [B. M.

2. Weltliche Gesangsmusik.

a) Opern.

Alessandro il grande. Opera seria in 3 atti. P. Ms. 17526. [Hofb. Wien. B.B. Musikfr. Wien. Letztere erklärt die Oper für ein „Falsificat" (s. Seite 65, 1780).

Armida. Op. in 3 atti. P. Ms. 18637 in Hofb. Wien. B. B. Ms. 9912. Dresd. Mus. Ms. 376. (1. Aufführg. Esterhaz 29/2 1784. Wien 1797.)

Avide festa teatrale, Ms. P. in B. Wagener.

La Canterina, Opera buffa. Intermezzo 1766. P. Ms. 9916 in B. B.

Comedia Marchese. Ms. P. in B. Wagener.

La fedeltà premiata (Die be'•hnte Treue). Opera 1780. P. Ms. 9923 in B. B.

L'incontro improviso. Die unverhoffte Zusammenkunft, Oper in 3 Aufz. P. Ms. 18641 in Hofb. Wien. B. B. Ms. 9918 „rappres. 1775".

L'infeldeltà delusa. Burletta 1773. P. Ms. 9922 in B. B.

L'isola disabitata, dramma in 2 atti (Die unbewohnte Insel), aufgef. 1786 in Berlin im Musikliebhaber-Konzert. P. Ms. 9913 und 9913 c in B.B. Hofb. Wien Ms. 19238 mit 1779 gez. Darmst.

Le jugement de Paris, Ballet-pantom. en 3 act. 1. Akt. von Haydn, représ. 6/3 1793, in der großen Oper zu Paris. Ms. P. [Paris l'opéra.

Laurette, op.-com. en 3 a. (Paris,

théâtre de Monsieur, c. 1791). Paris, Sieber. P. [Brüssel Cons. Darmst.

Il mondo della luna. Opera giocoso in 3 atti. P. Ms. 17621 in Hofb. Wien. B. B. Ms. 9910 mit 1777 gez. Brüssel Cons. in 2 voll.

Orfeo ed Euridice, Dramma per musica composto di ... Presso Br. e H. in Lipsia. P. 11 Nrn. fol. 90 S. [Musikfr. Wien. Proske. Dresd. Mus., der Kl.-A. ebd. B. B. nur 1 Chor und 1 Arie in Stb. Ms. 9927, Part. im Druck. Brüss. Cons.

Orlando Paladino (Der Ritter Roland). Opera eroicomico in 3 atti. P. Ms. 9915, deutsch 9915 a in B. B. Dresd. Mus. in 3 voll. qufol. und in Stb. br. Mus. Ms. 464. Hofb. Wien unter Roland Ms. 18636. Darmst. Brüssel Cons. 3 voll. u. deutsch 1 vol.

Le Pescatrice, op. in 3 atti. 1770. P. Ms. 9919 in B. B.

Il ritorno di Tobia. Opera 1774. P. Ms 18643 in Hotb. Wien (siehe auch unter den Oratorien).

Ritter Roland, siehe Orlando.

Lo speziale, op. in 3 atti, 1768. P. Ms. 9917 in B. B.

La vera costanza (Die wahre Beständigkeit), kom. Oper in 3 Akten, deutscher Text. P. Ms. 18638 in Hofb. Wien. B.B. italien. C. P: La vera Costanza, Opera repres. 1766 in Wien. P. Autogr. und Textbuch (Weckerlin 3, 281). Brüssel Cons. Ms. 2 voll.

Die wüste Insel, siehe L'isola.

b) Cantaten.

Cantata per un Soprano c. acc. (d'orch.) (Ah come il core). Vienna, Artaria & Co. P. und 10 Stb. qufol. [B.B. und im Ms. L 299 Nr. 51 und M.. 112. B. M. im Ms.

L'Abbandono d'Arianna. Cantata a voce sola e clavicemb., geschrieben in London. Ms. D 23 in Padua Ant.

Arianna a Naxos. Cantata a voce sola con acc. del Clavic. Vienna, Artaria & Co. P. qufol. [Hofb. Wien u. Ms. 18753. B. Lpz. B. B. Ms. 9954, P. Musikfr. Wien. B. Wagener: Paris, Imbault. 17 S. B. M. Antiq. Rosenthal: Lond., J. Blands. 18 S. In Berlin noch ein Originaldruck: London printed for the author. 4⁰. mit H.'s eigener Untorschrift. Brüssel Cons: Bonn, Simrock. Stb. u. im Ms. P. — deutsch, Lpz. b. Hoffmeister & Kühnel. [Berlin K. H.

Die Erwählung eines Kapellmeisters, Cantato f. Soli, Chor u. Orch. Autogr. P. Ms. 16616 in Hofb. Wien. Musikfr. Wien in P. u. Stb. B. B. Ms. 9931.

1663⁵ Johann-Wilhelm Simlers teutscher Gedichten die dritte, von ihme selbsten um einen Drittheil vermehrt und verbesserte Aussfertigung . . . – *Zürich, J. W. Simler,* 1663. 1 vol. in-8º, 608. p.

C. Diebold (16), D. Friderici (19), A. Steigleder (67), Anon. (2)

D Mbs - **GB** Lbm

1663⁶ Catch that catch can, or a new collection of catches, rounds, and canons: being three or four parts in one. – *London, W. Godbid for J. Playford,* 1663. 1 vol. in-8º obl., 168 p.

J. Barnard, Barnwell, T. Brewer, W. Byrd, W. Child, J. Cobb (6), W. Cranford (6), R. Dering, W. Ellis (3), Ford, R. Gibbes, J. Hilton (51), G. Holmes (2), T. Holmes (12), W. Howes, S. Ives (3), J. Jenkins (2), H. Lawes (6), W. Lawes (20), M. Locke, J. Lugg, E. Nelham (15), T. Pearce, H. Smith, Stoner (2), J. Taylor, W. Webb (5), White (6), Wilson, Anon. (23)

GB Ge; Lbm

1663⁷ Musicks hand-maide. Presenting new and pleasant lessons for the virginals or harpsycon. – *London, printed for J. Playford,* 1663. 1 vol. in-4º obl., 30 f.

W. Lawes (4), M. Locke (2), J. Moss, B. Rogers (2), B. Sandley, Anon. (43)

GB Lbm

1664¹ R. Floridus canonicus de ·Silvestris a Barbarano istaș alias sacras cantiones ab excellentissimis musices auctoribus, unica, binis, ternis, quaternisque vocibus suavissimis modulis concinnatas, in lucem edendas curavit. – *Roma, I. de Lazzari,* 1664. 5 vol. in-8º, 53 p. (Sᵗ) 27 p. (A), 42 p. (T), 23 p. (B), 82 p. (Bc)

O. Benevoli, G. Bicilli, A. Carpani, G. Carissimi, C. Cecchelli, G. Corsi, S. Durarₜ⁻ D. Florido, F. Foggia, B. Graziani, F. Mangiarotti, G. M. Pagliardi, M. Savₗ N. Stamegna, G. Tricarico, G. Vincenti

D MÜs - **I** Bc

1664¹ᵃ Sacri concerti del sig. Giovanni Carisio cieco torinese a due, trè, quattro, e cinque voci. Con trè motetti del sig. Gio. Battista Γrabattone, suo maestro. Opera prima. – *Venezia, A. Vincenti,* 1664. 6 vol. in-4º, 68p. (S₁), 52p. (A), 50p. (T); 42p. (B)

G. Carisio (19), G. B. Trabattone (3)

I ASc - **S** Uu (mq. S₂ Bc)

544

Fig. 27. *Répertoire International des Sources Musicales.* Recueils imprimés XVI–XVII siècles, Munich, Bärenreiter/Henle.

ARNE (Thomas Augustine) (contd.)

Britannia

Britannia. A masque [words by D. Mallet], etc. pp. 23. *Printed for I. Walsh: London,* [1755] fol. *According to an advertisement on "British Melody" this work was issued as No. X of the series beginning with "Vocal Melody."* BU, C, GE, L, LAM, LGC, LCM (2)*, O.

Cimbeline

Cimbeline. See infra: Cymbeline.

Comus

The musick in the masque of Comus. Written by Milton ... Opera prima. [Score]. pp. 47. *William Smith: London,* [1740] fol. *A comparison of the imprints shows that there exist 3 different issues of this edition. The first 2 issues are distinguishable by different addresses for both publisher and author. On the 3rd issue there is no mention of the author in the imprint. Some copies contain a privilege dated* 1740-1. C (3), GE, L*, LCM (2), LCO, LGC, LTM, M, O.

[Another edition]. The musick in the masque of Comus ... Opera prima. [Score]. *Printed for J. Simpson: London,* [c.1750] fol. G (2), CFM, L, LCM, Lc, LK.

[Another edition]. The musick in the masque of Comus ... Opera prima. [Score]. *Printed for I. Walsh: London,* [c.1750] fol. ER, L, LCM.

[Another issue]. The musick in the masque of Comus ... Opera prima. [Score]. *I. Walsh: London,* [c.1755] fol, C, CKC, OUF.

The songs, duetto and trio in the masque of Comus ... dispos'd properly for a harpsicord & voice, and may be accompanied with a violin or German flute & violoncello. pp. 25. *Printed for ... J. Cox: London,* [c.1752] obl. fol. C, CKC, L.

[Another edition]. The songs, duetto and trio in the masque of Comus, etc. *Wm Smith: London,* [c.1752] obl. fol. LGC, L.

[Another edition]. The songs, duetto and trio in the masque of Comus, etc. *Ja¹ and Jn° Simpson: London,* [c.1770] obl. fol. LVU.

The songs, duet & trio with the overture in the masque of Comus. Set for the violin, German flute and harpsichord. pp. 23. *Printed for Henry Thorowgood: London,* [c.1765] fol. CJC, CKC, L.

[Another edition]. The songs, duet and trio, with the overture in the masque of Comus, etc. *Printed for S. and A. Thompson: London,* [1778] fol. LCM, LK.

[Another edition]. The songs, duet & trio with the overture in the masque of Comus, etc. *Longman and Broderip: London,* [c.1780] fol. BU, D (2), DAM, G.

Comus ... for the voice, harpsichord, and violin, pp. 18. *Printed for Harrison & Co.: London,* [c.1785] obl. fol. B, BA, BU, C, CKC (2), EP, GU, L, LAM, LCM, LTM, LVU, M (2), OUF.

Comus. A masque, etc. [P.F.]. *In:* The Piano-Forte Magazine. Vol. III. No. 2. [1797] 8°. L.

The music in the masque of Comus adapted for the German flute, etc. pp. 26. *Straight and Skillern: London,* [c.1775] obl. 8°. CKC.

Comus, a masque ... for the German flute. pp. 20. *Harrison & Co.: London,* [1784] obl. 4°. G.

By dimpl'd brook. [Song]. See BY.

By the gayly circling glass. *A bacchanalian song, etc. R. Falkener: London,* [c.1770] s. sh. fol. L, LSL.

By the gayly-circling glass. [Song]. Sung by Mr. Reinhold, etc. *[London,* 1774] s. sh. 4°. *The London Magazine, Nov.,* 1774. L.

By the gayly circling glass. [Song]. See BY.

Fly swiftly ye minutes. [Song]. See FLY.

How gentle was my Damon's air. [Song]. See How.

ARNE (Thomas Augustine) (contd.)

Now Phœbus sinketh in the west. [Song]. See Now.

Preach not me your musty rules. [Song]. See PREACH.

Sweet Eccho. [Song]. See SWEET.

The wanton god who pierces hearts. [Song]: See WANTON.

Wou'd you taste the noontide air. [Song]. Sung by Mrs. Pinto in ... Comus, with graces. ff. 2. *[London,* c.1770] fol. L, LCM.

[Another edition]. The Noontide Air. [Song]. As sung by Miss Catley ... newly set by Dr. Arne. ff. 2. *Str[aight] & Sk[illern: London,* c.1770] fol. L.

Wou'd you taste yᵉ noontide air. [Song]. See WOULD.

[For other songs, etc., published anonymously:] See COMUS.

The Cooper

The Cooper, a comic opera ... [written and] composed by Dr. Arne. [Score]. pp. 29. *Printed for W. Napier: London,* [1772] obl. fol. L, M (2).

The Country Wake

The Country Wake. See infra: [*Songs, etc.* a. *Collections*]. The Syren ... with ... the new final piece at Vaux-hall Gardens called the Country Wake, etc.

Cymbeline

To fair Fidele's grassy tomb. *Dirge in Cimbeline, etc.* [Song, words by Wm. Collins]. *Sk[illern: London,* c.1780] s. sh. fol. *First published in vol. 2 of Arne's "Lyric Harmony,"* 1748. GU, L, LCM.

[Another edition]. To fair Fidele's grassy tomb, a favourite dirge in Cymbeline. Written by Mᵣ Collins, etc. ff. 2. *S. A. & P. Thompson: London,* [c.1785] fol. B.

—— Dirge in Cimbeline. Set by Dᵣ Arne. [Followed by an anonymous song "Ally Croaker"]. [Songs]. pp. 3. *Sk[illern: London,* c.1790] fol. L.

—— Dirge in Cymbelin. See BILLINGTON (T.). A second set of glees ... to which is added airs by Handel and Arne, harmonized by T. Billington, etc.

To fair Fidele's grassy tomb. [Song]. [For editions published anonymously:] See To.

Cymon and Iphigenia

Cymon and Iphigenia. A cantata ... sung by Mr. Lowe at Vaux Hall Gardens. p.p. 9. *[London,* c.1750] fol. CD, ER, L (2), LAM, LCM (2), Lc (2), LGC.

[Another edition]. Cymon and Iphigenia. A cantata, etc. *[London,* c.1760] fol. BU*, CKC, LGC.

[Another edition]. Cymon and Iphigenia. A cantata, etc. *Jo° Johnson: London,* [c.1760] fol. CFM, GE, T.

[Another issue]. Cymon and Iphigenia. A cantata, etc. *John Johnson: London,* [c.1760] fol. LSL.

[Another edition]. Cymon and Iphigenia. A cantata, etc. (*Thompson & Son: London,*) [c.1760] fol. BU, CKC.

[Another edition]. Cymon and Iphigenia. A cantata, etc. pp. 4. *Printed for C. and S. Thompson: [London,* c.1770] fol. CD, D, L, Lc, LGC, O.

[Another edition] Cymon and Iphigenia. A cantata, etc. pp. 4. *Longman, Lukey & Co.: London,* [c.1775] fol. CKC, LCM*.

Cymon and Iphigenia. A cantata ... for the voice, harpsichord and violin. pp. 8. *Printed for Harrison and Co.: London,* [1786] fol. *Plate number* 128 *being that of "The New Musical Magazine."* CPL.

The Desert Island

What tho' his guilt. *Mrs. Scott's Song in the Desart Island.* pp. (2). *Printed ... for G. Kearsley: [London,* 1760] fol. "*By assignment of Dr. Arne." Pp. 26 & 27 of a larger collection.* LCM.

FIG. 28. *British Union Catalogue of Early Music,* ed. E. B. Schnapper. Butterworth, 1957.

CHAPTER VII.

DICTIONARIES OF MUSIC.

E now come to the consideration of a large and a useful class of musical literature—the Dictionaries of Music, which range themselves under three groups—technical dictionaries, biographical dictionaries, and those which endeavour to combine both subjects.

It has already been pointed out that Music was the earliest of the arts to possess a special dictionary—the *Diffinitorium Musicæ* of Tinctoris, published, it is believed, as early as 1474, the interest of which now is purely antiquarian. But it is equally remarkable that, although such terms as fell within the scope of his work are explained in the well-known *Glossarium* of Ducange, no second attempt of the kind should have been made till the year 1701, when Thomas Balthazar Janowka, an organist at Prague, published his *Clavis ad Thesaurum magnæ artis*

144

FIG. 29. *The Literature of Music* by J. E. Matthew. Stock, 1896.

stellt) — Wien, Haslinger, Klavierwerke, Heft 36, 4. — Wien, Diabelli (Philomele 440).
V.-Nr. 7834. — Leipzig, Peters Nr. 299a (Friedlaender). Vgl. S. 1016.

Anmerkung: Erste Besprechung in der »Musikalischen Realzeitung« Boßlers, 6. Januar 1790. — Goethes Lied ist Mozart wahrscheinlich durch die Sammlung Deutscher Lieder (1779), I, Nr. 14 des Wieners J. A. Steffan oder die gleichnamige Sammlung Carl Friberths (1780), III, 14 bekannt geworden. Als Dichter ist bei Steffan nicht Goethe genannt, sondern Gleim [!]. Neudruck: DTÖ XXVII, 2, Nr. 7. Vgl. S. 1016.

Literatur: Jahn III¹, 350; II², 61; II³, 73; II⁴, 75. — M Friedlaender, Das deutsche Lied I, 46, 326; II, 164. — Abert II, 67, 258f. — Revisions-Bericht zur G.-A. (G. Nottebohm).

477. Maurerische Trauermusik für 2 Violinen, Viola, Baß, 2 Oboen, Klarinette, Bassetthorn, Kontrafagott und 2 Waldhörner   = 479ᵃ.

477ᵃ = Anh. 11ᵃ.
Cantata
für eine Singstimme und Klavier. Text von Lorenzo da Ponte
Komp. September 1785 in Wien.

Das Wienerblättchen meldet am 26. September 1785, p. 224: »Ueber die glückliche Genesung der beliebten Virtuosin Madame Storace hat der k. k. Hoftheaterpoet Abb. da Ponte ein italiänisches Freudenlied angefertigt: »Per la ricuperata salute di Ophelia.« Dieses ist von den berühmten drei Kapellmeistern Salieri, Mozart und Cornetti in die Musik zu singen beim Clavier gesetzt worden und wird in der Kunsthandlung von Artaria & Comp. auf dem Michelerplatz um 17 x verkauft.« Vgl. auch die Realzeitung 18. Okt. 1785, 42. Stück, S. 668. Mozart hat es in seinem thematischen Katalog nicht verzeichnet. Vgl. Jahn II³, 23; II⁴, 23. — Da Ponte, Denkwürdigkeiten (ed. Gugitz) II, 322; III, 356.

478.
Quartett
für Klavier, Violine, Viola, Violoncell
Komp. 16. Oktober 1785 in Wien. Mozart-Verz. 27.

Autograph: Im Besitz des Grafen von Hochberg in Rohnstock in Schlesien, der es im Dezember 1872 von C. A. André erworben hat. — Überschrift: »Quartetto di Wolfgango Amadeo Mozart mp. Vienna li 16 d'Ottobre 1785.« 20 Blätter mit 40 beschriebenen Seiten, Querformat, zwölfzeilig. André-Verz. 219. In Mozarts Verzeichnis steht

Fᵢɢ. 30. *Chronologisch-thematisches Verzeichnis sämtliche Tonwerke W. A. Mozarts.* Köchel-Einstein. Ann Arbor, Michigan, J. W. Edwards, 1947.

368 a = 341

Kyrie
für 4 Singstimmen, 2 Violinen, Violen, 2 Flöten, 2 Oboen, 2 Klarinetten, 2 Fagotte,
4 Hörner, 2 Trompeten, Pauken, Baß und Orgel

Komponiert angeblich zwischen November 1780 und März 1781 in München
Verzeichnisse: André hs. 160 – WSF (357) 367

Autograph: verschollen; früher Frankfurt a. M., Joh. Nep. Schelble (1789–1837); Offenbach, J. André.

Abschrift: Berlin PrStB (z. Zt. Marburg, Westd.B.), v. d. Hand A. E. Müllers, m. d. Bemerkung: „Nach Mozart's Handschrift copirt. Die Original-Partitur besitzt Hr. Kapellm. André."

Erstausgabe: Offenbach, J. André. „Nach dem hinterlassenen Original-Manuscripte herausgegeben"; V.-Nr. 4851 (um 1825). Eine ebda erschienene neuere Partitur mit derselben Bemerkung.

Ausgaben: *Partituren:* W. A. M. Serie 3, 5 – Vorabdruck NMA, Part., Orch.St., Chor-Part. u. Org. – B & H, Part.Bibl. 577 – London, Novello, Ewer & Co. (mit einem Orgel- od. Klavierauszug von Novello); Pl.-Nr. 206 – *Chorstimmen:* B & H, Chor-Bibl. 2007 – *Klavierauszüge:* Leipzig, B & H, hrsg. v. M. U. Arkwright; V.-Nr. 23182 – Offenbach, André; V.-Nr. 4851 (bei der Partitur, s. EA)

Anmerkung: Schon Jahn hat erkannt, daß dieses grandiose Kyrie „sowohl dem Charakter der Composition als der Zusammensetzung des Orchesters nach zu urteilen wohl nur bei diesem Aufenthalt in München geschrieben sein kann."

Literatur: Jahn [1] 674 Nr. 19, [III] 489 f., [2] 605, [3] 683, [4] 688 – Abert I 777, 798, II 857 – Rev.Ber. (Nottebohm) W. A. M. – WSF III 244 – A. Hyatt King, „Mozart in Retrospect", London 1955, S. 14 – K. Pfannhauser, „Zum d-moll-Kyrie", Mitt. Mozarteum 1956, 17. H., S. 1–4

368 b = 370

Quartett
für Oboe, Violine, Viola und Violoncello

Komponiert Anfang 1781 in München
Verzeichnisse: André hs. 173 – André 255 – WSF (356) 366

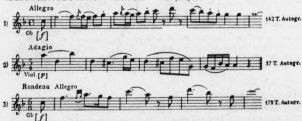

Autograph: Paris, Bibl. du Conservatoire, Slg. Malherbe; LLA Auktion 26 (29. Okt. 1900) Nr. 49; früher Offenbach, Aug. André (1862); Frankfurt a. M., Jul. André (1860). – 8 Bl. mit 13 beschriebenen S., Querformat 12zeilig. Überschrift: „Quarttetto [Par Mr Wolffgang Amadeo Mozart] à Munic 1781."

Fɪɢ. 31. L. Ritter von Köchel, *Chronologisch-thematisches Verzeichnis.*
Breitkopf, 1964.

KONZERTE

1041 Konzert a-moll

Besetzung. Solo: Violine. Begleitung: 2 Viol., Vla. u. Cont.

BGA XXI¹, 3. Vgl. auch XLVI¹, S. LXI und 233. — EZ Köthen etwa 1720. Bach gestaltete dieses Werk später zu einem Klavierkonzert um. (Vgl. Nr. 1058.)

Autograph. 6 Stimmen (27 beschr. S.) 4° mit d. Titel: „Concerto a Violino certato due Violini una Viola } obligati e Basso Continuo di J. S. Bach", BB Mus. ms. Bach St. 145. Faksimile der 1. Seite der Solo-Viol. St. in BGA XLIV (Bl. 21).

Abschriften. 2 Part. aus d. 2. Hälfte d. 18. Jhs., BB Mus. ms. Bach P 252 u. 253.

Ausgaben. Breitkopf & Härtel Part. PB 2724, Stimmen OB 2624a/b, Cembalost. von M. Reger. — Eulenburg Part, (Schering). — Peters Part. Nr. 229a u. Stimmen (S. W. Dehn).

Literatur. Spitta I 734f. — Spitta VA 142. — Schweitzer 385ff. — Wolfrum 125. — Moser 96. — Steglich 116. — W. Niemann, Bachs Violin-Konzerte a-moll und E-dur. Musikführer Nr. 237. Leipzig 1902. — BJ 1905: 115f.; 1912: 143; 1913: 21; 1914: 188f.; 1926: 80; 1928: 145f. — BFB 1908 (Chemnitz): 148ff. (Schering); 1914: 81ff. (Schering); 1925 (kl. BF): 4 (Heuß); 1929: 58 (Heuß).

1042 Konzert E-dur

Besetzung. Solo: Violine. Begleitung: 2 Viol., Vla. u. Cont.

BGA XXI¹, 21. — EZ Köthen etwa 1720. Bach arbeitete dieses Werk später zu einem Klavier-konzert um. (Vgl. Nr. 1054.)

580

FIG. 32. *Bach-Werke-Verzeichnis* by W. Schmieder. Leipzig, Breitkopf, 1958.

778a. **Cunnison, I.,** *Central African chronology* ('Man' LV, p. 143, No. 157), 1955.
BD¹GKL¹L²M

779. **Čurčin, M.,** *Das serbische Volkslied* (Leipzig, 1905).

Curtis, Natalie, see Burlin.

780. **Dal, Erik,** *Scandinavian Folk Music* ('J. of the Intern. Folk Music Council' VIII, p. 6 ff.), 1936. **ACJKL**

781. —— *Glimt af international folkemusikforskning* ('Nordisk Musikkultur' I, p. 340 ff.), 1952. **AK**

*782. —— *Nordisk folkeviseforskning siden 1800* (Copenhagen, 1956). **ACK**

783. —— *Opgaver og muligheder i folkemusikforskningen belyst gennem anmeldelser af ny udenlandsk litteratur* (= Problems and possibilities in folk music research, illustrated by reviews of recent foreign literature) ('Dansk Musiktidsskrift' XXXII, p. 69 ff.), Copenhagen, 1957. **AK**

783a. —— *The Faroese folk-song chain dance* ('The Folklorist' IV, No. 4, p. 106 ff.), Manchester, Winter 1957/'58. **A**

783b. —— *The linked stanza in Danish ballads: its age and its analogues* ('J. of the Intern. Folk Music Council' X, p. 35 ff.), 1958. **ACIJKL**

784. **Dalal, Navinkumar,** *Die Pflege der indischen Kunstmusik* ('Musica' VIII, p. 182 ff.), 1954. **CKLL¹**

785. **Dalberg, F. H. von,** *Ueber die Musik der Indier* (ein Abhandlung des Sir William Jones), translated from the English, with additions by ——), Erfurt, 1802. **C**

786. **Dalman, G.,** *Arabische Gesänge* ('Palästina-Jahrbuch' 1924, p. 77 ff.). **D¹K**

787. —— *Nachlese arabischer Lieder aus Palästina* ('Beiträge zur alttestamentischen Wissenschaft' 1920, p. 43 ff.).

787a. **Dalyell, John,** *Musical memoirs of Scotland, with historical notes and annotations* (Edinburgh, 1849).

788. **Dam, Theodore van,** *The influence of the West African songs of derision on the New World* ('African Music' I, p. 53 ff.), 1954. **AC**

789. **Damais, E.,** *Chants Africains notés* (in Hubert Caron, 'Rybani'), Le Havre, 1936.

790. **Dam Bo,** *The music of the Pemsians* ('The Journal of the Music Academy, Madras' XXI, p. 139 ff.), 1950. **AC**

791. **Danckert, Werner,** *Ursymbole melodischer Gestaltung* (Kassel, 1932). **A**

792. —— *Ostasiatische Musikästhetik* ('Ostasiatische Zeitschrift' N.S. VII), 1931.
D¹GKL⁵

793. —— *Musikwissenschaft und Kulturkreislehre* ('Anthropos' XXXII, p. 1 ff.), 1937.
BD¹GHKL¹L²M

794. —— *Musikethnologische Erschliessung der Kulturkreise* ('Mitteil. d. Anthrop.

Ges. Wien' LXVII, p. 53 ff.), 1937.
D¹GHL²

795. —— *Wandernde Liedweisen, eine Grundfrage volkskundlicher Musikforschung* ('Archiv f. Musikforschung' II, p. 101 ff.), 1937. **CDH¹KL**

796. —— *Grundriss der Volksliedkunde* (Berlin, 1938). **IL**

797. —— *Das europäische Volkslied* (Berlin, 1939). **DFHIJL**

798. —— *Die ältesten Spuren germanischer Volksmusik* ('Z. f. Volkskunde' XLVIII, p. 137 ff.), 1939. **AD¹KL¹**

799. —— *A félhang nélküli pentatonica erdete* (*The origin of anhemitonic pentatonic scales*) in 'Mélanges offerts à Zoltan Kodály à l'occasion de son 6oième anniversaire', p. 9 ff.), Budapest, 1943.
ACK

800. —— *Älteste Musikstile und Kulturschichten in Ozeanien und Indonesien* ('Z. f. Ethnologie' vol. 77, p. 198 ff.), 1952.
ABD¹GHJKL¹L²M

801. —— *Wesen und Ursprung der Tonwelt im Mythos* ('Archiv f. Musikw. XII, p. 97 ff.), 1955. **ACDFGKLL¹**

802. —— *Melodiestile der finnisch-ugrischen Hirtenvölker* ('Studia Memoriae Belae Bartók Sacra', p. 175 ff.), Budapest, 1956. **AC**

803. —— *Tonmalerei und Tonsymbolik in der Musik der Lappen* ('Die Musikforschung' IX, p. 286 ff.), 1956. **ACEFIKLL¹**

804. —— *Hirtenmusik* ('Archiv f. Musikwiss.' XIII, p. 97 ff.), 1956. **DFGKLL¹**

805. —— *Melodiestile der Ob-Ugrier* ('Acta Musicologica' XXVIII, p. 122 ff.), Basel, 1956. **ACDGH¹KLL¹**

806. **Daniel, F.,** *Note on a gong of bronze from Katsina, Nigeria* ('Man' XXIX, No. 113, p. 157 ff.), 1929. **BD¹GKL²M**

807. **Daniel, Gaston,** *La musique au Congo* ('J. de la Soc. Intern. de Musique' VIII, p. 56 ff.), Paris, 1911.

808. **Daniélou, Alain,** *Introduction to the Study of Musical Scales* (London, 1943).
ACJ

809. —— *The categories of intervals or Sruti Jatis* ('The Journal of the Music Academy Madras' XVII, p. 74 ff.), 1946. **C**

810. —— *The different schools of Indian Music* (ibid. XIX, p. 165 ff.), 1948.

*811. —— *Northern Indian Music* (2 vols.): I. *History, Theory and Technique* (London/ Calcutta, 1950); II. *The main Ragas. An analysis and notation* (London, 1953)
ACD (1 only), **G** (id.) **IKL**

812. —— *A Commentary on the Mahesvara Sutra* ('The Journal of the Music Academy, Madras' XXII, p. 119 ff.), 1951. **AC**

813. —— *Notes on the Sangita Damodara* (ibid. XXII, p. 129 ff.), 1951. **AC**

814. —— *Some Problems facing research on*

103

Music Librarianship

LINE, M. B. A classified catalogue of musical scores: some problems (*Library Association Record*, November, 1952, pp. 362–4).

In this article Mr. Line makes some criticism of the L.C. schedules and deals with a number of the difficulties in applying them in certain cases. He recommends a revision of the schedules (though no specific suggestions are made) together with an entirely new scheme for music written before 1750.

PRACTICAL EXAMPLES OF THE CLASSIFICATION OF BOOKS AND SCORES

These examples are provided for two reasons. First, they show the relative lengths of notations for the same book or score in different schemes; secondly, students can study, in so far as the necessarily limited number of examples allows, the relative merits of the schemes in showing the relationship between works that have a common factor (as in the first two examples, and the three Elgar scores), and in the provision or lack of provision for works that have some superficial relationship but for which separate places ought to be provided (as in the piano and string trios). Except for the D.C. placings, all have been checked by the appropriate expert mentioned under "Acknowledgements" at the beginning of the book.

	Brown	Cutter	Dewey (14th ed.)	L.C.	Bliss	B.C.M.
BEETHOVEN						
Piano sonatas	C647·9	VZP	786·41	M23(a)	VXPI	QPE
BLOM						
Beethoven's piano sonatas discussed	C647·9	VVB	786·41	MT145	VV9,S,I *or* VWJN, B3	BBJAQPE
DEBUSSY						
Preludes for piano	C647·9	VZP	786.4(b)	M25	VXPP	QPJ
ELGAR						
"Enigma" variations, min. score	C761	VYA	785·1	M1003	VXMY	MM/T
do. arr. piano duet	C647·9	VZPA	786·49	M209	VXPD	QNVK/MM/T
do. arr. 2 pf	C647·9	VZPB	786·49	M215	VXPD	QNUK/MM/T
SACKVILLE-WEST & SHAWE-TAYLOR						
The record guide	C330(c)	VXME	789·9	ML156·2(d)	VWYV	A/FD(WT)
NEWMAN						
Opera nights [synopses and criticisms]	C781	VV10	782·1	MT95	VWSO	AC
MOZART						
Don Giovanni: vocal sc.	C781	VYO	782·1(e)	M1503	VXL3(f)	CC
MOZART [i.e. Da Ponte]						
Don Giovanni: libretto	C781	VYOL	782·1	ML50	VXL5 *or* VWSI	BMSAC
SMETANA						
Bartered Bride, v.s.	C783	VYO	782·1(g)	M1503	VXL35(f)	CC
FORSYTH						
Orchestration	C760	VWT	781·632	MT70	VWVD	AM/D
BEETHOVEN						
String trios, op. 9 [parts]	C777	VYC	785·73	M351	VXNM	RXNT

182

FIG. 34. *Music Librarianship* by E. T. **Bryant**. J. Clarke, 1959.

Ausführliche Geschichte der Studien-Anstalten in Regensburg (1538–1880) in Verhandlungen des Hist. Ver. Bd. 35, 36, 37, Regensburg 1880 ff.; F. K r a u t w u r s t , Art. *Heilsbronn* in MGG; E. K o m o r z y n s k i , *Der Vater der Zauberflöte*, E. *Schikaneder*, Wien 1948, Neff; U. K o r n - m ü l l e r , *Die alten Musiktheoretiker* in KmJb II, 1887, 1; ders., *St. Wolfgang*, ebda. IX, 1894, 7; D. M e t - t e n l e i t e r , *Mg. der Stadt Regensburg*, Regensburg 1866, Pustet; ders., *Mg. der Oberpfalz*, Amberg 1867, Pohl; P. M o h r , *Die Hs. B 211–215 der Proske-Bibl. zu Regensburg*, Kassel 1955, BVK; H. N e s t l e r , *Der Regensburger Domchor*, Regensburg 1928, Pustet; J. P o l l , *Ein Osterspiel, enthalten in einem Prozessionale der Alten Kapelle in Regensburg* in KmJb 34, 1950, 35; J. S m i t s v a n W a e s b e r g h e , *Over het Ontstaan van Sequens en Prosula en beider oorspronkelijke Uitvoeringswijze* in Fs. Bernet-Kempers, 1957, 49–57 u. Kgr-Ber. der IGMW. Köln 1958, 251–254; B. S t ä b l e i n , *Regensburg, das Bild einer bayr. Musikstadt*, München 1948, Desch; ders., *Die Choralhs. der Regensburger Bibl.* in Caecilienver.-Organ 63, 1932, 198; ders., *Die zwei St. Emmeramer Kantatorien aus dem 11. Jh.* in 13. Jahresbericht des Ver. zur Erforschung der Regensburger Diözesangeschichte, Metten 1939, 239; ders., *Zwei Textierungen des Alleluia Christus resurgens in St. Emmeram* in Fs. t. J. Smits van Waesberghe (1961), in Vorb.; F. A. S t e i n , *Der Welt ältete KM.-Schule*, Caecilienver.-Organ 81, 1961, 75; J. T h a m m , *Das Musikgymnasium der Regensburger Domspatzen*, ebda. 81, 1961, 10; K. W e i n m a n n , *Die Proskesche Musikbibl. in Regensburg* in KmJb 24, 1911, 107; ders., *Regensburg als KM.-Stadt*, Regensburg 1928, Pustet; P. W i l d , *Über Schauspiele u. Schaustellungen in Verhandlungen des Hist. Ver. Bd. 53, Regensburg 1901; einschlägige Personen-Art. in MGG; eigene Arch.-Studien.

August Scharnagl

Reger, Johann Baptist Joseph M a x (imilian; hierzu Taf. 10), * 19. März 1873 in Brand (Oberpfalz), † 11. Mai 1916 in Leipzig. Regers Vater Joseph Reger († 1905 in München), als Lehrer 1874 an die Präparandenschule in Weiden versetzt, besaß vorzügliche mus. Anlagen, spielte mehrere Instr., bastelte eine Hausorgel und verf. eine pädagogisch wertvolle Harmonielehranweisung für die Schulen. Die Mutter Philomena († 1911), von der Max, das älteste von fünf Kindern, neben der zur Fülle neigenden Gestalt auch eine hinter oft drastischem Humor versteckte melancholische Sensibilität geerbt hatte, war eine Tochter des im Alter verarmten Fabrik- und Gutsbesitzers Joseph Reichenberger. Nach nicht eben methodischer Musikunterweisung durch die Eltern erhielt Max Reger im Okt. 1884 geregelten Unterricht bei dem Org. Adalbert Lindner (1860–1946), der 1921 eine Biogr. über Regers Jugendjahre veröff. Neben Beethoven und der romant. Kl.-Musik lernte Max die Inventionen von Bach und, im 4hd.-Spiel, die symphonische und KaM.-Lit. kennen. Als Org. konnte er bald seinen Lehrer im liturg. Orgelspiel vertreten. Mit fünfzehn Jahren empfing er nachhaltige Eindrücke vom Besuch der Bayreuther Festspiele. Im selben Jahre komp. er, gleich in Reinschrift, eine Ouvertüre *h* für das Weidener Liebhaberorch. Lindner sandte diese Kompos. heimlich nach Sondershausen an H. Riemann, der Regers ungewöhnliche Begabung erkannte und ihm zunächst einige seiner Lehrbücher übersandte. Im Apr. 1890 wurde er sein Kompos.-Lehrer. Vor der Übersiedlung nach Sondershausen hatte Reger noch ein StrQu., Präludien und Fugen für Kl. sowie Lieder komp. In Riemanns Nachlaß fand sich ferner ein 1890 komp. Symphonie-Satz *d*. Reger folgte seinem Lehrer nach Wiesbaden, komp. dort seine ersten bei Augener in London ersch. KaM.-Werke und Lieder und gab Unterricht am Kons. In dieser Zeit schloß er Freundschaft mit F. Busoni. Nach Ableistung seiner militärischen Dienstzeit kehrte er, durch Überarbeitung und genußfreudiges Leben („*Sturm- und Trankzeit*") erkrankt, 1898 ins

Elternhaus zurück. Er beschäftigte sich mit zeitgenöss. Lit. und komp. in unaufhaltsamer Folge neben zahlreichen KaM.- und Kl.-Werken und Liedern die großen Choralfantasien u. a. Orgelmusik, deren erster großer Interpret K. Straube wurde. 1901 verzog er nach München, wo er heftigen Widerständen durch die „Neudeutsche Schule" um Thuille, Louis, Schillings u. a. begegnete. Als inzwischen namhafter Pianist verstand er es, zusammen mit seinen Freunden H. Marteau, J. Hösl, J. Loritz, A. Schmid-Lindner u. a., seine oft angefeindete Musik durchzusetzen. Gemeinsam mit R. Strauss, dem er hohe Verehrung zollte, trat er in scharf formulierten Artikeln für die neue Musik und die Rechte der Komp. ein. Ferner schloß er Freundschaft mit Ph. Wolfrum, M. Hehemann und dem Dichter R. Braungart. Am 25. Okt. 1902 heiratete er Elsa von Bercken, geb. von Bagenski († 3. Mai 1951 in Bonn), sechs Jahre später adoptierte das Ehepaar die Töchter Christa und Lotti. In München komp. Reger u. a. das Kl.-Quintett *c* op. 64, das StrQu. *d* op. 74, die sehr angegriffene V.-Sonate *C* op. 72, die Bach-Var. für Kl., wesentliche Tle. der *Schlichten Weisen* und, als große Orch.-Werke, die Sinfonietta *A* und die Serenade *G*. Unzufrieden mit den Verhältnissen in der bayr. Hauptstadt, nahm er 1907 den Ruf als Univ.-MD. und Kompos.-Lehrer in Leipzig an, wurde kgl. sächs. Prof. und 1908, auf Veranlassung seines Biogr. F. Stein, Dr. phil. h. c. der Univ. Jena. Für diese Ehrung, der weitere akad. Titel folgten, bedankte er sich mit dem 100. Ps. für Chor und Orch. Sein Schaffen stieg sprunghaft an. Dem Freunde Marteau widmete er das V.-Konzert *A*, Frieda Kwast-Hodapp das Kl.-Konzert *f*, A. Nikisch den *Symphonischen Prolog zu einer Tragödie*, dem mit der Familie Mendelssohn verwandten Geheimrat Wach das StrQu. *Es*. 1909 hatte er große Erfolge mit eigenen Kompos. in London. Zwei Jahre später übernahm er die Leitung der Meininger Hofkapelle. Seine ausgedehnte Dgt.-Tätigkeit (die z. T. sehr kühnen Progr. sind in dem 1949 ersch. Briefwechsel mit Herzog Georg II. von Sachsen-Meiningen abgedr.) hat sein symphonisches Schaffen wesentlich gefördert. (Vier Zeichnungen von W. von Beckerath geben ein deutliches Bild von Regers Dirigierweise, Arbeiten des Hamburger Malers F. Nölken zeigen den emsig Schaffenden am Schreibtisch.) Am 1. Juli 1914 wenige Tage nach dem Tode des Herzogs, gab Reger den Posten ab und zog nach Jena, wo er seine letzten Werke komp. Auf einer Konzertreise ereilte den eben 43jähr. der Herztod. Die Aschenurne, sechs Jahre lang im Jenaer Arbeitszimmer aufgestellt, wurde 1922 in Weimar in einem Ehrengrab beigesetzt. Ihre endgültige Ruhestätte fand sie am 11. Mai 1930 in München. Unter Regers zahlreichen Schülern befanden sich die Komp. J. Haas, J. Weinberger, O. Schoeck, H. Unger, K. Hasse, H. Grabner, F. Lubrich, ferner R. Würz, der Musikkritiker A. Berrsche und die Brüder A. und F. Busch, die im In- und Ausland für die Interpretation seiner Werke berühmt wurden.

Werke (nur die Orig.-Verlage angegeben. Gleichzeitige oder spätere Übernahmen durch andere Verlage sowie Neuaufl. bis 1952 s. F. Stein, *Thematisches Verz. der im Druck ersch. Werke v. Max Reger*, Lpz. 1953, B & H; Sign. wie op. 79 m. Kompos. f. Kl., Org., Gsg., V., Vc., Chor oder op. 103 m. dem nachträglich hinzugefügten Obertitel „Hausmusik" sind aufgegliedert worden). Übersicht: A. Instrumentalmusik. 1. Orchesterwerke. – 2. Solo-Instrumente m. Orchester. – 3. Kammermusik. a. mit Klavier. b. ohne Klavier. – 4. Klaviermusik. – 5. Orgelmusik. – B. Vokalmusik. 1. Mehrstimmige Gesänge. a. mit Orchester. b. mit Klavier. c. mit Orgel. d. a cappella. – 2. Sologesänge. a. mit Orchester. b. mit

FIG. 35. *Die Musik in Geschichte und Gegenwart*, ed. F. Blume. Kassel, Bärenreiter, 1949–68.

N. 1, 4, 8 à 9—, N. 2, 6, 9 à 5—,
N. 3, 5, 10—12 à 6—, N. 7 7.50.
2. Le Berger, pastorale 5—.
3. Les Chasseresses, fanfare 6—.
4. L'Escarpolette, valse lente 6—, —30 *Gutheil.*
5. Cortège rustique 5—.
6. Pas des Ethiopiens 5—.
7. Scène et danse de la Bacchante 6—.
8. Marche et Cortège de Bacchus 7.50.
9. Barcarolle 5—.
10. Pizzicati, scherzettino 5—, —25 *Gutheil.*
11. Pas des Esclaves, et variations valse 5—.
12. Strette-galop 6—.
N. 4, 10 u. Roi s'amuse, N. 6. P 10/—, à 4/— *Schott.*
Barcarolle u. Piccicati, *VP* (M a r s i c k) 5/— *Schott*, —45 *Gutheil.*
Bouquets de Mélodies, P (R. d e V i l b a c), 2 suites à 7.50.
Cortège de Bacchus, 2P (A. W o r m s e r) 15—.
Intermezzo et valse, *VP* —60 *White.*
Introduction u. Valse lente, *VP* (M a r s i c k) 6/— *Schott*, 1— *White.*
Pastorale (E. F a v a n), P 2.50.
Pizzicati, P (F. F a u g i e r) 3—, (A. T r o j e l l i) 5—, 2— *Michow*, —40 *Brainard*, —35 *Century*, —30 *Church*, —40 *Fischer*, —30 *Gordon*, —40 *Kinley*, 4/— *Metzler*, —30 *Pond*, —35 *Schirmer*, —30 *Willig*, —30 *Windsor*, —25 *Gutheil, Idzikowski, Johansen, Jürgenson*, —50 n *Hals*, 1.50 *Bevilacqua*, 1.50 *Napoleão*, —50 *Wagner; 4ms* (R. d e V i l b a c) 6—, —50 *Ditson*, —40 *Gordon*, 5/— *Metzler*, —50 *Schirmer*, —30 *Leopas; 2P* 2— *Napoleão; 6ms* (J. A. A n s c h ü t z) 6—, *Ha* (B. F e l s, op. 13) 3—, *Banjo* —30, *P* acc. —20 *Jacobs, Mand* —25 *Fischer*, —30, *P* acc. —20 *Jacobs.* 1 —30 *Jacobs, OrgP* 5—, *MandP* 5—, —40 *Fischer, Mand* 5—, —40 *Century*, —40 *Fischer, VP* 6—, —50 *Century*, —75 *Fischer*, 5/— *Metzler*, —30 *White, VcP* 6—, *FlP* 6—, *MandGP* 5—.
Polka (A r b a n) 5—, *O* 1— n.
Quadrille (A r b a n)5—, *O* 1.25 n, (Strauß de Paris) 5—, *4ms* 6—.
Suite: 1. Chasseresses, 2. Valse lente, 3. Pizzicati, 4. Cortège de Bacchus, Part, *O* 25— n, p. sép. 25— n. N. 2. Part, *O* 4— n, p. sép. 6— n. N. 3. Part, *O* 3— n, p. sép. 4— n, *Harm*, Part, N. 1 4— n, N. 2—3 3— n, N. 4 6— n.
Suite, *4ms* (R. d e V i l b a c) 10—.
Suite concertante (T h. L a c k), *2P* 5— n.
Transcr. *P* (G. B u l l) 5—, (A. C r o i s e z) 6—, *4ms* (G. B u l l) 6—, *Cornet* (G u i b a u t) Airs 6—, *VVcP*, *VFlP* *VcFlP* à 12—.
Valse (O. M é t r a) 6—, *4ms* 7.50, *O* 2— n.
Valse chantante et pizzicati (A. H e r r m a n n), *VP*, *FlP* à 9—.
Valse lente (F. F a u g i e r) 5—, (A. T r o j e l l i) 3—, 2.40 *Michow*, —60 *Brainard*, —60 *Schirmer*, —60 *Willig*, —30 *Gutheil, Johansen, 4ms* 9—, —85 *Schirmer, Ha* (B. F e l s, op. 14) 6—, *Z* —30 *Mills, OrgP* 7.50, *VcP* 7.50, *FlP* 7.50.

- Сюзонъ открой —25 *Jurgenson.*
- Taxe sur la viande 1— n, *Ch. s.* —35 n *Gallet.*
- Trianon, *TTBB*, Part 1.50 n, *Ch. s.* —30 n *Gallet.*
- Trois oiseaux 6—.
- Valse des fleurs (d u C o r s a i r e) 7.50, *4ms* 9—.
- Vieille chanson du Roi s'amuse 4—, av. *Mand* 4—.
-2 Vieilles Gardes, opérette (1856, Paris), Ch. *P* 6— *Joubert*:
  Polka chantée. Vive la polka, *P* 2.50.
  Quadrille 5—.
- Voyage enfantin, 3 voix ég. av. *P* —50 n.
Delibes et Minkous. N é m é a, Ballet.
  Mazurka, *O* (S t r a u a ä d e P a r i s) 1— n, Polka, *O* 1— n.
Délices d'une jambe de bois —30 n *Joubert.*
Deliège J. Et mon mari? 5— *Stad.*
- Léon l'irresistible 4— *Stad.*
- Peintre d'histoires 3— *Stad.*
Delieu Mlle. Ni jamais ni toujours, duo 1— n *Durand*, —25 *Jurgenson.*
Deligand, Marche solenelle, *Harm* 4— *Katto.*
Deligny A. et Briollet, Conférence contre l'imoralite 1— n *Sulzbach.*
Delille, Rêve charmant, berceuse, *P* 3/— *Metzler.*
Delille L. Vignerons de Salntonge 1— n, *Ch. s.* —35 n *Labbé.*
Delioux Ch. *Schott*: Op. 1 Danse uapolitaine, *P* 1.75.
-2 Fantasie sur le Pommier fleuri, *P* 6— *Heugel.*
-7 Deux à deux, nocturne, *P* 1.70 n *Gregh.*
-8 Galop di bravoura 1.50, 2— n *Gregh.*
-9 Guarache, danse espagn. 6— *Sulzbach.*
-10 Capriccio nocturne, *P* 5— *Sulzbach.*
-11 Danse napolitaine, *P* 2.50 *Gregh.*
-12 Valse brillant 1.50, —60 *Gordon*, 7.50 *Heugel*, 1— *Cottrau.*
-13 2 Nocturnes, *P* 1.25. 1.70 n *Gregh.*
-14 Marche hongroise 1.25, 2— n *Durand*, —40 *Presser.*
-15 Un Dimanche en Bretagne, esquisses villageoises, *P* 1.50, 2.50 n. N. 1. A l'église 1.70 n, N. 2. Dans les champs 1.15 n *Gregh.*
-16 Confidenza, romance, *P* 1.25, 1.70 n *Gregh*, —40 *Neuparth.*
-17 Etude-Carillon, *P* 1.50, 6— *Sulzbach.*
-18 Chanson créole, *P* 1.25, 5— *Sulzbach.*
-19 Souvenir, mélodie, *P* 1.50, 6— *Sulzbach.*
-20 Grenade, souvenir espagn. *P* 1.50, 1.70 *Sulzbach.*
-21 Valse élégante 1.25, 7.50 *Sulzbach.*
-22 2 Mazurkas de salon 6— *Sulzbach.*
-23 Une fête à Séville, boléro, *P* 7.50 *Heugel*, 3— *Ricordi.*
-24 Rêverie sur l'eau, barcarolle, *P* 5— *Grus.*
-25 Ruisseau, étude de salon, *P* 6— *Sulzbach.*
-26 Forgeron, étude de salon, *P* 1.25.
-28 Mandoline, sérénade, *P* 1.50, 2— n *Durand*, —45 *Neuparth, MandP* 2.50 *Schott.*
-29 Cantilène, nocturne, *P* 5— *Grus.*
-31 Feuillet d'Album, *P* 1.35 n *Durand.*
-32 2 Mazurkas 7.50 *Legouix.*
-33 Tournois, marche 7.50 *Legouix.*
-34 Son du cor, chasse, *P* 1.50, 7.50 *Mathieu.*
-36 Loin du Pays, *P* 1— *Siegel.*

F I G. 36. *Universal-Handbuch der Musikliteratur* by F. Pazdirek. Vienna.
(Reprint, Knuf, Amsterdam.)

KEYBOARD INSTRUMENTS

STRING INSTRUMENTS

RS   ACCORDION

SK — *Arrangements*
LINDSAY, Charles
It's easy to play accordion: with 6 chords; edited by C.
Lindsay, Jr. New York, Consolidated Music; [London,
Fields], c1962. 126p. fol. *(Music for millions—vol.35)*
(B62-51228)

SM — Accordion band
HARRIS, Eddie
Six easy pieces: [for accordion band. Score & parts].
London, Hohner Concessionaires, 7/6. c1962. 3pt.
8vo.
(B62-52263)

SMK — *Arrangements*
SMK/CC — *From opera*
BIZET, Georges
Carmen: selection for accordion band; arranged by
Luigi Carboni. Score [& parts]. New York, [London],
Mills, 10/-. [1962]. 5pt. 4to.
(B62-50544)

SPM — Unaccompanied accordion solos
SPMJ — *Miscellaneous works*
NIEMAN, Alfred
Etude fantasie: for accordion. London, Hohner, 5/-.
c1961. 15p. 4to.
(B62-50545)

SPMK — *Arrangements*
SPMK/KDW — *From solo songs*
BERNSTEIN, Leonard
West Side story—*Excerpts*
Tonight; arranged for accordion by Pietro Deiro, Jr.,
lyrics by Stephen Sondheim. New York, Schirmer;
London, Chappell, 4/4. c1961. 3p. 4to.
(B62-50546)

RW   STRING INSTRUMENTS

KM — STRING ORCHESTRAL MUSIC
KME — Symphonies
OVERTON, Hall
Symphony for strings: string orchestra. [Miniature
score]. New York, London, Peters, 15/-. c1961. 53p.
8vo.
(B62-52264)

KMF — Concertos
CORELLI, Arcangelo
Concerti grossi. Op.6.
12 Concerti grossi: für Streichorchester; nach dem
Erstdruck herausgegeben und mit einer Cembalostimme
verschen von Waldemar Waehl. Partitur. Leipzig,
Peters; [London, Hinrichsen], 28/6. c1961. 211p.
8vo.
(B62-50547)

KMG — Suites
PITFIELD, Thomas Baron
A Keele garland: suite for string orchestra; tunes from
Sneyd MS. collection. London, Mills, Score 7/6, Parts
1/9 each. c1962. 6pt. 4to.
(B62-51229)

MJ — Miscellaneous works
GRAVES, William
Passacaglia and fugue: for strings. Score [& parts].
New York, London, Mills, 15/-. c1962. 6pt. 4to.
(B62-52265)

LONG, Robert
Lament: for string orchestra. Full score [& parts].
London, Chappell, Score 5/-, Parts 1/- each. c1962.
12pt. 4to. *(Music for orchestra)*
(B62-52266)

STRING ORCHESTRAL MUSIC—*cont.*
Miscellaneous works—*cont.*

MILNER, Anthony
Divertimento: for string orchestra. Opus 19. [Score].
London, Universal Edition, 10/-. c1962. 37p. 8vo.
(B62-52267)

RAPLEY, [Edmund] Felton
Elegy: for string orchestra. Score and parts. London,
Chappell, 10/-: c1962. 12pt. 4to.
(B62-52268)

STAMITZ, Carl [Philipp]
Quartet. Op.4, no.2.
Quartetto concertante, G-dur: für zwei Violinen, Viola
(oder 3. Geige) und Violoncello; herausgegeben von
Helmut Mönkemeyer. Partitur. Mainz, London, Schott,
6/6. c1961. 20p. 4to.
(B62-50548)

RXMK — *Arrangements*
RXMK/QRP — *From harpsichord solos*
RXMK/QRPG — *Suites*
PURCELL, Henry
Suite no.1 in D major; freely adapted [for piano &
strings] from pieces for harpsichord by Leonard Rafter.
[Parts]. London, Bosworth, 7/-. c1961. 6pt. 4to.
(B62-50549)

RXMK/R — *From organ works*
RXMK/R/T — *Variations*
FRESCOBALDI, Girolamo
Aria con variazioni detta 'La Frescobalda; elabora-
zione dall' organo per orchestra d'archi a cura di Roberto
Caggiano. Partitura. Padua, Zanibon; [London,
Hinrichsen], 8/6. c1960. 7p. fol.
(B62-51230)

RXMK/RXNR — *From string quintets*
BOCCHERINI, Luigi
La musica notturna di Madrid: trascritta per orchestra
d'archi e tamburo militare di Max Schönherr. [Op.30,
no.6]. London, Boosey & Hawkes, Score 15/-, Parts
1/9 each. c1962. 17p. 4to.
(B62-51231)

RXMK/SP — *From works for violin & keyboard*
RXMK/SPJ — *Miscellaneous works*
BACH, Johann Sebastian
Sonata for violin and harpsichord no.6—*Excerpts*
Adagio for the Brandenburg concerto no.3 in G;
arranged for string orchestra by Stanford Robinson. Lon-
don, Oxford U.P., Score 5/-, Parts 1/- each. c1962.
8pt. 4to. *(Oxford orchestral series—no.167)*
(B62-50550)

RXMP — WORKS FOR SOLO INSTRUMENT(S) & STRING
ORCHESTRA
RXMPQ — Piano & string orchestra
RXMPQF — Concertos
WILLIAMSON, Malcolm
Concerto for piano and string orchestra. Full score.
London, Chappell, 25/-. c1961. 59p. 4to.
(B62-50551)

RXMPQK — *Arrangements*
RXMPQK/MPQ — *From works for piano & orchestra*
FIELD, John
Concerto for piano, no.2—*Excerpts*
[Poco adagio]. Romanza; arranged for piano & strings
& flute (or violin) by David Branson. Score [& parts].
London, Bosworth, Score 3/-, Piano 3/-, Parts 1/- each.
c1962. 9pt. 4to.
(B62-52269)

141

FIG. 37. *The British Catalogue of Music, 1962.* British National
Bibliography, 1963.

TABLE OF CONTENTS

INTRODUCTION

PART 5 lists domestic and foreign published music and unpublished music registered in Class E. It includes also selected music materials in the form of books, pamphlets, and dramas registered in other classes.

Arrangement is by title. Each work is described in a main entry which includes information pertinent to the copyright claim. References lead from variant titles, from distinctive subtitles, and from other titles associated with the work. Works for which the subsisting copyright has been renewed are listed separately in the Renewal Registrations section.

The Name Index to the names of composers, authors of words, claimants, etc. given in the main entries covers both currently registered works and renewal registrations, the latter being distinguished by the symbol "(R)" following the title.

For unpublished works currently registered, each main entry includes the following items of information if available and applicable:

1) Title. If the piece is an excerpt, the title of the work from which it is taken is also given.
2) Descriptive data are given if the title names a musical form, e.g., Sonata.
3) Names of the authors, each preceded by an abbreviation indicating relationship to the work, e.g., "w" (words by), "m" (music by), "arr." (arranged by), etc.
4) Name of the employer in the case of a work made for hire, if so named in the application, together with the names of the employees when given.

5) Information contained in the application which relates to the registration of an earlier version of the work.
6) Brief statement of the new matter on which copyright is claimed, preceded by the abbreviation "NM," if this information is given in the application.
7) Copyright symbol ©.
8) Name of the copyright claimant.
9) Date on which the last of all the items required to complete registration (i.e., copy, application, and fee) was received in the Copyright Office.
10) Registration number.

For published works currently registered, each main entry includes the following items of information if available and applicable:

1) Title, and any descriptive data given in the work, including medium of performance.
2) Names of the authors with designations indicating relationship to the work.
3) Edition statement.
4) Place of publication for works published outside the United States.
5) Name of the first-named publisher when the publisher is not also the claimant.
6) Indication as to whether the work is published in score and/or parts.
7) Series statement.
8) Note giving the language of the text when it is not apparent from the entry.
9) Statement that the work is part of a collection or bound with another work.

vii

FIG. 38. *Catalog of Copyright Entries.* 3rd series, vol. 14, part 5, no. 2, Music, July–Dec., 1960. Library of Congress 1961.

Coleman, L o n n i e
Bum - Bum - Buerang: So wie ein Bumerang.
Couplet-Foxtr. — München: Siegel [1957]; f. Ges. m.
Klav. m. Bez. 3 S. 4°   2.—
Titel u. Text auch in engl. Sprache.

Colin, V l a d i m i r
Märchen (Basme [dt.]) Übertr. aus d. Rumän. v. A.
Margul-Sperber. Ill. v. M. Cordescu. — Bukarest:
Jugendverl. 1956. 210 S., 1 Titelb. 4°   Lei 5.75
Enth. u. a.: Die Geschichte vom Lied.

Collection tempo s. Collection t e m p o.

Zehn Jahre **Collegium** musicum, Zürich. Leitg: Paul
Sacher. Die Konzerte d. Kammerorchesters Collegium
musicum Zürich 1941–1951. — Zürich: Atlantis-Verl.
1951. 55 S., 2 Bl. Abb. gr.8°   Pp. sfr 6.—

Collegium musicae novae. 28. 29. 31. — Wiesbaden:
Breitkopf & Härtel 1957. 4° = Breitkopf & Härtels
Partitur-Bibliothek. Nr 3798. 3799. 3801 u. Breitkopf
& Härtels Orchesterbibliothek. Nr 3798. 3799. 3801.
    28. E d e r , Helm.: Op. 23, Nr 1. Musica semplice (1956).
    — 29. B e n k e r, Heinz: Praeludium pastorale. — 31.
    T r a p p , Klaus: Kleine Streichersinfonie (1956).

Collegium musicum. Nr 22. — Leipzig: VEB Breitkopf & Härtel 1957. 4° = Breitkopf & Härtels
Kammermusik-Bibliothek. Nr 1663a/c.
    22. F ö r s t e r, Christoph: Suite in G-dur.

Collegium musicum. Nr 59. 108. 109. — Wiesbaden:
Breitkopf & Härtel 1956–1957. 4° = Breitkopf &
Härtels Kammermusik-Bibliothek. Nr 1910. 2108.
2109.
    59. T e l e m a n n , Gg Phil.: Quartett in d-moll. — 108.
    R e i c h a r d t, Joh. Frdr.: Sonata C-dur. — 109. S a m m a r -
    t i n i, Giovanni Battista: Notturno à quatro A-dur.

Collins, A n t h o n y
Eire. Suite. [Neudr.] — Köln, Wien: Bosworth &
Co. [1956]; f. Orch. Klav.-Dir.-St. 15 S., V.-Dir.-St.
8 S, 16 St. 4°   Orch. 10.—; S.-Orch. 8.—
    1. Battle-March. — 2. To the Mourne-Mountains (Reverie).
    — 3. Fluter's Hooley (Reel).

Combo-Serie. Nr 32. 40–45. — München: Siegel (32.
40: u. Ed. Meridian) 1956–1957; f. S.-Orch. Ch.8°
                                                  Je 3.—
    32. 1. Du bist mein erster Gedanke. Rumba. Von Gonzalo
    Roig. — 2. Jim, der Frauenheld: Jim war der Held.
    Rumba. Von Irving Fields. — 3. Jonny, wenn Du Geburts-
    tag hast. Chanson-Foxtr. Von Frdr. Hollaender. — 4.
    Nimm diesen Goldring mit in die Welt! Mel.-Fox. Von
    Stuart Hamblen. — 5. Sonja-Waltz: Sonja, wie soll ich
    dich vergessen? Von Ralph Maria Siegel. — 6. French
    Cancan. Tonfilm. Daraus: Ich will ja nur Dich. Valse
    musette. Von Georges van Parys. [1957.]

    40. 1. Und es weht der Wind. Mel.-Fox. Von Stan
    Lebowsky u. Herb. Newman. — 2. Serenata: Heut' nacht
    sing ich mein schönstes Lied. Beguine. Von Lonny Ander-
    son. — 3. Nachtigall, sing' dein Lied an die Sterne!
    Beguine. Von Xavier Cugat u. George Rosner. — 4. Mein
    Sombrero: Mein Sombrero ist ein tolles Stück. Rumba-
    Fox. Von Xavier Cugat. — 5. Bring' deinem Chef ein
    paar Blümchen mit! Chanson-Foxtr. Von Jos. Niessen.
    — 6. Ganz privat: Ich bin inkognito. Foxtr. Von Ralph
    Maria Siegel. — 7. Tango americano. Von Henry Mancini.
    — 8. Tango im Regen: Ja, ja, nur deinetwegen steh' ich
    hier. Von Lot. Olias. 1956.

    41. 1. Cindy, oh Cindy! Langs. Rumba-Fox. Von Bob
    Barron u. Burt Long. — 2. Zwei Sonntagskinder: Zwei
    Sonntagskinder bummeln froh durchs Leben. Mel.-Fox.
    Von Ralph Maria Siegel. — 3. Oh-la-la, chérie! Tonfilm.
    Daraus: So ist Paris! Marsch-Fox. Von Léo Ferré. — 4.
    Bum-Bum-Bumerang: So wie ein Bumerang. Couplet-
    Foxtr. Von Lonnie Coleman. — 5. Mach doch 'ne Pause!
    Baion. Von Eddie Barclay u. Michel Legrand. — 6. Jonny
    hat recht! Rock-and-roll. Von Werner Scharfenberger. —
    7. Ticke-tack: Mein Herz das schlägt. Foxtr. Von Lot.
    Olias. — 8. Schlaf', mein kleiner Liebling! Griisches
    Wiegenlied.) Langs. Walzer. Von Ralph Maria Siegel. 1957.

    42. 1. Singender Blues: Warum strahlen heut' nacht die
    Sterne so hell? Foxtr. Von Melwin Endsley. — 2. Caravan
    (Karawanen-Song): Schau, wenn nachts. Foxtr. Von Duke
    Ellington u. Juan Tizol. — 3. Theo, Theo ... Calypso.
    Von E. Darling, B. Carey u. A. Arkin. — 4. In dem
    kleinen Café ... Beguine. Von Al Hoffman u. Dick

Combo-Serie. Nr 32. 40–45 (Fortsetzung)
    Manning. — 5. Schottische Polka. Von Helm. Zacharias.
    — 6. Liebling, heut' möcht' ich tanzen geh'n! Polka. Von
    J[aromir] Vejvoda. — Film-Sondercombo. 7. 8. Tante
    Wanda aus Uganda. Tonfilm. Daraus: Das Schönste
    auf der Welt ist doch die Liebe. Foxtr. 2. Uganda-Song:
    Wenn in Uganda ... Moderato-Fox. Von Ralph Maria
    Siegel. 1957.

    43. 1. Hale und kleine Fische. Tonfilm. Daraus: Wer das
    vergißt. Calypso. Von Lot. Olias u. [Karl-]Pet.
    Mösser. — 2. Weit, weit im Süden ... Foxtr. Von Eddie
    Curtis. — 3. Zwei blaue Augen, ein weißes Kleid ...
    (Das Mädchen in Seide). Beguine. Von Leroy Anderson.
    — 4. Muchacho: Muchacho, Muchacho, die Nacht ist
    dunkelblau. Calypso. Von Siegfr. Wegener. — 5. Jimmy
    Brown: Jimmy Brown, Jimmy Brown, du hast. Foxtr.
    Von Don Roseland, Ray Cormier u. Mel Van. — 6. Tele-
    fon, Telefon ... Moderato-Fox. Von Frdr. Meyer. — 7.
    Mein Schal: Mein Schal aus Havanna ... Rumba-Fox.
    Von Xavier Cugat.' — 8. Tante Wanda aus Uganda. Ton-
    film. Daraus: Cha-Cha-Negra: Cha-cha-cha. Von Ralph
    Maria Siegel. 1957.

    44. 1. Junge Liebe: Geliebt zu werden, ist alles Glück
    auf Erden! Moderato-Fox. Von Carole Joyner u. Ric
    Carrey. — 2. Wenn Verliebte träumen. Moderato-Fox. Von
    Ralph Maria Siegel. — 3. Buona sera, Annabell! Leb-
    hafter Baion. Von Willy Berking. — 4. Bella rosa Rosa-
    bella ... Merengue. Von Rafael Muñoz. — 5. Rocky-
    Tocky-Baby: Rocky-Tocky-Baby kommt aus Tampico.
    Foxtr. Von Heinz Gietz. — Rock right! (Und laß dir
    Zeit!) Rock and roll. Von Sherman Edwards. — 7. Leb'
    wohl. Schönste aus Gardone! Beguine. Von Hans May.
    — 8. Schade um jede Tränel Beguine. Von G. Fanciulli.
    1957.

    45. 1. Mi casa, su casa ... (Mein Haus ist dein Haus).
    Lied u. langs. Walzer. Von Al Hoffman u. Dick Manning.
    — 2. Du bist für mich ein Fragezeichen. Mel.-Fox. Von
    Ralph Maria Siegel. — 3. Herr Lichtenstein, Herr Lichten-
    stein! Foxtr. Von Ross Bagdasarian. — 4. Der Garten
    des Lebens: Schau dich um in dem Garten! Moderato-
    Fox. Von Dennise Norwood. — 5. Das macht die Liebe,
    Marie: So schön wie heut. Flotter Foxtr. Von Willy
    Berking. — 6. Nur wer liebt, kann das Glück und das
    Leid: Von dem Fenster in dem kleinen Haus . . Mode-
    rato-Fox. Von V[irgilio] Panzuti. — Film-Sondercombo.
    7. 8. Hoch droben auf dem Berg. Tonfilm. Daraus: 1.
    Rumbadi-bumbadi-Cha-cha-cha: Man spielt den Rumbadi-
    bumbadi. 2. Nach dem dritten Glase Wein ... Jodel-
    swing. Von Werner Müller. 1957.

Combo-Serie. Sonder-Combo. — München: Intervall-
Musik 1957. Ch.8°
Sonder-Combo. S c h l a g e r - K a r u s s e l l. 2.

Société internationale de musicologie. **Compte rendu**
s. Internationale Gesellschaft für Musikwissenschaft.
K o n g r e s s b e r i c h t.

Connor, T o m m y , J o h n n y Reine u. **Baguley**
Das kommt im Leben nicht wieder. Bounce; f. S.-
Orch. s. W i l s o n, Lee: Komm', Mister Tallyman!

Conrad v o n Z a b e r n
Die Musiktraktate Conrads von Zabern. Von Karl-
Werner G ü m p e l. — Mainz: Akademie d. Wissen-
schaften u. d. Literatur; Wiesbaden: Steiner in
Komm. 1956. 158 S. gr.8° = Akad. d. Wiss. u. d.
Literatur. Abhandlungen d. geistes- u. sozialwiss.
Klasse. Jg. 1956, Nr 4.   12.—
    Zugl. Diss. d. Phil. F. d. Univ. Freiburg i. Br. v.
    25. Febr. 1955, angezeigt u. d. T.: G ü m p e l, Karl
    Werner: Die Musiktraktate Conrads von Zabern.

Conrad, C o n
Zaubermusik: Ich küss' Dich beim Tanzen. Modera-
to[-Fox]. — München: Chappell & Co.; Seith [1956];
f. Ges. m. Klav. m. Bez. 5 S. 4°   2.—
Titel u. Text auch in engl. Sprache.
Verkauf nur in Deutschland u. Österr. gestattet.

Conrad, M a x
Im Schatten der Primadonnen. Erinnergn e. Theater-
kapellmeisters. — Zürich, Freiburg i. B.: Atlantis-
Verl. 1956. 208 S. 8° = Atlantis-Musikbücherei.
                                           Lw. sfr 12.05
Enth. u. a.: Wilhelm Furtwängler als Operettendirigent.

Conradi, R.
Aufi geht's s. B e t h m a n n , Siegfried.
Wir tanzen. Bd 5 s. W i r tanzen.

FIG. 39. *Jahresverzeichnis der deutschen Musikalien und Musikschriften,*
1957. Leipzig, Hofmeister, 1959. (This is the current form of
Hofmeister's *Handbuch*.)

LISTE INTERNATIONALE SELECTIVE N° 19

(âout 1962)

I. — Théâtre et films; II. — Musique instrumentale; III. — Musique vocale; IV. — Folklore;
V. — Ouvrages sur la musique et ouvrages didactiques

ALLEMAGNE (Bundesrepublik Deutschland)
Rédacteurs: Hans HALM et Alfons OTT (München)
(1. 12. 1961—1. 7. 1962)

I

HINDEMITH (PAUL). *The long Christmas Dinner. Das lange Weihnachtsmahl. (1960). Oper in e. Akt. Engl. T.: Thornton Wilder. Klav.-Ausz. u. Dt. T.: P. Hindemith.* Mainz, Schott 1961 (E. Schott 5175). DM 25.—

OFFENBACH (JACQUES). *Die schönen Weiber von Georgien. Optte. Musikal. Einrichtung v. Klauspeter Seibel. Als Ms. gedr.* Berlin, Wiesbaden, Bote & Bock, Klav. Ausz. DM 30.—

ORFF (CARL). *Ludus de nato infante mirificus. Ein Weihnachtsspiel.* Mainz, Schott (Ed. Schott 5265). Part. DM 15.—

II

BECK (KONRAD). *Sonatina f. Orch.* Ibidem (Ed. Schott 5022). Stud.-Part. DM 6.50

BENKER (HEINZ). *Spielmusik (1956) f. Streich-(Schul-) Orch.* Wolfenbüttel, Zürich, Möseler 1961. Part. DM 5.—
St. je DM 1.20

BIALAS (GÜNTER). *Konzert f. Vcllo m. Orch.* Kassel, Basel, London, New York, Bärenreiter (Bärenreiter Taschenpart. 112). DM 16.—

BLACHER (BORIS). *Op. 7. Divertimento f. Harmoniemusik.* Berlin, Wiesbaden, Bote & Bock 1961. Part. DM 25.—

DAVID (JOHANN NEPOMUK). *Praeambel und Fuga d-moll (1930) f. Org.* Ibidem (Ed. Breitkopf Nr. 5549). DM 4.50
— *Wk 32. Vier Duos. Nr. 3.* Ibidem (Ed. Breitkopf Nr. 5784) — 3. *Sonate (1945) f. 2 V.* DM 7.—

DEGEN (HELMUT). *Kleine symphonische Musik (1960) f. kl. Orch.* Ibidem (Collegium musicae novae Nr. 54). Breitkopf & Härtels Partitur-Bibliothek Nr. 3865. DM 18.—
St. je DM 3.—

HENZE (HANS WERNER). *Antifone per il Festival di Salisburgo (1960) f. Orch.* Mainz, Schott (Ed. Schott 5018), Stud. Part. DM 6.50

KRENEK (ERNST). *Basler Maßarbeit (1960) f. 2 Klav.* Kassel, Basel, London, New York, Bärenreiter 1961 (BA 3510). DM 9.60

RAPHAEL (GÜNTHER): *Drei Stücke in Cis (1956) f. Vcllo m. Klav.* Kassel, Basel, London, New York, Bärenreiter 1961 (BA 3746). DM 9.60

ROHWER (JENS): *Sonate concertante f. Blockfl. in f' (V.) m. Klav.* Wolfenbüttel, Zürich, Möseler 1961. DM 6.50

STROHBACH (SIEGFRIED): *Der Kuckuck. 1958. Trio f. V., Vcllo, Klav.* Ibidem 1961. Part. DM 9.80

ZBINDEN (JULIEN-FRANCOIS). *Op. 14. Quatre Miniatures. Vier Miniaturen (1950/55) f. Fl. m. Klav. (Git) ad. lib. Git.-Bearb.: H. Leeb.* Köln, Sidemton (Gerig 1961). Part. DM 3.50

ZILLIG (WINFRIED): *Streichquartett II. Zum prakt. Gebrauch einger. v. R. Keochert.* Kassel, Basel, London, New York, Bärenreiter (Bärenreiter Taschenpart. 131). DM 14.—

III

BIALAS (GÜNTHER): *Im Anfang . . . Die Schöpfungsgeschichte. Dt. T.: Martin Buber f. 3 Sopr. (auch chorisch) u. 6stgn. gem. Chor.* Ibidem 1961 (BA 4349). Chor. Part. (m. Soli) DM 30.—

GENZMER (HARALD): *Vom Abenteuer der Freude: Singen, singen, singen in dieser Zeit (1960). T.: Stefan Andres f. 4—8stgn. gem. Chor m. Orch.* Mainz, Schott (Ed. Schott 5168). Part. DM 10.—

KNAB (ARMIN): *Lautenlieder. Gesamtausg. Neudr. f. Ges. m. Laute.* Wolfenbüttel, Zürich, Möseler 1961. DM 5.—

KRENEK (ERNST): *The Ballad of the railroads: Railroads, railroads dinning in my ear. Die Ballade von den Eisenbahnen: Bahnen, Bahnen dröhnen mir ins Ohr (1944). Engl. T.: E. Krenek f. Ges. (m.) m. Klav.* Kassel, Basel, London, New York, Bärenreiter 1961 (BA 3956). DM 19.80

LANGG (HANS): *Op. 51. In dulci jubilo. Weihnachts-Kantate. Daraus: O Heiland, reiß die Himmel auf! Satz T. nach Friedrich von Spee f. 4—6stgn. gem. m. 1stgn. K.-Chor.* Mainz, Schott 1961. Chor-Part. DM —.45

FIG. 40. *Fontes artis musicae.* Kassel, Bärenreiter, 1962–.

16. Goyizi L'Ago   1480 ACP-P 79021 H
Se. Historical song on the founding of Gê villages, praise song for the dynasty of the Glidji, and adjigo song; with bell, (14) and rattle/*chant historique sur la fondation des villages Gê, chant de louange de la dynastie des Glidji, et chant adjigo: avec cloche de fer, (14) et hochet.*
Gê men/*hommes.*

17. Minɔdu miadu tʌsrɔ   1464 ACP-P 79020 H
Ss. Exhortation to prudence, with bell/*exhortation à la prudence, avec cloche de fer.*
Gê man/*homme.*

     8–17 Rec. Togo, 1946, p.

UNESCO. ARCHIVES INTERNATIONALES DE MUSIQUE POPULAIRE
10″, 78 rpm. dsr.

1. Nt.   AI 55 16/I
Se. Herdsmen's calls/*appels au bétail.*
Fulah herdsmen/*pâtres peuhls.*

2. Nt.   AI 55 16/I
3. Nt.   AI 55 16/I
Ss. Lyric songs/*chants lyriques.*
(2) Fulah man, (3) woman/*Peuhls:* (2) *homme,* (3) *femme.*

4. Nt.   AI 70 16/II
5. Nt.
6. Nt.
Id. and Is. Flute duet and solo, and musical bow/*duo de flûtes, solo de flûte, et solo d'arc musical.*
Felahs/*Peuhls.*

     1–6 Rec. Niger, 1948, p.

7. Nt.   AJ 2 1 II
Ss. Fragment of a story of a small bird fighting a heron/*fragment d'un conte du combat d'un petit oiseau contre une outarde.* (David & Goliath.)
Hausa professional story teller/*conteur public haoussa.*

8. Nt.   AJ 3 1 I
Ie. Drumming for an exhibition of fighters/*jeu de tambours pour une exhibition de lutteurs.*
Hausa drum ensemble/*batterie de tambours haoussa.*

9. Nt.   AI 57 II
Sd. Lyric song/*chant lyrique.*
Tuareg man and woman/*homme et femme touaregs.*

10. Nt.   AI 56 II
11. Nt.   AI 57 II
12. Nt.   AI 57 II
Ss. Lyric songs/*chants lyriques.*
Tuareg woman/*femme touareg.*

13. Nt.   AI 56 II
Is. Programme music: an attack on a herd/*musique à programme: attaque d'un troupeau.*
Tuareg reed pipe player/*touareg jouant une flûte de roseau.*

     7–13 Rec. Tahoua, Niger, 1948, p.

77

FIG. 41. *The International Catalogue of Recorded Folk-music.*
International Folk Music Council, O.U.P., 1954.

green as the rushes grow' or 'Lord Trowend").
Child 193. *The ballad describes an historical
event; Parcy Reed, owner of Troughend in
Redesdale was murdered by the Halls and the
Crosiers—a band of moss-troopers—in the
16th century.*

(THE) DEATH OF PARKER Ye powers
above, protect the widow: BGSWc. FSJ 34,
188-90. *Richard Parker, leader of the Mutiny
at the Nore, was hanged on June 30th, 1797.*

(THE) DEATH OF QUEEN JANE Queen
Jane was in labour/travail for six weeks/days
or more: BSP (*words only, from oral communi-
cation*), SEF (ii). FSJ 9, 221-3: 11, 67-8: 20,
257-8. Child 170.

DEEP IN LOVE, O WALY, WALY A ship came
sailing over the sea: BGSWa, BGSWb,
BGSWc; The water is wide: SFS (ii), SEF (i),
NSS (ii). (*Sharp gave the verses he noted the
title 'O Waly, Waly' on account of their
resemblance to those so-called in Orpheus
Caledonius. They appear, however, to be the
cento of a longer song in a group that includes
'The belt wi' colours three', 'Died of love',
'The prickly rose', 'T for Thomas', 'The Trees
they are so high'*). FSJ 27, 69-70.

(THE) DERBY RAM, OLD TUP As I was going
to Derby, Sir: BCS (*three versions, one from
Miss Mason—cf. Jewitt's Derbyshire Ballads,
and N & Q 1, ii, 71, 235, and cp. the tune
with the 'Hobby-horse dance' CPM 601;
another from Northumbria, communicated by
Mrs. A. J Hipkins as learned from her grand-
mother; and a third from Auston and Thorpe
(Yorks) with notes on the Old Tup pastime*).
WUP (*words only*), CDC. *See also FSJ 1946
'The Old Tup and its ritual' for a discussion of
the pastime, and other tunes. Although now
familiar as a "song of marvels or lies"—of
which other examples are 'As I was going to
Banbury' and 'The Crocodile'—capable of
embellishment according to the taste of the
company, 'The Derby Ram' properly belongs
to a winter luck-visit, pastime or masking
similar to the Old 'Oss of the Cheshire soul-
cakers, the Hooden Horse of Kent, the 'Osses
of Padstow and Minehead who perambulate in
May and the bull-masking of Dorset and the
Cotswolds. Such masking is of the most ancient
tradition, and representations, differing little
from the appearances of the present day can be
seen in the marginal decorations of the great
15th century Romance of Alexander. A visitation
from these animal-maskers is "lucky", and the
occasion is enlivened by the pastime which
follows, a traditional form, though varied
somewhat in the crudity of its humour according
to circumstance.*

THE DESERTER, RECRUITING SONG When
first I deserted: KG. FSJ 5, 234-5: 19, 153-4.

(THE DEVIL AND THE FARMER *see* (THE)
FARMER'S CURST WIFE.

DE'IL STICK THE MINISTER Our wife she
keeps both beef and yell [*i.e.* ale]:. SRSN.

(THE DEVONSHIRE/CHESHIRE (*etc.*) FARMER'S
DAUGHTER *see* (THE) HIGHWAYMAN
OUTWITTED.

Dick Turpin hero is my name *see* TURPIN
HERO.

DICK TURPIN'S RIDE Dick Turpin, bold
Dick, hie away WUP (*words only*).

DICKERY, DICKERY DOCK, the mouse ran
up the clock: MCSa, MCSb. ODNR 206-7.

DICKY OF TAUNTON DENE *see* RICHARD
OF TAUNTON DENE.

Did you ever hear tell, on a long Time ago *see*
(THE) BABES IN THE WOOD.

DIED OF/FOR LOVE, THE BOLD/BRISK YOUNG
SAILOR/FARMER, *etc.* My true love once he
courted me: KTT (*two versions*), KN (*as
first version in KTT*); There is an alehouse:
KTT (*tune, variant of that familiar as 'O Waly,
Waly'*); There is a bird in yonder tree: KTT;
A brisk young lad came courting me: BTSC;
A bold young farmer courted me: VWE;
A brisk young sailor courted me: BS, KG,
SEF (ii) (*text compiled from several versions*),
NSS (x); In Sheffield Park there once did
dwell a brisk young lad: GHS. FSJ 5, 252:
8, 155-60: 12, 188-9: 19, 181-9 (*notes*): 27,
70-5 (*notes; see also references appended to
'Deep in Love'. 'Died of Love' is the stock from
which many fragmentations treated as separate
songs have been made, including the modern
burlesque 'There is a tavern in the town'. It is
closely related to 'Deep in Love' though each
has distinct elements. Miss Broadwood has
pointed out that the tune most often associated
with it has a striking resemblance to the
Agincourt Song.*

(THE) DILLY SONG *see* (THE) TWELVE
APOSTLES (ii).

(THE) DISTRESSED SHIP'S CARPENTER *see* JAMES
HARRIS.

DIVES AND LAZARUS As it fell out upon a
day rich Dives made a feast: HSN (*words only*),
BCS, LVWC (*not the usual tune*). FSJ 7, 115-26
9, 239-42 (*under 'Gilderoy' q.v. · Appendix,
p. 120*): 11, 130: 17, 337: 18, 16-18: 19, 99: 31,
29. CPM 747 (*under 'We be poor frozen-out
gardeners'*). Child 56. *There are few tunes so
widely used as this, known to folk song collectors
as 'Lazarus', and still familiar as 'The Star of
County Down'. The moral ditty, one of those
cited in Fletcher's Monsieur Thomas 1639,
varies little, and though believed by Husk not
to have been printed before 1860, can be seen
in A Good Christmas Box, a chap-book
published at Dudley in 1847.*

[Do] Di ye ken Elsie Marley, honey? *see* ELSIE
MARLEY.

FIG. 42. M. Dean-Smith. *A Guide to English Folk-song Collections,
1822–1952.* Univ. of Liverpool Press, 1954.

GREECE

Words by
DIONYSIOS SOLOMÓS (1798-1857)

English versification by
T. M. CARTLEDGE

Music by
NIKOLAOS MANTZAROS (1795-1873)

Chosen as National Anthem of Greece by King George I and adopted in 1864.
Of the 158 verses, the first two which are given are those usually sung.
Music copyright J. B. Cramer & Co. Ltd.

FIG. 43. *National Anthems of the World*, ed. M. Shaw and Coleman
(2nd rev. edn.), Blandford Press, 1963.

Russian Maiden's Song
(Parasha's aria from the opera *Mavra*)
—— ARR. VLN. & PF. Dushkin & Stravinsky 1920-1
  ☆ J. Szigeti & I. Stravinsky (in ‡ C.CX 1100:
FCX/QCX 212; ♭ *Reg.SEBL 7022)*

III. ORCHESTRAL

Capriccio pf. & orch. 1929
  ☆ J. M. Sanromá & Boston Sym.—Koussevitzky
  (Copland, Fauré, Sibelius)   ‡ **Vic.LCT 1152**

(Le) Chant du Rossignol 1919
  ☆ Cincinnati Sym.—Goossens (‡ Cam.CAL 189)

Circus Polka (after Schubert)[1] 1942
  ☆ N.Y.P.S.O.—Stravinsky   in ‡ C.CX 1100
  (Fireworks, Ode, etc.)
(‡ FCX/QCX 212; ♭ *Reg.SEBL 7021)*
—— ARR. PF.
  T. Ury   ‡ *Argo.ATM 1006*
  (Berg & Prokofiev)
  ☆ A. Foldes (‡ *PV. 36104)*
—— ARR. 2 PFS.
  ☆ V. Vronsky & V. Babin (in ‡ Phi.N 02100L)

CONCERTOS

D major Str. orch. 1946
  Boston Orch. Soc.—Page   ‡ **SOT. 1062**
  (Villa-Lobos & Bach)
  ☆ Victor Sym.—Stravinsky (‡ G.QALP 132)

E flat major 16 insts. 1938 *("Dumbarton Oaks")*
  Rochester Cha. Orch.—Hull ‡ **CHS.CHS 1229**
  (below; & 3 Pieces, Str. qtt.)

Piano & Wind Insts. 1923-4
  S. Stravinsky & Vic. Sym.—I. Stravinsky
        ‡ *Vic.LM 7010*
  (Scherzo à la russe, Pater Noster, Ave Maria)
        (♭ set WDM 7010; ‡ ItV.A10R 0007)
  ☆ N. Mewton-Wood & Residentie Soloists—Goehr
        (‡ Cle. 6151; ‡ MMS. 64A, d.c.)

Danses concertantes 1942
  Rochester Cha. Orch.—Hull ‡ **CHS.CHS 1229**
  (above; & 3 Pieces, Str. qtt.)
  (Firebird on ‡ MMS. 64)
  ☆ Victor Sym.—Stravinsky (‡ ItV.A12R 0114) ·

Ebony Concerto Jazz orch. 1946
  ☆ Woody Herman Orch. (in ‡ C.CX 1100: FCX/QCX 212;
        ♭ *Reg.SEBL 7020)*

Fireworks, Op. 4 1908 *(Feux d'artifice)*
  ☆ N.Y.P.S.O.—Stravinsky   ‡ C.CX 1100
  (Norwegian Moods, Concerto, etc.)
        (‡ FCX/QCX 212; ♭ *Reg.SEBL 7020)*
  ☆ Chicago Sym.—Defauw (in ‡ Cam.CAL 162)

(4) Norwegian Moods 1942
  ☆ N.Y.P.S.O.—Stravinsky   in ‡ C.CX 1100
  (above)   (‡ FCX/QCX 212; ♭ *Reg.SEBL 7022)*

Ode 1943
  ☆ N.Y.P.S.O.—Stravinsky   in ‡ C.CX 1100
  (above)   (‡ FCX/QCX 212; ♭ *Reg.SEBL 7021)*

Scènes de Ballet 1944-5
  ☆ N.Y.P.S.O.—Stravinsky   ‡ *C.C 1815*
  (Pétrouchka)   (‡ *QC 5008)*

Scherzo à la russe 1944
  ☆ Victor Sym.—Stravinsky (in ‡ *Vic.LM 7010:*
        ♭ *set WDM 7010; ‡ ItV.A10R 1007)*

SUITES Small orch. (orig. *Pièces faciles*, pf.)
  Nos. 1 & 2
  ☆ Cha. Orch.—Oubradous (♭ *Pat.ED 37)*
  Little Orch. Soc.—Scherman (‡ *D.UA 343560)*

No. 1 ☆ N.Y. Cha.—Craft (in ‡ Cle. 6173)

No. 2, . . . Valse only 1921
  Philharmonia—Markevitch   in ‡ C.CX 1273
  (Chabrier, St.-Saëns, Sibelius, etc.)
        (‡ QCX 10172; Angel. 35154)

SYMPHONIES
No. 1, E flat major, Op. 1 1906-7
  Vienna Orch. Soc.—Adler   ‡ **Uni.UN 1006**

[No. 2], Symphony in C 1940
  Cleveland Sym.—Stravinsky   ‡ **EPhi.ABL 3108**
  (Cantata)   (‡ AmC.ML 4899; Phi.A 01149L)
  Berlin Sym.—Rubahn   ‡ **Roy. 1489**
  (Card Party)

No. 3 (in 3 movements). 1945
  Cento Soli—Albert   ‡ **CFD. 19**
  (Firebird)

Symphonies for Wind Instruments 1920, rev. 1946
  N.W. Ger. Radio Orch. Members—Stravinsky
        ‡ **AmC.ML 4964**
  (Histoire du Soldat; & Octet)
  U.S. Military Acad. Band—Resta
        ‡ **PFCM.CB 176**
  (Barber, Still, Ravel, etc.)
  ... Finale —— ARR. PF. Stravinsky[2]
  E. Ulmer   ‡ **CHS.H 12**
  (Dukas, Roussel, Goossens, Malipiero & Debussy)

IV. BALLETS

APOLLON MUSAGÈTE 2 Tableaux 1927
  Vienna Cha.—Hollreiser ‡ **E. & AmVox.PL 8270**
  (Pulcinella)
  ☆ Victor Sym.—Stravinsky (‡ G.QALP 132)

(Le) BAISER DE LA FÉE 4 Scenes 1928
  French Nat. Radio—Markevitch ‡ **C.CX 1228**
  (Pulcinella)   (‡ FCX 350; Angel. 35143)
  ☆ Victor Sym.—Stravinsky (‡ ItV.A12R 0114)

(The) CARD PARTY 1937 *(Jeu de cartes)*
  Philharmonia—Karajan   ‡ **C.FCX 163**
  (Roussel)   (‡ QCX 163)
  Berlin Sym.—Rubahn   ‡ **Roy. 1489**
  (Symphony)

(The) FIRE BIRD 2 Tableaux 1910
  (Oiseau de feu)
  COMPLETE RECORDING
  Suisse Romande—Ansermet   ‡ **D.LXT 5115**
        (‡ Lon.LL 1272)

  Revised Orchestral Suite 1919
  Philadelphia—Ormandy   ‡ **AmC.ML 4700**
  (Moussorgsky)   (‡ Phi.A 01187L)
  Leipzig Radio—Borsamsky   ‡ **Ura. 7157**
  (Moussorgsky)(& ‡ Ura.RS 7-18; MTW. 521; ACC.MP 25)
  (Valse infernale . . . only in ‡ Ura. 7096)
  London Phil. Sym.—Scherchen ‡**West.LAB 7032**
  (14ss—Honegger)
  Netherlands Phil.—Goehr   ‡ *MMS. 64*
  (Danses concertantes)
  (Concerto, pf. & wind on ‡ MMS. 64A)
  Cento Soli—Albert   ‡ **CFD. 19**
  (Symphony No. 3)
  Dresden Sym.—v. Berten   ‡ **Roy. 1462**
  (Kabulevsky)   (‡ *Var. 69128, 2ss)*
  ☆ Suisse Romande—Ansermet   ‡ **D.LXT 2916**
  (Symphonie des Psaumes)   (‡ Lon.LL 889)
  ☆ Minneapolis Sym.—Dorati   ‡ **EMer.MG 50004**
  (Borodin)
  (Debussy on ‡ Mer.MG 50025; ‡ FMer.MLP 7505)
  ☆ Sym. Orch.—Stokowski (‡ Vic.LM 9029 &
        in ‡ set LM 6113; ‡ ItV.A12R 0130; ‡ FV.A 630218)
  Danish Radio—Tuxen (‡ *Tono.LPL 33003)*
  ... Berceuse —— ARR. VLN. & PF.
        Dushkin & Stravinsky
  I. Stern & A. Zakin   ‡ & ♭ *AmC.PE 21*
  (Moussorgsky; Sorochintsy Fair—Gopak)
  ☆ J. Heifetz & E. Bay (♭ *Vic.ERA 94; ♭ DV. 26034)*

  New Orchestral Suite 1945
  ☆ N.Y.P.S.O.—Stravinsky   ‡ *C.C 1810*
        (‡ QC 5004; & ‡ AmC.ML 4882)

(L') HISTOIRE DU SOLDAT (Ramuz)
  Narrators & 7 insts. 1918
  M. Auclair, M. Herrand, J. Marchat & Ens..
  —Oubradous   ‡ **Pat.DTX 124**
        (‡ AmVox.PL 7960)
  F. Weaver, J. Harkins, F. Warriner & Inst.
  Ens.—Vardi (Eng)[3] ‡ **E. & AmVox.PL 8990**

---

[1] 'For a young elephant.'   [2] For *Le Tombeau de Debussy.*
[3] English text by S. Tillim after Newmarch.

Fig. 44. Clough and Cumming. *World's Encyclopaedia of Recorded Music.* 3rd suppt. 1953-55. Sidgwick & Jackson, 1957. (Supplementary data are kept on cards by the British Institute of Recorded Sound.)

Rom, schließlich große Erfolge an der Mailänder Scala. Bereiste Spanien, Portugal, England, Frankreich und Südamerika. 1955 kam er an die Oper von Chicago, 1956 an die Metropolitan Oper New York. Hier seitdem in Rollen wie dem Radames in «Aida» und dem Manrico im «Troubadour» gefeiert.

Zahlreiche Schallplattenaufnahmen auf Cetra (u. a. vollständige Opern «Bajazzo», «Simone Boccanegra») und Decca (vollständige Opern «Aida», «Der Troubadour»).

Bernac, Pierre, Bariton, * 12. I. 1899 Paris. Nachdem er zuerst an Kleinkunstbühnen aufgetreten war, kam er erst relativ spät zu einer Karriere als Konzert-, vor allem als Liedersänger. Debüt 1933 in Paris. Entscheidend wurde für ihn seine Begegnung mit dem Komponisten Francis Poulenc, mit dem ihn eine echte Freundschaft verband. 1934 gaben beide zusammen ihr erstes Konzert in Salzburg, 1935 in Paris im Saal der École normale. In den folgenden 20 Jahren unternahmen beide große Tourneen, die in den Musikzentren in aller Welt größte Erfolge einbrachten. Die typisch französische hohe Baritonstimme von Pierre Bernac hat in den Liedern von Poulenc, aber auch in denen anderer französischer und auch deutscher Komponisten, durch ihre Wandlungsfähigkeit des Ausdrucks und durch die Feinheit ihrer Diktion beglückt.

Schallplatten: Ultraphon und HMV.

Berry, Walter, Bariton, * 1929 Wien; wollte ursprünglich Ingenieur werden, studierte dann aber Gesang an der Wiener Musikhochschule bei Hermann Gallos. 1949 trat er in den Wiener Akademiechor ein, 1950 wurde er an die Staatsoper von Wien berufen. Hier hatte er seinen ersten großen Erfolg als Titelheld in «Figaros Hochzeit». 1952 bei den Festspielen von Salzburg, seitdem Jahr für Jahr dort aufgetreten. Walter Berry wie auch seine Gattin, die berühmte Altistin *Christa Ludwig*, haben in der gesamten Welt eine glänzende Karriere gemacht. Gastspiele und Konzerte in Mailand und London, in Chicago und Buenos Aires, in San Franzisco, Brüssel, München und Stuttgart; seit 1961 auch an der Städtischen Oper Berlin engagiert.

Sehr viele Schallplatten auf den verschiedensten Marken, u. a. auf Decca, Philips, Vox, darunter auch integrale Opern («Don Giovanni», «Arabella», «Der Rosenkavalier», «Ariadne auf Naxos»).

Bertram, Theodor, Bariton, * 12. II. 1869 Stuttgart, † 24. XI. 1907 Bayreuth (Selbstmord). Sohn des Baritons *Heinrich Bertram* (1828 bis 1905) und der dramatischen Sopranistin *Marie Bertram* (1838 bis 1882). Wurde durch seinen Vater ausgebildet und debütierte 1889 am Stadttheater von Ulm. 1891 kam er an das Opernhaus von Hamburg, 1892 an die Berliner Kroll-Oper, 1893–99 wirkte er an der Münchener Hofoper. 1899 wurde er an die Metropolitan Oper New York verpflichtet, wo er bis 1901 sang; gastierte in dieser Zeit auch in Philadelphia, Chicago und Boston. 1901 sang er

Fɪɢ. 45. *Unvergängliche Stimmen* by K. J. Kutsch and L. Riemens. Bern, Francke Verlag, 1962.

CORBETT (THOMAS). Bookseller and book auctioneer, London, 1715-32; Corner of Ludgate, next Fleet Bridge; The Child's Coat, down the Ditch side near Bridewell Bridge, or, by Fleet Ditch; Addison's Head, next the Rose Tavern, without Temple Bar, 1719-32. His name appears in an advertisement, June 1728, "This Day is published. Mr. W. Corbet's Bizzaria's or Concerto's, proper for all Instruments or the new Guito's of Italy. The subscribers may have their books by sending the rest of the money to Mr. J. Walsh . . . and Mr. Tho. Corbett at Addison's Head without Temple-Bar, where they are sold," etc. Succeeded by his son Charles Corbett.
P. II.

CORNISH (WILLIAM). Chromo and lithographic printer, London; 62 Bartholomew Close, c. 1847-49; 63 Bartholomew Close, c. 1849-86. Printed some illustrations in colour in "Jullien's Album for 1853."

CORRI & CO. Music sellers and publishers, Edinburgh, 37 North Bridge Street, 1790-1801, with additional premises at 8 South St. Andrew Street, c. 1796-1801. Natale Corri, younger brother of Domenico Corri, was connected with the business. Published in conjunction with Domenico Corri, and afterwards with Corri, Dussek and Co. in London; succeeded Corri and Sutherland.
K. G.
A Catalogue of Music. Vocal and Instrumental. c. 1790. 1 p. fol. (B.M. g. 272. v. (3*.))

CORRI & SUTHERLAND. Music sellers and publishers, Edinburgh, 1780-90; at 37 North Bridge Street, c. 1783-90. Partners were John or Domenico Corri and James Sutherland; partnership dissolved in 1790 when Sutherland died. Domenico Corri having commenced business in London in 1789, the Edinburgh business was continued as Corri and Co., with Natale Corri, younger brother of Domenico, as one of the principals; succeeded John Corri.
K. G.

CORRI, DUSSEK & CO. Music sellers and publishers, London, 67 Dean Street, Soho, January 1794-c. 1801. Additional premises at 68 Dean Street, c. 1795-96, and 28 Haymarket, c. 1796-1801, which became the principal place of business; continued by Domenico Corri alone. Jan Ladislav Dussek was a son-in-law of his partner Domenico Corri. Corri, Dussek and Co. published in conjunction with Corri and Co. in Edinburgh.
K. G.
Catalogues:—New Music. 1795. 1 p. fol. (B.M. Hirsch III. 800.); 1795 & 1796. 1 p. fol. (B.M. G. 806. h. (1.)); For the years 1796 & 1797. 1 p. fol. (B.M. g. 141. (15.))
See also Corri (Domenico).

[117]

FIG. 46. *Music Publishing in the British Isles* by C. Humphries and W. C. Smith. Cassell, 1954.

1650 aveva già incominciato a lavorare e firmare da solo *Carlo Francesco Rolla,* che continuerà la ditta per lo meno fino al 1659 pubblicando mus. sacra di : Grancino, Bagatti, Vanzoglio, Penna (Op. 1, 1656) e Cesati (Op. 2, 1659) nonché l'antologia *Canzonette spirituali e morali che si cantano nell'Oratorio di Chiavenna* (1653 e 1657). Marca tipogr. : S. Cecilia seduta all'organo.

ROSATI FORTUNIANO. Stampatore ducale di Modena attivo fra il 1695 e il 1702. Pubbl. belle ediz. di mus. soprattutto strumentali di : Corelli (Op. 4, 1697), Pegolotti (Op. 1, 1698), Iacchini (Op. 3, 1697), Fioré (Op. 1, 1699), Vitali (Op. 3, 1695, e Op. 4, 1701), Brevi (Op. 5, 6 e 8), Albergati (Op. 8 e 9) e altri. Si trasferisce poi a Venezia, dove si appoggia alla casa ed. di Antonio Bartoli (v.) per pubbl. i *Salmi a 4* del Giannettini (1717) e il *Tantum ergo* op. 9 del Brevi (1725).

ROSATI GIUSEPPE. Tipografo attivo in Parma fra il 1711 e il 1733. Pubbl. *Il tutto in poco, modo per imparare il Canto fermo* (1711) e due trattati del Vallara : *Teorico-prattico del canto gregoriano* (1721) e *Primizie del canto fermo* (1724). Nel 1733 pubbl. *Selva di varie composizioni ecclesiastiche* ancora del Vallara. Un *R. Ippolito* si trova più tardi in Parma socio con Dall'Oglio (v.).

ROSETTO (Rossetti) BLASIO. Autore del trattato *Libellus de ridumentis Musices,* ne sostiene le spese dell'ediz. del 1529 in Verona presso Stefano Nicolini e Fratelli (v. .

ROSSI. Attivo in Siena nella prima metà del secolo XIX, pubbl. nel 1828 *L'arte del contrappunto* di Lotario Gauleno.

ROSSI FRATELLI. Tipografia attiva in Macerata nel secolo XIX. Nel 1825 stampa uno *Stabat mater* del Brunetti.

ROSSI FRANCESCO di Valenza (Rubeus Franciscus de Valentia). Tipografo ed editore n. a Ferrara nel 1503, ivi m. intorno al 1573. Figlio di Lorenzo R. di Valenza, passato da Venezia a Ferrara dove lavorava dal 1485 al 1499, Fr. succede al padre dirigendo la tipogr. dal

FIG. 47. *Dizionario Degli Editori Musicali Italiani* by C. Sartori. Florence, L. S. Olschki Editore, 1958.

show that he does not. Dvořák certainly knows his themes; and indeed he invented a rather peculiar type of theme for variations. At all events, his three outstanding variation-movements, the wonderfully clever finale of the Terzet for violin and viola, the brilliant and poetic finale of the otherwise unsatisfactory Sextet for strings, and the present orchestral work, are all on themes of this peculiar type, which has since been made more familiar to the public in Elgar's Enigma Variations. Instead of relying upon any solid rhythmic or harmonic structure, the composer takes two alternating strains as full of different melodic figures as possible, and states them in the order A, B, A. It will be seen from my quotation—

Ex. 1.

that every pair of bars of this whimsically severe theme contains a very recognizable melodic figure (like $(a), (b), (c), (d)$); and that the second strain B groups its new figure (d) on steps of a rising scale reaching to a climax. These melodic facts are solid enough to allow Dvořák in some of his later variations to break away from the original rhythmic limits of the theme, and to indulge in considerable passages of development without seeming to break the backbone of his variation.

The theme having been stated in harmony of portentous bareness, the first three variations simply clothe it in all sorts of bright counterpoints.

The 4th variation disguises the first strain of the melody, although retaining its harmonic outline; but the second strain, with its rising scale, is easily enough recognized.

The 5th variation has brilliant running figures.

In the 6th variation there are symptoms that the theme is able to stretch itself, for the first strain begins by taking two bars for one of the original theme. The second strain, however, moves at the old pace.

In variation 7 the freedom of rhythm grows as the colouring becomes more dramatic, and in variation 8 it is possible for the strings to add a little introduction on a diminished version of figure (b) before the winds enter mysteriously with the theme.

Variation 9 again spreads out the first strain, and, apropos of the F sharp in its second bar, enriches the harmony throughout more boldly than hitherto.

FIG. 48. *Essays in Musical Analysis* by D. F. Tovey. O.U.P., 1935.